THE CHANNEL

———◆———

BY STEVEN EHRLICK

LOST〰
COAST
PRESS
Fort Bragg
California

Lost Coast Press
155 Cypress Street
Fort Bragg, CA 95437

www.cypresshouse.com

Publisher's Cataloging-in-Publication
(Provided by Quality Books, Inc.)
Ehrlick, Steven.
   The channel / by Steven Ehrlick. -- 1st ed.
   p. cm.
   Includes bibliographical references.
   LCCN: 99-97249
   ISBN:1-882897-49-8

   1. Reincarnation--Fiction. 2. Channeling (Spiritualism)--Fiction. 3. New York. (N.y.)--Fiction. 4. Spiritual biography--Fiction. I. Title.

PR9199.3.C53E37 2000   813.6
                                QBI99-1896

The following publishers have given permission to use extended quotations from copyrighted works:

From "I am the Walrus," by John Lennon and Paul McCartney, Copyright ©1967 Sony/ATV Tunes LLC (Renewed). All rights administered by Sony/ATV Music Publishing, 8 Music Square West, Nashville, TN 37203. All rights reserved.

From "Do Not Go Gentle Into that Good Night," by Dylan Thomas, from *The Poems of Dylan Thomas*, Copyright ©1952 by Dylan Thomas. Reprinted by permission of New Directions Corp. and David Higham Associates.

From "Accidents" by John Keen, Copyright ©1969 Songs of Windswept Pacific o/b/o ABKCO Music Inc., Towser Tunes, Inc., and Fabulous Music Limited.

From "The Clod and the Pebble," by William Blake, public domain.

Manufactured in Canada

*For Trish; and in loving memory
of my father, Murray.*

And God said unto Noah, The end of all flesh is come before me; for the earth is filled with violence through them; and, behold, I will destroy them with the earth.

Genesis 6:13

I am he as you are he as you are me and we are all together.

John Lennon & Paul McCartney

ADAM'S DREAM:

I fly. Far above the ground. In the clouds I fly. I see cities with lights strung together like a jeweled web. I move across the ocean. It is dark. The moon rises. In the moonlight an island appears before me. It is tropical with palm trees and towards one end climbs a volcanic peak. I circle the island. There is an overwhelming sense of fear emanating from the island people. I sense it. But I do not feel it. I feel instead the pure heart of the volcano beating in steady, rhythmic pulses. The volcano shakes and fissures spew gas and dirt; a drunken sailor of a mountain, cursing and foaming into the black night. It knows what it must do. There is no fear, no anger, only purpose and intent. I await, hovering above the quivering island. The volcano detonates; worlds touch, forced together by the seismic episode. The inhabitants are crossing over; they come towards me and we watch together as their terrestrial home vanishes beneath a wave.

I move north, the spirits of the island people following me . . . we are a spirit arrow, shooting across the firmament. There is a community of will, a collective imperative guiding us, directing us to our next destination. It grows cold but we are immune. The blue-black carpet of the sea is transformed into a bed sheet of white. The first crimson rays of morning are creeping over the eastern edge of the world. Without warning, we are sucked straight up and away from the earth as if a cosmic vacuum cleaner has determined to rid the atmosphere of our soiling presence. I sense, we all sense, a guiding hand redirecting our course. As we rise, I see the polar cap cradling the end of the world. We stop. And wait. We peer into the void with the impatient expectation of commuters. The train is coming. A giant, frozen train of rock and ice and gas. It whizzes by us not stopping, not stoppable, its final destination in the hands of gravity.

PART ONE

I

As ADAM FISCHER WALKED up Hudson Street, bent against a cold, wet wind, he attempted to concentrate on the mundane. There were, he noticed, more and more cracks in the sidewalk where thin tendrils of various forms of flora had broken through. How do they do that? he wondered. How does Nature give a blade of grass the strength and tenacity to plow up through the concrete of a New York city sidewalk? Adam looked up. There were orange and white lights highlighting the Empire State Building. Halloween was a few days away. How many blades of grass, he asked himself, would it take to bring that building down? Another thought intruded, one that had plagued Adam most of his life. Of course, Adam Fischer becoming disturbed by a thought was like a pincushion resenting being stuck by a pin.

You see, during its forty-nine years of waking existence, the left side of Adam Fischer's brain had proven incapable of turning itself completely off, permitting only the occasional shift into neutral, where it would reluctantly remain, impatiently idling, while the right side took temporary control of the wheel. During those times when most humans give themselves freely to the libidinal buzz of the right side— say during sex or while tripping on acid—Adam's reason refuses to yield, remaining steadfast, ever vigilant, continually scanning the psychic horizon for the irrational hordes. Nothing was beyond his inspection or circumspection. Until recently, that is.

Adam had been troubled all of his life by the impermanence of things, man-made things, like cars and buildings, roads and TVs. It disturbed him to see a building torn down. He did not understand it. Once it was up, a building should stay up. Forever. He mistrusted warranties. Five years or fifty thousand miles was just a euphemism to Adam for—this car will break down eventually and leave you stranded somewhere when you are least equipped to deal with it.

Adam returned his eyes to the sidewalk, as if the city lights might tell him something he did not care to know. The sky felt too close, and he was not sure what that meant. There was a full moon, and a bitter wind was kicking up grit and bits of dead leaves and aiming it all carefully into Adam's eyes. He noticed a card in his hand, almost forgotten; he went to shield his eyes and saw it pinched between his fingers, so he used it as a tiny visor.

He had a card in his hand yet had forgotten his coat, and only the chill penetrating his sports jacket brought its absence to mind. He thought of reversing and heading back to Lucia's apartment to retrieve it but no, he had left there on an impulse propelled by confusion and fear and the reasons for doing so were fresh and alive and it wasn't all that cold once you considered the alternative.

His mother checked in with an admonishing word, dead for a decade but still alive with a lead role in Adam's perpetually running internal play. The outside had been a deadly place to her, full of germs and invisible illnesses lying in wait for her child dare he venture out into its dominion without first fitting himself with snow pants, parka, gloves, toque and scarf. Adam would wait impatiently by the back door while his mother slid every button into its allotted slot, her irresistible smile converting his ill temper into something approximating tolerance as she twisted and knotted his woolen scarf over most of his face until it threatened to suffocate him, in part from its tightness against his mouth and nose, but mainly because of the putrid smell of unwashed wool still damp from yesterday's steamy breaths.

You'll catch your death out there, he would hear her say, could hear it now as he clutched the lapels of his sports jacket and pulled them close to his throat.

There was hardly any pedestrian traffic on the sidewalk. But Adam noticed something peculiar about each person who did happen to pass by. Normally he would be greeted with a familiar deadness of expression, a poker player's countenance, non-antagonistic, uninterested; I don't care about you so please do me the same courtesy. Tonight though, it seemed different—the odd lingering stare, the quickly placed furtive glance in his direction. It was as if there was an attention-grabbing wad of snot hanging from his nose or a possible resemblance to a recently released police sketch.

Lucia said he had filled up the room with light. Maybe he was blinding passersby with his brilliance. Or maybe he just looked crazy, like a homeless street crawler wearing a winter coat in the broiling heat of summer, only in reverse.

4

Adam checked his watch. If he hurried he could pick up the PATH train to Hoboken at Christopher Street and still make the connecting train to Montclair. He thought about going to the studio first to see how the mix was going, but he was far too preoccupied by his shadow, the way it swung over the sidewalk as he passed under a street lamp, and the cracks in the sidewalk were hypnotizing and then there was Lucia's voice. He would never be able to concentrate on tiny dials and plastic-knobbed faders. He would wait until tomorrow to hear the mixes. Tonight he had more thinking to not do.

The pavement was turning red. Dark then red then dark again. Adam reluctantly forced his eyes away from the pavement and saw that the intersection at Christopher Street was awash in a crimson whirlpool of spinning police beacons. And there, in the middle of the street, lay the twisted remains of a mountain bike and, twenty feet from it, the still, lifeless form of its recent occupant.

The courier lay in the center of the scattered remains of his bag; large envelopes, caught by the wind, toppled end over end down the street while his helmet, several feet away, rocked back and forth in mock prayer. A taxi cab, stopped in mid-turn onto Christopher Street, had its windshield smashed and there was this shrill dialogue, like the disturbing notes of a harpy, coming from the animated mouth of the cabbie who was in the midst of emphatically distancing himself from any culpability. Two cops, ignoring the driver, talked officiously into their lapel microphones.

The inevitable crowd had gathered, held back onto the sidewalk by a thin strand of yellow plastic, the taller stepping back a bit to allow the shorter an unobstructed view. Adam joined in the unspoken communal prayer offered up by the onlookers, grateful to be standing on the sidewalk because no one ever wants to draw a crowd.

The ambulance had arrived and the medics were hunched over the body. A stretcher lay next to the fallen courier but there did not appear to be any urgency to rush him to the hospital. Perhaps the way his head lay parallel to his shoulders had something to do with the lack of immediacy at the scene, thought Adam.

"Checking out early," came a low gravelly voice from behind Adam. He turned to face an elderly, withered black woman pushing a shopping cart. Her head was crowned by knotted gray curls that fell carelessly over her eyes. The skin of her face was creased with jagged lines that ran into each other like the tributaries of a mighty river. She wore a man's pale blue cardigan sweater that hung loosely over her bony buttocks. The cart contained all of her worldly goods, but what they were could only be guessed at since everything was hidden away in all manner of plastic bag.

"I suppose," said Adam.

"No doubt about it," she said. "Time's a-coming for everyone. Saw it in a book. Some ain't got the stomach for it. Checking out early."

She continued on her way, people standing aside to let her pass, leaving Adam to ponder her cryptic message. But all Adam registered when he looked back into the street was a person lying dead in the middle of it.

The courier had been riding against traffic, south down Hudson Street. Adam had an almost obsessive loathing for people who died of stupidity. He internalized it, letting it devour his calm. He was determined that when he died, stupidity would not be the cause. For Adam Fischer was certain that you were only granted so many bad decisions in one life. It was statistical problem, not a philosophical one.

Adam would be reading about a senseless death—Teenager dives into river and breaks neck—and become infuriated. He would think about the parents; how the mother bore the ingrate, nursed him and changed his diapers, rushed him to the hospital when he was sick; how his father helped him with his homework, kept him away from traffic and strangers and stray dogs; how they loved him and cherished him and then lost him due to one brain dead, thoughtless decision. What kind of world was it, Adam wondered, that brought forth human beings whose sole purpose, after years of being nurtured and cared for, was to serve as a bad example.

Adam crossed over to the north side of Christopher Street and headed west towards the PATH train entrance. He was uneasy. This was not his New York tonight. The street, the laughter rising and falling from passed restaurants, even the air seemed alien and unfriendly. He felt dispossessed and rejected, pushed out to the periphery, tolerated but unwanted.

Adam found himself nervously glancing every so often over his shoulder, so when the young girl came out of the darkness between two buildings and called out to him, he turned around so forcefully that he knocked into her, toppling her into the wall of the near building.

"You fuckin' dirtbag," she said, quickly getting back onto her feet.

"I'm sorry. Really. I didn't see you. Are you all right?"

"Try watching where you're going, dickhead. Look at my bloody elbow."

She pulled back the over-sized hooded sweatshirt she wore and there was indeed a little blood oozing from a scrape.

She was probably not more than twenty years of age, although the yellow rings under her eyes and the nether quality of her affected stare made her age irrelevant. She could have been pretty; her features were strong and she was tall but she was slowly wasting away so all one could do was fill in the places where she had imploded into herself and imagine the attractive figure that had once pressed out from her frame.

"So how about it, mister . . . you look like you could spare a few bucks. I'll use it for food, promise." She held out her hand and it was a pretty hand, long and slender, but marred by broken nails and chocolate-coloured dirt stains.

Adam hesitated. His wallet was in his absent coat. All he had in his sports jacket was a credit card folder and some train tickets but then he remembered the wad of walking-around money in his pants pocket.

"So maybe you want a little company, then. I give a hell of a BJ. Ten bucks. Only take a minute and that's a promise."

On another night, Adam politely says no thanks and walks quickly away. At any other time, he is certain to be appalled at being accosted by yet another of the depraved characters who inhabit New York's hidden underworld, the lost ones who exist within the murk and murderous mayhem that lies one thin layer beneath the day-to-day experience of most New Yorkers. But tonight, with the full moon turning the girl's pale skin a deathly blue, he takes her filthy hand and tells her to come with him and although she probably figures she's looking at ten bucks, he leads her instead into a nearby café and sits her at a table, ordering her to stay put.

There was nothing unusual about Idaho Eights, except maybe the name, which was not so cleverly rendered on the menu as *idahoei8hts*. A service counter on the left contained sandwiches with exotic names and predictable fillings, while a huge mirror, which created an illusion of space for the cramped eatery, dominated the right-side wall. Below the mirror was a counter with stools, newspapers and weekly magazines neatly placed, inviting loners and losers to take their place in quarantine. Littering the floor was standard diner furniture; small square tables, blood-red surfaces rimmed with chrome, soft black cushioned chairs, also chrome framed, made to resemble another time but they were too pretty, too unblemished, to fool anyone. Patsy Cline was playing on the sound system, loud enough to interfere with table eavesdropping.

Adam ordered the girl a chicken salad sandwich and a mineral water, then added a banana muffin because he liked them and she might not want it. He watched her from a mirror, this one behind the cash register. She sat staring out to the street—the front of the restaurant consisting of five glass panels that could be opened up in summer—but staring at what Adam could not imagine, as the only thing in view was an empty playground across the street dominated by one of those fancy coloured plastic climbing, sliding, swinging apparatuses designed, Adam supposed, to put children in touch with their primordial ancestry.

He brought the tray back to the table. The girl needed no encouragement. He watched as she devoured the sandwich, chewing two or three times before swallowing each mouthful. She had taken off her coat and, despite the fall weather, was wearing nothing more substantial than a white T-shirt with several moth holes near the shoulder seams. Her nipples were erect, attesting to her chilled body temperature, and Adam could not help but admire her youthful firmness, which had so far resisted her otherwise gradual degeneration.

"You must really want to screw me," she said and only then did he realize that she had stopped eating and was staring up at him.

Adam blushed, his olive skin taking on a subtle sunburned glow, not normally given to lusting after girls half his age and embarrassed by even a hint of desire for this ravenous waif scavenging before him with little gobs of mayonnaise bookending the corners of her mouth.

Adam was not looking forward to his next birthday. He did not feel fifty. Well, maybe his knees felt fifty, and his waistline was succumbing, little by little, to the force of the earth's gravity, yet the same thoughts and dreams that had floated around his head when he was twenty even now resided there and deceived him into believing he was still a young man. You knew you were getting old though, when the Playboy centerfolds started sharing the same ages as the daughters of your friends and associates. Or so he'd been told recently by Derek. For more than a decade his interest in female companionship had not strayed beyond the companionship part of the equation, despite, he had to admit, several valiant but fruitless attempts by some wonderful and desirable women. And this disturbed Adam, as his reticence was not an intentional decision on his part. Yet, no matter how successfully he rationalized the need, desire even, to re-enter the world of romantic love, there would always come the moment when he looked inside, and every time he did, there was only a dark, desolate hole where love and romance had once lived and filled his meager life with unimagined bounty and given to him the mirage of infinite possibility. The hooker couldn't have picked a worse mark.

"You don't talk much," said the girl, half of the muffin stuffed into her mouth.

Adam decided it was a rhetorical comment and said nothing.

"What's this?" she said and reached for the card Adam had put down on the table. It was lying face down and as the girl reached over to pick it up, Adam reacted and tried to grab it, but youth was quicker and the card was in her hand while Adam's was still grasping at air.

Adam tried to snatch the card from the girl's hand but she easily pulled it out of reach and teased him with it, laughing while she danced it above his head, daring him to try to get it from her, and after a couple of vain attempts, Adam became embarrased, so he got small and quiet and asked her politely to return the card.

"I know what this is," she said, turning the card over in her hand. "It's a tarot card. There's a girl I know who has a nice little sideline going reading the other girls. Not that it ever means shit. I gave her five bucks once. She said I'd meet the man of my dreams soon. Yeah, well, she ain't seen any of my dreams or she wouldn't have said that. So, where's the rest of the deck? You don't seem to me like the fortune teller type."

"I'm not. What's your name, by the way?" asked Adam.

She introduced herself as Apple but Adam was too preoccupied to even consider the possibility of her not having been baptized with such an unusual appellation.

There was no reason to attach such importance to the card. He had been holding it in Lucia's apartment and in his haste, had forgotten to release it. But that did not really play very well, Adam had to admit. Nothing was playing well tonight, as if all of the normal signs and signals had somehow become crossed or short-circuited. And nothing pointed this out more than finding himself sitting across the table from Apple, the cracked-out prostitute street urchin.

"It's from a friend's deck. I picked it up by mistake."

"So, what does this one mean?" and she held it face up so he could see it, but he already knew what it looked like and its meaning was still fresh in his mind.

"I really have no idea. May I please have it back?"

Apple handed it over and started licking her fingers, pressing them onto the remains of the muffin then sticking them into her mouth, two at a time, sucking at them in a way that Adam figured was supposed to be construed as seductive.

Adam glanced at his watch again. He quickly thought of and discounted heading to the studio or going back to Lucia's place. There was still time to make the train.

"How old are you, Apple?" asked Adam.

Apple said she was twenty-five and he was not sure why she would lie but he was certain she was at least five years younger.

"Do you have any family in New York?"

"Oh sure, and we visit every Sunday for brunch."

"Seriously, where's your closest relative who's still talking to you?"

Apple gawked at Adam, her expression similar to that of a confused puppy when it tilts its head at something unfamiliar.

"Why do you want to know? You're not going to save me. You're not calling anyone to come get me or any bullshit goody-two-shoes crap like that."

Adam paused. What was he trying to do? It was an impulse, nothing more. He did not have the time to reflect upon it.

Apple finally said, "My brother lives in Albany, but what's it to you?"

Adam tried to think of the right thing to say as he replayed the little episode at Lucia's, then decided it was best not to think but to react, an unfamiliar position for someone whose idea of an impulse was choosing Burger King over McDonalds.

"I've been nice to you, right? Not weird, bought you some dinner, so maybe you'll do something for me, something totally crazy, without thinking about it or analyzing it."

"I knew it. I knew sooner or later you'd get around to it. But it's going to cost you more than a sandwich."

Adam placed his hand over hers and stared into her eyes with an intensity that paralyzed her momentarily.

"I don't want sex. I don't want anything from you, but I want you to do something for me. I want you to do it because I'm a nice guy and you're probably a sweet kid underneath the dirt and what do you figure a bus ticket to Albany would cost? Thirty bucks?"

Adam reached into his pocket and pulled out three twenties from the pile.

"Here's sixty. There is no reason for you to do what I'm going to

10

ask other than to humour me. I want you to call your brother and ask him if he'd like a visit from his sister. Then grab a cab and go to the Port Authority and hop on a bus. Go to Albany. Do it tonight."

With that, Adam, feeling the vagaries of his mind unleashing, got up and headed out of the restaurant and made for the PATH entrance where he quick-stepped down the stairs and into the train station.

Submerging into the depths of New York's subterranean world was not unlike a peek behind the Wizard's curtain. All pretence was stripped away; down there the glitz and glamour was replaced by exposed pipes, worn concrete and oppressive heat. The Big Apple's core was rotting, as decay and technical malfunctions easily outpaced the city's reactive attempts at maintenance.

Adam approached the turnstiles, fumbling in his pockets for some money. He could easily have called a car service to take him home, but his cell phone was in his coat and it still embarrassed him, after all these years, to be driven home in a limo. Adam passed by a bank of IEU's. There were several different types of Identification Exchange Units from which to choose. First in line was the original fingerprint reader standing next to a retina reader. And then there was the latest development in privacy intrusion—a chip reader.

It amazed Adam how readily people were allowing microchips to be surgically implanted into their wrists, all in the name of commercial convenience. On the wall near the chip reader was a print ad; a young housewife is shown sweeping her wrist over a grocery store checkout scanner, everyone smiling—the customer, the clerk and the two kids in tow. The caption read, "You're not chopped liver, but you just paid for some!" One quick swipe and somehow a signal was sent to a bank's computer, telling it to remove funds you never really possessed and move them into the grocery store account which never takes actual receipt of any cash. Neat, clean, and in Adam's opinion, terrifyingly surreal.

Adam imagined supercomputers, instantly pouring over this poor, unsuspecting woman's grocery list, dissecting her choices, analyzing her movements through the aisles, evaluating the pro rata ratio of carbohydrates to protein to fat purchases. Adam was certain that during her next visit to the same store, subtle differences would be introduced; a new end rack with her favourite cereal, a slight alteration in the positioning of the vegetables, perhaps a different light intensity in the meat section to highlight the marbled texture of the fresh cuts of beef.

A voice broke the introspective rant as a hand touched his arm. Adam turned suddenly, causing the old beggar to step back and stumble.

"I'm sorry, what did you say?" Adam asked as he reached into his pocket for coins. Some might say that giving beggars money only encouraged them, but to Adam, there could be no encouragement in desperation.

The old man gained control of his wavering, hunched-over body and repeated himself. "I said . . . you think it's kinda funny."

"Oh, I'm sorry, I thought you wanted money."

"I do," replied the beggar, "indeed I do. Have you ever tried sticking your hand in that thing over there?" He motioned towards the fingerprint IEU. "Come on, come over here a minute."

This is ludicrous, thought Adam, but then he recalled his encounter with Apple and remembered the full moon.

The man led him over to the machine. He could have been anywhere from fifty to seventy, it was impossible to tell. He was wearing schizophrenic chic—torn pants, ruined Nike cross trainers and a filthy neon-blue nylon parka, which, given the frosty evening, blew a big hole through Adam's psychotic apparel theory.

"Watch this," said the old man as he wiped his right palm up and down his pant leg. The machine looked like an arcade video game. The fingerprint reader was located at waist level, the monitor sitting above it. When operating, the screen would identify your fingerprint, acknowledge your debit and the turnstile next to it would unlock temporarily. The old man placed his hand into the reader. The monitor awoke, switching off a default instructional screen and replacing it with its reaction to the old man's touch. Adam, sans reading glasses, drew closer and read the message:

WE HAVE NO RECORD OF YOUR EXISTENCE.
PLEASE WASH YOUR HANDS AND TRY AGAIN.

"Can you believe that?" said the vagrant with a twisted smile that accentuated the rugose crevices of his gnarled face. "Those fuckers say I don't exist. Wash my hands, my ass. The day I sign up for one of these god-suckin' things is the day they install a cock detector. If I'm gonna sell my soul to some machine, I might as well get fucked for it!"

The image both amused and repulsed Adam. *Why am I indulging this guy?* "You've got a point. I haven't signed up either. Here, take this."

"I don't want your money," said the old man as he pocketed a five-dollar bill. With his other hand he reached out and grabbed Adam's forearm. There was a mad intensity in his eyes; two black holes of hurt and fear that have peered over the precipice and struggled vainly to maintain a semblance of normalcy ever since.

"It's over, you know," he said. "We're all finished here—my bones can feel it. Dreamt it too. You know it. There's still some colour left in you. Don't deny it—you know what I'm talking about. Better go. Get out while you can—no escape for me. Nowhere to go. I'll wait a bit. Maybe ride the rails tonight. Should be interesting from in here. Go. Think of me—you know me—been through this before, you and I."

Adam pulled back, unable to break the man's grip. He grew dizzy and nauseated, the old man letting go before the blackness became complete. There was an odour in the air, metallic and burning. When Adam's vision cleared, the man had disappeared into a group of commuters exiting to the street.

Too much weirdness. He had to get home. Adam took a few deep breaths and headed for the manned token station. He could not decide which was worse, being confronted by the old hoot or, in a curious way, understanding what he was talking about. How was he able to make sense of such babble? But he did. Not so much the words—more of a visceral communication, subatomic, subliminal. Adam wondered if there was a normal person on the streets this night. Was he normal tonight? Even a stoned-out Apple had probably not thought so.

Adam closed his eyes as soon as the PATH train cleared the Christopher Street station. It was cool and bright in the car and not too crowded. Adam did not qualify for the business class car. The latest development in subway travel, the upgraded compartment was neatly appointed with soft seats, newspapers, a stock ticker and vending machines. But it cost a dollar more a trip and only a wrist chip could activate the special turnstile for those compartments.

The train rumbled underneath the estuary that was the Hudson River and Adam tried not to think about it. He had a real problem imagining himself being transported beneath a sea bed. All that water above his head. He was terrified by the thought of drowning. Not so much of dying, but of gasping for air and sucking water into your lungs, then gagging and choking during those last horrible moments.

Adam jerked out of his delirium. Eyes closed, eyes open—there was to be no peace tonight. *There's still some colour left in you.* What did that mean? And what was it Lucia had said, something about a ring, that he was protected by a ring. It was all making sense, all of it, but Adam did not want it to make sense. He resisted putting the pieces of the puzzle together; Lucia's predicament, his own unease, the old man, the girl in the café . . . Sedona. He was seized suddenly by panic, felt a terrifying rush rise up from his stomach straight to his racing heart, realized he had a few heartbeats left to calm himself down before his thinking mind relinquished control to a mind unhinged.

The dialogue commenced: *Take a deep breath. Nothing to be afraid of. You've been here before. Isn't that what the old man said? Yes, that's it, think about something else. Oh shit, here comes another rush. It's claustrophobic in here. I've got to get out. I won't make it to Hoboken. Please God make this go away. Okay, okay, that's better. Calm down. That's it. Take a deep breath. This isn't such a bad one. You've had worse. Remember that time in the airplane, walking up and down the aisle. This one isn't nearly as bad. I think it's over. Yes, it's receding. Close call. Just relax. You're almost home. You'll feel better at home.*

By the time Adam Fischer reached Hoboken Station he had finally achieved his evening's goal. His mind had shut down. A walking automaton, force of habit alone led him to track 8 where he boarded a Boonton Line train bound for Mount Olive, with a 10:10 P.M. scheduled stop at the Walnut Street station in Montclair.

II

ADAM FISCHER'S EGO was of a less than average size, stunted over the years by his shyness and diffidence. It also bruised easily. Tonight though, it was taking a beating. Adam was not feeling too cool or celebrated. He found it extremely difficult to believe he was talented or worthwhile or destined for historical greatness as he sat on his knees, his arms embracing a black porcelain bowl half-filled with water while he regurgitated the dinner he had forgotten to eat. Adam had reached a degree of nausea so claustrophobic that only God's mercy could save him. His heart was still racing, generating dread and loathing as a queerly coloured fluid spewed out of his mouth. The stench of this effluvium from digestive purgatory caused disbelief that something so foul could be part of someone so admired by others. He remembered, with fondness, what life used to be like, mere minutes past. He sadly said goodbye to the good times as the next wave of nausea hit and he realized with certainty that it would always be like this, the old life gone, the cars, the restaurants, gone, gone forever. And then it was over and his dignity reappeared. But a chunk of bruising humility was left behind, as a reminder, like the admonishing whisper of a Roman slave—'*All glory is fleeting*'—into the ear of a victorious general as he parades through the streets of Rome.

If Adam had had a larger ego, the size of his home would easily have accommodated it. Two years before, he had abruptly sold his Upper East Side brownstone and left Manhattan for the tree-lined streets of Montclair, New Jersey. This action was perceived as more than a move to the suburbs. To his friends and business cronies, Adam's abandonment of their beloved city was an act of treachery.

Clearly there were mysterious forces at play, but no one could figure out what they were, exactly. Adam would obliquely mention the need for a change; he needed quiet, he needed to get away. This from a man who spent successive days and nights secreted away in a recording studio, cut off from the rest of the world, oblivious to time or events, a man as divorced from mainstream life as a person could be and still be able to function within it.

What was most subversive about Adam's move, the one possibility no one who knew him well wanted to face, even had they been able to verbalize it, was that by removing himself from the scene, Adam was clearly making a declaration. The scene no longer mattered to him. And if Adam didn't think something was cool anymore, then maybe it wasn't.

Not that he paid much attention to the gossip surrounding his departure. Adam went about the business of producing hit records with a preoccupation that made him oblivious to his celebrity within the music industry. There were mornings when he would pause before the Grammy Awards sitting on his dresser. He would read the inscription and wonder how it was that these trophies had happened to end up in his bedroom with his name engraved on the shiny brass plates.

It was nearing midnight when Adam called Derek Eaton to see if his perpetual houseguest was in residence. After having renewed himself with a cool shower and a late night snack of plain yogurt with almonds and strawberries, Adam had found his way to his favourite chair, winged back with a muted beige floral pattern, located in front of huge bay windows in his study, had been sitting there for some time, admiring the panoramic view, when the desire for Derek's counsel struck him. I must be desperate, thought Adam. Derek's advice, like the Devil's, was always heavily mortgaged.

It was far more house than Adam Fischer, middle-aged Jewish widower, required. The Tudor mansion was located on the west side of Upper Mountain Avenue. The property rose steeply from the street, resting comfortably high on a hill. Worn down by epochs of erosion, the north-south running ridge currently gave only a hint of its past majesty, yet remained a formidable one-mile climb on nearby Route 280, where transport trucks and vehicles laboured up its eastern slope.

The backyard of the estate melded seamlessly with the Eagle Rock Nature Reserve which sat on the crest of the ridge, while the front afforded a spectacular view of the Manhattan skyline, fifteen miles or so distant to the east as the helicopter flies, which they sometimes did when Adam's services were immediately required downtown. Built of stone, three stories tall, the house was stately yet charming, one's eye drawn to the portico that arched over the driveway on the right side, protecting the side entrance.

Adam's profession was not a natural fit with those of his neighbours, a street with as many Ivy League degrees as Adam had gold records adorning the walls of his study. And there might have been some talk about the world famous record producer who had moved into the Barnes estate, except no one on the street knew he was world famous and most had not seen him or talked to him, nor had they any idea what he did for a living.

Montclair, the suburb with a conscience, a bedroom community with the aspirations of a town, cultivated, integrated, its citizens involved, vocal and committed to cloning the best of New York's liberal, inclusive, free expression lifestyle and transplanting it fifteen miles to the west. All of these things made Montclair an attractive alternative to living in Manhattan and perhaps would have lured Adam there had he been aware of them. But no, it was a full moon that did it, casting its reflected light on the Barnes estate as Adam drove by one night, late for a dinner party at a friend's house. In an instant he knew where he would next live without examining why. Sometimes you imagine your dream home and sometimes, as was the case with Adam, you just dream it.

Adam and Derek met backstage at an outdoor rock festival during the summer of 1969. Derek Eaton was not there for the music; he was promoting an open-air festival of his own outside of Toronto, funded by two wealthy fathers whose sons had been classmates of Derek's at private school. To label his friends as classmates was a bit of a technicality since Derek had managed to miss more classes than any other student in the school's eighty-five-year history. The school administrators had tired of keeping tabs on Derek. His parents were spending a lot of money so that Derek could hone his pool game. Eventually, the school decided the tuition was inequitable compensation for the aggravation and he was expelled. Since going home was never an option, Derek, at age fifteen, hitched a ride out of Toronto to Buffalo, eventually ending up in New York.

The festival was called Woodstock, named after a quaint town in upstate New York that was generously seeded with artists and musicians. The actual event took place in Bethel, seventy miles away. For months, the promoters had cleverly advertised and promoted their concert into the consciousness of the youth underground.

Three days of peace and music.

Adam was making a name for himself as a sound engineer at the time, specializing in live outdoor events. He couldn't imagine a better life. He didn't get laid as much as the rock stars did, but they would generally fuck anything conscious and female, although the former was not an absolute prerequisite. Adam hated himself every time he walked away from a sure thing, but there was always a voice inside sabotaging the lecherous advances of the wolf, finding some fault—maybe she bit her nails or had a zit on her chin or didn't know Captain Beefheart from Captain Kirk—that would short-circuit the attraction. He was bored by the ones who were incapable of saying anything intelligent and was smothered by those who had mastered the rhetoric of sixties angst. He was picky in an age when they were giving it away for free. It was like kicking the tires of a borrowed car.

Adam did not really know Janis Joplin. He was generally pretty shy around the musicians, no, not the musicians, but the stars, the head-liners. They were constantly engulfed by a human swarm; entourage, sycophants, label executives, managers, agents and friends and Adam lacked the will—he was missing the chutzpah gene—to break through and make contact. He wasn't the star-struck type, but something about Janis appealed to him. There was a shyness he could read in her eyes; a backstage room full of weed smoke and alcohol vapors, the constant clashing dissonance of voices one-upping each other, and there sat Janis, the eye of the hurricane, a pint of Southern Comfort in her hand maybe; those sad, searching eyes half hidden behind her stringy, coarse hair, and you knew she was somewhere else, searching for that safe place, anesthetizing the fear with booze, nowhere to run, events consuming her and pushing her faster than her mind could digest. And you wanted to reach out and tell her it was all right, it was okay, there was some-one else who shared the pain, but you didn't, you couldn't, either do the reaching or really feel it.

Adam is backstage late Saturday night, having been relieved tem-porarily from the sound board, is weaving his way through canyons of speakers and amplifiers with a dying flashlight, desperately search-ing for some microphones to sacrifice later in the evening to the equip-ment bashing Who. Sly and the Family Stone have left the stage, hav-ing taken everybody higher, when he sees this guy tucked in behind a Marshall amp, all crouched down, then he pops his head up at the wrong time and Janis sees him too.

"You son of a bitch!" she screams as she brushes by Adam, her love beads slashing upwards and smacking Adam in the nose as she runs by and he wonders where the shy, scared girl has gone, but then he knows that she's next to hit the stage and the stage transforms her, turns up her pain full blast, especially if she's had a few; only now she's chasing this guy around the amplifiers, and the dude's playing that game you learned as a kid—it must have a name but Adam doesn't know it—where you keep a large object between you and your adversary, in Adam's case, usually his older brother, Kevin. Sometimes it was a tree or maybe a parked car, and it was frustrating as hell for Kevin, because every move he made to get Adam, Adam countered with a move of his own, a carousel dance of self-preservation. The guy, long blond hair flying across his face, is keeping a Fender Bass amp between himself and Janis. She's jumping and lashing out, trying to dig her nails into his face, the bangles on her left wrist a sonic warning, and he's laughing, can hardly breathe he's having such a good time, all the while keeping her at bay.

"I'll fuckin' kill you for this!" and you wonder what he's done, but then while you're wondering if you should intercede, you hear Chip Monck over the P.A. introduce Janis Joplin to a crowd the size of a small city. Adam knows he has to do something because the band is starting to make those little musical hiccups always heard before the set starts—a short, machine-gun drum roll, guitar tuning, test, test, one, two, three, test, and their leader is still backstage attempting emergency eye surgery on a recalcitrant patient. But at last the guy bolts, disappearing further into the backstage area and darkness, his leather vest flapping behind him and Janis turns, the fire in her eyes momentarily doused.

She looks at Adam. It only takes a second but he absorbs it all, watches as the vibe reaches her, sees the rage redirected, channeled and focused. A smile, just the hint of one, closed mouthed, and she runs past him to bask in the warmth of half a million strong.

Derek had never really explained to Adam what he'd done to make Janis so mad. In truth, he had, over time, given Adam so many variations on a theme that it had become impossible for Adam to extract the mushroom from the horseshit.

"Adam, it's midnight for Christ's sake. You wouldn't call a normal person at this hour."

"Your point?"

Adam was not concerned with the lateness of his call. Derek was a night owl and besides, he lived in the coach house for free; Adam could take certain liberties.

"Right. I forgot. Normal people have jobs and go to sleep by midnight."

"And pay rent," replied Adam.

"A low blow, given, I take it, due to the time of night and the import of the call?"

"I saw Lucia this evening."

"Great, and I had a tuna salad sandwich for lunch."

"Dolphin killer."

"Listen soybean boy, no lectures. You called me. So what did she see in her crystal ball this time?"

"I don't want to talk about it over the phone. Jump into your bathrobe and come over."

"Jenny's here."

"Jenny's always here. Give her a kiss for me and come over. I really need to talk to you."

Something in Adam's voice must have made Derek belay an internal command to respond with a witty rejoinder.

"Give me a minute," he said then put down the phone and reached for a pair of jeans. He didn't own a bathrobe.

Derek Eaton was no relation to the Canadian Eaton department store dynasty, although Derek's father claimed the existence of a common ancestor. This, his father had believed, entitled him to a storewide discount which he was not shy in demanding from every beleaguered cashier he encountered, and to a young Derek's astonishment and embarrassment, more often than not, a ten percent deduction was granted, as if it was a store policy to offer price reductions to bastard relatives. Derek believed his parents, who had emigrated from England to Toronto in the late '40s, were Communist spies, deep cover moles, waiting a lifetime in obscurity for the cipher that would instantly activate their dormant other selves. Derek's father claimed to have known Kim Philby, which only added to the credibility of Derek's suspicions.

Derek entered without ringing, proceeding down the central hallway, past the stairs on his right leading to the second floor, straight through the living room to the study. The house gave him the creeps, so he'd told Adam many times; not the house so much as Adam living in it, alone, something obscene in the amount of space being preserved for one person. This, of course, from a man who had yet to meet a couch he couldn't crash on, a man who considered roots to be invisible chains, designed to bind you to one place, one person, one destiny.

Adam was seated with his back to the door.

"Something bad is going to happen," said Adam without turning.

"If you continue leaving your door unlocked, you're absolutely right. I read it in the Montclair Times today . . . there are at least two or three break-ins in Montclair everyday."

"I saw Lucia this evening," Adam said, ignoring the admonishment.

"So you said on the phone. Just spill it, man. You're starting to weird me out."

"She said there was a ring around me."

"I see . . . could you please translate that into English from whole earth cookie language?"

How long had it been, three hours? And already the details were hazing over, eluding his inspection, a mental hide-and-seek game where coherent thoughts appeared, nearly recognizable, then ducked down and disappeared into an infinite network of electrical impulses and chemical reactions. Adam spent the better part of an hour describing to Derek as best he could, sometimes verbatim, other times hesitatingly, unsure of himself, the gist of what had occurred in Lucia's apartment.

First there had been the frantic phone call to the studio. Adam was in Soundtrax, a small studio in Chelsea, mixing a track for a very popular act. He was doing a friend a favour, troubleshooting the final mix for the band's next album. He was working on drum sounds for the first single when the call came into the studio.

"Hi Lucia, how did you find me?"

"Your assistant gave me your number. You have to come over here right now."

"Right now? Where are you? Is everything all right?"

"Yes, at home and no."

"Huh?"

"I mean yes, right now, I'm home and no, everything is far from being all right."

"Are you sick?"

"Yes, I'm sick . . . and scared, and I need you to come over and stop asking me questions. Will you please just come? I need you. I'm freaking out. Now please, tell your little musician friends that uncle Adam has some personal business to take care of and get over here. I mean it."

This was hardly the first time Adam had received a distress call from Lucia. He had absorbed a steady diet of them for the last ten years, beginning very early in their relationship when he was one of the most sought after producers on the planet and she was going to be the next big thing, his next big thing.

21

The feeding frenzy was in full gorge when he arrived at the Mercury Lounge on that night so long ago. Every label had their A&R people at the gig, some jostling for position near the stage, some hanging in the far corners—cave denizens waiting for their next meal to be served up.

Adam hated clubs. He hated the cigarette smoke, he hated the smell of beer, mostly he hated waiting until 11:30 for the band to come on stage. Never comfortable with small talk, Adam found it unbearable to attempt it with ninety or so decibels coming through the sound system. "You have to come down and see this girl," his manager had insisted over the phone. "Someone from Elektra found her in some shithole bar in her hometown—near Albany I think—and now everyone wants to sign her. I have her demos and it's the real shit. You have to come."

So there stood the snob producer in a dark corner, dressed a little too refined for the setting in a three-quarter length calf-skin coat, wearing smartly creased dark wool pants and Italian leather shoes, smug in his aloofness, casually holding a regulatory beer bottle, a member of rock's ruling elite, to whom deference was paid and isolation was more or less respected.

Just give me a food pellet, Adam thought.

Adam was a big fan of B.F. Skinner. He had seen a laboratory film of a rat pressing furiously on a bar until a food pellet fell out of a hole. And Adam identified with the rat, always pushing the bar, always wondering when the next pellet would drop.

What had Skinner done to elicit such extraordinary behaviour? Nothing more radical than noticing that when a girl smiles at a guy, the guy invariably smiles back and maybe goes so far as to start up a conversation, having subconsciously digested the smile as a primal green light to proceed. He says something clever, the girl smiles again and another food pellet drops from the slot. Adam was in the club because every now and then, after dozens of nights of enduring mediocre talent, sophomoric lyrics or poor musicianship—or all of the above—he was revitalized by the dazzling presence of pure, raw talent. And so long as another gifted singer or band came around every year or so, the behaviour was reinforced, guaranteeing that when Adam's manager called and asked him to please come see 'this fabulous girl', Adam dutifully came, always aware of the forces manipulating his own shaped behaviour which led him, like a cow with a nose ring, to the edge of the swarm now moving slowly towards the front of the stage to check out the latest buzz band to arrive on the New York club scene.

Lucia was great that night. Her presence filled the room like a narcotic gas. He could not take his eyes off her, switching between her long tanned legs—exposed between her Doc Martens and an extremely short black cocktail dress—and her face, chiseled to perfection, dark hair pulled back severely, allowing her bone structure to dominate and inspire, her liquid green eyes searching the audience, unafraid, a Greek goddess turned art house temptress. Adam watched, mesmerized, her energy an electric thread weaving its way through the room and for a moment taking everyone away from themselves. But only for a moment.

As the cab pulled onto Christopher Street, Adam asked himself a question that had plagued him for years—what had gone wrong with Lucia's career? All of the ingredients were there. Everyone thought the first album was brilliant or at least a promising start. The reviews were for the most part positive, the live act was first rate; she got all the press she could have wished for and the record label worked its brains out to get the first single on the radio. And nothing. Not a dent. Sure, it went on to sell about thirty-five thousand records, but with over two million invested in the project, her record label lost interest and Lucia's career was over before it really had a chance to begin.

While reaching into his pocket for his money clip, the answer began to percolate up from the depths of the right side, past the analysis, past the postulation and second guessing, ignoring the gates and walls, a feral dog of an idea running wildly through the ordered neatness of Adam's manicured mindscape. Adam knew why Lucia could never become a star. She already was a star.

He got out of the cab; the squeals of children playing on Grove Street where it was barred to car traffic unnerved him momentarily. He was suddenly reluctant to take the steps to the front door of Lucia's trendy West Village apartment, a premonitory moment paralyzing him as every neurotic impulse he owned began clearing its throat to be heard; paranoia taking the stand first, demanding a hasty retreat; obsession next, warning that any awful thoughts brought on by this visit would be examined and cross-examined for days, even weeks; anxiety in the gallery making too much noise, threatening to drown out the others. But reason still held the gavel, pounding the others into temporary submission as Adam placed his index finger on the button next to Lucia Dillane's name and depressed it gently.

III

LUCIA DILLANE'S APARTMENT resembled her mind—scattered, disorganized and cluttered to overflow. Big overstuffed purple pillows belonging to the couch had been left end to end on the floor in front of the TV, little elbow cavities permanently installed in the fabric of the pillow closest to the screen. The coffee table, a curved device resembling a paramecium, was inlayed with a black and gold-tiled mosaic that Lucia believed was only decipherable from above, the design currently obscured by cardboard pint boxes of half-eaten Chinese food, fashion and music magazines, some costume jewelry and a clear glass bowl of coloured condoms which were really chocolate mints. An odd assortment of unmatched shoes lay scattered near the front door.

There was a desk in the corner by the door, more of a bridge table really, Lucia having retrieved it from the sidewalk one garbage day. On it a deck of tarot cards had toppled, lying scattered neatly like fallen dominos. There were dozens of small, dark vials of essences—lavender, sandalwood, yin yang, frankincense—all pushed together where the table met the corner.

Pictures clung haphazardly to the two converging walls, above the desk, some torn from magazines like the black and white picture of a male model, visible from the shoulders up, intently applying nail polish to a very feminine foot in his hand, while others were obligatory family pictures; sister and baby, sister and baby and hubby, parents and grandchild and one picture of Adam, hunched over a forty-eight track SSL board, intently writing something on a piece of masking tape that had been placed lengthwise along the bottom of the controls. Lucia would often stare at his picture then at the nail polish ad and wistfully replace the male model with Adam, and the exquisite foot with her own.

Lucia believed a home should be an externalization of one's hopes and dreams, an expression of who you are, where you've been and what you wish to be, a shrine and nest and refuge, rolled into one.

This belief was being sorely tested as Lucia ran around, desperately straightening up. Odd expression, *straightening up*, she thought. Straighten up, clean up, get up. If you could get down, why couldn't you straighten down? Oh, shut up, Adam is going to be here any minute and he already thinks I'm a slob. Well, I am a slob, but why hand over more incriminating evidence to the prosecution.

Lucia heaved the pillows back onto the couch, adjusted a framed print of Picasso's *Two Acrobats with a Dog*—the painting always made her feel hungry—turned on her lava lamp with its yellow ooze, checked herself in the mirror by the right side of the front door, then waited for the buzzer. She looked around the apartment and decided it was a showcase for either a creative genius or a schizophrenic. And in Lucia's world, there wasn't all that much difference between the two.

She was pleased by her reflected image. And Adam would be pleased as well. Thirty-five and her breasts were still full and perky, legs long and smooth, the waist narrow, and buttocks round and firm. Clinique and limited exposure to the 'harmful rays of the sun' had kept the small lines around her eyes small, cute even, adding character when she smiled. "Yeah right, character my ass," she said to the mirror.

She had chosen a short skirt, a sort of Halloween-influenced design with different hues of orange and brown swirling about, an orange T-shirt with a V-neck so that Adam could cop a peek when he thought she wasn't looking, her silky soft, dyed-black hair pulled back and held in place by a scrunchee high up on her crown.

She studied her eyes, green cat-eye ovals that ruled majestically above her high cheekbones and wondered for a moment why she cared so much about pleasing Adam, about being attractive for him, wanting his gaze to contain the hunger of a wolf sizing up its prey. With most men, that look disgusted her along with the incessant, vulgar taunting. What do men think—that they're being complimentary, making themselves desirable? Adam once told her men like that were merely playing the law of averages—something about rats and food pellets—and all they needed was one smile, one unsuspecting dullard of a girl who actually stops and smiles and perhaps even thinks it's complimentary to have guys hanging out of vans with large company advertising painted on the sides, shouting crude praises at her. God, men are jerks, she thought. But you can't live without them and you can't have them neutered.

Yes, she liked what she saw in the mirror and would surely burn in hell for the pleasure derived from her own image. She wasn't one of those pure, unaffected beauties who are blissfully unaware of the sweet pain their countenance brings to the world they inhabit. No mock modesty in this girl, no contrived innocence. What was that old saying? If you've got it, flaunt it.

The odd thing was she didn't much care about it in others. She admired beautiful men and women both, but she admired Van Gogh and Picasso more. Adam was handsome; he didn't look fifty, barely forty, but he was fifty, almost, and everything was softening and sagging just a bit. And yet she had to concentrate to see it. She had to be mad at him to point it out. Mostly, she saw Adam, the sweet, gentle whelp of a soul who made her laugh, who always had something interesting to say, whose advice was sound if not always taken and who loved her mind more than he loved her body. Not that she would mind if for once he reversed the two.

Funny, Lucia no longer felt as desperate as she had when she first called Adam. Was that manipulation? Or denial, perhaps? Probably the latter. This was serious. She had never experienced this . . . this total block. It reminded her of songwriting, her guitar on her lap, strumming chords, struggling for lyrics, with nothing coming out of her mouth more profound than drool. But this was different. This wasn't about her livelihood—this was about her life. About life.

When Adam walked through the door, he immediately settled himself into the purple couch, his eyes drawn to the table in the corner. He still had his coat on and was obviously uncomfortable; if he wore a fedora, he'd be fiddling with it in his lap. His expression was as blank as someone suffering from amnesia who has been taken to a location intended to arouse lost memories.

"Had any live ones today?" he asked, throwing his head in the general direction of the table.

"That's what I want to talk to you about."

Lucia joined Adam on the couch, curling her long legs underneath her buttocks while keeping her knees pressed together. There were things a girl could reveal and things Mother said should never be seen with the lights on.

"Adam, I know we have a kind of unwritten rule, you and I. You've made it very plain to me countless times that you don't want to talk about my, you know, my . . . gift."

"The 'C' word, you mean," said Adam.

"Yes, the 'C' word," she said and the exasperation in her voice was not lost on Adam.

26

"It's not so much I don't want to hear about it, it's more that I'd rather not be around when you're opening it."

"Opening it?"

"Your gift."

"Very funny. May I assume by your presence that I am free to discuss it now?"

Adam nodded.

"Thank you." Lucia, using her hands like crutches, moved her torso across the couch until her knees were next to Adam's thigh. She stared into Adam's brown eyes; he looked away, suddenly finding something important about the front of his coat to inspect. There was no pretence in her eyes but she could see the forced approbation in his.

"Adam, why do you live in a huge house by yourself, away from your work, away from your friends—and me?"

"You're the clairvoyant—you tell me."

"Fuck off, I'm serious. I need to know."

She watched as he struggled to swallow whatever flippant retort he had planned for her. She could see him search, first for an appeasing answer, then for an ancillary answer, and finally for some piece of the truth.

"It's not so much the house as it is where the house is located," he said and there was resignation in the sound of his words.

"That rather begs the question, don't you think? Why is being away from all of this, all of us, so important to you?"

"I told you when I bought the house. I needed to get away. I practically stole the property. The old gal just wanted to unload it. She already had more money than God. And it gave me all of the room I could ever need and besides, I like being alone." He had to stop to take a breath.

"Why have you never told me what happened to you in Sedona?"

"Because nothing happened to me in Sedona." Adam shifted and made much drama out of finding a more comfortable position for his body. "It was so long ago. Why would you ask me something like that? Has my good buddy Derek been opening his yap?"

"No. He once told me something very strange had happened there but he wouldn't elaborate. I don't know why I asked. It comes into my head sometimes."

"Why am I here, Lucia?"

"Okay, okay, forget it. Here's why I called you. I was running around, doing errands earlier, just regular stuff; I had to pick up some film, do a little grocery shopping, and I'm walking along the sidewalk, la dee da, when I decide to play my little psychic spying game. You know what I'm talking about. I love people, I love New Yorkers and when I'm in the mood, I just open up and watch the colours. You have no idea how entertaining it is. I'm bombarded with all of this energy; weird stuff, ancient stuff, sick, twisted, happy, sad . . . whatever. So I'm walking along, I open myself up and nothing. Not a vibe, not a colour, nada, nothing. I freaked. Got dizzy. I had to sit down at a doorstep and put my head between my legs. I mean, this has never happened to me before. As long as I can remember, I've been able to see people's auras without trying."

"Maybe you're tired. Maybe you need some rest to recharge your batteries."

"Thank you, thank you for that wonderfully condescending remark. The weird thing is, Adam, I can see your aura right now. It's yellow in case you were wondering, a glorious bright, sunshine yellow."

"I wasn't and I wish you wouldn't do that."

"I can no more stop it than I can stop breathing."

Adam turned towards Lucia, releasing his body from its temporary paralysis, taking her hands in his. He looked at them admiringly; long and narrow, golden fingers, tapering to oval racetrack-shaped nails. She knew he hated the purple nail polish.

"The day you stop breathing I stop breathing."

"Bullshit!"

"All right. How about—I don't mean to belittle you and your weird, crystal ball, hocus pocus."

"How about admitting what you're so deathly afraid to admit—that I do have the gift of clairvoyance. You know it is real and I know you hate not being able to think it away." She withdrew her hands and stared at them as if they were not hers, as if they were some trinket or bauble she had picked off a store shelf to examine.

"Adam, I am so very tired of tiptoeing around your universe. I need you on my side. I need you, of all people, to believe in me, believe in my world. You know I believe in yours. Why can't you do the same for me?"

Adam fell back into the couch. He bought some more time by removing his coat.

"I've decided to stay—don't try to talk me out of it." He turned again towards Lucia. "The fact is, I have always believed in your talent, musical and otherwise. I have no doubt that you possess what-

28

ever it is you possess. What exactly is it you possess, anyway? You've never actually told me what you think is going on in that gorgeous head of yours."

She answered with a kiss. It was long and hard, and it lit her insides with the intensity of a propane gas explosion. Adam returned it eagerly at first, his fingers finding her waist, then he disengaged, embarrassed.

"There. Ten years in the making. And don't tell me you didn't enjoy it," said Lucia.

"Okay, I won't," said Adam. "Was it something I said?" He unconsciously took two fingers and gently rubbed his lips, massaging her wetness into his.

"No, it was something I've been waiting for you to do but I couldn't wait any longer."

"You know why I can't," he said and an uncomfortable silence came between them. Adam finally broke the spell. "So tell me what you think is going on. How does this all work?"

"For whatever reason they aren't letting me see."

"They? Not he or she?"

"No, it's definitely *they*, a collective. They decide what I see and what I am not allowed to see. But *they* have never drawn the curtain down like this before."

"Can you communicate with them?"

"No, no Adam, you're missing the point. This is not a two-way dialogue. I don't see spirits, I don't hear things. It's more like a waking dream. I can't explain to you how I know it is being directed to me by a spirit group. It's like going to the movies—you don't need to go upstairs to the projection room to confirm there's a guy up there changing reels. You just know he's there. It's the same with my abilities. The movie I'm watching is being sent to me, or more accurately, I'm looking out a window and can only see what is paraded past."

Adam took a sudden interest in Lucia's lava lamp. Lucia watched as his eyes followed yellow lumps of the lava ascending to the top of the glass cylinder. My god, she thought, he's actually digesting what I have to say. Would he consider it, analyze it, then dismiss it as PMS or some other insignificant ailment? But that wasn't fair. This was a hot spot for Adam, forbidden territory and she must tread with careful, dainty steps.

"I don't see how anything you have said so far explains your ability to see colours," Adam said.

"They don't control that, but if you don't mind another analogy, I drive the car but they pay for the gas. Today the tank is empty. Today they're leaving me at the on deck circle without a paddle."

"You're mixing your metaphors, but I catch your drift."

"It's as if they are protecting me from something they don't want me to see. It's scaring the crap out of me."

"Now, let's think about this for a minute. You normally have no difficulty zoning in, as it were. You see auras at will. How about when you're doing a reading, do you ever come up dry?"

"Sure, sometimes I can't pick up anything from a person, but it's usually them, not me."

Lucia explained how a client will show up at the appointed hour. Lucia may offer tea, if she's in the mood, or have the person sit on the purple couch while they chitchat aimlessly about the weather or the news of the day. Meanwhile, Lucia is circling her prey, folding into herself to that other place, a place here but not here, as if this world had a double image, one world slightly out of synch with the other. Like a time-lapse photograph, Lucia begins to see both worlds simultaneously, begins to watch the drama unfold, a silent movie of imagery and vistas; it's as if she is being taken blindfolded to a foreign country, dropped off into the countryside and told—Go ahead, try to figure out where you are. But occasionally Lucia would need to buy more time because nothing was coming up—she'd keep the small talk going, offer cookies with the tea. After a while, she would draw out why the client had put up mental walls. There was nothing to see because the client was jamming his or her own spiritual circuits.

"I've had bad days. Days when my head is so messed up it feels like I am at a loud party and I can only hear fragments, psychic gobbly goop, but nothing coherent, nothing useful. Today I feel like I've been exposed to green kryptonite. Today I feel mortal."

"You said you could still see my aura? What's the deal with that?" asked Adam.

"Maybe it's because I know you so well and just think I see it. Maybe that's what's happening. I'm so used to seeing your aura that I can call it up when it's not really visible to me."

Adam got up and started pacing in front of Lucia. She watched as he walked back and forth, quick turns—there wasn't much room—worry lines building on his forehead, five parallel creases, and she drew imaginary musical notes on them and a treble clef by his right temple. She liked her serious friend. She liked him far too much.

30

Adam's six-foot frame probably measured five-foot-nine as he walked back and forth listing forward at about twenty degrees. His hair was full and straight, the brown locks only suggesting gray near his temples. He wore it in a dated way, almost collegiate with a side part and long bangs pushed off to one side, shorter than his sixties shoulder length hippie style, but much longer than the current trend of fifties crew cut styles. He looked like James Taylor with hair. He had one hand up over his mouth, playing with a non-existent goatee; long and slender hands, too pretty for a man. His skin was too smooth, his nose too slender. He would have made a great girl.

Adam turned and stood above her.

"How familiar are you with Edgar Cayce?" he asked.

"I've read a few books. He's the real deal. Why?"

"I saw a program about him once. His talents seem very similar to yours."

"Similar perhaps, but you're talking about a guy whose trance-reading transcripts can be found in the Library of Congress. My sessions can be found on Maxell cassette tapes, hidden in my clients' dresser drawers. I'm a little surprised you know anything about him."

Adam smiled. "I read a lot of occult books in the sixties when you were discovering the joys of going diaper-free."

"I was toilet trained at one and a half, asshole."

"Overachiever. Anyway, there's this story about Edgar Cayce. Seems he was visiting a department store, might have been in New York, I can't remember. So he's standing at the elevator waiting for the doors to open when a young woman appears next to him to await the arrival of the elevator. Now Cayce had claimed being able to see auras since childhood. Like you, it was second nature for him. Cayce becomes somewhat disconcerted by the fact that this woman is giving off no aura. I suppose, like you, he initially passed it off as an anomaly. Just then the doors to the elevator open. There are four or five people in the elevator. Cayce is paralyzed by what he sees. Or more accurately, by what he doesn't see. Like the woman beside him who has preceded him into the elevator, none of the occupants has an aura. Cayce remains stationary as the elevator doors close. Moments later, a malfunction causes the elevator to plunge several floors, killing those trapped inside. "

There was an uneasy silence. They looked away from each other. Adam finally got up and walked over to the window. He moved the drape with his finger.

"What are you doing?" Lucia asked.

"I'm playing Where's Waldo, my own paranoid version. Come over here and tell me what you see."

Lucia approached the window.

"What am I trying to see?" she asked.

"Colour."

"I don't see any."

"Read me."

"What?"

"Read me. You can see my colour. Let's see what else you can see."

Lucia recoiled into the corner of the couch.

"I can't read you, Adam. Even on a good day. We're too close. I know too much about you. I'm too vested."

"Too vested?"

"Adam, do you want a road map? I care about you. I don't read friends, relatives or lovers or my clients' significant others."

"I guess that makes us friends. Hey, I won't sue if you give me bogus lottery numbers. Let's just see what happens. Let's try to make some sense of all this."

"I'm afraid, Adam. You don't understand what it's like to live in my world. When I was small, I was terrified by images I couldn't explain, thoughts I hadn't thought. It felt like there was a radio in my head and I couldn't turn it off. I remember a day in grade school; the teacher asked the class if anyone knew how many Americans died in the Civil War. I stood up. I could hear myself talking but the words were spilling out without my having to think of them first. I told the class it was too smoky to see much of anything, what with the shells landing in our yard and musket fire, but even over the din, I could hear men screaming. Then I stopped talking. All of their eyes were on me—on the freak. Then followed a trip to the nurse's office, and a few weeks later I was put into a private school. I'm telling you all this because this talent of mine, this gift from the gods is an awful weight. I didn't ask for it and I'd be happier without it. I've helped a lot of people along the way, and that makes it worth it. But there has always been a warning, a message from my masters. And it goes something like this: Don't fuck around in the spirit world."

Adam walked over to Lucia's desk and absently picked up a tarot card. He turned it over in his hand. It was a medieval scene. A young boy is leaning down towards a small girl child, perhaps his sister, his legs bent to compensate for the disparity in their height, holding in his outstretched hands, a large chalice full of flowers. He is dressed in long sleeves, a short skirt with knee socks, his face peering out from a liripipe hood with shoulder extensions, the pointed tippet flowing halfway down his back. The little girl, preparing to accept the chalice, almost the same size as she, is wearing a peasant's dress with a shawl draped over her head and shoulders. She wears mittens. Beyond them, in the background, a house and larger building appear, sturdily built, one resembling a castle or some sort of public building. Almost hidden, a guard with a lance, his back to the scene, patrols the entrance to the castle. To the left of the boy, another chalice sits upon a small stand. In the foreground, four more chalices on the ground. All are filled with flowers.

"What's this?" asked Adam.

"It's the six of cups."

"What does it mean?" asked Adam.

"It's a card representing nostalgia, the past, memories of childhood or an old love, some precious memory carried with you always. It says that dreams can still be realized."

Adam flinched. He saw his wife's face, it filled his mind, the way she looked at him when he had first told her that he loved her, her eyes so wide and dark and filled with reflected feeling. He was momentarily seized with painful longing and unrelenting regret.

"Adam, picking up a card randomly can have tremendous meaning or mean nothing. Besides, you're showing it to me upside down."

"What difference does that make?"

"It makes all the difference to some tarot readers. There is a reverse meaning to every card. The reverse of the six of cups is prophetic in nature. It represents that which will come to pass presently; a new relationship, new knowledge, a new environment. It foreshadows change, from the familiar to the unfamiliar."

Adam continued to examine the card. He tried to glean some meaning from it. But all he could see was a scene out of Robin Hood.

Adam said, "A single card drawn can mean something or nothing. Does this card mean anything to you, Lucia? Will you read me?"

"I already am. As soon as you picked up the card, the whole room was lit by your aura. I've never seen anything quite like it. There is a yellow ring around you, emanating from your solar plexus. It's like you are being protected from something."

"So you haven't been totally shut down."

"I can read you. But I've never seen anything like this before. When

I say you have a yellow aura I mean that's your dominant colour right now. It can change. If you get mad or aroused for instance. But normally the light is in the shape of an egg. I don't understand the ring thing. Let's not try to analyze it though. We'll just go with it for now."

Lucia was still seated on the couch. She stared to the left of where Adam was standing, focused far past the confines of the apartment, in the manner of a shipwrecked sailor scanning the horizon for a passing ship.

"What do you see?"

"They won't let me really see it. Usually I sense their presence; like I said before, I know the visions are directed. But right now, I can almost hear them, as if they are calling out to me. Oh no . . . "

Lucia jerks violently. Her legs shoot out from underneath her like a released switchblade, extending over the couch onto the floor. Her hands press down against her sides. She is frozen at attention, a mannequin lying over the end of the couch. Then her body relaxes slightly and she begins to speak:

"We are the guides who communicate through this incarnate body. We speak to the entity known in this plane as Adam, as we so speak at this time to others by way of other incarnate beings. Seek out the others. Seek out those who listen. The earth is a living body. She must cleanse herself as she has done before. Leave this place. The entity Adam must help. The entity must discover its soul purpose. The entity must connect to the fibers of energy flowing through it and all things. There is much to learn. There is little time. The entity already knows what it must do. The way and the means have been previously revealed. Guard this incarnate being. Leave this place."

Adam is stunned. He staggers back from the couch in mortal fear. The voice emanating from Lucia's mouth is hoarse and masculine, the volume, ear splitting. If there is a voice of God, then he has heard it. He falls back into the chair by Lucia's desk. He sits there for several minutes in stunned silence, his eyes unwavering from Lucia's face, wishing away what he has just witnessed, dreading the return of the voice, knowing in one instant what he has heard, denying in the next the possibility of its existence.

A half hour passes before Adam feels he can rise from the chair. He goes over to Lucia and bends down close to her face. She appears very peaceful in sleep, more beautiful than he has ever seen her. Although her eyes are closed, he swears he can feel her emerald-encased pupils observing him. He carefully lifts her legs onto the couch, one hand still pinching the tarot card, and covers her with a blanket. He leans over and gently kisses her cheek. He is suddenly filled with desire for her, but a desire not driven by lust. He gets up and closes the door quietly behind him.

IV

THE GRAND MARNIER SWISHED AROUND the snifter, adhering to the circular movements of Derek's hand. In one deft movement he emptied the last sip into his mouth, embracing it momentarily before releasing it to his throat, smiling as the warm sensation followed in its wake.

Derek had been listening from behind Adam's chair. Now he placed himself in front of Adam, blocking his view of the Manhattan skyline.

"You actually believe it might be true. Your perceptions tell you it is true. But you cannot know if it is true. And it's driving you nuts. You have no faith, my friend. That is your problem."

Derek drifted back to the built-in wall cabinet and poured himself another drink. He had listened patiently during Adam's moderately coherent description of the evening's events and now his patience was spent.

"In case you haven't noticed, good buddy, you're in love with Lucia, but you can't admit it to yourself because you have already experienced the love of your life and, even if you were able to get past that, Lucia has a fatal flaw in your estimation. She thinks she's psychic and you can't handle it. Because in your world we are born, we live, we eat and sleep and shit and screw and maybe squeeze out a bit of happiness, or at least some occasional joy, then we die. End of story. There is no way to know what will be until it happens. No other possibilities. To admit there may be forces at work on some airy-fairy spiritual plane, without scientific evidence to support it, runs counter to your button-pushing, cause and effect mentality. I can't believe Sedona left no lasting impression on you."

"Have I ever told you how much I hate you?" said Adam. He had been sitting in his chair in front of the windows since Derek had first walked in. During the last couple of hours, he had rarely turned to face his friend, preferring to focus his eyes on the Manhattan skyline, waiting, but for what he had no idea.

"Several times. But only when I'm right."

There was truth in Derek's words, hard, hurting truth. Did he re-

36

ally hold Lucia in contempt for claiming a talent he did not believe she possessed? Did he really disbelieve it after tonight? Adam marveled at how easily his mind vacillated between conflicting positions. Earlier this evening, Adam had been plagued by doubt, afraid to acknowledge Lucia's performance as anything more than hysteria. Now, listening to Derek, he realized that the structures upon which he had built his world were crumbling. Sedona had been the initial trumpet blast from Joshua's horn. But the walls had remained steadfast, until now.

"What are you waiting to see? What do you think is going to happen out there tonight?" Derek's voice was agitated but there was a timbre of concern as well.

"I don't know. Nothing, I guess. Have you ever told Lucia about Sedona?"

"No, but you should."

"She knows something. She said you told her something weird happened there."

"Something weird did happen there."

"I don't want her to know."

"Fine. Maybe our friend the gardener told her something."

"Not a chance."

"Well, she is psychic after all."

"You are so helpful. You should become a therapist. Oh . . . wait a minute. Never mind. That's a job."

"Take your best shot," said Derek. "You're the miserable one. It drives you crazy that I'm able to subvert the system, survive on my own terms and have fun doing it. I de-legitimize everything you've carefully constructed around you."

"You needn't remind me. I am, after all, currently footing the bill."

Derek went back to the bar. "Speaking of which, we're running out of Grand Marnier."

Derek turned and lifted the snifter in Adam's direction in mock salute. Adam reciprocated by poking the middle finger of his right hand into the air.

"Were you planning to go into the city with Jenny tomorrow?" asked Adam.

"I'm touched. Chicken Little is concerned about me."

"Jenny, actually. Doesn't she waitress at that Soho bar on Wednesdays?"

"You're serious. You want us to stay put tomorrow. This does not sound like the concern of a skeptic to me."

Adam shifted uneasily in his chair, his thoughts creating phantom aches in his lower back.

"I've got a bad feeling, is all. Lucia really spooked me tonight. I don't want to be alone tomorrow."

There was a sharp crack of expanding metal, the radiator system coming to life as the autumn evening chill crept into the century-old house. The sound startled Derek; it had a gunshot quality.

"Have I told you how much this house gives me the creeps?"

"Yes. I'll see if I can get a permit to move the coach house further back."

"That would be super. You are absolutely my best friend."

Even in jest, Adam knew it to be true. It was impossible to explain the strong connection he felt for Derek. He had long ago abandoned all hope of finding a logical reason. They each approached life from opposing angles yet had intersected and wound around and around each other until a Gordian knot of shared history and uncensored affection had made unraveling impossible.

"I'll see you tomorrow, then," said Adam, "but before you go, tell me what you really think is going on. If Lucia is for real, then what am I supposed to make of what I saw and heard tonight?" Adam was turned completely to one side of the chair now, one leg hanging over the armrest.

"How do I explain it? I don't have to explain it because I know something about the forces at work in my world . . . and yours. But even someone of your limited intuitive inclination must recognize the possibility of invisible influences at work during any encounter between two people. Maybe she's like a seismic detector, naturally more sensitive to spiritual vibrations or electro-magnetic waves. Hell, I don't know. But whatever it is she is tapping into, her information is real. The source may be unknown. And her interpretation is her interpretation. But the information is real. I'm going to sleep. Good night."

"Good night. And thank you, Sigmund."

"I thought you didn't believe in reincarnation. Sedona was a dream, you said." Derek threw the remaining drops of Grand Marnier into the back of his throat, placed the snifter on the bar, and was gone before Adam could respond.

"Sedona was a dream," he said to the empty room.

Adam thought of heading for the bedroom, but something kept him in his chair. He had a ringside seat for god knows what. He'd never fall asleep now. Better to sit in the peaceful confines of his study and appreciate his antique collection of Gramophones and radios that were sheltered and softly lit behind a wood and glass display case. Adam admired the craftsmanship of the cabinetmakers and the genius of the early radio and recording pioneers—Edison and Marconi—men who had done for amplified and transmitted sound what Gandhi had done for civil disobedience. He looked out over Montclair and further to the lights of Manhattan and wished he could think of a way to put a display case around his life, big enough to hold his world and the lives of those he cared about. Soon, the weight of his thoughts made him weary and sleep came when it was least expected.

Adam awoke from a dreamless sleep. The eastern sun temporarily blinded him. Must be near eight, he thought. He squinted to read an antique mantel clock. It was 8:10. His back was sore from the strain of sitting in one position for the entire night so he rearranged his body in the chair while reaching for a remote control unit on the nearby side table.

It was an elaborate device, custom-made to cater to Adam's high tech needs. The stereo and video equipment had been cleverly concealed in the room so as not to infringe upon the esthetic repose of the room's interior design. It had been a challenge for the engineers and architect to meet the incompatible desires for turn-of-the-century study and cutting edge entertainment center. With a little ingenuity and a fair portion of Adam's hard earned currency, the effect had been achieved. With the touch of a button, the middle shelf of a bookcase, located on the opposite wall from the display case, pneumatically lowered itself like a drawbridge, revealing a cornucopia of blinking equipment. The depression of another button and the tuner awoke.

" . . . so if you've been putting off getting the wrist chip because you think you can't afford it, think again. With our four easy payments plan you can be in and out of our premises in minutes and never have to wait in a subway token line again. So give us a call. That's one eight eighty-eight, nine seven six chip."

They make it all sound so cheerful. Hasn't anyone read George Orwell? He was about to change to a music station when a familiar voice caught his interest.

"I am Imus in the morning and we are coming to you from our flag ship station, WFAN The Fan, as well as being simulcast on the nearly bankrupt MSNBC. We are continuing to talk to my brother Fred who is in just a hideous mood. Fred, by the way, is being brought to you by your Tri-State Jeep and Eagle dealers. Good morning Fred."

"What do you mean hideous, you wrinkled old brillo head?"

"Now Fred, no one wants to talk to you if you're gonna be nasty."

"Well, you try getting to sleep when your blow-up doll keeps losing air."

"Okay, you've got a point there . . . hey, what the hell was that. Charles . . . Jesus God, did you feel that . . . ?"

Adam did. At first it felt like the shudder his house gave off when a commercial jet flew overhead. The house was directly below a flight path into Newark Airport. But there was no accompanying jet noise and the shudder did not stop.

" . . . Christ, what's happening! Fred . . ."

The remote fell away from his hand, unnoticed. Adam gripped the arms of his chair, clawing at the fabric as he pushed himself further into the back of it. He stared out the window with an intensity that should have melted the glass or caused it to explode into an uncountable number of pieces. It felt as if his heart was enveloping his entire being, as if he had unzipped a ventricle and climbed in. The throbbing was unbearable, liquefying his mad scrambled attempt at cohesion.

Now children, sit still while the car is moving, he could hear his mother say, heard it now, wished she was there to cuddle him and make him whole, kissing away the pain from the congealing red mess that used to be his knee or stroking his hair and holding him close, weaving fibers of encouragement with her soft grainy voice, her lips millimeters away from his ear, smoothing away the fears, reducing his Sunday sadness that always appeared at the wrong end of the weekend.

There must be noise, but he no longer heard it, not the radio or the clatter of crystal goblets as they spun out of control on the bar, careening off their mates, making tinkling sounds that in another place would have prompted a kiss from the groom, some crashing into the sink, others, the more fortunate, taking a brief trip through space to the carpeted floor where they landed with the grace of a space capsule splashing into the ocean.

We're not moving until you sit still, mister.

He loved it when she called him mister. It was meant as parental bluster, a signal that future behaviour in keeping with the present would not be tolerated, but he knew it for what it was, a signal of her love, her tone betraying the message, the jocundity in her eyes signaling how much she adored him, her conspiratorial smile reinforcing his position at the center of her universe.

He remembered once seeing buildings sway, flowing back and forth like tall grass in the wind, shimmering fluid things, amorphous, spineless, hotels mostly, full of people who must be holding onto bedposts to prevent themselves from being tossed from one end of the room to the other. It's that LSD will make you see things you don't want to know about. You want shape and structure, lines and angles, hard concrete and smooth asphalt; instead you receive an overflowing platter of curves and colour, vibratory sinews of cosmic papier-mâché, beautiful, unstable, changing. You die a little to watch it. But even if you close your eyes, it takes a piece of reality away from you and never returns it.

How long would it take how many blades of grass to reduce the Empire State Building to rubble?

They're going to have to change all those postcards.

What was he trying to remember? There was a voice, not his but not coming from out there either, out where he observed glowing dust particles, illuminated by the sun's rays, not slow dancing in the ether but oscillating with a seizure-induced frenzy, rhythmic movements, sidetracking his thoughts, parking them momentarily.

The voice. His mother's voice. His friend, the gardener's voice.

There is much to learn. There is little time.

Wasn't that one of his Gramophones catching his eye, out there on the periphery, positioned unnaturally, end over end, free falling, turntable momentarily facing him like a moving target, needle arm flailing in mad pendulum strokes, the antique striking the carpet on its edge, splintering, losing contact with the past? Poor Mr. Edison.

They'd go for ice cream in Daddy's convertible. Mommy turning and saying, no horsing around, I don't want one of you flying out of here. And he could imagine it. Almost wished for it. Flying through the air. Free falling. No seatbelts back then. His dad's '61 Thunderbird, a sleek mechanical great white shark, slicing through the invisible ocean, him and Kevin giggling in the back seat, turning their heads, letting their hair whip their faces, eyes watering until the landscape blurred, like looking through a milk bottle.

If only the chair came with a seatbelt.

Clockwork Orange. At the end when poor Malcolm has those devices in his eyes, preventing him from blinking. So he could watch the horror to Beethoven's Ninth. I'll never be able to listen to Imus again.

The earth is a living body.

The earth is having a fucking heart attack before my unblinking eyes.

A red glow in the distance. It appeared harmless enough from where he sat. A marshmallow fire, glowing red coals. Dad was always making them wait until the fire had burned down. You don't want the marshmallow to catch fire, he would admonish, delivering yet another perfectly browned gooey lump of whipped sugar for them to devour. But Adam loved to burn his, watching with delight as the black burning mob overran the pristine, virginal, snowy landscape of the mallow, black ash lodging semi-permanently in the crevices between his teeth.

Diamond pieces of glass were falling, slow-motion prisms reflecting the morning sun rising in the east. He felt the cold, damp blast of autumn air, smelled its pungent scent of death and decay, smelled it at night, tucked in his bed, the odour drifting up from the compost pile of clothes deposited next to his bed, grass stains and wet leaves embedded in his jeans, wide awake and reliving a diving lunge for an errant pass, catching the pigskin—the grownups called it a pigskin of all things—bringing it into his body, protecting it against the impending impact with the leaf-strewn grass.

A shower of falling glass. He thinks he should put his hands up, protect his face, his eyes, but he's afraid to let go of the arms of the chair, can't let go.

He loved the smell of fresh laundry, would watch his mother make his bed with military precision, standing at the foot, flicking the sheet in the air, letting it float to the mattress, then flicking it again because it hadn't landed just right, and, as he watched it descend with its undulating hills and valleys, he thought, for a split second, that he could see trees and rivers and hills, with little alpine villages tucked away in the folds.

You have to watch out for your dreams, he thinks as he watches a long stretch of ground before him buckle and undulate, trees uproot-ing, houses being engulfed into the folds of his mother's sheets.

There's still some colour left in you.

Lucia, he wanted to think about Lucia but the chair would not stop shaking and he could not remember what he wanted to think about, knew there was something dreadful he should be recalling, but it re-mained hidden, like some forgotten traumatic event from your past that, no matter how vividly recounted by others, remained a mystery, outside of your experience, a stranger you couldn't recall having met.

There was this screen door, see, and it was forever wedging itself against the door frame, as if it had a mind of its own and it was dark out, his football under one arm, yanking the door handle with the other. He'd been holding it in for the whole walk home from the play-ing field, and now he was ready to burst, only the door wouldn't open and he could feel the hot burning liquid right at the tip of his peepee—that was the acceptable word in his house and he really didn't know any other except penis, but that word made him laugh—and he was screaming for his mommy to let him in, didn't want to suffer the embarrassment only a pissing-in-your-pants eight-year-old can know, but then he felt it, like he felt it now against his thigh, the guilty pleasure of release.

Senses. There were five of them. Touch, check. His innards were being violently massaged by invisible waves of pressurized air currents. What else. Sight, check. But what the hell was he seeing out there? Making sense of the sense. That was the challenge. No context. It was a problem of context. There were certain things you absolutely counted on. Like your mother being home at lunchtime. Peanut butter and jelly sandwich waiting on a blue plastic plate. And you'd better eat your carrots mister or you're not going anywhere. Carrots skinned alive, sweating on your plate. Made you feel guilty if you didn't eat them. Your mother home at lunch, frilly apron covering a summer dress, her calves exposed down to her bony ankles, little alpine mounds of bone and flesh, neatly inserted into half heels; you were going to find a girl just like her. But you had time, being ten and all.

But then one day she was gone. Forever. The girl you found who was just like mom.

What did they call it? Terra firma—firm land. Another lie. A lie told to your body, a thick fluid inside your ear convincing you that you're rooted firmly to the ground—an illusionist's trick. All the while this celestial rock you're standing on is hurtling through space at ungodly speeds, spinning towards infinity. What were you thinking? Push and pull, up and down, round and round. Couldn't feel it before, was blinded to it, saw it now, not out there but inside, just behind the eyelids, hot molten blood-red ooze, and the pulse, a pre-natal thumping, Earth Mother awakening her sleeping children.

The entity must connect to the fibers of energy flowing through it and all things.

Entity. So impersonal. A unit. A discrete amalgam of blood and tissue and bone. Being lugged around by a prescient dictator; look at this, pick up that, time for lunch, nice legs, hurry up I'm late, wipe my ass, I need a new life. But the body always demanded revenge; it tired, sustained injury, caught colds, succumbed to disease, got old, died.

He remembered the face dancing before him. Two painted eyes and an exaggerated grin, weaving and dipping as he held onto the hose. One of those summertime garden toys some genius had convinced a toy company to produce. The TV ads were effective. He begged his mom for one. Just some hose with a rounded cone-shaped piece of plastic secured over the top of the exposed end. With a silly face. Turn on the water and watch it dance and weave, defying gravity. And the whole idea was to get as soaked as possible. Water flying out from beneath the face. Kids screaming as they ran to escape the rampaging hose, water shooting in all directions. There was no escape. Adam could still feel the water hitting his face. He smiled, remembering those warm days in the backyard and his little plastic box of a wading pool. Dad had to empty it everyday or there'd be a square yellow spot where green grass had once been allowed to photosynthesize. So warm and safe. Warm and safe. And wet.

It was the water sobering him up, spraying him, irritating his eyes and slowly drawing him out. Adam could feel the rain, his clothing clinging to his body. He opened his eyes and watched large droplets hitting the Persian rug, each drop staining the bright colours with darker versions of themselves.

He thought a rational thought. It seemed foreign, as in he'd gone on sabbatical and had lost track of the familiar, forgetting in which drawer the underwear was kept or opening a closet door expecting the bathroom. The fire sprinkler system had been activated. Very expensive but the architect had insisted. His vanity would not allow his creation to be carelessly burned to the ground.

Better check for smoke, he thought. He tried to get up but his legs refused the signal from his brain and he collapsed in a heap. Oddly comfortable, he surveyed his immediate surroundings, lying on his side, arms outstretched, a perfect model for a police chalk drawing.

The room had been redecorated, he couldn't help noticing, in early California earthquake. He searched for something left in its proper place but only his chair had managed the feat. He felt nothing seeing his treasures lying in various grotesque positions about the floor, pieces cleaved off, cracks and bends and smashes. No pathos or sense of loss. A vain attempt at immortality. Better to lose it now, get it over with and free yourself from the inevitable parting.

People. People you wanted to collect, the right sort of people to populate your life, nurture you, lift your spirits, offer you hope. Because maybe you could take them with you. Eventually. A treasure waiting for you in heaven.

He thought of Lucia then, and the magnitude of the horror he had just witnessed sickened him and he let the bile and assorted stomach juices free themselves, felt better for having done so. So many smells; his pants, the vomit, a mildew odour rising from the Persian rug, but the discomfort they elicited paled in comparison to the agony the thought of her caused, of her dead, lying crushed under beams and concrete or trapped alive or horribly disfigured or crippled or worse.

It was time to act. He did not want to think anymore, was tired of it, the experience beyond his comprehension, so why bother? There would be time enough to decipher it, ponder it, read about it, watch talk shows and CNN for the latest updates, then wait for the books and mini-series to arrive.

Some mental debilitation had dissolved away because he found himself standing, able to move about and function normally. He put his hand on the doorknob; it was cold, no fire on the other side of the door waiting to turn him into a cinder.

Other than water everywhere, ruining those things that water ruins, the house did not appear too damaged. It was so messed up though, you would not have had a problem believing it had been broken into by burglars with attitude. Or by CIA operatives who had searched everywhere for something very small. Juanita would have a fit when she saw the place. She had an unnatural disrespect for dust.

Adam had no idea how to disable the sprinkler system so he kept pushing buttons on the security panel until the water stopped flowing. He then made his way to the master bedroom where he immediately removed one watch, a quartz Seiko, and replaced it with his Rolex, an automatic. He would have normally asked himself why he had done such an odd thing, but he was sworn to non-thought so he proceeded to peel off the wet clothes and enter the shower. The hot water touching his skin calmed him. Liquid gold bringing blood and clarity to his body and mind. And so he lunged at the taps and turned them off. Hot water, precious stuff, don't want to waste it. Again the eccentric behaviour, but this newfound acquiescence, this kind of go with the flow, trust your body instinctual pattern, felt good. He touched his head for bruises. Maybe something had fallen on him during the earthquake. But no, there weren't going to be any easy explanations for anything anymore. No cheat notes, no clues, no rulebooks.

The walk-in closet off the bedroom was pretty much intact—a few boxes had fallen from the overhead shelf—but the only thing dry was his tuxedo, having been sealed in a suit bag and zipped up. Don't think about it, he said to himself as he grabbed the bag and pulled out the jacket and slacks. Now where's my cummerbund, he mused and was happy for the gallows humour, like having an old friend drop by. He found a pair of fairly dry cowboy boots to wear, then put on a white T-shirt and some underwear and socks from his dresser drawer. Fully clothed, he could pass for a rodeo MC.

He was lucid, almost giddy from O.D.-ing on adrenaline, his body rewarding him with a little high for having survived one more of life's little calamities. But this was not going to be one of life's little calamities. This was going to rock the very foundation of everything Adam had come to rely upon. The deck had been re-shuffled.

From the familiar to the unfamiliar.

What was it the gardener had said to him? There were no coincidences. You attracted the destiny you deserved. How could so many people have deserved this? What god could be so pissed at humanity? Then again, he thought, this is New York we are talking about.

The screen door to the coach house had separated from the frame and hung precariously from the uppermost hinge. Adam pushed it away and tried the door. It was unlocked and opened easily. The living room on the right was dishevelled, but it was difficult to tell where Derek's lifestyle ended and the earthquake began. Beer bottles lay upended on the floor and there were a few books freed from an IKEA bookshelf but structurally, the building appeared to have sustained little damage. A wide zigzag staircase led to the loft area containing the bedroom.

"Derek!" Adam called out, halfheartedly, spooked by the silence and half hoping the pair had made their way out of the building. Receiving no answer, he proceeded up the stairs and as his head cleared the floor of the loft, his eyes immediately turned towards the queen-size bed in the middle of the floor.

He could see two bodies, still and lifeless. A cold, gut-wrenching wrongness grabbed him violently and threatened to relieve him of the ability to stand. He willed himself towards the bed, his mind rapidly cataloguing an infinity of thoughts, from funeral arrangements to recalling correct CPR procedures. He reached the bed and was nonplussed by the sight.

Christ, they're asleep! Adam was astounded. It was impossible. Unconscious he could accept, but not asleep. Adam walked over to the night table, having spotted a prescription vial. He picked it up and read the label. Chloral Hydrate. A couple of these and Adam knew you could sleep through a root canal.

He smiled down at the pair. Derek, a man who had never attended an event he couldn't enliven, a man who had been asked to leave far more times than he'd been invited, had missed the biggest show New York had ever hosted.

He went back downstairs. There was no point in attempting to wake Derek now. Better to have him somewhat coherent when he surfaces. He'd need all of his faculties to take in what had occurred in his absence. And Adam knew a sober Derek would be mandatory if they were going to attempt to find Lucia.

He walked out of the coach house. Adam had not noticed it before but now he could hear it, the sounds of disaster; sirens off in the distance, the cascading resonance of sprung water hydrants, electrical hisses from downed wires and the scattered cries of the wounded and terrorized. Who had changed this world? Why do I want to attach blame? It was an earthquake, pure and simple. Happens all the time.

Then why didn't he believe it? What was his gut trying to tell him?

No, he would not think about it. Lucia would have the answers. Or maybe the disembodied voice he'd heard ascending from her throat would tell them. First though, he had to find Lucia. She was only fifteen miles away but as Adam stood on his driveway, surveying the devastation, the smoke and ruin blurring his view, as he cast his gaze eastward to the Hudson River, surely uncrossable, it occurred to him that if she was still alive, Lucia might as well be sitting on the Moon.

V

SHE SAW HIM FIRST. Not him exactly, but the spectral glow of him, the suggestion of his presence about twenty-five miles away. She glanced down to the desert ten thousand feet below, unmoved by its stark beauty, quickly calculating whether she had enough floor if she decided to trade altitude for power. She looked back into the cockpit. The heads-up display, called a HUD, was a kind of teleprompter, a transparent screen in the pilot's line of sight which dispensed all types of valuable information, from altitude, pitch, weapon selection and air speed to G force and targeting information, all in a soft green glow. The HUD allowed the pilot to absorb information without having to take his or her eyes off the horizon. Below the HUD was the Radar/Electro-Optical Display or REO, a green lit screen, translating the radar beams emanating from the aircraft into little dots and numbers, all designed to tell you where the enemy was, how fast he was moving and in what direction. The HUD and REO had turned air combat into a deadly video game.

Joey checked on the bogey. That's what they called the enemy. Bogey, Charlie, Jerry, it was important to trivialize those you had to kill. You gave them all the same name and marginalized their individuality. You didn't kill people in war, you killed a name, you killed the same person over and over again.

The bogey, a little square on her REO was now bearing 135°, on a heading of 315°. She checked her airspeed on the HUD. 460 knots. She estimated an intercept, if she maintained her present course, in less than three minutes. She switched off the Normal Air Mode radar and the blip disappeared off the REO screen. No sense in advertising her presence. He probably hadn't picked her up yet. She was counting on it.

She felt the two sticks in her hands, the sidestick controller in her right and the throttle in her left, could feel the awesome power of the F-16's engines flowing deep into her muscles, making her bones vibrate, better than sex, hell, way better than sex, and besides, the Falcon always did what it was told, the fly by wire control system responding almost to her thoughts. She flicked her right wrist and the warbird banked left and up while her left asked the turbofan engine to suck on its own fumes, kicking in the afterburners for a surge of power that felt like someone ramming you from behind with a pillow. She thought about going head to head with this one but decided to decrease the aspect angle and increase her odds of a clean shot. It was a flanking maneuver designed to put the Falcon inside the bogey's turn circle and behind for a high percentage missile or gun shot. If she got on his "6," she could unleash her heat-seekers then sit back and watch the show.

She climbed to fifteen thousand feet on a heading of 135°, running the opposite way almost parallel, she hoped, with the bogey's heading.

She checked her airspeed again. She pulled the aircraft back to 450 knots. She wanted power but she also wanted to be able to turn on a dime and nothing in the air could out-turn her F-16, not at this speed. Any faster and the bird would resist her, any slower and a quick turn would bleed speed like a slaughtered pig.

It was time to check in on her friend out there. All of the training, the years of fighting her way through a system determined to keep her and her gender at bay, a way of life that abhorred weakness, saw even her monthly flow as a defect of design, it was all on the line. Today it would be set right. Today she would prove her mettle, although in her mind it was spelled metal and she wasn't sure what it was supposed to mean, but she was going to prove it nonetheless.

She flicked on the radar, this time set to Situation Awareness Mode. She panicked. He was gone. How did she know it was a male? Just playing the odds. No time for this. She hit another button and widened the azimuth scan of the radar beam. Maybe he had made her and taken evasive action. Still no blip on her screen. She increased the elevation scan to 0525. If he was still out there . . . shit.

He had friends. Two of them. They had climbed to just under twenty thousand feet and were bearing down on her at 600 knots. They had elevation, speed and firepower on their side and she wasn't sure anymore what she had on hers. She corralled the closest bogey on her REO display and hit the IFF button. A squawk would mean friend, silence would mean foe. She prayed a silent prayer for a squawk but she knew there would be none.

She activated the AIM-120 AMRAAM missiles under the wing tips of the Falcon. With a range of twenty-five miles, she had no trouble locking onto the closest bandit fourteen miles away and closing. She brought the blinking diamond on her HUD into the Center Point of the display.

Two things happened almost simultaneously. She observed one and heard the other. The lead bandit, probably spooked by the howl in his cockpit triggered by her radar lock on his aircraft, took immediate evasive action, pulling up and away from the fight. Chicken shit, she thought, but then in an instant she had the opportunity to re-evaluate her enemy's lack of courage when her own instruments screamed at her that one of the other fighters had missile lock on her. Take evasive measures, her trained mind told her, the text books showed her, her instructors taught her, but up here something else took hold of her, a primal sort of sanity, instinctual, not rational or reasoned, the hare and the hound, she was both and neither, determined with a myopic blindness for self-preservation.

She pressed the firing button.

Fox one.

The missile left the rail, irresistibly following an electronic trail to the fleeing bogey. By turning away, the pilot had reduced the aspect angle to a negligible degree. The missile was about to crawl right up his ass.

Magic Magic. She said it to herself because she didn't have any wingmen to call out to. Lights were flashing in her cockpit, reminding her in a not-too-subtle manner that an all aspect, heat-seeking missile was heading straight for her fuselage.

The two other fighters were less than five miles away. The missile was on her screen, less than a mile and seconds away from impact. She switched to Air Combat Mode radar, which immediately painted the closest jet. She got tone, fired an AIM-9M this time, if for no other reason than to give them something to think about while she attempted to evade the missile.

It was coming straight for her. Wait. Wait. At about a thousand yards, she pounded out flares and chaff, big orange farts exploding behind her, while thousands of shards of aluminum attempted to confuse and thwart the incoming missile. At the same time she pulled hard on the controller, the Falcon pitching up 90° to straight vertical. She was climbing to heaven, her body crunched into the back of her chair, pulling at least 8 or 9 G's, she couldn't tell, the readout on the HUD beginning to blur as she momentarily blacked out. It was an odd sensation; they made you go through it, part of the training, like forcing someone who planned to become an alcoholic to vomit a few times so he would know what it felt like when the real sickness sets in. It literally felt like someone pulling down the blinds. She thought she was awake but there was no sensation, no sensory input, just blackness. Then the blood started to return to her brain and the lights turned back on.

Joey was bleeding speed as she came out of the climb and back to her senses, the nose of the plane arching back towards earth. Upside down now, she could see the ground, relieved that the missile had missed her. She saw that she had climbed to twenty-seven thousand feet, frantically searched below her for the enemy aircraft, could see smoke in the distance, the first bogey probably, no time to think, the other two were on her screen, needed to find them before they acquired her. She spotted vapor trails—there they were, pulling up towards her, the last missile buying her some time, but if they got their noses around first, she knew she'd never get another missile off. A flick of her wrist and the Falcon rolled left and down, gravity her friend, pulling the nose straight on the two pursuers, head-on, too close now for missiles so she switched to guns, fired wildly, neither plane totally within the EEGS gun sight, six thousand rounds per minute of spewing destruction from the muzzle of a six-barrel cannon, located just behind her head. The sensation was indescribable, her right hand directing the plane and line of fire, tracers directing her aim, the noise nearly splitting her head open, while her adversaries separated, gyrating madly to avoid the deadly rain.

She flew between them upside down, flicking her wrist again, the jet turning on its axis to an upright position then another tug and she was pulling up and left, nosing towards the red jet exhaust of one of her remaining pursuers, the other breaking off—perhaps she'd tattooed him with a few rounds—the cat and mouse rolls switching in a heartbeat.

One to go. He was dropping flares and chaff. She headed for the smoke, driving for the entry window to his turn. She reached the spot and started to pull G's. She was inside his turn circle. All of the instruction, the simulators that made it seem so simple without the G's and the vertigo and the incredible howl of the General Electric engine whizzing her through the air like a modern-day circus act being shot from a cannon, the years in the air, the hazing and razing and tears and study and it all came down to this, and here she was, inside, watching for a yo-yo maneuver because this guy probably had more experience, couldn't lose him now. She pulled her nose to lead pursuit, monitored her speed while easing up a bit on the throttle, her corner velocity vital now. She played with the throttle, controlling her overtake. He was slowing down; she was moving out of his turning plane. She hit the air brakes, rolled the jet, orienting her lift vector out of the bandit's turning plane. She pulled hard then eased off, bleeding more speed, saw the bogey moving across her canopy as she pulled back into lead pursuit. Target about three thousand feet and pulling about 7 Gs now. She had him. The turbo driven heated gas made a perfect target as she eased up on the throttle, armed the AIM-9M, radar locked on the target and let it fly.

Lieutenant Joey Eaton did not bother to wait to see if the missile made its mark; instead she pulled on the stick, the machine responding with a right slicing bank. There was a fighter jet running almost parallel with her, a couple of hundred feet below. She could see down into the canopy of the F-15. The pilot, one of her instructors, looked up and gave her big thumbs up.

Joey's radio cackled to life.

"Nice show there, Queenie," said the man with the thumb, Captain Jerry "Snakebite" Springfield.

"Notch another for the Blue Team," she replied, thinking there had never been a happier moment in her life.

Another F-16 sidled up on her left flank.

"You crazy bitch, splitting us apart with cannon fire like that," but there was laughter in his voice. Joey knew it was the kind of maneuver that Captain Lance "Thunderbolt" Jeffries would try himself.

"They're blanks, you know. You afraid of the noise?"

"Okay, cut the chatter. Red Team, Blue Team, back to base for debriefing." The call came from the tower, Nellis calling her children home.

"I can't believe you pulled an Immelman. Lame man, so lame," said Jeffries.

"Kept that simulated missile from crawling up my ass, shithead." She was loving this, had been waiting for her turn, trash talk, guy talk, could almost feel big brass ones rolling between her thighs.

"See everyone at the base." It was Captain Springfield, pulling towards home.

"Permission to stay out late. I need to savour this. I need to commune with the warrior gods." She didn't want this to end, just one more dance, please . . .please.

"Okay, but I want you in before dark and no talking to strangers."

"Aye aye, Captain."

The jet angled north, away from the base, away from the obtrusive wart on the desert landscape that was Las Vegas. Her fellow pilots loved to spend their free time and money there, but Joey never gambled and the odds of meeting a decent guy in a place like that were smaller than at the roulette table. Joey didn't get it, gambling that is, though she didn't get much of the other thing either. Dating a fellow serviceman was out of the question, not that a few hadn't tried, with one or two succeeding, like the dashing young captain who flew in last year as a guest instructor, what was his name, Lester, right, Lester Browning, now he was tempting, tasted so yummy but she had pushed him away, had been pushing things away for as long as she could remember.

Joey was pretty sure she did not need a man in her life. Pretty sure because she had no point of reference, no boyfriends to speak of, no brothers and a father who was seasonal at best. Her dad was great, she loved him to pieces, but he was more of a friend, more like a friend of her dad's than her dad. He had never been around long enough to become involved, to find out who she really was and what she really needed. It was always about Daddy, about some investor he had to see about a show, or a rock star in need of coddling or probably it was a girlfriend who was growing impatient while he played family man for a day or two.

Joey could see Humboldt National Forest, watched the tree tops pass under the wing of the Falcon while fathers, men, sex, all of the late-night, can't-fall-asleep topics dissipated, a rare peace descending upon her, permeating her body like a slow-release barbiturate, a woman and her jet, alone in the universe, untouchable, deadly, peacemaker or hellraiser, you choose.

Daddy used to say by way of apology that the problem with what he did for a living was loving it too much. Which may have helped him rationalize his absence but made Joey think that maybe he loved her too little. Now, sitting a few inches away from an engine capable of Mach 2, having earned the respect of her peers and superiors, defying the gods with every second spent in the air, she had to begrudgingly acknowledge she finally understood her father's passion. This was her drug. Sure, others shared the experience, spoke enthusiastically with her about it, but here, it was hers alone, she was a part of something that took her out of her life, made her shine with a brilliance otherwise hidden, a tinder box of a life, small sparks igniting her passions and bursting them into flame.

Joey tapped on her fuel gauge out of habit. She'd never live it down if she was forced to land on a county highway. There was more than enough fuel to get back to base but this baby was a guzzler so she banked and headed south for Lost Wages.

Nellis Air Force Base was a few miles east of Las Vegas. Visiting tourists and gamblers had no idea of the number of times the city had been destroyed by simulation. It was too close, too gaudy with its lights and glitter and too easy a target to ignore. For fun, Joey turned on her air to ground radar. The REO display immediately began picking up the terrain, then the skyline. Joey targeted Caesars Palace. Maverick, Maverick. She imagined the air to ground missile leaving its position, snug under the wing, a smart bomb, knowing its destination without further guidance, imagined it hurtling down towards the building, blowing a big beautiful hole through the casino, a naughty idea, a 'go straight to hell' idea.

At first, she thought it was her imagination. A hallucinogenic extension of her little prank. Caesars appeared to shimmer, almost sway as Joey flew parallel to the city. She had no explanation for it, thought maybe it was the movement of her craft in relation to the ground. Joey banked the plane for a second pass. She was flying into commercial airspace without notifying any tower so she had to be careful. She saw the North Las Vegas Air Terminal off her starboard wing and McCarran International Airport was only six miles off to her left. But her curiosity was up and something else, a dreadful premonition, a flash pot of a thought, quickly smothered by a mind too busy to cope with other than piloting her plane and uncovering the mystery.

The inner voices stopped their chatter as Joey came around 180° heading southwest. All of the buildings were trembling, smoke and dust flying up into the air where telephone poles had fallen; cars leaving the road, crashing into sidewalk storefronts; a part of a wall from Caesars Palace crashing to the ground as she flew past.

"Nellis Tower, this is Queenie, do you copy?"

Static.

"Nellis Tower, this is Queenie, do you copy?"

The voices inside returned, got a bit louder, started to intrude on her thoughts and actions.

"Queenie, this is Nellis Tower."

"Tower, I am witnessing an earthquake in the Las Vegas . . ."

"Queenie, bring your bird down immediately. Do you copy?"

"Copy that. Returning to base."

She turned northeast for the short ride to the runway. She flicked on the ILS and immediately picked up the runway transmitter. The ILS HUD mode was used primarily for night landings. Joey checked the Glide Slope Deviation Bar, saw that she was too low for her approach and pulled back on the stick for more altitude. When she leveled off she scanned the terrain. The ground was obscured by clouds of dust. She was cruising at about fifteen hundred feet and should have been able to pick out the backyard laundry but all she saw was brown haze.

She mechanically went through her landing procedures. Flaps down, air brakes on; at five hundred feet she lowered the landing gear. She was floating towards the ground at just under 200 knots. The runway was in view, so small and narrow from up here. She worked the foot pedals, yawing slightly to the left, aligning herself perfectly for the landing.

Joey searched the ground for evidence of disturbance around the base. She could see details now, people on the ground, other warbirds outside the hangers, silhouettes in the control tower. The earthquake did not appear to have reached out this far.

Two hundred feet now. The runway looming before her. A quick adjustment to her air speed, one ninety and dropping. Nose slightly up, AOA indicator in a perfect glide position. A hundred feet now, speed dropping, easing up on the throttle. God, I hope all of those people are okay. How can they be okay? The voices again. An unexpected and unwelcomed emotional jolt of sadness.

Her rear wheels on the ground now, the nose slowly coming to rest, front wheel pounding into the runway, she's reaching for the wheel brakes when she sees it—a huge crack in the earth, ripping the runway in two, maybe three hundred feet in front of her.

"Abort landing!" she hears over the radio but her left hand has already asked the Pratt & Whitney engine to get her the hell off the runway, her right hand pulling back on the controller stick as the Viper begrudgingly drags itself back off the ground.

The tower is telling her to find an alternate air strip, a panicked voice, then nothing, static, so she turns off the radio, doesn't want to hear anything but the mantra of her engine.

Um money pay me Hank—Um money pay me Hank.

She hated the smell of incense. It gave her a headache. But worse than the smell was the embarrassment of having a hippie for a father, having to explain to her friends what her dad did for a living, why he was never around and when he was, what was he doing at home in the middle of the afternoon in his pyjamas—a crimson robe he bought on a trip to India—when everybody else's dad was at work.

Um money pay me Hank. She knew that wasn't really how it went, that the first word was Om, some Hindu spirit word, yet every time she walked by her parents bedroom, smelling the combined miasmas of incense and pot escaping through the cracks in the door, she could not shake the vision of some timid creditor, asking for money from a guy named Hank. Over and over and over, she would hear it, like a broken record, the bass of her father's voice penetrating almost every room of the house, until she felt like bursting into her parent's room and screaming—Just pay him already!

The jewel is in the lotus.

Why would anyone want to repeat a phrase like that? Dad said it meant the jewel is in the lotus. Like that explained everything. It was the hippie way. You could explain away the world in a sentence, cure the ills of mankind with a phrase, end a war with a word.

Om mani padme hum.

When she was older she learned how to say it, from a roommate at college who was taking an Eastern Religions course. It did not help her understand her father any better although the image of a debt-ridden Hank eventually disappeared.

She had maps—topographical maps, maps with secret military locations, Rand McNally maps—started yanking them out of their tucked away location. The logical place to land would be Williams Air Force Base southeast of Phoenix near Apache Junction, but that was about two hundred miles away and the fuel indicator was giving her maybe half that distance. There was a small airport at Kingman and another in the Grand Canyon National Park but she wasn't sure either had a runway long enough for her to land.

Joey was flying about two thousand feet over the Colorado River as it ran almost due south. Ahead she saw Bullhead City, sitting below the Davis Dam. Then the water came so fast, Joey was unable to frame a thought to adequately explain what was happening on the ground. There was a town, then there was water—mad, furious, dirty water engulfing everything. Everything. She looked east and saw the surging mass spreading out into Mohave County.

High ground. I need high ground.

Can't think about this now. I'll think about it later. Life imitating art. Isn't that what they called it?

Prescott. Nestled in the Juniper Mountains. There was an airport there so Joey pulled the plane around to a southeast heading of 135°.

It ran down from Utah, along the Wasatch fault zone, a tectonic flux belt now tearing the state in two. As if self-directed, it had bent slightly southwest, heading straight for the spot where Utah, Arizona and Nevada congregated, the Hoover Dam its apparent destination. This structural marvel, the manifestation of the twin human attributes of ingenuity and arrogance, had been crushed into humbled chunks by the seismic fury of the earth. Like a healing salve over an open wound, the water spilled over the breached dam, inundating the landscape, surgically removing all blemishes—vegetation, houses, cars, people—there was no hint of prejudice in its actions, no preferential treatment for any of its victims. It was an equal opportunity disaster. There were other disturbances to the west, most notably the unstable San Andreas and Hayward Faults, the Pacific and North American tectonic plates tiring of each other's company, creating significant and catastrophic distance between each other.

The effect to the area was devastating, but no more so than the terrain two thousand feet below the undercarriage of the Falcon F-16 being piloted by Lieutenant Joey Eaton. Travelling now at 200 knots to conserve fuel, Joey was hard-pressed to stay in front of the surging water travelling with an irresistible force, swallowing up everything in its path.

She crossed over the Aquarius Mountains, could see the green of Prescott National Forest about fifty miles ahead. The water was behind her now, some of the panic dissipating, a safe haven only a short distance away.

Low fuel warning lights were flashing but she ignored them. Joey tried to raise the Prescott tower but received no response. Despite the low fuel, Joey felt it prudent to make a racetrack approach. She would guide the jet on a low parallel course with the runway, gauge it for length, then turn 180° and land.

Over a ridge covered by forest, Joey could make out the town of Prescott, the territorial capital a century before. She adjusted her flaps and played with the air brakes. She wanted as long a look-see as she could afford without stalling.

Her heart sank because when all seems lost, a space is created for it to fall into. It finds a place to hide in your stomach and starts beating from there. It pumps faster and makes your brain swim with blood, intoxicating your thinking with an oxygen and adrenaline cocktail. The airport was gone. Oh, there were hangers and planes and a runway and tower. But the airport she needed, the runway her bird required was not up to spec.

Most of the tower lay on the tarmac, shattered glass and bent metal strewn in a radius around the impact of the fallen building. A small plane, a Cessna, was burning dead center in the middle of the landing strip. There were people running about, none with any determination that Joey could detect. Even from her position high above the devastation it was easy to see the confusion, feel the panic of those on the ground. As she passed the end of the runway she saw a crack running perpendicular to the asphalt, a ten- or fifteen-foot crevice cutting the runway in half. Black smoke arose from the terminal building. Her last glimpse was of a fire truck making its way to the downed Cessna.

Joey could not pick what to be most afraid of. Her plane would run out of fuel in minutes. This was an aerodyne she was flying; heavier than air, a lot heavier. Her plane did not really fly through the air; it was pushed. It had the glide characteristics of a boulder. The jet was kept aloft solely by the science of aerodynamics. All bets were off when the fuel was spent. If she was more than a few feet off the ground when the last of the jet fuel burned through the engines, there was little chance of her walking away from the crash.

Then there was this thing devouring the countryside. It seemed to take particular delight in her situation, like it had a personal stake in seeing her dead. Later she might feel pretty selfish having those thoughts, but right now, the animal spirit in charge of survival was flying the plane, and it didn't give a damn about anything except finding a safe place to land.

Flagstaff. It was her only choice. There was no airport closer. She read the map resting on her lap, took her index finger and thumb and measured out about an inch or so between Prescott and Pulliam Airport. Fifty or sixty miles. There was no way. These machines did not run on fumes.

What the hell, she thought, as she adjusted her course to the northeast, might as well enjoy the view.

Um money pay me Hank.

She passed over Jerome, an old mining town built on the side of Mingus Mountain, now converted into a hippie refuge, an artist colony cum tourist trap where the sixties still lived, propped up by love beaded, tie-dye-shirted, peace-loving shopkeepers who kept alive the faith so long ago abandoned by their generation, a generation whose members had promised to change the world but instead discovered that luxury cars are so much damn fun to drive. Jerome was her father's kind of town.

She knew this area, had been here before with her parents on one of those rare occasions when her father had made a real effort to create the illusion of normalcy for her. A family trip, two parents and a child in a VW Van of course, making their way from Los Angeles to Sedona. She hated it, hated the drive, hated the music—who in their right mind really enjoyed listening to Hendrix—hated the heat, the dust, Frank Lloyd Wright's Church or whatever it was, the red rocks and cool dude talk the locals spoke. Her mother pleaded with her to give Dad a break, that he was trying to connect with her, trying to be a father but her mother was so blinded by her love, forever the flower child, in awe of her guru, her prince of peace. It never seemed to matter to Joey's mom how often her husband cheated on her, abandoned her, came crawling back, borrowed money and made promises so he would have another reason to break her heart. He was allowed to be whom he was, the free spirit, blowing in and out of their lives. Given her heritage, Joey was actually grateful to her parents for not naming her Tulip or Kashmir or Venus.

She was named after Joey Heatherington, a passable actress who could sing and dance her way through a number on the Ed Sullivan Show, but whose career had faded along with the decade that spawned her. Amongst the dozens of celebrity pictures adorning the wall of her father's den, mostly rock stars, there was a picture of Joey Heatherington with her arm around her father—big smiles. They are backstage somewhere, a lot of people milling about behind them and a bleacher in the distance, the two of them grinning like cartoon characters at the photographer. She has short blonde hair with pointed sideburns, very sixties, wearing a turtleneck and jeans. Dad is in his uniform, bell bottoms, cowboy boots, frilled leather vest and a T-shirt. He was always vague about how well he knew her. He claimed to have only met her once, the day the picture was taken. He was a big fan, he said. She lit his fire, he said. He admired her versatility but mostly he loved her look, he said. Not to cast any aspersions on her father's taste, and she liked her name, but all things considered, she would have rather been called Marilyn or Bridget or even Raquel. Then she would have understood her father's fascination.

Cottonwood was off her starboard wing now. Route 89A, making its way to Sedona, was below her. She figured it must be twenty miles as the crow—or F-16—flies from Sedona to Flagstaff's airport, although to drive there would take you an hour or more. She inspected her instruments. Such beauty, such grace. Every dial, every knob and toggle switch, every wire and nut and bolt had a reason to be there. There was economy and extravagance but never extravagance at the expense of economy. Her machine was the manifestation of mankind at its evolutionary finest.

Defying gravity, defying physics, defying God.

She felt so proud. Proud to be an American. Proud to wear the uniform and fly the plane. Proud to be a woman. Everything working as it should. You pressed a button and the right thing happened. You studied hard, worked diligently, and got promoted. Cause and effect. Action and reaction.

The jewel is in the lotus.

Her roommate said her father had gotten it wrong. It was, *The jewel is in the heart of the lotus.* Who cares. How big can a lotus be. You put a jewel in it and it's got to be close to the heart, right.

She's out of fuel.

The buttons and dials were doing the right thing, the displays were properly activating. A blind and deaf person could detect that this aircraft was trying to tell her something. But she was still in the air. Fumes. She was driving on fumes. Or on a little bit of fuel resting below the indicator float in the tank.

Sedona, it's going to have to be Sedona. Of all the places to land, red-rocked, hippie-laden, Sedona. Planned stopover on the infamous family outing. Her father could even be there, having several friends in the area to mooch off of, but no, he had called her yesterday from Adam's house in New Jersey. He didn't come right out and say it but he was fishing for some money. So he was not going anywhere.

She activated the flaps and hit the airbrakes. Then the landing gear. She nosed down; the red earth filled the canopy. Route 89 was littered with cars so she angled north, searching for anywhere to land. There was a road, heading up towards Boynton Canyon—she thought she knew it, remembered her father had a friend up that way—pulled out of her steep descent, flaps fully extended now, descending slowly, then silence.

Joey had never heard it before. Not even sitting alone in the cockpit on the ground. Silence, but not a pure silence; the wind hissed as it passed over the fuselage.

She pulled hard back on the controller stick but the bird barely responded. The rudders yawed her nose around parallel with the road. She was only about fifty feet off the ground but her nose was too low. The stick was all of the way back but this was no Cessna and the plane was too heavy to care anymore.

The front wheel hit first, collapsing under the weight and concussion, but the rear wheels held fast. Joey activated the wheel brakes and her job was done, her fate in the hands of Newton's second law, or was it the first. Bodies in motion tend to remain in motion unless acted upon by an external net force. Acting upon the underside of the Falcon was a dirt road and, unseen, gravity. She proceeded in a fairly straight line but the road did not, so the plane slid off the shoulder and into the desert, carving a furrow through the dirt, uprooting small shrubs and cactus, scattering sunning lizards and scavenging scorpions. She could no longer see anything, the dirt being thrown up onto the canopy, was frightened but knew she had somehow survived, would open the canopy in a few seconds and walk away. And finally, the awful sounds ceased and there was only stillness and the sound of her breathing.

The damage was surprisingly minimal. The front wheel had jack-knifed back into its bay, was probably inoperable but still in one piece. The pitot head, the needle-like probe jutting out from the nose of the craft, had been shorn off and left somewhere back up the road. The fuselage forebody had been beaten severely but Joey did not detect any breaks. A good collision repair shop could probably bang out the dents. The IFF aerial was missing but the last thing she would be needing was a friend or foe detector even if she could get her plane in flying condition. All of the bogeys were earthbound now. After a quick inspection, she sat down and pondered her next move. She needed a mirror. Having removed her helmet, even the hot air felt cool against her forehead. Her short blonde hair was plastered, wet and sticky to her forehead. She had soft blue eyes, but they were hidden behind the mandatory aviator sunglasses she produced from a breast pocket. She was tall, you could say statuesque, though not to her face; tall enough to fly. The fact was, every airman at the base openly fantasized about her, joked about her, left comments trailing behind her as she passed by.

She had sat in the cockpit for a while after the crash landing, letting the dust and her thoughts settle. Looming ahead and to her right were the famous red rock formations that compelled thousands of tourists, artists, pensioners and counter culture vagabonds to put on their hiking boots and follow the trails leading to the energy vortices reputed to be in the area.

They had stayed for a few nights in a place called The Tennis Enchantment. The VW van could not be missed in a parking lot full of BMW and Mercedes sedans. For all of her father's power to the people, make love not war political rhetoric, he liked money and he liked comfort. The Enchantment required a lot of the former and provided nothing but the latter. It was an enchanting place, justifying the resort's namesake, her favourite part of the trip, the red rock cliffs so close you felt you could reach out and touch them. How aptly named, box canyon, because while sitting in the dining room, with its floor to ceiling windows, the entire horizon was obscured by the red cliffs rising sharply just beyond the tennis court and they made Joey feel contained within a wondrous giant painted container.

They had hiked up a trail to a vortex located near the resort property. Adam was with them. And his beautiful wife, Donna. Joey was eleven at the time, and if she was in need of a role model, there were few to be found in this motley crew. The grownups were so excited, anticipating god knows what when they reached the vortex. The group climbed slowly up through a forest that reminded Joey of the woods of Northern Ontario, where she had spent a summer with her paternal grandparents at their cottage on an always cold lake. It seemed odd to her to be tramping through a deciduous forest just a few miles away from desert and cactus, and not knowing the word deciduous or its meaning did not take away from the strangeness.

The vortex, according to their guide, was situated above a steep slope of a rock outcropping at the end of a box canyon. They climbed up the trail for an hour, once delayed when her mother skinned her knee on a rock. After struggling up the last rock face, they rested at their destination.

And nothing.

The adults were in a state of exaltation. Can you feel it? her father had asked. I feel wonderful, her mother had said. Feel what wonderful thing Joey had no idea. She remembered Adam being the only one who said nothing. He was sitting there watching the others and she felt the kinship of shared experience. He was as lost as she. Years later, when studying psychology in college, she learned about the placebo effect in scientific experiments. It made her think of her trip to the vortex and her blissed-out parents, high on an impression, getting off on a sugar pill of constructed illusions. It hardly came as a disappointment to Joey when during the next couple of days at the resort, the men went off on their own and her mom and Donna spent most of the day at the pool, leaving Joey in the hands of the resort's excellent youth program, or so the room brochure had promised.

There was a man approaching the aircraft. Joey had been on the ground for about twenty minutes. She was sitting on a boulder that the plane had narrowly missed, munching on a chocolate bar she had shoved into a zippered pocket before the Red Flag exercise began. It did not seem likely that she would know any time soon whether her Blue Team, composed of visiting pilots and junior officers like herself, had beaten the veteran Red Team. Funny how important it had all seemed a few hours ago, she thought. Now, it barely registered on her radar screen.

He wore the smile of a kindly priest, a Spencer Tracy smile. His face was weathered and lined—no sunscreen had ever graced its folds and crevices. He was probably in his fifties but Joey was lousy at guessing age. He had sharp Indian features, high cheekbones, plenty of forehead and a nose that divided his face like a mountain range. He was fiercely handsome, his hair long in the traditional manner, braided and pulled back and covered mostly by a creased cowboy hat. He wore denim—shirt and pants—and Joey wondered how he managed to fit the skin-tight jeans over his beat up cowboy boots. And there was something oddly familiar about his eyes.

He walked past her without a word. Hands on his hips, he circled the crippled aircraft slowly, inspecting it, occasionally reaching out and touching the fuselage. Joey did not know what to make of him. His silence was disturbing to her. She felt intimidated in his presence, which only fueled her confusion. One part of her insisted that she was in the presence of an ordinary man, a rancher maybe, and she had made a profession out of dealing with ordinary men. But another part of her, a part she did not put much faith in, an aspect of her makeup seldom used, intuition, was letting her know that this man was no curious hayseed.

He came around the nose from the far side of the plane.

"You always land them like that?" he asked.

"I ran out of fuel."

"Having trouble finding a place to land?"

"I suppose you could say that."

Joey reactively turned westward. The sun was low in the sky, heightening the redness of the terrain to a vein-blood hue.

"Have you felt anything today?" she asked, afraid to come out and tell the stranger what she had witnessed.

"You mean the earthquake?"

"Yes, the earthquake."

"No," he replied.

He reached for her hand. She recoiled involuntarily, pushing herself a little higher up the boulder.

"You'd better come with me. This isn't safe ground." His hand still reached out for hers. Reluctantly, she moved her hand into his and he helped her off the rock.

"What do you mean, not safe ground?" she asked.

He turned and faced the low sun, his eyelids squinting so tightly that it was hard to imagine he could still see through them.

"What you saw from your plane, the thing that chased you here— it's coming. This isn't safe ground. You must come with me now."

Joey had to this point managed to hold herself together. What she had witnessed, her miraculous escape from certain death, and now this bizarre man, were conspiring to unhinge her completely. She detected two choices in amongst the chaos disrupting her mind. She could come completely undone trying to make sense of a world she no longer recognized or she could place her faith and fate in this man's hands. There it was again, the seldom-heard voice deep within her, gaining strength, cutting through the chatter, pleading with her to let faith have a turn.

"What about my plane?"

"No problem. My brother Tom has a pickup truck. I'll have him haul it some place safe. My truck is down the road a bit. We should go now."

He gestured for her to follow him. Joey pulled a few things from her cockpit, some classified material and a carrying bag containing a first aid kit and a semi-automatic handgun, standard issue, then followed the old man down the road.

She had to lengthen her stride to keep up with him.

"My name is Joey Eaton."

"Nice of you to drop in on us, Miss Eaton. My name is John Walker. Welcome to Sedona."

"I was here once before when I was a child . . . with my parents."

"Is that a fact?"

"I think we stayed at a place not far from here."

"Probably The Enchantment."

"Yes, that's it. How did you know?"

"Like you said, it's not far from here. I used to work there off and on before it changed hands."

"Really? What did you do there?"

The wind was coming up. The Indian quickened the pace slightly, his eyes never leaving the western horizon.

"Handyman mainly, a bit of this, a bit of that," he said. "Mostly I tended the grounds."

"So you're a gardener."

"I suppose you could say that," he said.

VI

IT WAS NOT SO MUCH the structural damage that made evacuating the building difficult. It was the human wreckage that was providing the obstructions. The roof of Lucia's apartment building had caved in, destroying the fifth floor along with its occupants, the weight of the debris then causing most of the fifth floor to cave into the fourth. Miraculously, the rest of the building remained standing, the third floor and below still mostly intact—which was more than could be said for the mental condition of Lucia's neighbours.

Lucia's third-floor apartment looked like it had been placed in a martini mixer and shaken, not stirred. Dust particles sat heavily in the air, slow-motion moving, ancient stuff, dormant for decades, now awakened, displaced by the earth's maniacal fury. A waist-high book-case had fallen over, books splayed across the room as if dealt by a drunken gambler. The Picasso print lay facedown on the floor, impaled by an overturned high-heeled shoe. The galley kitchen shelves had been relieved of most of their contents. Broken glass was spread across the counter, trapped within a multi-coloured goo of syrups, jellies and exotically-flavoured cooking oils, all of which were dripping off the counter's edge to a widening pool on the kitchen floor.

When Lucia first awoke, it was from hitting the floor. The initial shockwave had not disturbed her sleep, however, her precarious position on the sofa was finally lost when the second wave hit, sending her free falling to the carpet. She awoke with a long-forgotten sensation, a childhood memory, the dull panic of finding herself on the floor, asleep but suddenly not so, sitting nonplussed by the side of her bed, then wailing, her mother magically appearing to pick her up and assure her it was nothing, she'd only fallen out of bed, go to sleep darling, everything is all right, a little pat on the head and then the welcoming darkness.

Only this time the room was moving.

At first Lucia clutched the ground madly, digging her nails into the carpet, trying to find a hold in order to keep herself from bouncing. Beyond the glass breaking and the sounds of books and pictures and whatever else was falling and hitting the floor of her apartment, past all of the rumbling and crashing noises from outside, was a deep, resonating sound, a low growl being absorbed into Lucia's body. She did not so much hear it as feel it enter her. It had an emotional quality, a compassionate rage.

She had no doubt about what was happening. No denial, no confusion. She had seen this coming, had felt it, unable initially to articulate it or expose the meaning behind the symbols, but now that it was here, she had not the slightest doubt of its portent.

She had no fear of her own death. As the room shook and rocked in fits, she could feel the suffering around her, the naked, mind-numbing fear, multiplied and focused by the thousands from people unmasked, lost within themselves, strangers to their own spiritual essence.

But that wasn't all. She could also sense the radiant brilliance of love around her, felt herself an interloper to an explosion of feelings from lovers and parents and friends.

There were tremendous crashes outside, and incredible gushing sounds as air exploded into her small apartment, the pressure causing her ears to pop. Lucia closed her eyes and let her mind slip slowly inside, away from the noise, to a quiet place. She often wore her Walkman headphones to bed, slowly drifting off as the band played on. Sometimes she would fall into an in-between state of consciousness, not asleep but not aware of the waking world, and the music would disappear. And sometimes a street noise or a body movement would rouse her back to consciousness and the music would jolt her awake. And she would wonder, where had the music gone? Or rather, where had she gone? Now she knew and as she withdrew further into her self, she saw the place clearly, unaided by the veil of sleep.

There was a center to her universe and she had found it. Mostly it was a warm, luxuriating light, inviting and soothing. She allowed herself to fall into it, travelling up a path that passed out of the top of her head.

Lucia could see her body on the carpet. She felt a kind of pity for the form lying prostrate next to the couch. It was so leaden and awkward, dense and crude, a blood and tissue machine enslaved by its bodily functions and the weight of living.

What a pigsty, she said to herself, then remembered whose sty this was. She hovered above the coffee table. Well, I'll be damned, she thought, it does mean something.

Lucia knew what was happening. She had never left her body before but had always felt the potential to do so was within her reach. It felt so good, there was such joy in this reality; it felt like a thousand Christmas mornings rolled into every second.

She heard a voice, a familiar voice, not communicated in words but the meaning was clear, telling her it was time to return. Recess was over. With reluctance came a powerful sense of discipline and duty and as quickly as she had left, Lucia felt the old suit of her body, squeezed her fingers into a fist, and then opened her eyes.

It was still. The room was still, the air was still, even the screams had silenced. Lucia lay there for a while, allowing herself a little time to regain all five senses. It took a while to actually feel the floor of her apartment beneath her. She slowly moved her head, her chin burying itself in the soft pile carpet. Her tarot cards were scattered in front of her. A group of ten or so were neatly spread a few inches from her face. All but one were face down. The one exposed card depicted a tower sitting on a small, rocky island, crumbling and ablaze at its summit, the ocean swirling around it, a fierce lightning storm above and, in the foreground, two unfortunate souls tumbling head first from the heights of the tower to the ground.

It figures, thought Lucia as she reached for the card. The Tower. A card of calamitous change, representing the exposure of false or outdated values, the stripping away of those man-made structures, both physical and cultural, designed to conceal the beast within, an indictment against human institutions, professions, governments and a society designed to hide a shameful truth—that we no longer know who we are. The Tower bore witness to the superficiality of lives wasted by the worship of power, position and youth.

The card, when selected by one of Lucia's clients would be a warning to get in touch with your true self, to stop being what you do and start being who you are, eliminate the role playing and start playing. Stop being the high-powered lawyer every waking hour, weekends included, and start spending some time with your kids, or, forget plastic surgery, your nose is fine but your life is a vacuous spiritual desert, filled with goods but no good. Lucia had no need of her psychic abilities to tell her how New York had just drawn the Tower card, she didn't need to go outside to see the devastation, to bear witness to ruined buildings and downed wires. There was something divinely fundamental going on. A cleansing, she thought, as she raised herself off the floor. A sweeping away of the old, the corrupt, the empty, the evil. Tell me you are surprised, she told herself. It had to happen here first. This city was the logical choice. But who was doing the choosing?

Once on her feet, Lucia disovered that she was covered in a fine white dust. She shook her head and patted her clothes, creating a cloud around her. The sounds from the street became increasingly louder and more distressed. There was movement in the hallway outside her door. Then a knock, which scared her so, she instinctively placed a hand on her heart.

"Is there anyone in there?" a male voice yelled. He pounded on the door once more.

"Hello, is everyone all right in there?"

Lucia went to the door but did not open it.

"I'm fine, just a little shaken up," she said.

The man said, "You'd better grab what you can and get out of here. There are gas leaks all over the building and I'm not sure it's going to stay standing for much longer."

She heard him walk away and start pounding on her neighbour's door.

It was desert island time. That game you played when you were bored; what ten books would you take to a desert island or what ten albums, or which supermodel would you want to be stranded with, or if you could only eat one thing for the rest of your life, what would it be? She saw the cards on the floor and gathered them up. She put on a coat—a big winter full-length one, leather, with lots of big pockets—and stuffed the cards into one of them. It was Adam's, the one he was wearing yesterday. How could he leave and forget his coat? No time. She ran to her bathroom and grabbed a toothbrush and some makeup, a bottle of moisturizer and a few tampons. In her bedroom she opened a few drawers, stuffing socks and underwear into her pockets. Seeing a sweater she took off the coat and put on the sweater, then another, then replaced the coat.

She kept scrounging around. What should I take? What will I need? She was frantic. How do you pack for the destruction of a way of life. Maybe I'm overreacting? she thought. Earthquakes happen all over the world everyday. Buildings collapse, people die, the place is declared a disaster area, relief aid appears, and eventually, the place is re-built. Why should this be any different? Happening as it had in New York did not make it an extraordinary seismic event. Oh, but it did. Lucia knew it did. Because New York was special, its geographical location no accident. Lucia realized that that was what she had felt during the earthquake—the energy beneath this city coming up through the earth.

Lucia chastised herself for not realizing it sooner. New York, New York. Of course. It was so clear now. Why else would millions of people crowd onto this modest island, pouring in by the millions each day, building it up vertically so more and more people could fit onto it, piling on top of each other like in a rugby scrum. There was a flow of pure energy rising straight up from the ground. Lucia felt it. And she began to understand how it had been distorted, twisted and bent by the people and institutions sitting on top of it for generations, corrupting the source, polluting the well, to the point where the earth had said, enough already, and had purged itself of the blight causing it such malignant discomfort.

We have done this, she thought. We have brought this upon ourselves. There were forces at work here and she did not pretend to understand them, yet she was certain that a collective gestalt of negative energy was at the root of this destruction.

She had her hands in her pockets. One of them was playing with the bottle of moisturizer she had grabbed. I won't be needing this, she said to herself, and threw it on the bed. I won't be needing anything.

Lucia walked out of the bedroom and headed for the door. She turned back to consider her meager possessions, assessing her life's inventory with the detachment of a mortician. Her scattered belongings created a kind of collage, a memorial to her rapidly receding past, events conspiring to constrict time, eliminating the sense of present, leaving only a fast-approaching future.

Lucia thought of Adam, then. Where had he disappeared to last night? Something had happened, a reading, she was doing a reading, then what? She was stunned suddenly by the fear of Adam being caught somewhere in the city, unprotected, dead or injured. It quickly passed and more reasonable, pacifying thoughts waylaid her paranoia. Adam was fine, she knew. She must find him or contact him. Adam was the one thing in her life to which she must cling. He was the bridge between her past and whatever may lie ahead. How or why didn't matter. Only Adam mattered.

They were standing at the third-floor landing, a group of tenants, squeezed together in the narrow hallway, preventing Lucia access to the floors below. A few she recognized—one or two she knew by name. There was Leonard Deblasio, the cellist, a member of a quartet that rented itself out to small parties, providing eighteenth century muzak

70

to hors d'oeuvre-munching guests. He was dressed in his pyjamas, a coat thrown over them, sporting a nasty gash slightly above his receding hairline, his cello, sheathed in a canvas-carrying bag, clutched close to his body. He was on his tiptoes, reconnoitering from above the heads of those blocking the staircase. An elderly couple stood back from the group, the wife supported by an intravenous stand, a plastic tube looping down from a bag of clear fluid to a place hidden by a bandage on her wrist. Her husband, a short man with a glistening pink face and a yarmulke on his crown, bobby pinned to the remnants of what was once a full head of hair, was soothing her with cooing sounds. But her crazed eyes were not appeased. He held a small torah in his free hand and had wrapped his tallis around his neck like a scarf.

People had various items in their hands; photo albums, clothing, one girl, about eight, clung to her teddy while her older brother, Walkman in hand, headphones on, had his music set to full blast, perhaps out of defiance, perhaps to shut the world out. There were people talking loudly and people not talking at all.

Lucia pushed her way gently through the tenants and approached Leonard, partially because she knew him but mainly because he was tall and could see what was going on.

"Hi Leonard. What's happening?" she asked.

"Oh, Lucia. Thank the Lord you're not hurt. Isn't this awful. It's so awful. I can't stand it. I'm going to burst I'm so afraid. They say the building is going to collapse."

"So what's the holdup? Why are people just standing here?"

Leonard had large blackheads on his nose, and his face was flushed red from distress. He looked so frantic, Lucia thought he might burst and rain his puss-clogged pores all over her.

"There's a man down there," was all he said.

She made her way to the top of the stairs, becoming necessarily more aggressive as she pushed past the last of the obstructing tenants.

On the landing between floors, five or six steps below her, lay a man. She did not recognize him. A long piece of railing with wrought iron spindles attached had broken loose from the floor above and the spindles had impaled the man, entering his chest and stomach, punching their way clean through his body. He was not laying flat but rather, was suspended over the landing, one end of the railing having wedged itself against the outer wall, the other mounted on a step leading up to Lucia's floor. His arms hung lifelessly behind him, his hands just grazing the floor. His face was frozen in the astonished expression the impact must have caused. Blood covered the landing, spilling over in a reluctant waterfall to the steps leading down to the second floor.

People are like cattle, thought Lucia, and this obstruction, this man who has died a most horrible death and bled himself dry was nothing more to these people than a cattle gate.

Lucia started down the stairs, oblivious to the gasps and murmurs behind her. She stood on the last step before the landing. There was no way to avoid the blood unless you made your way over the railing at the point where it U-turned to the second floor. She fixed her gaze on the man. He was vaguely familiar to her, though it might have been the archetypal image of the crucifixion that made the scene seem familiar and not the man. She had never seen so much blood, had never realized how much there could be in one person. The colour had a hypnotizing effect and she had to force herself to turn away. She grabbed the rounded wooden ball atop the baluster, it must have a name but she didn't know it, and hoisted herself onto the railing, cowboy style, slid down a few feet past the body, then dismounted on the staircase leading to the second floor.

The tenants were astonished by the ease with which she had circumvented the seemingly impassable obstacle in their path.

"He's dead. That's blood," she said, pointing down at the darkening pool. "I guarantee you there is more of the same outside. Wake up. Things are not going back to the way they were when you went to bed last night. Not ever."

With that she started down the stairs. She heard the girl with the Teddy complain to her mother about her party shoes getting dirty. But Lucia didn't care. She was dropping a steel curtain around her emotions. That girl will surely die, and thousands like her, and there was nothing to be done about it, thought Lucia. Humans in transit, moving over to the other side, leaving behind on this horrible, black morning, only those with the stomach to face it. Lucia did not even understand what she was thinking on a purely cognitive level, but on a visceral, emotive level, it made perfect sense.

From the familiar to the unfamiliar. When had she said that recently?

The ground floor was no more than a cubbyhole, deserted, debris scattered everywhere. Most of the floor was covered with false ceiling tiles, broken and trampled upon. The front door was ahead, only a few feet away and Lucia's heart was pounding in anticipation of setting foot outside. She was afraid of the imagery that would engrave itself into her memory forever. She went through the security door, then, without hesitation, she reached for the handle of the outer door, pulled it open and stepped out onto the street.

It was terrible and terrifying. The light of the sun in the cloudless sky was filtered through the haze of the dust and dirt that continually drifted up from the collapsed buildings, creating a surreal unfocused visual effect up and down Bedford Street. Lucia walked down Grove Street the short distance to Hudson Street. There, the full impact of the force of the earthquake was in full evidence. Most of the commercial storefront buildings were lying in the street. The contents of their second and third floors were strewn everywhere. Beds, cabinets, clothing and many dead bodies littered the street. There were people clawing at rocks to free trapped family members and people sitting on the ground weeping, people walking aimlessly in a daze and people running past as if being chased.

Lucia was unsure where to go. She was certain of the necessity to keep in motion, to not stop and give anyone any time to observe her. Already the looting had commenced. Some of the runners, all men, had TVs and cameras and CD players in their hands—Lucia could not recall an electronics store in the neighbourhood—racing back to their homes to plug the equipment into what exactly? To watch what exactly?

A fire hydrant had been decapitated, sending a geyser straight up into the air, people standing nearby with buckets to catch the water that no longer flowed into their homes. Some buildings were burning out of control, igniting the adjacent buildings in an infernal game of dominoes. Further north she could see fire trucks, attempting, in vain, to make their way clear through the debris.

Up ahead Lucia saw two black men in army fatigues, each sporting a baseball bat. A man, a white man, was the first victim she saw, his head crushed by the home-run swing of the larger of the two black men. Payback time. Everyone wanted in on the action, and everyone had a role—victim, survivor, avenging angel. For some reason, Lucia remained on the same side of the street. People began to give the men a wide berth. An unsuspecting young boy—he must have been around eight, Asian, probably Korean, Lucia guessed—walking in a kind of hypnotized state, passed unharmed between the two men. Behind the boy, an old black woman, dragging a bulging green garbage bag along the ground, stopped in front of the two men and raised herself erect, her gigantic breasts pointing out at the men like twin-draped cannons.

"What's got into you boys?" she said, one hand on her bag, the other pointing a crooked, accusing finger in the direction of their arrogant faces. "You two's acting like a couple of mad dogs. Don't you have any sense between you? Go home now and leave these people be. Nobody needs any more trouble. The Lord's seen to that."

A quick swing and part of her skull and brain splattered against a storefront window that had somehow remained unbroken, the gooey mess flattening, then slowly sliding down the pane, leaving a bloody trail before it lost its hold on the window and fell to the ground.

Lucia tried not to react, but found her hand covering her mouth anyway so she consciously placed it back by her side and made herself breathe, deep and slow, in through the nose, out through the mouth.

I must be an idiot, she thought, staying her course, the two men thirty feet in front of her. I am invisible, she commanded and, as her stride gained purpose, she detected a slight change in the light, a purple filter diffusing the scene before her. She passed between the two men, like a U-boat slipping between two destroyers, unnoticed or not suitable prey, take your pick. She had survived the gauntlet and did not glance back, not even when she heard another dull slap of wood against flesh and bone.

There was a strange squeaking sound over to her right. A two-storey building lurched forward, its front façade of brick falling into the street, lengths of wooden beams and chunks of plaster and drywall spilling out in almost symmetrical fashion, a huge cloud of dust obscuring the scene momentarily. There were screams, then moans and the pitiable mewing of the trapped.

Lucia kept going north along Hudson Street. She let her feet guide her, her mind receding further away from stimuli she could no longer assimilate. How often had she witnessed long lines of refugees on TV, fleeing floods or volcanoes or advancing armies or pestilence? So distant, so remote, another world, a third-world phenomenon, bad karma to be born to such a fate.

And now it was our turn, Lucia thought. Payback time. The avenging angel. The Tower. The tearing down of false idols. Starting over. A cleansing. A non-denominational ethnic cleansing.

What was left of the Whitehorse Tavern was before her now. She stopped in front of the wrecked place. Warm memories crept up; she often met friends here—even Adam would occasionally show up if the planets were aligned correctly—and they would command a table in the front room if it wasn't too crowded, throwing back a few, digging their fingers into a pile of greasy french fries, Dylan Thomas glaring at them from his bar stool, larger than life, immortalized on the wall of the second room, his passion, his pain, his genius glaring at you and making you feel guilty for having disturbed his solitude.

The roof of the venerable old building had collapsed, the walls exploding outwards, but there amongst the rubble, stood an inner wall, Dylan Thomas, mug in his grasp, wide-eyed, glaring.

> *Do not go gentle into that good night,*
> *Old age should burn and rave at close of day;*
> *Rage, rage against the dying of the light.*

Dylan Thomas, bohemian poet, acerbic observer, reckless drunk, iconoclast and nonconformist, writing for the generation to follow and now witnessing the natural conclusion of the degradation and suffering that had followed him and revealed itself to him and had finally claimed him.

> *Though wise men at their end know dark is right,*
> *Because their words had forked no lightning they*
> *Do not go gentle into that good night.*

Lucia stood there in homage, verses she remembered playing across her mind like a player piano, old meanings discarded, new impressions, a deeper understanding bubbling up, each word a catalyst, old worlds remembered, revisited, footprints in the snow, bleak and white, leading her past the confusion and pain.

Amongst the crumbled bricks on the ground, she spotted a black star, made of iron, she thought. It was one of many that had adorned the front wall of the building. She picked it up and put it in one of the large pockets of Adam's coat. A souvenir.

What a day.

A scream broke the epiphanic spell, pulling her eyes back south and across the street. There was a derelict gas station now serving as an indoor parking lot, painted a colour not red, not pink but some mutated bastardization of both, two ancient gas pumps, years having passed since their last taste of fossil fuel, standing erect on the driveway, appearing from a distance as one-armed robots. The garage was below ground with a short steep driveway serving as the only entrance. Lucia had walked by it countless times, eyes always drawn to the cavernous service bay. She had never noticed more than a couple of cars parked inside despite the relatively cheap parking rates boasted by the sign near the street. The place had always given her the creeps as had the unsavory characters who operated the parking service— dark, greasy men with moustaches and faded green parkas, lurking behind drawn blinds, holed up in the station's service office.

It was a young scream, a child's scream, gender indeterminable, with the sonic quality of amplified feedback. For the first time since venturing out of her building, Lucia felt curious, more than curious, felt drawn towards an unwanted responsibility, as if she had no choice but to respond, to involve herself in a drama not her own. Something inside was doing the picking and choosing; she did not question the process, a moral lassitude slowing her reaction to the compounding tragedies playing out before her eyes.

She walked over to the gas station. The screams had ceased but there was a commotion, a scuffling sound coming from the garage. She had her hands in her pockets, feigning indifference while an unfamiliar fear made it difficult for her to breathe.

At first she could not see them, the light from outside preventing a clear view of the darkened cavern. She stepped into the shadow thrown by the building and the light dispersed, revealing three people, a frozen scene of final judgment; perpetrator, victim and avenger.

> *Good men, the last wave by, crying how bright*
> *Their frail deeds might have danced in a green bay,*
> *Rage, rage against the dying of the light.*

The Korean boy she had seen earlier was lying on his side, his pants pulled down to his ankles, moaning but seeming more scared than hurt. Near him, still and misshapen with one arm flung behind his back and legs twisted, lay an adult male, his head an island in the middle of a bloody pool. He was white, in his early twenties, a multitude of earrings in both ears, orange stubble, eyes wide open with a scream on the tip of a tongue that would form no more words. He too wore his pants below his knees, his thing thankfully hidden from view. Standing over him was a man, so still he could have been a mime from Central Park, a two by four in his hand, a big man, probably fifty years old or more, his benevolent face distorted by the trauma his deed had unleashed.

There seems to be a run on head bashing today, was the first coherent thought Lucia had.

The boy continued to moan, crawling away from the widening pool of blood threatening to consume his sneakers. Lucia was absorbed by the paralysis of the moment, her eyes on the man and the blood-stained piece of wood. The killer, probably sensing Lucia's presence, turned his head. Without consciously trying, Lucia saw his aura, an emerald green, with a purplish border, thick with colour, a magnificent display. It occurred to Lucia that his was the first aura she had seen all day. The little boy spotted Lucia and grabbed for the waist of his pants. She saw no colour from him.

"I had to do it. He was hurting the boy," said the man, his voice weighed heavy, a gruff voice, but a kind one.

"I know," said Lucia, coming down the ramp.

He had gentle, round eyes, full of tears, a big bear of a man, the friendly neighbourhood cop or gym teacher, a family man, someone accustomed to minding his manners, the sort of man who would find this deed incomprehensible.

"I had to. He wouldn't stop. Said, go away nigger. Nobody's called me that in a long time."

"You had no choice," said Lucia, but she was only scrambling for something to say.

"I had no choice. I was so mad. Ain't got nothin' 'gainst white folks or fags, but he was hurting the boy, see. Plenty of both in the Navy."

"Plenty of what?" asked Lucia.

"White folks and fags," said the man.

He said it so seriously it almost made Lucia laugh.

"They'll put me in jail for sure for this," the man said as the plank slipped from his hand, its impact with the floor startling Lucia and the boy.

"I don't think so, not today," she said as she walked over to the boy.

"Are you all right?" Lucia asked the child.

"I'll live," he said, and Lucia heard a lifetime of anger and shame born in those words.

"Where are your parents?" asked Lucia.

"In heaven," answered the boy, and she realized how young he was, maybe young enough for this day to fade into a stale house smell of a memory, in the air, lingering, unpleasant but not always noticeable.

"What's your name, son?" asked the man.

He said his name was Brian Kwon. He was eight years old and lived with his parents somewhere off Center Street. He said their flat had collapsed on top of them, burying his parents and younger sister, although he did not say flat, he said house, and from the vantage point of eight years on the planet, his family was under the rubble, not dead. He was bright and articulate but there was no reference point for him, for any of them, no foothold, words free falling, rambling conversation, bits and pieces of fact becoming legend, a story placed in the family album, the beginnings of myth.

There were no more coincidences, Lucia decided—as if there ever had been. And there was no more fate or destiny. There were only choices. Every second, every heartbeat, another decision, another fork in the road taken. She stood there watching the man—whose name it came out was Sydney—talking to the boy, and knew she was supposed to be here, at this moment, not because it was written down, but from a universe of choices made, little decisions, selections on a menu, delivering her to this ugly little hole in the ground.

> Wild men who caught and sang the sun in flight,
> And learn, too late, they grieved it on its way,
> Do not go gentle into that good night.

"We can't stay here," and it sounded so dumb after she had said it that she quickly added, "these buildings are all collapsing . . . it's not safe in here," as if a body with its head smashed in was not a compelling enough reason to leave.

They were blinded by the intense sunlight as they exited the parking garage, each of them instinctually raising a hand to block the sun, a lunatic salute to the passing parade.

A woman ran by, her arms clutching three fur coats. You could tell they were hers, not stolen, the only things she had grabbed from her closet. Maybe it was their value or they were her favourite possessions or maybe she hated the cold and winter was coming soon and warmth would be more precious than gold or stereo equipment. It was her choice, but it weighed on her, the fear; maybe she's thinking her diamonds would have been so much easier to conceal and these coats are heavy and visible. She knew she was a target, knew she would regret the decision, but second-guessing was a luxury the day would not allow.

Activity on the street was increasing; as more and more buildings threatened to collapse, people instinctively gravitated closer to the middle of Hudson St., away from the debris and falling buildings. The mass of them were forming a serpentine procession leading nowhere in particular, not stopping, defeated, unsure of the way or what further horror would accost them before a safe haven was reached. Many were injured and marched by with a walking-dead sort of gait, part lurch, part misstep, some part of their body—an arm or leg or side—favoured, not working, wrapped in bloodied clothing.

> *Grave men, near death, who see with blinding sight*
> *Blind eyes could blaze like meteors and be gay,*
> *Rage, rage against the dying of the light.*

The boy, Brian, started walking away, drifting back into the thick, sun-blocking dust that seemed worse behind them than ahead. There was no goodbye, no thanks for the man who had saved him. The world had temporarily foreclosed on courtesy and manners.

"Where are you going?" yelled Sydney.

The boy stopped. He did not turn around. He was thinking, it was plain to see. Indecision, because you knew he wanted a reason to stay, was deep-down traumatized and was scared by what he imagined he would find by returning to his neighbourhood, but maybe he was brought up to distrust non-Asians, because whenever you belonged to a group, everyone else was a *non*. In Lucia's family, there had only been Catholics and non-Catholics.

He turned around, a scared little boy with tears rolling down his face, so big and juicy that they made stains the size of quarters when they hit the pavement.

"I know a place," said Sydney. "I know a place where we can go. We'll be safe there. All of us."

They were sweet words, words of reliance, words with the ring of truth to them. She did not need to know this man to know she could trust him, not only to say true things, but to deliver on them. If he knew of a safe place in this living purgatory, then such a place must surely exist.

> *And you, my father, there on the sad height,*
> *Curse, bless, me now with your fierce tears, I pray.*
> *Do not go gentle into that good night.*
> *Rage, rage against the dying of the light.*

So too the boy, who introduced the smallest of smiles, he also understood and recognized the truth of Sydney.

And with the smile came the glow, so sudden and bright that Lucia flinched, not green like Sydney's but orange, thin, extending not further than a few inches from the boy's skin, but bright and alive.

It could only mean one thing—a choice, another small decision, one way leading to oblivion, another to promise. A microscopic neuron triggering a synapse this way and not that, had changed the universe. Maybe tomorrow another path would lead the boy down a treacherous course, but for now the child was safe, they were, the three of them, safe, moving in the footsteps of Sydney—stranger, deliverer from evil and into whose hands Lucia had just placed her life.

"Let's go," said Sydney, taking Brian's hand, putting his other on Lucia's shoulder briefly, turning her in the right direction, giving a little push against her inertia.

"Where are we going, precisely?" asked Lucia.

"I have a boat," said Sydney.

VII

MAN WHAT A DREAM, Derek Eaton thought as he tried to raise his head from the pillow. Except it wasn't a pillow, it was soft and fleshy and smelled of good, sweaty sex. He opened one eye to inspect. The rounded curve of Jenny's butt rose majestically beyond his line of vision. Ah, the firmness of youth, he thought, as he passed a hand over Jenny's ass, up the small of her back to her shoulder blade. He wanted to roll her over and start all over again, pit his experience once more against her youthful explosiveness.

But as much as he willed it, he could barely raise his head, let alone anything as fickle as his dick. What was that shit we took last night, he wondered, then remembered, a pharmaceutical, a downer and one of his favourites. They had needed something to cut through the coke buzz. Jenny was wired and he couldn't get it up anymore so they had swallowed a few Chloral Hydrates just before dawn. The last thing he remembered was the gel cap dissolving in his stomach, sending an ether-smelling fume straight up his throat.

I'm getting too old for this shit, Derek reflected, but he didn't really believe it, didn't for a moment consider that a fifty-two-year-old man lying half-stoned and totally naked with a twenty-five-year-old Columbia University graduate and part-time waitress, in a coach house owned by his best friend, might be pissing off the following persons:

1. His daughter Joey, macho airforce pilot, coincidentally twenty-five years old and stiff enough to pass for a broom handle; or,

2. Jenny's parents, Connecticut residents, connected up the yin yang, could probably have him deported to Canada or worse, her father a big muck-a-muck at NBC, street rat made good, started-in-the-mailroom kind of success story; or,

3. Adam's neighbours, but fuck them; or,

4. Adam, but he's just jealous, hasn't been laid in so long, peeing has become an exciting event for him; or,

5. Jenny's boyfriend Daniel, a Harvard law grad, the trophy she likes

to bring home to mommy and daddy, a ruse, a smokescreen, someone she trots out for public display while the real Jenny dips behind the curtain and pursues her natural inclination for debauchery, crazy making, shit disturbing and anything else conjured up by a mind freed from the restrictions normally imposed upon a girl of her social station; or,

6. Gloria, estranged wife, perennial flower child, coniferous in her dedication to a sixties lifestyle no longer taken seriously by its original progenitors or at best, paid lip service to or rolled out for an occasional airing. Of course her disapproval of Derek's current fling would rank about two hundred and fifty-three on her all time list; or,

7. Lucia, the closest thing Adam has to a main squeeze, spooky lady, attractive as hell, disapproves of Derek's relationship with Adam, doesn't need her clairvoyance to see through Derek's game; or,

8. Derek himself.

Self-recrimination—not Derek's strong suit. A life spent second-guessing or self-flagellating one's self for every misdemeanor, each bad decision or ill-mannered act, was not Derek's idea of time well spent. Sure, he tried to learn from his mistakes but he had more fun making them.

He shifted, rolling onto his back, his head sliding down Jenny's thighs. That's when he noticed it.

"Jenny, we've been fuckin' robbed! Come on, get up."

He started to shake her, her head rolling back and forth, unresisting, on the pillow.

"Go away, I'm tired," she mumbled, then buried her head beneath the pillow.

"I'm serious," said Derek. "Someone snuck in here while we were zonked out and ransacked the place. It's a fucking mess in here."

He got up and whipped the pillow off her head. She reluctantly and with great effort, lifted her head high enough to survey the surroundings.

"Derek, you're an idiot. We weren't robbed." She sunk back into the bed and closed her eyes.

Derek walked over to the railing of the loft. Anything capable of movement by anything less than two strong men, had moved. The umbrella stand was knocked over, a couple of paintings normally hanging horizontally now hung at an unflattering angle, dishes on the floor, spilt beer on the coffee table—the house was a mess.

"Get up and come see this. Someone has totally trashed the place, probably your uptight boyfriend. What an asshole. If I was him I would have killed us but no, the chicken shit takes it out on the furniture."

With more determination, Jenny raised herself on her elbows and said, "It wasn't Daniel. He wouldn't stoop to anything as silly as this. I thought you said you spent years in L.A."

"And that is relevant because . . . "

"Please. Does any of this look familiar to you? Would you care to have it spelled out in block letters? We slept through a bloody earthquake, my sweet. Aren't my drugs fabulous!"

She said it so casually, Derek had a hard time taking her seriously. It did resemble an L.A. apartment after a major shake. Whatever it was, he'd slept through it so why not an earthquake? What else could it be? Nothing appeared to be missing.

"Oh shit," said Derek.

"What?" Jenny was out of the bed, picking up her clothes from a heap on the floor.

"She called it. Right on the money. Lucia. She is fucking amazing."

Jenny straightened and turned to face Derek, absently clutching her stomach.

"Lucia knew this was going to happen? Oh god, my parents, I've got to call them."

She ran to the phone but there was no dial tone.

"Derek, how am I going to find out if my family's all right?"

She was frantic, started biting her lip, still naked, her distress shrinking her, her forehead showing you where the permanent creases would one day lay their claim.

"We'll get some news. Don't worry. Nothing happened to us so there's no reason to think the earthquake was any worse where your house is. Put on your clothes. Let's go see if Adam is okay."

They entered the main house through a back door. A thorough search and lots of calling out failed to locate Adam's whereabouts. Derek had gone to the study first and now led Jenny back there. Derek wasn't feeling good about any of this, not about the earthquake, or the squishy sound their footsteps made in the soaked carpet, or finding the house empty. Mostly though, he wasn't feeling good about feeling good, of making contact with the part of him that was taking delight in everything—the wrecked house, the busted Gramophones, the smoke rising over the Manhattan skyline, the 'scared out of her wits' look on Jenny's face, the fact that no one was going to work today, the disabled phones—it all made him feel good, it justified his

existence. It was an old, familiar feeling, the taking delight from someone else's misfortune feeling. He could not help himself. It was his
job to point out the futility of taking life so seriously. He was living
proof of how it could be done. And he was suddenly very afraid that
he was about to have the time of his life.

"God, look at you. What a freak." Jenny had picked up a framed
picture from off the floor. She had never noticed it before.

"Your hair is so gross. And that can't be Adam. Where is this?"

Derek took the picture from her hand. It was a photo of him and
Adam, sitting at a table, contorted by laughter. It was taken on the
day they first met.

"Woodstock," he answered.

"I can't believe I'm sleeping with someone who went to
Woodstock." She found a hook on the wall and put the picture back.

"I didn't *go* to Woodstock. I was there on business."

She didn't believe him, you could see it in her face. Adam hadn't
either, more than three decades before.

Derek is in the food tent in the backstage area, scarfing down anything he can lay his hands on. It's Sunday afternoon and he hasn't
slept in three days. He has a nice buzz going and a severe case of
the munchies so his brain is sounding like a waiter calling out food
orders to a short order cook. Everything tastes great, even the veggie
and rice shit they're serving, but nothing is dousing his cravings.

There's another helicopter landing. They can't get the acts in by the
roads anymore so they're flying them in. It's pretty cool what's happening but Derek is mainly trying to figure out how he can attract a
crowd this size to his show, to be held outside Toronto at a speedway,
and make sure that every last blissed-out music lover pays for the privi-
lege. This free concert bullshit is not his idea of a good time.

There's a bit of a commotion outside the tent. It's Hendrix who's
just been flown in. Derek wants to go over and say hello but there are
too many people around him—his Band of Gypsies, not the same deal
without Noel. That would be an angle. Get the Experience back together for his show. Good press.

He's sitting at a table by himself, and he sees the roadie from the
night before, approaching, plate in hand.

"Mind if I join you?" he asks.

"You heard the man—it's a free concert," says Derek.

"I'll take that as a yes. My name's Adam."

"Derek."

They shake hands, hippie style, hooking thumbs. There's a sizing up, a hint of recognition, a distorted reflection in each other's eyes, then the hands release.

"You move pretty fast," Adam says.

"I was on the relay team at school."

"I doubt she was trying to pass you a baton."

"She was trying to scratch my bloody eyes out, the bitch."

"So why was she so mad?"

Derek can tell the dude is trying to be casual but it's so obvious he's dying to know, it's killing him, this not knowing, like after a date when you go meet your buddies and they want to know, well, how was it, did you get any, details, we need details, man. This guy is digging into a pile of potato salad and it's a funny brown colour; he is trying to be nonchalant, but it's eating him up inside, the not knowing.

"Simple case of mistaken identity," Derek says.

"And you just happened to be hiding behind those speakers."

"I wasn't hiding. I was checking out some equipment."

Derek lets Adam sit there while he goes and refills his plate. He's so full he feels like he's going to burst but he needs something sweet, a doughnut maybe, only they don't have any, just some granola cookies, so he takes three, then a fourth. Derek strikes up a conversation with Neil Young, wants this Adam dude to see him talking to Neil, doesn't really know why it's important to impress the guy, but shit, he's got this tight ass attitude. Derek and Neil are talking about Toronto and The Riverboat days and how's your old lady and what's this I hear about you hooking up with Stills' new band and Neil tells him he's going to sit in for a couple songs tonight, see how it goes.

He wants Neil to come sit down but Neil has to go, has to learn a few songs before their set but they can't find Crosby to rehearse and Neil is telling Derek that Stills is freaking out because he figures Crosby's walked out into the multitude to catch the vibe and they'll probably never see him again, not to mention they've only performed these songs live once before so it should be fun, you can't faze Neil, and they're walking while they're talking, heading towards the table.

Derek makes the introductions. But it's not going right. Adam gets up and gives Neil a big hug, Neil saying, "Great to see you man," and he's smiling, a rare facial expression by rock's serious young man, so you know he means it.

Derek fades, the brilliance of the two men's affection for each other too intense. Neil is inviting Adam to come spend some time with the band, Adam pulling a paper out of his back pocket, scanning a list and saying maybe he'd have some time after Country Joe's set.

"So whose equipment did you say you were checking out?" Adam asks, deadpan, after Neil has departed. It's a shot, well placed.

Derek says, "Janis's. She caught me putting Spanish Fly on her microphone," and Adam doesn't believe him but the image takes him by surprise and they can't stop laughing, it's not even that funny.

People at other tables are starting to watch them. A photographer notices the commotion, raises his Asahi Pentax at the two pranksters, focuses his 200m lens, and engages the shutter.

"So why were you backstage?" asked Jenny.

"I was with The Band."

"Which band?"

"Not which band . . . The Band."

"Is this like, who's on first?" she asked.

"No and I can't believe I'm fucking someone who doesn't know who The Band is."

"Sorry. I don't listen to old fart hippie music."

"Well you should if you're going to hang out with old fart hippies."

It did occur to Derek that the world was coming undone, his friend was missing, he had no idea if he should go searching for him, report him missing, or prepare dinner and instead, he was having a generational tennis volley with his cradle-plucked girlfriend. Which did not particularly bother him.

"The Band played at Woodstock. In fact, The Band lived in Woodstock. But three of them were from Ontario. I used to hang with one of the members, Rick Danko, and got to know the rest of the group when they were called the Hawks. They played for years in Toronto, fronted by this wild man from Arkansas—Ronnie Hawkins—before they started playing with Dylan. That's Bob Dylan—you've heard of him, haven't you?"

"Sure," said Jenny, "he's Jacob's dad."

She was loving this and he knew it so he didn't bite.

"Anyway, I was hanging out at Big Pink that summer and when the boys went to play Woodstock, I picked up a guitar case and went along."

"So you were one of their roadies."

"No I was a friend pretending to be a roadie. I had business to attend to there. I was planning a big festival of my own outside Toronto and was making contacts with the bands and their managers."

"Did you pull it off?"

"As a matter of fact, I did. It put me on the map as an outdoor pro-moter. With a little bit of help from my friends."

"Adam," said Jenny.

"Adam was a big help. He worked the show, did all the sound plus used his connections to get a lot of the acts to show up."

"But I never got paid," said Adam, startling the two so badly that Derek staggered back a foot and Jenny gave out a feeble gasp.

Adam stood in the doorway, a couple of shopping bags in one hand, a shotgun in the other. The combination of his dishevelled appearance and formal attire had transformed him into a mad version of himself.

"Shit, I forgot. It's dress-up Thursday," Derek said.

"It's my new look."

"For shopping . . . with a shotgun?" Jenny asked. She appeared terrified by its presence, or perhaps by what its presence represented.

"No. I heard some gunfire on the way back home so I thought I should unearth this baby just in case."

Adam put down the bags, activated the tang safety on the pump-action 12-gauge Browning shotgun, placed it carefully against a wall, then hugged his friends.

It wasn't true, of course. He hadn't just taken the gun from the walk-in vault that the original owner of the house had installed to protect his silverware from the pickpocketing moves of his staff. Adam had retrieved it much earlier, after he ventured down to the end of his driveway and saw the dented Cavalier go past.

Five guys in the car. Taking in the sights. Driving by real slow, faces framed by the windows, not the driver's though because he was hav-ing a lot of trouble avoiding tree branches and wrought-iron fences and everything else that had fallen into the street, with mixed re-sults if the dents and paint scrapes were any indication.

It had a movie quality, a scene he had seen played out many times in violent action films, a slow-motion scene, close shot of the car, camera moving with the vehicle, the stares, soulless, vacant of any human emotion past hate.

They were black, the five of them, and he tried to ignore it but the truth was, it scared him, made him wonder if they had driven up from East Orange or Newark to scope the place out, do some damage, make a quick score. Like it would make a difference if they were white and desperate. Like it would somehow hurt less or feel more comfortable to be robbed by his own skin colour. He knew it was irrational, knew it was racist, but they scared him. He was buying into their culture of hatred and intimidation because it was real and it was honest.

He owned a couple of firearms, the shotgun and a Remington bolt-action hunting rifle. Adam didn't like handguns; they were too seductive, too blatant in their purpose. But the shotgun, it was a weapon of self-defense, somewhat indiscriminate, literally capable of hitting two birds, a frontier weapon, just point and shoot.

Adam had taken up skeet and trap shooting for a while. There was a gun club about twenty minutes from his house. He went through all of the paper work to obtain the gun permit, bought the guns, joined the club, took lessons, made shooting dates with the people he met there, took guests—musicians were lousy shots for the most part— did all these things to convince himself he hadn't really bought the guns just in case a carload of hoodlums drove by his house with eyes coveting everything he was and owned—but he had.

After the car disappeared, Adam went back to the house and retrieved the shotgun from the vault. He walked back down the driveway, unsure what he would do if he actually had occasion to draw a bead on a human target. He had never in his life killed anything bigger than a cockroach—there was that car incident with a squirrel but that was an accident—and he wasn't sure the resolve was there to follow through with the provocation an armed person would provide.

Most people are killed by their own guns, and Adam could never figure out if that meant suicide or deranged family members or accidents.

When he was sure the car was not going to make a return visit, he crossed the street, reluctant to leave his house and a vulnerable Derek and Jenny unprotected, but he had an insatiable, voyeuristic urge to survey the damage and get a feel for the state of the infrastructure, or what was left of it.

It was an obscenely beautiful day, crisp—you could see your breath, but just barely—the sun now high in the southeastern sky. There was no wind and the temperature was precisely at the point where Adam could never decide which coat to wear because his parka or long coat made him sweat, and his leather bomber jacket left him slightly chilled. He had always loved the day his mother marched into his room, removing his T-shirts and shorts, packing the pastels and Madras patterns away into a box marked *Adam/Summer*, and replacing them with the grays and browns of winter; sweatshirts and flannel pyjamas, and his winter parka, the friend he had left behind in spring, forgotten during the warm weather, relegated to a hook on the basement storage rack, now back, a one-dollar bill or stick of gum he'd left in a pocket, waiting patiently for his return.

It was the bomber jacket today. The long coat was in New York, along with his wallet and whatever else was in the pockets. He was not sure how he had managed to forget it at Lucia's but that was not really true. His mind had been elsewhere when he left the apartment, the cold air unnoticed.

Adam turned down Bellevue Avenue and headed towards the commercial section of Upper Montclair. He suddenly felt silly carrying the shotgun and concealed it in a hedge. There was much activity ahead—noise, fish-market noise with a vitality bordering on manic. From a distance you would have thought there was a sidewalk sale in progress, merchants lording over merchandise dragged outside, makeshift counters erected on the sidewalks, people milling about but with an urgency that belied the carnival atmosphere.

There were plenty of policemen about, some directing traffic, others erecting police lines along the jagged boundaries of collapsed buildings, but most were watching the crowd, unsure of their role, perhaps trying vainly to remember catastrophe day at the police academy.

There was a huge line of cars, snaking out of sight along Valley Road, waiting their turn at the Mobil gas station on the corner. A makeshift sign said "$10 Max." and a couple of cops were playing gas jockeys.

Al Bolestki was standing across from the gas station, on a doorstep, grabbing a smoke and catching the action. He was the manager for a huge rock act, an ego band that Adam despised. Al lived the next street over from Adam but they did not socialize nor had their professional careers crossed paths. They knew each other the way everybody knows everybody in the business, especially the heavy hitters.

Adam took a position next to Al. Al was a big man, claiming a majority of the small space, his addiction to tobacco contrary evidence to the notion that smoking keeps you thin. His face was always smiling even when he wasn't, which was most of the time. He was essentially an unfriendly person but his eyes danced in their sockets—maybe he had a thyroid problem—seemingly attached to a different part of his brain than the rest of his face. He was wearing a flannel shirt and jeans piled up over a pair of ratty Adidas running shoes; a shlub, Adam's father would have called him, a Yiddish word no one in the family had ever bothered to translate, its meaning was so clear.

They said hello and nothing more, silenced by the embarrassment of having nothing in particular to talk about on a day when you could find something to say to a chipmunk.

"The band's in Australia," Al finally said.

"That's good," Adam said, because like all artist managers, Al would be thinking first and foremost about whether his meal ticket was still safe, still able to generate the gross revenue from which Al extracted his twenty percent. Managers weren't necessarily bad people, it was the parasitic nature of their profession that made them consumed with self-interest. There could be no joy in another artist's success, it only meant another entertainment dollar going into someone else's pocket. There were no managers' associations or clubs devoted to their patronage. They worked alone or maybe with a partner, drawing the world close around them.

"How's the house?" asked Adam.

"It got roughed up a bit. Karen and the kids are cleaning it up right now. They don't like it when I light one up in the house so I said I'd go get some milk and cigarettes. Well, good thing I've got half a carton at home cause there's about two thousand people trying to get into Kings."

"I wonder when things will get back to normal," said Adam but he said it more for Al, because for Al, this was just an inconvenience, a few days without cigarettes.

A group of five boys, young teenagers, walked by, tossing a basketball between them. And you knew what they were thinking—no school. They were alive and invincible and this was someone else's problem, an adult problem. With any luck, the high school would be reduced to rubble.

"So are you coming home from an awards ceremony or are you supplementing your income as a waiter?" asked Al.

"My sprinkler system went off. Soaked all my clothes."

"Nice boots."

There was a commotion at the gas pump. A man had gotten out of his BMW and was berating one of the police officers. There was much other noise but Adam still managed to hear bits and pieces, how the man had every right to fill his car up, he knew the police chief, don't try to stop me, I'll have your badge so get out of my fucking way, as he attempted to wrestle the nozzle away from the cop. He was in his forties, wore his success well, the clothes fake casual, too expensive— who would ever throw a football around wearing clothes like those?

It's drawing many onlookers and Adam can't tell who they're cheering for, then Adam sees the other cop draw his gun, watches him extend his right arm while his left hand wraps itself over the bottom of the gun stock and his right wrist, his legs bending slightly.

The driver's blood is up, the neatly-tied green cashmere sweater around his neck falling onto the ground, the two men fighting for control of the gas hose, hoisting it over their heads and one of them has his finger on the trigger because gas is spraying into the air, it's raining gas, soaking the two men, the trajectory of the gasoline following the struggle, the crowd drawing back like you do when the ocean breaks on a beach and you've got your shoes on.

A warning shot is aimed at the innocent sky, and you expect the sound of it to explode in your ear, make a big impression, stop you in your tracks, but it's only a pop, you could do better with a stick and a tin can. And, as Adam is wondering where bullets land when they are shot in the air, the policeman lowers his gun, because these two guys are going to kill each other and he has to do something, only it's obvious he doesn't want to try to pull them apart because of the gas so he shoots low, maybe aiming for the driver's leg but he's probably never aimed at anyone before or he's missed his last few scheduled turns at the firing range so is it a surprise when he misses the citizen completely?

The heat from the explosion was suffocating, Adam gasping for air that was no longer available, having been diverted to fuel the flames shooting sixty feet into the air. It was too hot to open his eyes and the force of the concussion had knocked him backwards into the door, Al's body slamming into his which was the bad news, but Al absorbed most of the initial blast which was the good news, only in reverse for Al.

Adam lay still, spread-eagled, pinned down by a two hundred and thirty pound bag of flesh, his head and shoulders pinned against the door. Adam leaned his head so he could see around Al's body and as he did so, another of the pumps blew up, straight into the air, just like in the movies. People were screaming, running past, one, Adam could see, with her blouse ablaze, a quick-thinking man tackling her on the street and rolling her over and over, until the flames were killed, leaving small, erratic, smoldering red lines that continued to eat away at the synthetic, wash in cold water only, fabric.

Adam wanted to help, wanted to get up and see, was dying to see the conflagration, seduced by the flame, no more sense than a fly, but he could not push Al Bolestki—infamous artist manager to the stars, now doing a pretty good impression of road kill, only he was still breathing—off of himself. Al's head was wedged up under Adam's throat, and past the gasoline fumes, past the smoke that was not too thick down near the ground, past all the smells produced by burning rubber, wood and flesh, was the damp, mildew, basement smell of Al's hair, forcing its way uninvited down Adam's nasal passage.

Al started groaning, something about his back and Adam was able to extricate himself from under Al's bulk and stand up. Al's down vest was smoking out of a small hole, an errant hot cinder, Adam removing the vest, then pulling Al to his feet. Other than maybe a concussion and singed eyebrows, Al appeared to be not too damaged. There was a change in his eyes though, the casual, disassociated observer eyes replaced with eyes alive with fear; he had seen the light, the terrible flash of combustible fluids and now all he wanted to do was go home.

"Call me if you need anything," Adam said, but the phones weren't working, he had checked.

A fire truck arrived, another one not far behind. Adam watched as the pumper was attached to a hydrant; he half expected nothing to happen when they turned the valve and was relieved to be wrong. If the water mains weren't ruptured then the town was not in bad shape, he thought. He cared not to think what New York must be like but he was unable to avoid it. He imagined hydrants spewing water, buildings collapsed and people, only two kinds, dead or crazy. They will need to write textbooks to catalogue the new forms of mental illness born on this day in that place. If insanity were a sport, Adam thought, today would be the start of the Olympics with New York, the host city.

And in the midst of the craziness, the extremely sane Lucia Dillane. He felt guilty, he felt useless, it was a relentless drone in his head, this issue of—I'm over here and she's over there and why didn't I stay with her last night or take her home with me—and he knew he had to try something only his mind could not find the peace and concentration necessary to formulate anything even remotely resembling a plan. All he could hear was a voice saying that if he didn't do something soon, if he didn't think of a way to reach her, to free her from that place, then at least he had her CD to listen to.

There were more police now, and they were clearing the place, asking people to go home. There was an edge, polite, but Adam knew it would not take much to set one of them off. They had lost two of their own, they were angry and scared and Adam knew better than to hang around.

He thought about his prescriptions, took a mental inventory; quantity and need. What he needed most was an antacid; Pepcid or Zantac would do.

There was a pharmacy not too far away and Adam hurried towards it. He was a block away when he saw the horde, maybe a hundred people, and they had all thought the same thoughts as Adam, only they had thought them sooner.

The police were literally beating people back from the front door of the CVS Pharmacy. Customers were being let out but no one was being let in. Adam recognized a woman from his train commute into New York. She held a small girl above her head, waving her like you would a sign at a hockey game, screaming something about insulin to the unhearing police. People more brave than smart were pushing to the front, demanding to be let in, only to be struck by the club-swinging police officers. The scene made the acid in Adam's stomach churn, at least that's what people said but how did they know, how does something churn by itself, without a stick or something to get it going.

This is bad, Adam thought. Not just his dwindling supply of stomach pills—everything. *I'd like, I'd like to know, what this whole show is all about, before it's out.* It was something printed next to a friend's grad picture in their high school yearbook. Of all the captions, it was the only one he remembered. Adam had always wondered what it meant. Now he thought he knew. His high school friend had seen something coming and wanted to stand in its way and let it run through him, enlighten him, give meaning to his life before it flickered out.

Adam wanted to know. Lucia had been trying to tell him something, the voice, whatever it was, was trying to get through to him, commanding him to find out, find out what it's all about, before it's out.

He had to go home. There was no good reason to be on the street. It was going to get worse. He reversed his tracks to retrieve the gun. He turned up the street where he had left it. He reached in and pulled the gun out and as he did so, he heard something behind him and turned.

A man stood, fifteen feet away, white-faced, a plastic bag in each hand. He was trying to speak but his eyes were stuck on the shotgun. Adam swung the rifle to a cradle carry, a safe and non-provocative presentation, but it had the opposite effect. The man dropped both bags, turned and ran down the street, screaming "Don't shoot me, don't shoot me!" Adam was going to call out but the only word in his head was 'halt', so he said nothing.

Adam walked over to the bags. He nudged them open with the muzzle. There was a God after all. Two bags, six bottles of Pepto Bismol in each. Adam picked up the bags, smiled, first time all day, and headed back to his house.

VIII

ADAM FISCHER LOVED DRIVING MUSTANGS, even this anemic 1966, 289cc automatic that a member of the production crew at the site had lent him. It had no air conditioning and even with the windows down, the air in his face felt as if it were being blown by a hair dryer. By the time he pulled into the parking lot and turned off the key, his back had fused to the leather seat so that when he finally stepped out, his T-shirt was sweat-glued to his body. Adam untucked it and pulled it away from his skin, sending a chill up his back. He was from the north, from Canada, and the Miami heat made him feel like a licked postage stamp.

Adam stood out front and peered in through the shop's windows. He had never seen anything like it before, not even in New York. Most head shops were narrow cubbyholes, off the street and down a few steps, a few square feet of crummy retail space squeezed in between other equally low-end shops; massage parlours, pawnshops and arcades. There was always incense burning and a long glass counter containing roach clips, hookahs, bongs, beedees for the faint of heart, pipes, papers, and the same guy working there; bearded, granny glasses, bell bottoms, vest with no T-shirt, love beads caught up in a hairy chest, and you could smell him, part stale pot, part hippie b.o., which was different than say, construction worker sweat or street bum stink.

The Great Train Robbery was a one-storey building devoted to a lifestyle owned by Adam's generation. Adam found it hard to believe any straight person had allowed a store like this one to open, a store whose customers slept on the beach or in parks, smoked pot, and sullied the otherwise pristine commercial beauty of Miami Beach. For tourists coming off the Arthur Godfrey Causeway, heading for their ocean front hotels with their American Plan meals and cheesy nightclub entertainment, The Great Train Robbery was a billboard, declaring, *Beware—we've come to seduce your daughters and ruin your sons.*

Adam walked in and the air-conditioned atmosphere immediately coaxed goose bumps out of the skin on his arms. He stood in awe as he took in the store, trying to remember his schedule because he knew he would want at least an hour to rummage through the place. He had another sound check in about two hours so he relaxed and took in a deep breath of patchouli-tinged air.

The place was a shrine to a lifestyle fueled by pop music, recreational drugs, sex and a political climate that pitted generations against one another. Somewhere a stereo was playing Steppenwolf's *The Pusher* over tinny speakers, horrible sounding to a professional like Adam who had finished his third sound check of the day less than an hour ago and still had a hundred and twenty phantom decibels ringing in his ears. All of the requisite paraphernalia was present but there were also cool and unique items like a Lyndon Johnson dart board or you could choose the Richard Nixon if you were a Democrat. Adam lingered at each display, stopping to idly watch the yellow globs in the lava lamp float lazily to the surface. He flipped through some psychedelic fluorescent posters glowing under the purple luminescence of a black light. There were tie-dye T-shirts and frisbees, a case full of provocative candy like a chocolate hand giving the bird on a lollipop stick, a bookcase full of books about the occult, marijuana cultivation and Eastern Religion and next to it, a stand dispensing incense with names like Nocturnal Delight, Sunshine, Serenity and Meadowland.

Adam spotted something hanging from a Chinese screen. As soon as he saw it he knew he had to have it. It was a plastic sign, a sign of the times hanging from a linked chain. Adam read it over a few times, laughing to himself; he couldn't wait to show it to the crew.

DRUGSTORE

GRASS.......$20/oz.
ACID.........$4/tab.
HASHISH...$10/gram.
BENIES.......25¢/5 for $1
NO-DOZ......7 for $1
    ?   ....17 for $1
COCAINE.....$30/spoon

REQUESTS FOR SMACK
AND METH MUST BE AC-
-COMPANIED BY A NOTE
FROM YOUR PARENTS
OR LEGAL GUARDIAN
(WE DO NOT HONOR CREDIT CARDS)

Adam had seen her when he first came in, the girl behind the cash register, but she was on the phone and turned away from him, so he hadn't really checked her out. She was still on the phone, leaning against the counter with her back to the store when he approached. Not a good security move, thought Adam, as he assessed her from behind. It was a little game he liked to play; see a girl from the rear, gauge her sway, the curves, the quality of her skin, her ankles, then make a guess. It could be a very disappointing exercise.

This might be one of those, thought Adam, because she looked fabulous from this side, long dark hair halfway to her waist, wearing tight blue jeans, bell bottoms, Adam guessed because he couldn't see past her bum, and even that he was seeing through the distortion of two panes of glass. She wore one of those frilly white, Mexican blouses, drawn tightly above her exposed bellybutton—except from his viewpoint, the small of her back—with puffy shoulders and short sleeves, usually fairly revealing in front but again, it was only a guess at this point. Her skin was immaculate, golden almond, tanned but not overly so; Adam could see the minute blonde hairs that fanned up from her waistline following a path up her spine.

She was talking to a girl, a friend, and it sounded like a rehash of last night's party; there was silence, then laughter, a full, low octave laugh, not forced and automatic, no, this was authentic laughter, and the sound of it sent a chill through Adam. It had a seductive quality and it made Adam dread the moment when she would finally decide to notice his presence.

There was a quick glance over her shoulder, but Adam was captivated by those blonde hairs again, imagining his hand on her waist, walking down a sidewalk in some place his mind had not yet made up, so he missed seeing her eyes, and was embarrassed by the possibility of her having caught him with his cast approximately in line with her ass.

She was telling her friend she had to go, she had a customer, then she put down the phone and turned around.

The girl said, "That sign is so far out, I love it. I copped one for my brother for his birthday. Of course, when was the last time you scored a lid of pot for twenty bucks?"

She took the novelty item from the counter where he had laid it, and started ringing in the sale. Adam tried desperately to come up with the right reply, the winning comment to make her notice him, see beyond the eight dollar and fifty cent sale plus tax and see him, to see him seeing her, because never before had he been in the presence of someone so intensely beautiful; big round eyes, warm and brown, her face covered with slightly freckled skin drawn tightly over high cheek bones and a slender nose. He forced himself to look elsewhere because he wanted to stare at everything—her lips, her eyes, her skin, everything.

"I don't usually have to pay for it."

Wrong, that was wrong—she'll think I'm power tripping, he thought.

"Well, lucky you," she said as she took his money, giving him a raised eyebrow but it might as well have been a .22 caliber bullet to the forehead.

Now he only wanted to leave, get his change and walk out of the place so he could immediately commence a day and a half or so of self-recrimination, then daydream about her for a bit, maybe even fall asleep to a fantasy filled with her, replay the scene, rewrite the script, too late come up with the sure-fire lines, irresistible words, feel the vibe between them, develop a plot, replay it, catalogue it for future reference then sigh sadly as sleep came, another life not lived for dreaming.

He took carriage of the package, his stupid, juvenile sign in a brown paper bag, receipt included, and headed for the door.

"Are you going to the festival?" she asked before he had made it to the door. He smiled and turned. Be subtle, he told himself.

"I'm working there."

"Really. My girlfriend got us backstage passes. She knows the guys from Three Dog Night."

"Well, I spend a fair amount of time backstage."

"Far out," she said and she seemed to mean it although Adam had heard the expression used in the past to describe events as exciting as watching an ant carry a much larger dead insect, so he could not be sure how impressed she really was.

She asked what he was doing there and he looked away once more, as if he feared her beauty might permanently damage his retinas.

"I'm doing the sound for the grandstand stage," said Adam. "It's called the Flower Stage in the program, I think."

"That is so cool. To work with all those rock stars. I can't wait to go. My girlfriend wants to get there as early as possible and spend most of the day backstage so maybe I'll see you there. I'm Donna Preston."

She extended her hand. It had five of the loveliest fingers Adam had ever shaken, long and brown with perfect nails, no polish, soft and warm, the kind of hand you wanted to hold and never let go.

"Adam Fischer."

"Well Adam, I guess I'll see you there."

Adam had worked a number of outdoor concerts but never anything of the magnitude of the Miami Pop Festival. The festival's producers had secured Gulfstream Park racetrack as the venue, the grandstand making a perfect location for the first stage, with a second stage, dubbed the Flying Stage, in a huge field to the southwest of the track. Between the two stages was an arts fair, part carnival, part tourist trap, booths set up hawking T-shirts, posters and psychedelic art. Pot was being smoked openly throughout the grounds, countless joints being lit by their owners and passed into the crowd, disappearing down a daisy chain of hacking tokers.

It was still the early days for the hippie movement, now gaining momentum—the summer of love a year and half past and still a fresh memory—insinuating its way into a youth culture that readily embraced its hedonistic and anarchic lifestyle. It was a period of transition where pampered youth, the privileged and the moneyed, toyed with street culture, partly out of curiosity but mostly to piss off their uptight parents. And there was no better place for kids from the right side of the tracks to cross-pollinate with those from the wrong than a pop festival, Levi's and T-shirts imposing a socialist commonality between imposters, weekend hippies and the truly committed.

Adam had no time to consider the historical importance of the event. He knew he was part of something big, over twenty thousand people expected the first day, but he was busy, oblivious to the sociological curiosities out in the audience, more concerned with microphone placements for the long list of artists who would perform on the grandstand stage this day.

Adam wasn't cool by nature, didn't think about it or fret over it. He wore jeans because they were cheap and easy to clean, T-shirts for the same reason. He wore his hair long because he hated getting it cut and wore a headband sometimes to keep it out of his eyes while he worked. He worked with wires and buttons and electricity because he liked to play with sound, to work his magic behind the board so that the bands on stage were able to reach the crowd, draw them in with the throb of the bass and kick drum, stun them with the highs of the electric guitar and soothe them with blended vocals.

Adam could see what was going on, how the whole scene was designed basically to achieve one thing—getting chicks. All the peace-love stuff, the dope and the music, the meditation and incense, the political posturing and railing at society, deep at its core it was about getting laid. Events had conspired to disguise the motivation but all Adam saw were guys trying to be hip while on the make. The hippies had rewritten the rules for everybody, giving the world free love. What a laugh, thought Adam. There was always a price tag.

Adam knew he looked like he belonged, like a hippie, a freak, but he did not really feel that way inside. He lived for the music and he lived in an age when music was king. What did it matter if he rarely smoked pot or took acid or meditated or had yet to read *The Tibetan Book Of The Dead*? He worked behind the scenes at music festivals and that made him a member of the privileged elite, at a time when musicians held court and everyone vied for access.

All Access. Those were the magic words, the secret code into the guarded castle. Adam wore his backstage pass the way a doctor wore a stethoscope. It meant nothing more to him than, leave me alone to do my work. But he saw it in their eyes, the people on the other side of the fence, a young girl, maybe sixteen, calling out to him, pleading with him to go find so and so because she was promised backstage passes only none were at Call Waiting, and she's desperate, she doesn't want to mingle with the plebeians who have to watch the show from the stands, never mind the fact you can't see a damn thing from backstage, she hasn't come for the music anyhow. And maybe one of the musicians had promised her passes, anything to separate her from her bell bottoms, only after he kicked her out of his room he may have entertained himself by finishing off a 26'r of Jack Daniels before passing out, and even sober, chances are he wouldn't be able to pick the girl out of a police lineup.

Backstage was an uncomfortable place for Adam. He much preferred to be out in the crowd, sometimes suspended overhead on a scaffold, or sequestered in the middle of a sea of drug-crazed fans, a cordoned-off island of efficient, focused calm, Adam at the controls, feeding off the communal energy, playing with the switches while he watched the fans sway and shimmy to the hypnotic beat, to the jungle rhythms, an electronic puppeteer, fingers riding the faders, up and down, highlighting a guitar solo then fading it back and riding the vocal mike for that never-to-be-reached perfect mix. There was no time to think about politics or religion or the state of his mind.

But there was time to think of Donna.

He had asked some of the local crew about her. A lighting tech knew her and said he thought she had a boyfriend, leaving Adam to fret over whether a) it was true and b) how serious was the relationship.

He had seen nothing of her all day and was getting tired of having his heart leap every time he saw a longhaired brunette. His stomach was nervous and even in the heat his sweat was cold. It was a marvel to him how the female of the species could elicit such a visceral response without doing anything other than being beautiful and speaking in tones designed to fry some portion of his brain and short circuit it.

It was late Saturday night and Adam was backstage storing away some equipment. There was a bit of a party going on. Jose Feliciano was entertaining a small but rapt gathering composed of various band members, roadies, and the ubiquitous guests with their proud guest passes. Adam paused for a moment, saw the fascination in a couple of girls' faces as they watched Feliciano's hands caress the fretboard of his acoustic guitar, and he figured they were wondering what it would be like to sleep with a blind man, like there was something he could do with those hands that the seeing members of the gender had no idea was possible. And Adam was wondering it himself.

He was bending over an equipment box when he felt a hand on his back.

"Hello Adam."

He shot up and straighten himself, self-consciously wiping his hands on an already soiled white shirt.

"Hi. I was starting to wonder if I'd see you today."

Donna stood before him, a halo around her head from the lights in the grandstand, making the features of her face almost invisible.

"I spent most of the day travelling between the two stages. I think this has been the best day of my life, so far. It was so groovy out there," Donna said, jerking her thumb at the security gate the way hitchhikers flag down cars.

Not that she needed to, but she won him over with that one. He noticed her backstage pass and knew she was a bit embarrassed by it, had concealed it as she made her way through the throng, how she wanted to avoid appearing elitist or apart from what was happening, wanted to connect without any pretense and besides, there was always the danger of someone ripping it off.

"What was your favourite act?" he asked.

"Procol Harum blew me away," she said. "But I loved Three Dog Night and Jose Feliciano too."

"So you spent most of your time at the other stage. I'm hurt."

"Hey, Fleetwood Mac are not my bag, what can I say."

What is your bag, Adam wondered, and could he fit inside.

She went on about some of other acts she saw, but Adam wasn't listening although he could hear her talking and thought he was understanding the words, yet every time he snapped back and tried to remember what she had just said his mind was a blank. He felt a little dizzy, the way you do when you jump out of bed too fast or bend over for something then rise up quickly after you've found it. It was her, she was making his head spin, literally. Maybe it was an allergic reaction.

" . . . so what do you think, you want to come?" and Adam said yes, as soon as he was done, only he was not at all sure where they were going, but was insane with pleasure at the prospect of going with her, of showing up anywhere next to her.

They ended up at a house party in Coconut Grove. A record producer Adam had never met owned it. Adam saw a few people he knew. It was the backstage set transplanted.

The Beatles' White Album was playing in a sunken living room—*Dear Prudence*—lines of cocaine being vacuumed up by an assembly line of volunteers as fast as a girl in a crocheted sweater with a weave wide enough to allow her nipples to peek through could make them. She was holding a six of hearts in her hand, using it to separate bits of white powder from a pile large enough to make a snowball. Adam had never seen so much coke and guessed he was looking at his salary for the year.

They walked up a few steps to glass doors leading out to a pool. Everyone was naked, boys and girls running and laughing around the pool's edge, tits and cocks flying every which way, one couple on a lounge chair copulating madly, another doing it in the pool, Adam hoping the chlorine would kill the sperm so some kid would not have to grow up with the legacy of having been conceived at an orgy by two zonked-out strangers.

They found a bit of quiet out by the gazebo.

"Good wholesome fun," said Adam, as another high-pitched squeal reached them from the pool.

"Does it bother you, the carrying on?" Donna asked, lighting a cigarette and offering one to Adam, who put his palm up in refusal.

"It's not the carrying on. It's the sex and drugs."

"You don't like sex and drugs?"

"Not in public."

"Well I don't think anyone can see us right now," and she reached into her bag, pulled out a joint and lit it from her cigarette. Then she got up and straddled Adam's lap, put one hand behind his head, sucked hard on the joint so that the ember burned red hot, lighting up Adam's face for a second in a hellish glow, then took the joint away from her lips and buried her tongue in Adam's mouth, swishing it around as she exhaled the warm moist smoke from her lungs into his, co-mingling vapors and juice from the center of her being to his.

Adam rarely smoked pot. Mostly it gave him a headache. But as he responded to the kiss—no, kiss did not adequately describe the assault to his mouth—and as he pulled her close, mad for her, insatiable in his appetite for her tongue, for the consumption of every inch of skin on her face and neck, he was no longer able to discern the vertical from the horizontal or the lighted Chinese lanterns dancing in the air by the pool from the blasts of light igniting behind his eyelids.

In a dream they floated down to the ground, Adam following her lead, letting her take him to the place she had created for him, bringing him down to her, out of the light and into her darkness.

IX

BRIAN SAID NOTHING AS THEY WALKED. He held Lucia's hand, really only her fingertips, his grip fierce, digging his little nails into her soft flesh but she ignored the pain. It was a day for ignoring pain.

She wondered what could be going on in his child's mind. She thought of her own childhood and the ability of children to alter time, slowing it down or speeding it up to their own rhythm; turning weeks into years, especially around Christmas or a pending birthday or making hours of play disappear into a few seconds, so who knew where this boy was now, maybe reliving each prolonged second of this morning's terror or perhaps so far past the images that he could barely see them through the haze of receding memory.

They had turned west onto 14th street, meatpacking warehouses on either side. Lucia was desperate for any sign of diminished damage as they moved away from the Village; she knew what an epicenter was and maybe the West Village had been hardest hit, God taking aim at the breeding ground of beat poets and musicians. But it was a vain hope, for as they plodded along the street, past burning buildings and twisted debris, as people passed them by, evoking the forlornness of the homeless, it became readily apparent that there was no escape from the damage, no imaginary safety line to cross over.

They walked in the middle of the street, Sydney slightly ahead, running interference, Lucia with the boy a step behind, other people jostling for position. Another stream of people headed east, passing on the trio's left, like traffic. It reminded Lucia of a war film she had seen, or maybe it was a scene in every war movie, one group of GI's heading for the rear, weary, with gray faces, another group, fresh, green, heading in the other direction, eyes nervously watching the veterans file past, the veterans averting theirs, unable or unwilling to acknowledge the walking dead. Only here there was no rear to retreat to.

Lucia figured Sydney was leading them towards the Hudson River. He said he had a boat. It must be tied up at a pier on the West Side. But where was everybody else going? Were all the left-handed people going one way, the right-handed the other? Or was it even and odd license plates?

There was a fair bit of pushing and shoving. Everyone was vying for the middle of the street. At first Lucia thought it was the fear of buildings collapsing that was driving them, like frightened wildebeests, into the middle of the pack. Then she saw the real reason; there were human jackals nipping at the heels of the weak, the infirmed, and the old. On the perimeter of the human sea were several street toughs, having transformed their toques into balaclavas, pulling people out of the pack, beating them senseless, some of the hooded men using sides of beef to pummel their victims, then robbing them of whatever it was they held precious. And the pickings were good because in most cases the victims had grabbed valuables to bring with them on their journey into oblivion—jewelry, watches, money—their first instinct to maintain the highest degree of material wealth in the smallest possible form. It was a hoodlum's version of shooting fish in a barrel.

Did these thugs really think their haul would be worth something, that it would carry them through when things got back to normal? There would be no going back to normal. A new normal had taken over. The rules had changed. These scumbags were no more than pathetic actors, called in for the last act of the final performance on the old world's stage.

But they were still beating the shit out of people so Lucia slipped her hand through the bend in Sydney's elbow and kept a steady pressure on the hand of her charge, who followed dutifully a step behind her.

"How big is your boat?" she asked Sydney.

"Big enough."

"Big enough for three people or big enough for a catered office party?"

"Big enough for you," he said and he turned around and smiled at her. He had big beautiful white teeth, and his voice was deep and strong, and Lucia thanked her lucky stars, not that she had any, for sending him to her.

They continued past the meat warehouses, people running out of the loading bays with armfuls of animal carcasses. Better than stereos, Lucia thought. She saw some people inside a refrigerated truck. A family had set up shop; there were a couple of mattresses and cardboard boxes arranged as night tables, the mother having found some flowers, god knows where, and she was placing them in a McDonald's soda cup while her husband arranged the bedding, their two small children sitting at the edge of the container, legs dangling, waving at passersby.

There was no evidence of city officials anywhere, not police or firemen or utility personnel. Lucia wondered if there was a secret vault in the bowels of the city where all civil servants could go during catastrophes like this one.

Lucia heard a familiar noise overhead as a helicopter came into view. It was a tourist helicopter. It hovered at about a hundred feet, kicking up paper and dirt with its prop wash, a baseball hat flying down the street, skipping and rolling, compelling its owner to overtake it as people egged him on.

A man on the passenger side of the chopper leaned out of the cockpit with an electronic bullhorn in his hand.

"Attention New Yorkers. Manhattan has been devastated by the earthquake. There is no way off the island. The tunnels have been ruptured and the bridges are either down or unsafe for passage. Anyone carrying ten thousand dollars in cash or goods should make their way to the Liberty heliport at 12th Avenue and 29th Street for evacuation to New Jersey. Make your way to the heliport as soon as possible." Then the helicopter banked towards the Hudson and flew away.

A man near Lucia broke from the middle of the street and started to run briskly down the street, dodging people like a halfback as he went. This, Lucia realized, was going to be a big mistake on his part and, sure enough, the man had not proceeded more than about two hundred feet before some men pounced on him and punched him and kicked him motionless then ripped at his clothes in search of anticipated treasure. As the threesome walked by, they glanced down in unison at the mostly naked beaten man, blood trickling from his nose, mouth and ears, dead probably, one of his attackers standing over him, swinging a money belt, his compatriots jumping up, trying to snag the thing like a bunch of school kids reaching for the ball that the tallest kid always managed to keep out of reach.

The boy left Lucia's side and grabbed Sydney's hand, latching onto two large fingers.

"Why are the men hurting each other?" asked Brian.

"There's a lot of bad men in the world, son. Most times you don't see them. Today is their day and for some of them, this will be the first day they are really bad. Some men are going to find out how bad they are today."

"But not you, right Mr. Sydney?"

"No not me, son. My bad days are all behind me."

Sydney put his hand over the side of Brian's head, pulling him gently close to him, covering his right ear in a vain attempt to protect his innocence. Lucia grabbed the back of Sydney's coat, partly to make sure she didn't lose him in the crowd and partly to complete the chain and amplify the glow of their combined energies.

They were on 11th Avenue now, walking north. At W.22nd Street the road forked, the left fork becoming 12th Avenue and the West Side Highway. The Hudson River came into full view and across the river, the cliffs of Weehawken. There were gigantic gouges in the cliff sides where buildings had given way and slid down into the Hudson.

Sydney kept them on the east side of the wide boulevard. There was a lot of action on the west side. Outside Chelsea Pier, a half dozen boys were playing road hockey on Rollerblades while the truly insane were over by the riverside driving range screens, climbing them for reasons Lucia was unable to decipher.

Lucia returned her thoughts to Sydney. He had not said much since the parking garage, a few encouraging words to herself and the boy and even then without looking at them, always staring straight ahead, full of purpose in his manner, his walk, a man used to taking charge, but of what?

"You have any kids, Sydney?" she asked as she overtook him, then began matching his stride.

"A son and a daughter," he said without turning.

She searched for the right words but he saved her trouble.

"They don't live around here any more. George is in school in Ohio and Martha is married to a man in Detroit."

A patriot.

"And their mother . . . "

"She died in 1982."

He turned at that and there was hurt still there, fresh for thinking about it.

"I'm sorry," she said because nobody had invented anything better to say.

"She was a wonderful woman. Raised two fine children. Don't know what she saw in me. I guess some of us are just plain lucky."

"I'm sure she saw the same fine man I see before me."

"Don't know about that. You're not exactly seeing me on my best day."

"I doubt that."

They walked in silence for a while then Lucia asked, "Do you believe in God, Sydney?"

"Yes, I certainly do."

"After today?"

"Especially after today."

"You figure He had a hand in this?"

"It's His world."

"And the man in the garage . . . "

"I think he was working for the other guy."

"The Devil."

"That's right, the Devil. Maybe I did some of his work today as well. I don't know. It weighs heavy on my mind right now. For a few seconds it feels right, it feels like I did the right thing. I see this boy here and I know it was right. Then this thing happens, a thing I ain't never felt before, even during the war, something crawling down from my mind and into my stomach, a horrible feeling of wrong. I can't explain it."

My god, Lucia thought, the man is so good he is incapable of recognizing guilt for the lack of having experienced it. Was it any wonder his aura was so pure and thick?

They were near the heliport now. There were dozens of people milling about, some attempting to scale the wire fence to the launch pad area but being beaten back with sticks by the men on the other side. Two helicopters hovered a few feet off the ground, ready to evacuate if the barricade failed. For the first time this day, Lucia saw policemen, two on horseback, attempting some crowd control, useless against the numbers and the quality of the frenzy. Rocks and debris were being thrown at the cops, the horses shying away from the barrage. One of the officers had a radio device on his lapel, was speaking into it, trying to maintain control of his mount with one hand holding both reins, cowboy style, but his horse turned on its haunches so abruptly that the policeman lost his seat and fell awkwardly to the ground.

Everyone's blood was up and Lucia watched, horrified, as the downed officer was pummeled senseless, fists and shoes finding their mark all over his body. His partner attempted to put his horse between the mob and the downed cop but he too was eventually overcome and dragged from his saddle.

Sydney pushed Brian towards Lucia, barked at her to stay put and crossed the boulevard. It's the uniform, thought Lucia. A Pavlovian response to the uniform, the good soldier responding to a comrade in harm's way.

Sydney barged through the mob, his aura thickening and turning a deep red. Lucia could barely see his body for the light. A man in a camouflage parka jumped on Sydney's back and with a flick of Sydney's shoulders, the man flew into the paths of three men, knocking them all onto their backs. He reached in and pulled people off the second fallen policeman, tossing them aside like a gardener pulling weeds. He pulled the policeman to his feet, who immediately headed for his partner while Sydney knocked people out of his way.

Lucia took Brian's hand and crossed the street. Out of habit she looked both ways. There were no cars on the street although the roads were fairly free of debris. Even if you could get into your car and drive, where were you supposed to go? The helicopter man had been right about that. There was no mass exodus because there was no way off the island.

Lucia imagined people swimming across the Harlem River, like rats abandoning a sinking vessel. And they were right to try to leave. She had no idea what else was coming—maybe another earthquake or famine or mass rioting—she only knew everybody had to get off the island before something worse happened.

Lucia reached the edge of the surging mass of bodies, a palatable single-mindedness pervading the air, herd mentality, individual thought given way to the lynch mob collective. There was no regard for her gender by the men in the crowd. She was caught up in the violent ebb and flow, moving with the shoving so as not to be trampled. As she tried to reach Sydney, the throng reversed and began to back away from the convergence point. The bloodied officer was now straddled over his unconscious partner, revolver pointing wildly at the crowd, all of the training useless now, no control, no discharge protocols to follow, this was something else, not in the books, no instructor having explained what to do when an angry mob wants to rip you to shreds. Sydney stood beside the crazed cop, extolling him to put the gun down but he was not being heard. There was a perverse expression of joy on the cop's face each time he waved the gun and the people along the gun sight surged back from the line of fire.

Every group like this has one, a brave fellow, belligerent, shit for brains, a guy who hasn't considered the damage a single bullet can do when it propels itself through your gut. Tough guy, he was standing up to the cop, telling him to get the fuck out of his way or he's going to rip his tongue out and strangle him with it, was about to supply some more invective when the cop fired a round, caught the poor schmuck square in the throat, severing an artery, blood spraying out as if from a garden hose and the guy was dead on his feet.

Something is wrong, though. The instant the gun goes off, Lucia sees a blinding light, stars really, her head exploding in pain as she crumples to the ground.

She hears Brian screaming. "She's been shot!" he screams. "She's been shot!"

Sydney is beside her, she can see him, can see the others, but they are so far away, or she is, as she slips into a starlit darkness.

It's only a flesh wound, she hears Sydney say as he presses his hand against the side of her head above her ear. Easy for him to say. It's getting darker inside her mind, then she sees him, approaching her from out of the darkness, beatific, serene, not stern and overbearing like the last one, yes, now she remembers the last one. He was pushy and demanding, leaving no conscious trace of his coming but this one's different, this one is coming with love.

She begins to speak, not in the voice Sydney knows, not in the voice Adam had heard from the couch. This one is husky, deep, yet lyrical and serene.

"Do not approach this entity. She must not be disturbed. Know that fear is your enemy. You must conquer your fear or you will not survive the completion of your trial. Many of you will perish. Transition is inevitable. All entities are on the same path. Some leave off before others. What matters is to leave with knowledge of the goals set for your life and the realization of those goals. To ignore your true self is to ignore the truth. You are not forsaken. The body is meant for pain. You will be judged on how you accept your pain. Fear is your enemy. It disconnects you. Connect. There is little time."

Sydney kneels down and takes her hand. Her eyes flutter madly, lids closed. Someone says she is having a seizure.

"Lucia ma'am, are you all right?" Sydney asks.

"The entity known as Sydney knows what it must do. Take this entity. Guard it. There is little time. Your pain has been but little. Do not dwell on the past. Learn now what you already know. Protect this entity. Leave this place."

Then there are words for Lucia only, words of comfort and instruction. They see her nodding her head, up and down, and smiling, a conspirator's smile.

When Lucia sat up suddenly and opened her eyes, those gathered close to her jumped back with fright. There was no human sound, only the incessant thumping noise from the two helicopters. Sydney put his arm around her, hand under her armpit and raised her to her feet. She fought the initial dizziness, let her weight be held by Sydney's massive arms and fought for enough clarity and strength to stand on her own.

Little Brian hugged her leg with a ferocity that declared he was unwilling to let anything more happen to the adults who were supposed to be caring for him.

Lucia studied the mass of humanity before her. Rich in clear sight she saw total despair in their timid eyes. She felt pity, then anger, for what she really saw was failure.

There was a man, tanned with a cashmere long coat and attached fur collar, shiny shoes and not a hair out of place, a GQ poster boy in the middle of a holocaust.

"You," she said, pointing at the man. "Do you know why you are here?"

"Hey lady, I'm just trying to get off Manhattan like everybody else."

He turned to his audience with a shy smile, canvassing for some sympathy, some camaraderie amongst the gathered. But everyone was focused on Lucia.

"Getting off Manhattan is the least of your problems. It's the steps you took to get to this place, right here, right now, that you ought to worry about. You're probably going to die. We, all of us, are going to die, today, an hour from now . . . doesn't much matter when. It's not too late. Better get ready. You want to be ready."

The man stood there, the blood drained from his face. He backed up, pushing his way through the crowd.

"You can't run away from yourself," Lucia yelled. "None of you can run away. Go ahead, get on a helicopter. Go a thousand miles away. It doesn't matter. Don't you see? We have all done this. We have all failed. And there is no escape. No escape for any of us."

One man, a bystander who had happened upon the scene, an older man, small in stature, wearing a dated gray suit with a burgundy V-neck sweater, standing to the side, fiddling with a fedora of all things, stepped out to the front and addressed Lucia.

111

"I think you are wrong. About me at least. I know what you are saying. I have prayed to Jesus every day to deliver me from the evil that surrounds me in this place where I have lived most of my adult life. I have seen all things horrible. I am not afraid to die. It's good riddance, I say. But I need to know. Will He be waiting for me? Will Jesus be there waiting for me when the end comes, like the Bible says?"

Lucia paused, the agitation in her mind receding, already her rational side replaying the last few minutes and wondering what the hell her brain was up to, calmer now, more herself.

"Somebody will be there," she said.

"But will it be Jesus?" he asked.

"I'm sure he'll make it if he can."

On a day when faith was the only option, even the atheist was praying for deliverance. Lucia's otherworldly outburst had both frightened and soothed the gathering, turning a unified mob into a group of desperate individuals, alone with their fear, and many, hearing the words, must have heard something else, inside, something other than the animalistic howling ringing in their ears. It was the sound of chilling reality. For a fraction of a second maybe, because it held the emotional discomfort of a hand on a hot stove, they, each of them, saw the unsanitized version of themselves.

The assembly was dispersing. The cop coddled his unconscious partner. Someone had placed a coat over the dead man. A man behind the fence was yelling, half price, five thousand dollars, and there were a couple of takers, but most were numbed, drained by the gamut of emotions the day had drawn from them. They drifted away, some heading up 29th Street towards the center of town, others back south towards Greenwich Village or who knew where.

Sydney had his two charges under each of his arms, Lucia still a bit unsound in her footing, Brian staying close to Sydney's right leg, mindful of not tripping over the massive limb striding next to him.

"Is that a normal sort of activity for you?" asked Sydney.

"It's getting to be, I think. I'm not really sure what just happened but I think a similar thing occurred last night in my apartment. I'm pretty sure I scared the hell out of a friend of mine."

"You keep doing that to your friends and you're gonna die lonely."

"Was it really bad?"

"No, it was that good. You one of those ladies who speaks to the dead?"

"No," Lucia said and her body stiffened inside Sydney's arm.

112

"How's your head feeling?" he asked. Sydney had ripped most of his shirtsleeve off and had wrapped it around Lucia's head, Ninja-style.

"It's throbbing like crazy."

"I've got a medical kit onboard. You're lucky, it's only a flesh wound."

Lucia smiled. "Next time I hear that in a movie I'll feel a lot sorrier for the victim than I ever have before."

They continued walking, few people passing by, the devastation of Mid-town extracting a painful silence. The pencil building—Lucia didn't know its name, so that's what she called it—was missing its lead point. Other buildings were missing windows, or parts of walls had fallen away exposing outer offices to the elements, creating a dollhouse effect.

There was something missing, thought Lucia, and then she gasped.

"It's gone," she said but it was more of a question and Brian and Sydney turned to the east, towards where 34th Street must be, where the Empire State Building stood, and maybe they thought for an instant their bearings were off, but it was more wishful thinking than disorientation.

"The top of the Empire State Building is gone," Brian said. "Where is it?" he asked.

"Where did they put it?" he asked again, only this time it was more of a demand to know—I'm the kid, you're the adults, tell me what's going on—except the adults were standing there, silent.

Lucia watched tears fill Sydney's eyes. Lucia wanted to cry too, wanted to mourn so much, the loss of life, of home, of this great city, only the words came back to her, words whispered only to her in a deep monotone voice, the message unmistakable, unbearable.

She reckoned there was not much time.

"Sydney," she said, but he did not respond. She tugged on his elbow and he slowly turned to her, silvery streams running vertically down his face. His green illumination engulfed the three of them.

"Sydney, do you know what an aura is?" she asked and there was a bit of hesitation in her voice.

"What?"

"An aura. There are people who claim each person gives off a visible aura, the thickness and colour differing for each individual and each emotional and spiritual situation. I've only known a few people who can see them."

"But you can see them."

"Yes. I can. I can see your aura. A deep and beautiful thick green colour."

"And yours is purple."

"Excuse me."

"I've been seeing these colours since I was a little boy. Never thought much about it. Never said much about it. I figured everybody could see them. It's like, someone gets mad and how do you know that? Could be they're yelling at you, or they got this real cross look on their face, or the colour around them changes to something fiery. It's all the same information, only different clues, know what I mean?"

She nodded, knowing absolutely what he meant, only she'd never heard anyone describe it so succinctly before. She had met a few people in her life who claimed similar abilities as her own, but they usually fit a stereotype and were wrapped up in their occult artistry. Never had she met someone who treated this ability like nothing more than souped-up 20/20 vision.

"You can see my aura?"

"If that's what you call it. Didn't know they were called auras. That's a fine name. I've always searched for the right word. Never could come up with one I liked. Aura. Has a nice ring to it. Aura. I always called them a person's light bulb."

"How about today, Sydney? What do you see today?"

"*You* know," he said, as his eyes averted hers.

"Tell me," she said.

He was still except for one hand absently patting Brian's shoulder.

"The people."

"What about the people?"

"When I saw you standing there, at the garage, I couldn't see you because of the light, the light behind you from the street and the light around you. You were the only one. The only one. I was afraid. Then when Brian came with us, I could see his, too. So I knew. I knew I was meant to protect you and Brian. It was a sign. The others, I don't know. I can't see them. Never happened like this before. But today isn't like any other."

"So you understand. You know why Brian's choice to come with us changed things."

"I guess I do. I guess something goes dead inside before you go dead outside."

A tremor charged up Lucia's legs, and the three clung to each other,

114

the boy smothered between the two adults, Sydney and Lucia trying to keep their balance until Sydney decided it was safer on the ground. He pulled Lucia and the boy down to the pavement, Brian half buried beneath Sydney's bulk, whose arm extended over Lucia's back as if he feared she might somehow slide away.

Lucia felt the cold pavement on her cheek, her ear flush against the surface, a dull roar escaping from the concrete. Not far away a building collapsed, sending more dust into the air. People were screaming but Lucia closed her eyes, did not raise her head from the ground. She was infused with the energy being released along the fault line.

She thought of Adam, was mad at him for leaving her here, was afraid for him, imagining all manner of horrible fates for him, death a hundred different ways or crippling injuries, knew he would be taking this all badly, this reshaping of his world, he wouldn't like it, would probably blame it on her somehow, put two and two together, but he will come for her, if only out of guilt, no, guilt born of love because she knew his heart, even if he refused to.

So unnatural this most primeval of natural phenomenon. She knew what everyone was thinking—she could sense it—a communal disbelief that the earth could move of its own volition. She was sinking into it, getting comfortable with it. Then it stopped.

The disturbance had lasted for thirty seconds, or maybe a minute. So much thinking in such a short period made it impossible to know unless you were timing it with your watch, and if you were, well, surely there's some idiot out there who had.

They got up, did the things people do with dirt on their clothes, even the child brushing the bits of stone from the indentations in his palms then rubbing his hands against his trousers to loosen the dirt.

"Aftershock," said Sydney, like it needed clarification.

Lucia saw that the pencil had lost some more of its point. There were three thick black plumes of smoke spiraling up to the sky, bending slightly to the west with the wind and further north, towards Central Park, she figured, the sky was filled with a dark gray haze. She had not noticed the smell until now, the pungent smell of burning wood.

"Sydney, where's the damn boat? I have a really bad feeling and the one thing I know is we have to get off this god-forsaken island."

"They bought it from the Indians for twenty-four dollars," Brian said.

"That's right, sweetie," Lucia said, "and pretty soon they'll be selling it back to them for about the same amount."

"Come on," Sydney said, taking Brian's hand and grabbing Lucia by the elbow, "we're almost there."

They walked steadily for another ten minutes, seeing no one, hearing the occasional siren, the fires more frequent, the sky blackened by the smoke, Lucia's eyes tearing and painful, Brian shielding his view with his hand. Sydney marched on, either impervious to the smoke or uncaring of the discomfort, his eyes unwavering.

Lucia and Brian had their heads down, avoiding the smoke when Sydney came to an abrupt halt. Lucia had slipped in behind Sydney for the last few hundred yards so her forehead bumped into his back before she realized he had stopped.

Lucia asked, "Why are we stopping?"

"We're here," Sydney said.

"Where?"

"Here," he repeated, his hand gesturing towards the dock.

She hadn't noticed it because her head had been down.

Its clipper bow rose in a massive Y from the water's surface to a flat deck almost a hundred feet from the ground. A plane's nose was jutting out over the deck. The thing had to be a hundred feet wide. It sat stone still in the water.

"What do you mean, we're here? This isn't your boat. This can't be your boat. This is a fucking museum. I thought you had a boat. Where we'd be safe. You're kidding, right?"

She was beside herself, at least she thought she was because she was never sure what that really meant. She had trusted him. He had played his role perfectly—until now. He would protect them. It was a little late to find out the guy was out of his fucking mind.

"How's my aura doing?" he asked, his eyes doing the laughing he wouldn't allow his mouth.

"It's fine."

"That's strange, 'cause yours is starting to fade just a tad."

"What are you trying to say?"

"I'm trying to say, welcome to the aircraft carrier, USS Intrepid, finest ship in the Navy, survivor of one direct torpedo hit, three Kamikaze hits, a typhoon and I'll bet whatever it is you think is about to happen."

And in an instant Lucia saw what would happen and how right Sydney had been to lead them here.

116

X

John Walker got up from the ground, grabbed another log and tossed it into the fire. The concussion created a dazzling display of red sparks which spiralled skyward, momentarily blinding Joey who sat wrapped in an Indian blanket, cold despite the warmth being thrown off by the flames and glowing cinders.

He said his name was John Walker and she had no reason not to believe him but it was such a common name for an uncommon man. Joey had been observing him all day; during the ride to his home, throughout dinner, and now, outside under a clear black sky pierced by billions of stars. After building up the fire, John Walker returned and sat next to Tom, a younger version of his older brother. Tom ran a small gas station outside of Sedona.

They were brothers, there was no questioning the similarity, but the comparison ended there. John Walker was Joey's notion of the modern day noble savage, a notion encouraged by the way he carried himself and his attire. His clothes were unremarkable; blue jeans, flannel shirt, cowboy boots that had done the things that cowboy boots were meant to do, and a cowboy hat made of some sort of tightly woven straw material. Strategically placed on his body were accents of Indian apparel; a turquoise and silver bracelet on his right wrist and an exquisite turquoise and red coral necklace hanging from his neck. In his left ear was an odd earring, odd only because it did not fit in with the rest of his jewelry. It was a gold peace sign. She hadn't noticed it until now. No, that wasn't it. She had seen it and its familiarity had hidden it from her scrutiny. Seeing it now made her think of her father. He had worn a similar earring for as long as she could remember. It only added to her strange attraction to this man who had rescued her. She felt as if she knew him or perhaps it was how comfortable and safe she felt in his presence that gave off the illusion of familiarity.

Tom could dress like his brother and not come across at all the same, Joey thought. She was searching for a word. Assimilated. His clothes were not much different than John Walker's. He wore overalls and construction boots. His hair was very short. His eyes were as dark as John Walker's but they sparkled when he talked, lacking the involuntary sadness of his brother's. Tom was a regular guy who happened to carry Indian blood in his veins. It was not difficult to figure out the dynamics here. Like scores of other children of minority groups living in the United States, Tom had been seduced away from his heritage and the traditions of his parent's tribal culture, embracing instead the America found in magazines and on TV. And Joey could relate, having broken away from the liberal values held dear by her parents.

Joey would periodically steal a glimpse of the silhouette of her Falcon, parked next to a pickup truck, the one John Walker had walked her to after her emergency landing. She refused to think of it as a crash. Tom said he might be able to fix the housing for the front wheel but the hydraulics were pretty beat up and it was sophisticated stuff and parts would be a problem so he didn't think he'd be able to handle the repairs. Not that she had anywhere in particular to go at the moment.

The desert made her uncomfortable, nervous even. It was too open, too sparse, lacking in definition and colour. It caused her mind to wander and she didn't like that. And she was afraid of scorpions, afraid of dying from the sting of a miniature lobster with attitude. But try as she might, she could not deny the unadorned beauty of her surroundings, all of which made the sight of her warbird at rest next to the ranch house such an incongruous sight. Pick out the one that doesn't belong, she thought, remembering those aptitude tests they gave you when you were in grade school, and in her mind she saw successive pictures of a cactus, a scorpion, a coyote and an F-16 Falcon.

She had gone through survival training. All Air Force pilots had to do it. The test was rough and she was accorded no advantage nor was any favour curried on her part—she could handle the physical demands. But the worst part had been at night, the sounds coming out of the blackness, real and imagined, the scurrying of nocturnal fauna, Joey burrowing herself into her mummy sleeping bag, inspecting every crack, every seam for the possible incursion by the imagined swarm of scorpions gathering around her, no doubt waiting for her to fall asleep and loosen her grip on the exposed end of her bag.

Sometimes she hated being a woman.

Well, that wasn't really true now was it. I mean, who in their right mind would volunteer to be a man, she reminded herself. They were crude and thoughtless, and most of the ones at the base had managed to turn self-centeredness into an art form—and they had penises. What god thought that was a good idea?

Unfortunately, men were too stupid to be afraid of scorpions and that put her at a disadvantage. Being practical and exercising common sense was no edge in a world dominated by men. And competing in a male-dominated profession, no, male-dominated was not strong enough, male-ruled, male-dictated, male-controlled—actually there was not one word she could think of to adequately convey the pervasiveness of the male ego in all things martial—made her job so unattractive at times that it was a wonder she had survived the training to become a pilot.

John Walker lived alone as far as she could tell. There was not a hint of feminine influence in the bungalow. It was an austere place limited to essential items; two chairs and a table, a fridge and a stove, some books, an Indian rug not unlike the one around her shoulders, lying in front of an ancient television—nothing terribly native about the place.

She had wandered into the living room, catching a glimpse of herself in a small mirror, the first time she had seen herself since earlier that morning when she had stood in front of a full-length mirror after donning her uniform. There was a little desert dust on her face and her short blonde hair was having a bad day after being cooped up inside her helmet. But a little bit of dirt could not hide her beauty, which was both intimidating and approachable, the girl next door with centerfold potential. Even without a trace of makeup, her big, blue eyes dominated her face. Her golden brown skin was populated with even darker brown freckles which were scattered across her angular cheeks and nose, making it difficult to convince anyone she was twenty-five. She wanted to hate her lips, hate their redness and prominence and the way men leered at them. She wanted to but she was still a woman and beneath all the mental posturing, she liked being attractive, even if it meant fighting off unwanted attention and dealing with the double standard annoyances that came with it. She patted down her uniform, felt her breasts beneath its camouflage, happy to hide her curves and long legs beneath its masculine cut.

The only picture adorning a wall was a small, five by seven, grainy, black-and-white photo of a young John Walker with his arm around a goofy-looking toothless man who was wearing a jump suit and an oversized, tattered cowboy hat. John Walker was bare chested in the picture, strong, slim, with massive biceps, a bandana holding back long, black hair that fell behind his shoulders to an indiscernible length. Behind them there were numerous people and trees but the depth of field for the shot was short so most of the background was blurred.

They had not said much to each other in the car. John Walker asked her a few questions; he asked her about the water, about where she had seen it, whether she'd seen the dam burst—she hadn't—whether she'd seen any evidence of earthquake activity—put a check mark next to that one—he asked her about the plane, where she had taken off from, where she was going. Then he asked her if her parents were living and when she said yes, he said good, as if he half expected her to say no.

"Is it hard to fly?" he had asked, pulling her thoughts and eyes back into the cab of the pickup.

"The jet? No, not really. It takes a lot of study and practice, of course, and it is full of sophisticated equipment but it's designed to allow the pilot to react instinctively instead of mechanically."

"So could you teach me to fly it?"

Joey explored John Walker's face for a hint of levity but he remained impassive, eyes unblinking, concentrating on the road and waiting for an answer.

"I don't think the United States government would approve," she said, unsettled by the question and trying to make light of it.

"Okay," he said, and something in the way he dismissed the idea made the hairs on her forearms stiffen.

He had a cellular phone plugged into his cigarette lighter, an older model, like a big walkie-talkie, a gray hunk of plastic with black tape holding the keypad in place. He had called his brother on it, giving him directions to the plane and imploring him to take some back road route to his house—Why?—"Because you're hitched to a U.S. Air Force jet and you don't want to be answering too many questions as to how you came to be towing it."

Joey had asked to borrow the phone and had called the base. Not surprisingly, she failed to get through. Maybe there's some news, John Walker had said when they reached his house, so he turned on an old RCA set, did not seem too interested himself since he immediately walked over to the fridge, grabbed himself a beer, after inquiring whether Joey cared to wet her whistle—she didn't—twisted off the cap and flicked it into a wastebasket in one blurred motion, then walked outside, leaving her alone in the dull glow of the black and white tube. Local television was awash in disaster coverage, the main story being the lack of any network feeds. CNN was missing the best ratings opportunity since the Gulf War. None of the networks were broadcasting.

Joey went out after John Walker. He was standing by the edge of the driveway, if you could call it that since the only thing separating it from the desert was a haphazard line of stones. He was facing west, the low sun accentuating the redness of the earth and his skin. He seemed to be waiting for someone—or something—eyes expectant, searching, vigilant.

"You wouldn't happen to have a computer with a modem?" she asked, drawing up beside him, knowing the answer before the words had cleared her lips.

"No. A modem?"

"It's a device like a telephone that lets you link up over a telephone line to other computers, like the Internet, for instance."

"Why would you want to do that?" John Walker asked.

"To communicate, to talk to other people, get information, that sort of thing."

"What's wrong with using the telephone?"

"There's nothing wrong with it, but with the Internet, you can communicate with hundreds, even thousands of people."

"You know that many people?"

"No, of course not."

"Then what do you need it for?"

She had good reason to believe he was toying with her, playing the proverbial turnip truck passenger, because even out here in the middle of nowhere, it was impossible to have avoided the digital revolution of the last few decades.

"I thought I could use it to communicate with my base."

"Didn't you try to call before?"

"Yes, but I couldn't get through."

"And this Internet, it not only uses telephone lines, but repairs them at the same time? Maybe I should get me a computer."

She flushed red and it made her think of her father, how he delighted in embarrassing her, how easily he could push the right buttons and humiliate her, make her seem the fool for having followed dreams he considered nightmares.

She started to turn back to the house when she felt his hand on her arm. He was smiling, and it was warm and engaging and disarmed her.

"I have a friend a couple miles from here. He has a T-1. Right in his house. I told him he was crazy to spend that kind of money for a bloody phone line. He said it was worth it though. He said the live sex shows weren't worth the bother without a T-1 or at least an ISDN line. We'll go see him tomorrow. Maybe he's still wired."

She felt like whacking him one, only it was hard to be upset when he smiled. He was having a bit of fun with her, not attempting to justify his existence by shitting all over hers the way her father tended to do.

"I hate smart asses," she said.

"I only hate the stupid ones," said John Walker.

They stood there in silence for a while, watching the sunset, the red turning to purple before the light faded behind the screen of the western horizon.

"What sort of Indian are you?" she asked as they headed back to the house.

"I'm a Hopi sort of Indian. Most people prefer to call us Native Americans."

"I'm sorry if I offended you."

"Not at all. I like Indian. It's a good word. It's short and to the point. So what if Columbus got it all wrong. Most tribes called themselves People. So if you've got People and then some more people come along, how are you going to be able to tell them apart unless you give them a name? The problem is never the words, it's the meaning people attach to words. If there's hatred for a race, then any word you use for them will sooner or later come to represent that hatred and bigotry. And besides, we aren't really Native Americans, we just got here first. They should've called us, Got Here First Americans."

She searched for something intelligent to say, thoughts bouncing around her brain but nothing coherent forming up. She was not an intellectual, she knew that. Not stupid, just not articulate. She felt meaning more than heard it in her head. Facts, now facts were something else again, she digested facts. Got Here First Americans. Maybe he was having her on again.

"Is that an Indian name—like Stands With A Fist?"

"Who is Stands With A Fist?"

"Kevin Costner's love interest in Dances With Wolves."

"You watch too much television."

She hated it when a man patronized her, only she couldn't remember that word.

"Then what does it mean? You're talking in some sort of code I don't understand."

"I believe it's called humour."

"And I believe you are patronizing me," because she finally remembered the word, "and I would appreciate it if you would stop."

He turned and faced her. His eyes were laughing at her. Slowly, he raised his right arm and saluted her.

"Yes sir," he said.

He held the salute and stared beyond her, the way cadets are trained to do, unblinking, his chest not rising, even his hair seemed frozen. She wanted to be angry but he looked so ridiculous she started laughing and then started nudging him, trying to knock him off balance until she dislodged him and he fell backwards, still holding the salute, only when he hit the ground, he somehow bounced instantly back onto his feet.

Then he hugged her and told her he was glad to see she'd removed the stick from her ass and somehow the comment failed to bother her.

She said she knew about the Indian tribes migrating from Asia across the Bering Strait thousands of years ago.

"That's not how it happened," said John Walker.

"Oh really."

"That's not how the People came to this land. You Whites seek answers by digging into the ground or by experimenting in your laboratories. And all you end up finding are more questions.

"So if you know so much, why don't *you* tell them?" Joey asked.

"Because no White has bothered to ask."

"So, tell me then. I'm asking."

"Okay. But you won't believe me."

They made themselves comfortable in two chairs on the front porch and John Walker told her a story of the Underworld where many spirits lived after the end of the Third World. But many of the human spirits were unhappy there and when they heard someone walking on the surface of the earth, they sent birds to the surface and the third one they sent found Maasaw.

"Who is Maasaw?" asked Joey.

"He is the Guardian Spirit of the Earth. He gave the human spirits and the Kashina spirits permission to leave the Underworld and eventually, they found their way to the surface by climbing up the hollow insides of a long reed. They came out through a hole called Sip-papu, somewhere in the Grand Canyon."

John Walker described how the People met the Creator and Maasaw, who divided them into groups.

"Maasaw told the leaders of the Pueblo groups to pick an ear of corn from a pile. When the last of the leaders reached the pile, there was only one shrivelled piece left. This leader took it without complaining though. Maasaw saw this and called the leader's people, Hopi, meaning peaceful."

John Walker told Joey of a great migration of all of the People, each tribe instructed to spread out through the land, to erect shrines to the Earth Mother, and to search for Maasaw along the way.

"Many generations later, the Hopi found Maasaw tapping on a rock. He made a Covenant with the Hopi people. He had a horrible face because his message was equally horrifying. He told of the end of the Fourth World. He told the Hopi people to follow his Instructions and heed his Warnings. He gave them a Pattern of Life and a Road Plan to see them through to the end of the Fourth World. And on stone tablets he inscribed future events for them to recognize and prepare for. He said he was the first and he would also be the last."

"He sounds Jewish," said Joey.

"Actually, I have often wondered about that myself. Maybe Maasaw was sent to the Hebrews as well. But I think he trusted the Hopi more."

"Why do you say that?"

"He didn't ask for our foreskins to seal the bargain."

John Walker let out a hearty laugh, but Joey had no idea what he was laughing about.

"There's a path that runs from Northern Canada to the equator," John Walker said. It was a couple of hours later and they were in the house having some dinner. Tom had deliberately arrived after dark with the jet to avoid curious eyes, and the three were eating canned beans with hotdogs. John Walker had cut the hotdogs into bite-size morsels, the same way Joey's mother had prepared the dish. Joey loved hotdogs and beans. She asked for ketchup and the brothers watched in mute amazement as she circled the pile of steaming legumes and hotdog lumps with the bottle, creating a neat spiral effect.

"I knew a guy once who ate spaghetti between two pieces of white bread," said Tom.

Joey looked up from her artwork to confront four eyes staring at her plate.

124

"That doesn't sound too appetizing," she said, moving her fork through the beans, disrupting her design until the ketchup bled into the brown sauce, turning it a colour Joey thought was called oxblood.

"I plan to walk that path some day," said John Walker.

"I'm sure it would be very interesting," she said because what else do you say to a proposed five-thousand-mile hike.

"Interesting hell. I'll probably die along the way."

"Then why do it?"

"Because my brother prefers the past to the present," said Tom, his mouth full of brown liquid that threatened to escape his lips as he spoke.

Over dinner Tom asked a lot of questions about the F-16, questions about the engines, the HOTAS system, mechanic-styled questions and Joey felt good being on familiar ground, losing herself in the conversation, blocking out the nagging questions that were buzzing around her head like hungry mosquitoes. She wanted to make sense of the things she'd seen. The devastation she had witnessed weighed heavily upon her. So did being cut off from the chain of command and the systems she had learned and adopted, all designed to keep her life in a virtual stasis state. It had all disappeared in a single afternoon. And she knew this to be utterly true because at no time during her training had she been told to expect one day to be eating canned beans and hotdogs with two Indian brothers, in a house that wasn't ramshackle but could use a good dusting, discussing her plane, which happened to be parked outside—like this was a normal circumstance.

The two brothers were talking quietly. Their faces were bathed in the red glow of the fire. They sat on the ground, intent upon the flame, the tone of their voices serious, low and clear. They had been talking continually ever since John Walker had gotten up to put the last log on the fire but Joey had been off in a world composed of her own thoughts, oblivious to their conversation. Their voices carried easily over to where she sat. It was like opening a book in the middle and she could not easily catch the drift of the conversation.

Tom said, "So tell me, has the day finally arrived?"

John Walker did not respond. His eyes penetrated through the flames to where Joey sat. Their eyes locked.

"What day?" asked John Walker.

"The Fourth World. The end of the Fourth World."

"You think she is the White Brother?"

"She did drop from the sky."

"Yes, but from the West, not the East. And since when did you start believing in our traditions?"

"I don't, but you do."

The flames seemed to climb higher into the blackness just as John Walker returned his consideration to the fire. He was doing it again, that staring thing.

"I'd like to go in. I'm getting cold," said Joey.

"No, we can't go in yet," John Walker said.

She was used to taking orders, only there was always a stripe or bar attached to the uniform giving them and you could always tell yourself you were obeying the uniform, the rank, not the person inside. John Walker was just a man, a middle-aged handyman, living alone in a three-room glorified shack and she was a lieutenant in the United States Air Force and why didn't that fact seem to matter to anyone around here?

She stood up and wiped some imaginary dirt from her pants. She walked around the fire and confronted her host.

"I am cold and I am tired. Unless you can give me a damn good reason why I can't go to bed then I will say goodnight."

"Go ahead if you want. But I wouldn't if I was you."

"Am I missing something here? Are you going to perform a dance around the fire or is there a meteor shower expected or what?"

"Better."

Tom said, "Better? What could be better than watching you dance around the fire, John?"

John Walker ignored his brother. He stared at Joey. There was no mockery in his eyes—it was more akin to pity or sorrow.

"What you saw today, wouldn't you say it ran from the north to the south?" asked John Walker.

"Pretty much, sure."

"I'm no geologist but I'm guessing it started up by Salt Lake City. There's a fault zone up there called the Wasatch and it's part of a belt running under the mountains on a southwesterly direction, straight for Las Vegas."

"I'm sure this has something to do with why I can't go to bed, but I can't quite put my finger on it."

"There's no basement in my house."

"You know, Mr. Walker, I've had a really long, really bad day and I do appreciate your coming to my aid and giving me a place to stay over-night. I'm just not in the mood for riddles, so why don't you spit it out, say what you're trying to say and be done with it."

Tom now rose, nodding at Joey with an empathetic smile on his face, his white teeth reminding Joey of Chicklets; there were so many Joey wanted to count them to see if there were any extras.

"Yeah John, you're confusing the shit—pardon ma'am—out of me too. And it is getting kind of cold out here."

John Walker kept his eyes on the fire. He appeared unmoved by either plea. He raised both his hands and beckoned with his flexing fingers for them to sit down beside him. Joey's eyes slid back into her head momentarily, her head shook, mostly for Tom's benefit, then she plopped herself down next to John Walker. Tom, defeated in his attempt at gallantry, returned to his place on John's right.

"Look at the flame," John Walker said. "Look closely and it will reveal something to you. The flame is a portal through which we can see the earth's intention. The flame swallows the air in order to survive. The air does not mind. It knows it will turn into something else. Nor does the log mind as it transforms into ash. All is energy and energy cannot be destroyed. But energy can destroy. There is great energy being re-leased by Maasaw to purify and punish. Many will die, but like the air and the log, it does not matter, for they will transform into something else and be removed from this world. Look at the flame. See how it flutters to the pulse of the earth. The flame is a wick to the earth's candle. We sit here tonight and await Maasaw's decision."

Joey sat still, confused once again and afraid.

"Is that why we're out here? Waiting for a spirit to appear?"

"No," said John Walker, turning and putting his arm around Joey. "We are out here because there is going to be an earthquake and it's not safe to be in the house."

"John, how do you know there's going to be an earthquake and don't give me any Maasaw crapola."

"Tom, the only crapping being done here tonight will be by Maasaw so you'd best mind your tongue."

Tom said to Joey, "Do you have any idea what he is talking about?"

"He told me a little bit. What do you know?" asked Joey.

Tom leaned forward so he could see around his brother's giant frame.

"Maasaw's this god, a deity. The Hopi believe he welcomed them into this world, the Fourth World, and gave them land and rules to live by. It is believed he will return at the end of the Fourth World like an avenging angel to punish all the wicked people and ready the good ones for entry into the Fifth World."

"So you *were* listening when our father spoke. He never thought you heard a word he said."

"Yeah well, you try falling asleep with someone hitting you on the head with a stick."

"Can you blame him?" John Walker stopped talking and let the emotions inside recede before turning to Joey and saying, "Our grandfather was sent to Alcatraz Prison because he would not let our father attend the White's school. Both my grandfather and father were known as Hostiles because they would not agree to adopt the ways of the Bahanna, the white man's ways. When my grandfather returned to Hopi land he left our sacred village with his family and, with others, started a new village in order to keep our traditions alive. So you see, Lieutenant, my brother, with his Bahanna ways, was a great disappointment to my father. Tom might have benefited from a stick to the head although he is lying when he says my father used one."

Joey said, "So, according to your beliefs, you believe I saw something more, more . . . I don't know . . . more significant than an earthquake."

Joey pulled the blanket close around her, cocooning herself from words she did not wish to hear.

"I think you saw a significant earthquake," said John Walker.

"And we are going to sit here and wait for another one?"

"Where would you suggest we go?"

"There must be somewhere safe. A mineshaft or a shelter of some kind."

John Walker picked up a stick lying by his side, more of a pole with a dulled pointed end blackened by repeated incursions into the heart of the fire. He poked at the fire, sending more sparks dancing up into the blackness.

"There is a Hopi proverb: *Kaiitsivu, kapustamokca, konakopanvungya hakapii hihita ung kyataimanii.*"

"That sounds somewhat ominous. What does it mean?" she asked.

"Why don't you ask Tom?"

"Very funny, chief. That's his way of letting you know I don't understand the Hopi language. But fortunately for you I happen to remember this one. It means something like 'He who is slow to anger, frustration and self-pity will live to see and wonder at the many changes.' So what I guess my big brother is trying to say in his cryptic, shaman's way is, if we sit tight and think good thoughts, nothing should happen to us no matter where we are. Except apparently, in his house."

"Not bad for a mechanic. Lieutenant, we are a people few in number. We have no prophets but we are a people of prophecy. Maasaw's Instructions are ethnocentric, meant for the Hopi people, to guide us and lead us towards the true path. Maasaw taught our people how to lead honourable lives, with humility and grace. But Maasaw's prophecies are also meant for all of the people of the world. Much of the true meaning of our prophecies has been perverted by well-meaning New Age adherents and environmentalists, bent and shaped to fit their own political concerns. Yet there is one thing you cannot change. There is truth in the traditions of our People. Maasaw will return. Maasaw is coming. He was the first and he will also be the last. And he will protect us."

"As long as we stay out of the house?" said Joey.

"Why make his job more difficult."

"So tell me brother, what happens after we witness all of these changes? Do I go back to the shop and change a few more spark plugs or will I have more noble work to do?"

"Your work is as noble as your attitude towards it. I do not know what will be once the Fourth World ends. It is believed the White Brother will show us a new way prior to Maasaw's return. "

John Walker addressed Joey. "The White Brother is a kind of messiah, a shower of a new way of life. Many times in the past, the People have been fooled into thinking the White Brother had arrived."

Tom said, "The Mormons were the worst."

"No worse than the Catholics. They all attempted to replace our beliefs with their own. The Mormons had a better story. They convinced many of our people to believe Maasaw was actually Jesus, resurrected in North America and any reference to the appearance of the White Brother must surely be reference to the Christ."

"I had a Mormon girlfriend once," said Tom.

A coyote's howl rose up into the night air and was answered by a second then a third refrain. Even though she knew they were harmless, the sound froze her skin, and even the two men stopped and listened.

There was another sound. There was no mistaking its high pitched shrill. It was a raven's call.

"Isn't it odd to hear a raven in the middle of the night?" Joey asked.

"Yes," said John Walker, who sat forward now, his head bent slightly to the right, as if trying to locate the direction of the sound.

"It's time," he said.

They awoke in consonance with the first light of the sun. Joey found her head resting on John Walker's massive bicep. She lay still for a moment and thought she could hear his blood passing by her ear. She raised her head. Tom's back was to her. He was curled up in the fetal position, scratching his scalp and using his left construction boot to scratch the inner side of his right calf.

She sat up, disturbing John Walker, whose eyes were open and red as if from crying.

It had been anti-climactic, the earthquake, but terrifying nonetheless. There were a few tremors, not severe enough to disrupt even a mah jong game in Burbank. A deep rumbling sound, almost a growl could be heard far to the west. John Walker had stood then, raising his arms up to the sky, and watching him had made Joey dizzy. There were small sparks on his finger tips, the kind you made as a kid when you rubbed your feet in the pile broadloom then touched a brass doorknob.

She remembered seeing Tom's hair, standing straight up, stretching towards the sky, threatening to uproot itself. He was staring at her hair too, and when she touched it, she heard little crackling sounds of static.

The fire, she noticed, had died down considerably; the flames were actually receding back towards the hot coals.

John Walker then started making an incantation, if that was the word. His body began to jerk spasmodically, as if possessed, his hands forming claws, arms out before him, palms facing the sky. He tucked his chin against his shoulder; his eyes were closed tightly creating size 12 crow's feet on either side of his face. He began to sing. It was a soulful song sung with pleading urgency, the words squeezed out of John Walker's mouth, his teeth almost clenched together while he sang. And it was familiar. Joey knew this song but she could not quite place it. It was a Beatles song. But he sang it so weirdly it was difficult at first for Joey to make it out.

John Walker bent forward and back as he sang, raised his left hand in a mock guitar pose and strung a few phantom bars with his right. He swiveled and shook his head back and forth. It was quite possibly the most ludicrous and inappropriate behaviour Joey had ever witnessed as well as the funniest and she and Tom were laughing so hard at the sight of John Walker's performance that Tom began to cough uncontrollably and somehow the coughing seemed funny too and Joey rolled to the ground in a fit.

By the time John Walker's performance ended, so too, had the earthquake. As the earth's energy bled back down into the subterranean levels, the energy of the three dissipated as well and they were soon, the three of them, asleep.

The house had survived intact—only a few items had fallen from shelves; there was a half beer still standing on the kitchen table.

Before they entered the house John Walker pointed to the west up towards the sky. There were hundreds of birds in the air, circling, perhaps three or four miles away.

"Gulls," said John Walker. "Can you smell it?" he asked.

"Smell what?" asked Tom.

"The sea."

Joey took a deep breath and yes, there was a hint of salty air in her nose.

"That was quite a performance you put on last night," said Joey as they wandered into the living room, she with a bowl of yogurt, John Walker eating a banana and Tom satisfying himself with an early morning Coke.

"John does one hell of a Joe Cocker impersonation. I haven't seen you do that in years. What on earth possessed you?"

"I don't know. Maybe the earth possessed me. It just felt like the right thing to do at the time."

Joey said, "You don't seem the rock 'n' roll type."

"Neither do you," said John Walker.

Joey walked over to the one window and looked out at the brilliant blue sky, still dotted with shrieking birds. The idea of seawater being only a few miles away was terrifying. She backed away from the window and stepped on something. The picture from the wall was lying on the ground. There was a crack in the glass. She picked it up and was about to re-hang it when something about the picture caught her eye, something she hadn't noticed the day before.

There were four people walking past and behind John Walker in the shot, but only two, a boy and a girl were even a little bit in focus. The girl was in profile but the boy, perhaps noticing the photographer, had cocked his head towards the camera. Joey could clearly see the boy's impish grin, so familiar, but what finally caught Joey's eye was the peace sign earring in his left ear. She unconsciously dug her fingernails into the back of the frame as goose bumps raised themselves on her arms and thighs because there was no questioning the identity of the two passersby as anyone other than her mother and her father.

XI

ADAM SAT ON A STEP HALFWAY up the staircase leading to the loft of the coach house, chugging Pepto Bismol when what he really needed was something stronger, something dramatic to slow his beating heart. He feigned interest in whatever it was Derek and Jenny were going on about, his head bobbing up and down, his lips manufacturing a smile, all the while his mind preoccupied with quelling the panic attack that was gathering critical mass in the bottom of his stomach.

He was in familiar territory, this managing of his private terror while the outside world went on without him. Adam had divided into two; his body on automatic pilot, going through the motions, playing normal, camouflaging the demon inside who threatened to burst him wide open and turn him into a blithering bag of mush. It was a difficult job, like keeping your eye on the puck while someone is smacking you in the head with a hockey stick.

The nurse is speaking to him now, saying the right things, pulling out the stock phrases; *You're going to be fine, this will pass, you've been here before*, but it is too late as his guts are turned inside out by a rush of fear and he feels like he has just swallowed a tumbler of adrenaline and he wants to cry out for help, he wants to fall in a heap and hug his knees and rock back and forth and cry, only all that comes out is . . .

"I don't feel so good."

Derek knelt down in front of Adam, resting one hand on his knee.

"No kidding," said Derek. "Panic attack?"

"How'd you guess?"

"I was there the first time you dropped acid, remember."

"Yes, and it was mescaline," and talking made it better, brought him into the world and out of his nightmare.

"You got any downers?" asked Derek.

"No, and nobody calls them downers anymore."

"Nobody takes them either which makes them so damn hard to get hold of. Anyway, I don't believe you. You've always got something stashed away."

"Maybe."

"Tell me where it is. I'll go get it."

"That's okay. I'll go. I could use the fresh air."

"Let me know if you find any. And don't pull an Acapulco on me."

"What's an Acapulco?" asked Jenny, who had been preparing odd bits of food to feed the three of them, pretending she was deaf but unable to resist the question.

"We dropped acid with our wives one night on the beach, and Adam decided he wasn't feeling too well so he walked off and we didn't see him again for twenty-four hours."

"Where did you go?" asked Jenny.

"I went for a walk, which I'm going to do right now. I'll be right back."

The shotgun was leaning against the outside wall of the coach house. Adam picked it up and took it with him.

The police were out with their megaphones or loudspeakers or whatever it was they were using to rouse the population, rolling slowly up and down the long streets of Montclair, imploring the citizenry to be calm and stay in their homes.

"A state of emergency exists . . . "

Like they needed reminding, thought Adam as he went through the back door of his house.

"A curfew has been imposed beginning twelve P.M. *today . . . "*

There goes the massage.

" . . . and anyone found breaking the curfew will be subject to arrest and prosecution."

Adam was passing through the living room when he caught sight of the car in his driveway and heard a noise coming from the second floor.

"Crews are currently working to restore water and electricity . . . "

Adam froze. The water from the carpet began seeping through the leather soles of his cowboy boots. He turned his head, could see the car, which also put his good ear in the direction of the disturbance upstairs.

How different real fear felt from panic. Panic was all self-indulgence, a luxury for those with the time. But this, what he felt now, it was primordial, it had meaning.

It was the same car. Damn but he couldn't remember if he had seen

134

five or six kids. Like it mattered. Like he could handle five.

"Do not attempt to use your automobiles prior to the curfew. All automobiles found on the road will be pulled over and the keys confiscated."

Adam froze, his senses in overdrive. The muted colours of the living room appeared to glow with a new sun-like vitality. The grandfather clock in the corner of the room was suddenly ticking so loudly that Adam found it hard to believe he had ever been able to sit in this room and read the newspaper without wanting to hurl a shoe at it.

Something hit the floor above him. They were in the master bedroom. Not all of them. Five, there had been five in the car, he finally remembered. And two were still in the car. He felt naked, exposed. If he could see them could they not see him? But no, there was no light reflecting out of the room so the windows would appear blackened from the outside.

Three in the house. He didn't want to shoot anyone. He didn't really care what they took. But he was between them and the front door. Not a good tactical position. Move. Quietly.

He turned to retrace his steps when he noticed the antique barometer on the wall. It was one of those decorative, wooden-framed hanging wall units with a barometer and thermometer combined. He had found it at a flea market upstate near Woodstock one summer while visiting friends in the area. Adam habitually tapped on the barometer as he went by it every morning, stopping momentarily to set the brass pointer over the black indicator hand. It was one of his quiet pleasures, a morning ritual like his first cup of coffee; he enjoyed watching the progress of the black hand as it mysteriously moved a few millimeters away from the brass marker. Only now it was doing something he did not think was possible. The black hand was visibly moving, counterclockwise, falling past 29 inches, now touching the T of STORMY, now slowly moving towards the O.

"We have been informed there may be aftershocks from the earthquake. If you have not already done so, remove all wall hangings and items on open shelves."

They were coming down the stairs. Adam moved into the kitchen, located in the back of the house. No one robs the kitchen, he figured.

Adam heard their voices, their laughter; this was a lark, a game, the playing field provided by Mother Nature. It made him angry. He minded the theft less than the mockery.

What am I doing? he heard a small inner voice say, as if it were a statement coming from behind him, dissolving in his wake as he approached the open front door and walked through it into the daylight.

The sound of the pump action from his shotgun froze them in their tracks. It was a sound they understood, a sound with its own meaning, a declaratory statement of intent.

"We encourage everyone to be patient, to help those in need and to remain calm."

Adam mechanically pushed the safety button to the off position. One live round in the chamber and four in the magazine. One for each of them. Then that same little voice asking if he was going insane.

The three men turned slowly around, in a weird ballet movement, arms away from their sides, palms down, in practiced fashion. They had not taken anything big. There was nothing in their hands, only unnatural bulges in their pant pockets and loose fitting team jackets.

They were young. No more than twenty. Two looked scared but the third had a big, engaging smile on his face. He stepped forward a bit and Adam noticed he was blocking Adam's sight line to the two in the car.

"Tell your friends to get out of the car," said Adam.

The smile remained. "And then what? You gonna shoot us all?"

"Just tell them to get out of the car."

"And if I don't?"

Adam raised his gun, like he'd done so many times before while skeet shooting and let loose a round.

The lead shot from the 12 gauge 8½ shot shell tore off the left headlamp and most of the front corner of the near side of the car. The three men jumped involuntarily and the two in the car needed no further prompting, exiting with their hands held away from their bodies.

Adam was new to this and he knew he was dealing with seasoned street veterans. He was on offense but it was still their game. And the smiler knew it. And he knew Adam knew it.

"We got us a live one here, boys," the smiler said. "Still not convinced though. Pretty easy to shoot at a car. Little different when it's flesh and blood. Wouldn't want to get any blood on those fine threads you have on."

"I don't want to shoot anybody."

"Now that is a relief. See boys, richy here don't want no blood splattering all over the place."

"Let's see what you've got in your pockets."

A nod from the smiler and the other two started emptying their pockets; two watches, a small jewelry box containing, Adam knew, a couple of rings and a thick silver bracelet with a round medallion in the middle, inlaid with turquoise and coral. The smiler had Adam's money clip, a wad of bills still attached.

Adam asked, "What's your name?"

"So now he wants to make it personal. Okay. It's Jeffrey . . . only nobody dares call me that 'cept my mom."

A few giggles.

"All right, Jeffrey."

The giggles stopped.

"Who else do we have here?"

There was Robert, only everyone called him Boo, skinny and missing a front tooth; the driver's name was Edward, Edna for short, though it took the same time to say either name, he with dull, drugged eyes, compact frame, ill-suited for the baggy T-shirt and oversized pants hanging loosely from his body; Luther, riding shotgun, massive, arms like tree trunks, bemused expression, itching for some action, hardly a poster boy for his namesake; Patrick, called Switch because his last name was Blades—get it—brutally handsome, the chick magnet for the group, worth his weight in gold.

Jeffrey said, "So now we all got names. 'Cept for you, that is."

Adam lowered the muzzle towards the ground, pointing it a few feet in front of Jeffrey. They all inched forward and the muzzle came back up. They stopped. Simon Says with a shotgun.

"Adam Fischer."

"The producer?"

"That's it."

"Wow boys, we got ourselves a real celebrity here."

"I'm impressed. Didn't think you fellas would be into my kind of music."

Jeffrey let out a snort. "You mean white boy rock? You're right. We're not. I don't know your music from shit. I don't know you from shit. I saw those gold albums on your wall and you're too fuckin' old to be in any of those bands. Grammy Award gave it away. Producer of the year. Ooo wee."

The smiler gestured towards the house. "The music business been very, very good to me," he said, then started dancing in a small circle.

The other four started to clap and chant; this was a schtick they had perfected, fifties doo-wop time warped to a half century later.

"How 'bout recording us, Mr. producer man?" said Switch.

"Yeah," Jeffrey piped in, "We could use a new limo, specially since you done shot up our transportation—and some pussy to go with it."

It was a planned move. Jeffrey, the smiler, had manoeuvered in front of Switch. Now he flopped to the ground and the gun was out before Adam could react.

But Switch did not fire.

He held the gun in both hands, a semi-automatic. Adam could see what had prevented a possible shot. Switch had not had enough time or foresight to pull back the slide. That was the *semi* part of semi-automatic. He needed to pull back the slide to cock the gun. Only after he fired would the gases from the explosion do the work for him, expelling the spent shell and forcing the slide back against the hammer, reloading and re-cocking the gun before you heard the bang.

"Now what we got here is a Mexican standoff," said Jeffrey.

"Except I've got a live round in the chamber and you guys are standing close enough—I'll probably hit at least three of you. And you, being dead center, well, you'll just be dead, period."

Bravo, Adam thought, spoken like you meant it, only you're shaking so badly you can hardly keep the barrel pointed on the smiler's stomach and you know you can't pull the trigger, you don't want to do it, you'd rather take the hit then supply it.

"So what do you propose?" said Jeffrey.

"Tell Switch to lower his gun."

"Then what?"

"Then open the jewelry box. There's a silver bracelet inside. Throw it over."

"Then what?"

"Then pick up the rest of the stuff and leave."

"Just like that . . . leave with your stuff?"

"That's right."

"Shit man. You're crazy. You're fuckin' crazy. I like that. Boo, do like the producer man says."

Boo knelt down and removed the bracelet from the box. He gently threw it over near Adam's feet.

"Tell Switch to throw the gun into the car."

"Do it."

The gun landed on the floorboards with a thud.

"Now pick up the stuff and leave."

They were stuffing their pockets when the patrol car pulled into the driveway. Adam's view was obstructed by the five men. Without wondering why, he lowered his weapon then dropped it, nonchalantly, into the bushes by the side of the front porch.

Two officers approached, their right hands resting on the grips of their holstered revolvers. Jeffrey took a half step towards the car, then froze. Adam gave him a subtle shake of his head.

"Do we have a problem here?" said the bigger of the two policemen.

Jeffrey's eyes remained on Adam, while the others turned to face the officers.

"I said, do we have a problem here?"

His partner drew his revolver, while the one doing the speaking came around and between Adam and the five men.

Adam broke into a smile. "We do have a problem, officer, and maybe you can help us out. My name is Adam Fischer and I'm a record producer. I was working all night with these gentlemen—I have a recording studio in the house—and as we were wrapping up the recording session the earthquake hit. Now with the curfew, my associates have no way of getting back to East Orange. They're desperate to be reunited with their loved ones, as you can imagine."

The cops made a few calls and arranged an escort for the quintet out onto Highway 280 where an East Orange cruiser would lead them back to their homes.

Before getting into their car, Jeffrey approached Adam, hugged him theatrically while whispering into his ear.

"You one crazy sonofabitch. How'd you know we're from East Orange?"

"Lucky guess," Adam whispered back.

Another cruiser pulled up and the boys piled into their car.

"Hey, you better get that headlight fixed," said the cop, who was still standing near Adam while his partner briefed the other car.

"Interesting friends you have there, Mr. Fischer. I'd love to hear that recording some day."

"We encourage everyone to be patient, to help those in need and to remain calm," said Adam. "Just doing what I'm told."

"Yeah, I always say that to myself before I draw my gun. Don't forget your shotgun there."

The wounded car began backing up, pieces of the headlight falling out onto the driveway like a trail of breadcrumbs. The smiler stuck his head out the window, yelling, "You one crazy sonofabitch!"

It was almost noon. Just two and a half hours since the earthquake and several lifetimes of experience. Time was moving so slowly, the way it did when Adam was young, sitting next to his grandfather in synagogue during Yom Kippur or Rosh Hashanah. Every second a minute, every minute an hour, every hour a lifetime. And he was not allowed to talk, not to his cousin Ronnie on his right and certainly not to his grandfather, who was wholly absorbed in the sanctity of the ritual, a believer, ringing reverence from every Hebrew consonant. His grandfather would occasionally lift his head from his book and say, *Pray, pray,* and Adam would sit on his hands and refuse to even hold the book. Ronnie was far better indoctrinated, boldly davening the liturgies, singing so badly off key, it induced a kind of claustrophobia in Adam, his mind daring him to stand up and scream shut up or fuck off to the entire congregation. But he never did. He often fantasized what it would be like to, though. It was tempting but he was sane and sane people only think insanity.

All bets were off now, though. Go ahead and think the most insane thought and it will seem normal. Revenge fantasies, dreams of mass destruction, the end of the world, it was all at your doorstep. Gone was the need to dream up demons or to rely on psychosis or chemical imbalance or a missing gene because it was all on the outside now, available to everyone, exposed, as if normal was a suit of clothes and someone had turned it inside out and all you can see are the seams and the threads, and you wonder how something so ugly could be so beautiful on the other side.

Adam felt a great release but not without a measure of guilt because it did not feel right to feel good, not while he sat on his front step, appalled by the mauled skyline of New York City. But there was no denying the liberating effect chaos had produced. School was out. For good.

After the police left, Adam hurried back into the living room and checked the barometer. He could not detect any further movement, the black hand having come to rest past *Stormy,* Adam counting the dashes and coming up with 28.6 inches of barometric pressure. The sun had disappeared during his altercation with the gang from East Orange and now it was so dark beyond New York to the east, it appeared as if the night was time-lapse approaching.

"Are you sure they won't come back?" asked Jenny, Derek rendered dumb by the story, astounded by the sober account given by his friend.

Adam had gone and retrieved them, found them making love on the floor of the coach house living room, told them to get dressed and Derek to act his age, to which Derek replied he was acting his age, the age of Aquarius, and Adam had to laugh, because it seemed so appropriate for Derek to be getting it on, oblivious to the life and death decisions being made by Adam a couple hundred feet away. Derek always had all the fun so why should this day be any different? And Adam had to admit to a little envy. He could almost remember what it felt like.

"If they do ever come back, they'll probably have demo tapes to play me."

Derek finally stood up and walked down the steps of the porch, turned and faced Adam. Then he knelt on the step below the one Adam was perched on, pulled Adam's face to his and kissed him hard on the mouth. Adam struggled and finally managed to push him away.

"What did I do to deserve that?"

"Yeah, you never kiss me that way," said Jenny.

Derek said, "Welcome to the other side. I've been waiting years for you to let it all hang out and float downstream for a bit. I didn't realize it would take the destruction of civilization but what the hell, if that's what it takes then so be it."

"I chased a few burglars out of the house with a shotgun. It's no big deal. Float downstream . . . I'd probably drown."

The two men smiled at each other, ignored by Jenny who was no longer listening, her eyes and concentration stuck on the eastern horizon.

"What is that?" she said, barely audible, words more for herself.

Adam and Derek turned and the three sat in mute testimony to the magnificence of the wall.

Adam is calm. The earthquake had been a surprise. Lucia should have warned him about the earthquake. If you know about an earthquake, you tell people, especially people you claim to love. Then again, if you did know and do nothing to save yourself then maybe you didn't really know. Or maybe she told him and he had not understood it. Or maybe he was afraid to know.

But if the earthquake was Lucia's then the wave is Adam's. The wave of his dreams these years since Sedona. The countless rides he has taken, always the same, a relentless surging mass, travelling at speeds that pull the skin away from your eyeballs, massively destructive, energy exploding as it hits dry land, rapidly consuming real estate along the way, a tremendous thrust into the mainland before receding and then gone.

141

His house on the high ground, smart move. He had let it out once, the reason, a small reception in his house, a rare glimpse inside the Fischer mansion, a group of record company executives and musicians plus their manager, a celebration in honour of a newly finished album, and he remembers telling them, between their lines of cocaine, about a dream and a wave and how he figured this house was built high enough up the ridge to survive it and everybody is getting so stoned that it sounds like logic, for haven't powerful men been building impregnable castles for thousands of years, says an extremely attractive, college educated, marketing vice president with killer legs, more to ingratiate herself with Adam, but everyone says she has a point and for the rest of the evening he is Sir Adam, Knight of the round coffee table where he is forced to anoint his guests' shoulders with a fire poker every time they snort a line of coke.

There's still some colour left in you.

Crazy old man. Dead now for sure.

Been through this before—you and I.

Well I guess I have, Adam thinks as the curtain comes down on New York City, a shimmering green wall, having appeared moments before to the east, rising up like a velvet backdrop on a Broadway stage, its crest taller than the tallest buildings, crashing into the brick and steel and tossing everything aside as if it were made of balsam, travelling at well over two hundred miles an hour, a miserly percentage of its force drained by the struggle to scale the giant teeth of Manhattan.

There is again the sense of time slowing as the water climbs over buildings and through thoroughfares, some buildings stubbornly refusing to give ground but it is useless; what the first wave misses, the subsequent waves will pummel into nothingness.

Adam pulls his eyes away for a moment. Jenny is lying in the grass, fainted. Derek is deadpan, a rarity, but not scared.

"You knew this was coming. You knew this. Me being here. The coach house. You knew. But how?"

"Sit back and enjoy the show, Derek. It's not over yet."

There is no sense of joy or satisfaction in Adam's voice.

He isn't sure he had been warned. He isn't sure he had been singled out for special treatment.

Lucia is dead—she has to be. His rescue fantasies will go unrealized. He is too numb to feel the pain he knows will strike him down and tear at his heart for years to come. Replaced in time by heartbreak's ugly sibling, regret.

142

It swallows up the Hudson River estuary and rolls into the marsh lands northeast of Newark, following the path of least resistance, while further north a wall of water takes on Hoboken, Jersey City, Weehawken, West New York and all the other river communities.

"How far can this go?" asks Derek, as if Adam is an expert in all things tsunami.

"We'll know in about five minutes."

"Know what?"

"If I picked the right house."

"Not much of a margin of error. If you knew this was even a remote possibility, wouldn't say, Iowa have been a better location?"

"Too far from really good restaurants."

"Good point."

It is ten miles away, Adam figures. He can hear it. It has a voice, a deep baritone and it's calling out to him, he feels it calling him and his mind plays tricks as he hears *Remember me, remember me*, the rumbling sound of the water saying, *Remember me.*

It's a horrible scene to watch. And a thing of breathtaking beauty. Which is probably why Derek is sitting there, mouth open, spittle in the corners of his mouth, casually smoking a cigarette and taking in every moment, every detail. Derek has never had any discernable left brain activity as far as Adam can tell. What must that feel like, Adam wonders as he watches the water roll over eastern New Jersey.

It surges forward, reminding Adam of his little wading pool—hadn't he thought of it earlier?—and how his father would drain it part way then lift one end and Adam delighted in standing in front of it, the onslaught of rushing water spilling out and running over his feet and ankles, the water spreading over the lawn, drenching it before disappearing into the soil.

There are things he can only imagine, of course. It is autumn and most of the leaves have fallen, allowing a clear view all the way to the city. Can't see everything, though. The Passaic River is hidden from view, so is the Hackensack River. Giant Stadium must be over to the left. He can see it all in his mind as the water continues to roll towards Montclair.

It's halfway now; maybe two minutes have passed since Jenny spotted it. She is moaning, holding her head, must have hit it on the ground. He wants to help her but he'll miss the show. Blink and you'll miss it. She is dazed. Derek is helping her onto the step. She screams when she sees the wave.

Adam's heart leaps when the second wave appears. It is smaller than the first and easily rolls over what little is left of the Manhattan skyline because it all appears to be underwater. His mind can't decide which wave to follow, switching back and forth. The first wave is near, the thunder preceding it, a sound of pure energy unlike any he's ever heard. A deep roar fills the air, shaking the windows of his house. Jenny's screams become a muted drone against the backdrop of the water's exhortation.

He thinks to run. The might of the water will surely wash over the Watchung Range. He has miscalculated. His arrogance has put him in harm's way. He thought he had a bleacher seat and now he finds himself on the playing field.

It's clearly visible now. Not a solid green colour anymore; green and brown and blue, swirling and bubbling, chunks of trees and floating pieces of humanity, man-made things, a potluck stew of confusion, only a couple of miles away now, still racing forward, unabated, a spectacular sight, surely the reason he was born, to bear witness, to perish with this fantastic image still glowing on his retina, an image for eternity.

He feels something, a tightening on his arm, a blood pressure cup kind of pressure, knows it's Derek's hand, a final gesture, a squeeze goodbye, no time for words, wouldn't hear them anyway.

She must cleanse herself as she has done before.

She must flush the toilet, flush all the shit down the drain.

The horizon is filled by water, in every direction, its distance from the house measurable in yards, time measured in seconds. The scene resembles a tub filling up, the water continually rising, engulfing Glen Ridge, breaching Montclair Township, slowing or maybe only appearing to slow as it creeps closer to where they sit. Trees are snapping off as the edge of the swell slices through the neighbourhood, rooftops yanked off and sent spinning before disappearing, debris crashing into itself, horrible sounds then suddenly quieter, Adam hyperventilating, noticing his breath, hearing it and wondering how, the water still rising, slowing as it meets the foot of the range, probing, flowing sideways, pulling against its own inertia, gravity beginning to assert itself.

Still, the boiling, angry mass continues to rise below them. It is consuming the neighbourhood, still voracious, insatiable, people running, caught, digested, the ground trembling, sagging under the weight, tremors, the previously weakened substrata buckling, Adam

144

past fear, too much fear to process for one day, letting it all slip away, relaxing, detached, the water crossing his street, climbing towards the house, losing momentum, undecided, slipping, the lawn immersed, Adam noticing waves on the surface reversing course, heading back, the musty smell of the sea filling his nose, Jenny jumping up and running into the house, Derek statue still, the water almost touching Adam's cowboy boots as he instinctively lifts his feet, the water washing over the step, nothing but ocean, beachfront property, real estate value certain to skyrocket, Derek yelling something, something inane, "Far out, man!" he's saying, like he's stoned on acid, the water, icy cold, waist level, circling around the house, waves pounding against the foundation, then a high wave, its force knocking Adam and Derek right through the open front door into the hallway, Derek smashing into a wall, Adam flung into the kitchen, stopped by the counter, choking, gagging on the awful salty stuff, the room filling, Adam fighting to stand, grabbing for the sink, pulling himself to the counter, the water continuing to fill, windows breaking, water flowing through, rising, panic, drowning, horrible, certain death.

He is grasping the track lighting, slipping on the counter, keeping his nose above the surface, the fixture loosening, considers letting go, letting it all go because what's the use, then he feels something, a change. He is standing in front of the window and the pressure is coming from a new direction, the water passing through the window and into the house, reversing itself, spent, hurrying back to meet the second wave, oh god, Adam thinks, there was another, and it only takes a few seconds for the water level to recede to a few inches.

He is standing on the counter, alive, too cold to shiver, a muddy high water mark ringing the tiled walls of the kitchen a couple of feet from the ceiling, brown rivulets running between the deposits left behind on the floor, attempting to find their way back out of the kitchen, abandoned by the receding tide.

He is faint and nauseous, can barely stand, manages to climb off the counter and slumps to the ground, lying, uncaring in the sloppy mess on the floor, adding to it with what little remains in his stomach, tired of seeing his own vomit, tired of catastrophe on top of catastrophe, feels the seductive call of insanity, the allure of total withdrawal, must fight it off, resist the temptation.

The entity must discover its soul purpose. Or was it sole purpose. A deliberate play on words? A cosmic pun? Was there a difference in the end?

He lays still for a moment, letting his heart find a more comfortable rate, allowing it to pour some blood back into his thirsty brain, knows he almost went into shock, or worse, then slowly and deliberately he pulls himself up with the help of a couple of drawer handles.

Derek lay unconscious in Jenny's arms, Jenny sobbing and caressing his face. They were on the staircase and Adam could tell by the water damage where Jenny must have pulled him out of the water and up to a dry portion of the staircase.

"Is he dead?" she asked, looking up at Adam, tears running down her face and it struck Adam as odd how he could differentiate her tears from the rest of the water rolling off her hair onto her face.

She was a pretty girl, Adam knew she was, but now there was only the essence of her, no makeup, no airs, no upbringing, only her self, so naked, afraid, a strong fear, a woman's fear, holding the limp body of her man in her arms.

His chest was rising, Adam could see it. There was a bruise on his head, an ugly red thing above the right eyebrow.

"He's alive. He'll be fine," he said, meaning it, not believing it. "We'll carry him upstairs. First I have to check on something."

Adam walked to the doorway and searched the horizon. It wasn't there. The water was receding back to the coast, the massive undertow of the receding first wave having undermined the second. That's what happened. It was the only explanation. How many times had Adam watched the surf crash onto a beach, one huge wave climbing up the sand, then racing back down and cutting down the next wave, rendering it powerless to do anything but kiss the beach and return to the ocean.

The edge of the wave was a few miles away, having withdrawn at least halfway back towards New York. Adam's front lawn was littered with the new relics of a lost civilization; an overturned car with New York plates lay near the house, water seeping out of the seams, the windows closed and unbroken. There was a body inside, a man, his back pressed against the driver side window, floating in purplish water, his head only visible when it bumped into the window before disappearing again into the murk.

A stop sign had impaled itself nearly upright in the middle of the lawn—what were the odds—and the irony caused a painful smile to appear on Adam's lips. For as far as he could see, the landscape was covered with wrecked cars, huge pieces of destroyed buildings and houses, wires and snapped telephone poles. A toilet lay smashed on the roadway while wood siding and trees made walking in a straight line impossible.

Adam made his way through the maze of junk to the end of his driveway. Most of the trees in the vicinity of his house remained standing, the weakened force of the wave unable to uproot them. He found another body, this time a young girl, hung upside down from a large oak tree on the far side of the street, bent in a horrible, unnatural way. There were no other bodies within view, which was strange, but he was thankful for the small mercy.

He found himself climbing up the tree and extricating the girl—no easy feat—and it occurred to him he should be attending to Derek instead of the dead but he could not let her hang there. Derek had Jenny and this poor little broken thing had no one so he reclaimed her and carried her up to the house, intent on burying her, laying her down and forcing her broken limbs back into a facsimile of their normal position, wiping the long strands of her hair from her face, oddly unscathed by the brutal pummeling she was unable to endure, and there was peace in her expression, a final serenity and Adam sobbed convulsively as he laid her out and fixed her clothes, his hands trembling as he rebuttoned her blouse, several buttons missing, and flattened out her skirt. She was missing a shoe and sock and Adam thought to go looking for it, realized he was crazy to even think the thought.

He called into the house for Jenny, asking if Derek was all right and Jenny came out and covered her mouth with her hand when she saw the girl and the extent of the devastation. Adam wondered how she would ever get over the images locking themselves forever within her memory. She stood there, a silent scream forming in her mouth. Adam yelled at her, broke through her shock, and ordered her back into the house to take care of Derek. Adam could hear Derek's moans, him calling out for Jenny, relieved to hear his voice, as distressed and pained as it sounded.

He walked around to the back of the house. There was a tool shed where the previous owner had stored gardening equipment. The shed had been driven to the edge of Adam's property, upended, the floor facing Adam as he approached. It had missed striking the coach house by only a few feet. Adam pushed aside a few bushes and forced the door up, like a hamper, climbing in and letting the door slam behind him.

It felt like being in a fun house, part of the ceiling on the ground, a few items still hanging on a wall now pretending to be a ceiling. Adam quickly found a shovel and spade and pushed the door open and crawled out.

He was walking past the front door of the coach house, eyeballing the water mark on the front wall, about two feet above the ground, when he heard the telephone. He stopped and moved his head to determine the location of the ringing. It was coming from the coach house.

He ran into the house, his heart pounding. He was scared, scared he would miss the call, scared by the sound, an unnatural sound now, the signature ringing of a cell phone. The sound was coming from the loft. Adam slipped on the wet surface as he stepped towards the staircase, falling heavily and hurting his hip. Despite the pain, he pulled himself up and hopped up the stairs. Don't hang up, please don't hang up.

There was a coat, Derek's, hanging from a chair pushed tightly against a small desk. Adam frisked the jacket, cop style, felt the bulge, pulled the phone from a side pocket, flipped down the speaker and pressed 'Send'.

"Hello," he said, barely able to enunciate the words, the pain in his hip and the need for oxygen robbing his voice of any real force.

"Adam, is that you?"

"Lucia?"

"You were expecting someone else?"

"Oh my god, I can't believe this. Where are you?"

"Adam, you have to come get me."

"Are you okay? Are you hurt?"

"I'm fine. I'm a little banged up. This phone doesn't have much battery power left so listen carefully. You have to come get me before it's too late."

"Where are you? How am I going to get to you?"

"Not to state the obvious, but you're going to need a boat."

Adam listened, quickly scribbling notes on a pad, not wanting to lose a syllable, his mind clear, concentrating on every word, extracting an unexplored delight from every sentence, from each inflection in her tone, surprisingly certain that he would kiss her mouth long and hard when next he had her within reach and even after her phone went dead he continued to hear her voice, the anticipation of seeing her, of being with her again intoxicating him momentarily with unadulterated joy.

But first he had to find a boat.

XII

IMMORTALITY MISSED Sydney Johnson's gun crew by only a couple of feet. And that was just fine with him, he said as they stood, Sydney, Lucia and Brian, on the port side of the flight deck of the Intrepid. Before them stood a plaque commemorating the first Kamikaze attack on the Intrepid in October of 1944, a memorial for the friends Sydney had watched die.

"I was envious, sure. They were the only all black gun crew, and they were a proud bunch. Good shooters, too. I was in the next crew over."

He paused for a moment, and Lucia knew he was replaying it over again in his mind, like he must have done a gazillion times before, practiced, the tourists hanging on every word, because this was real drama and not a made-up-for-TV mini-series.

She let him go on, listening politely, all the while glancing to her right, to the smoke and fire. They had told her about the wave, they had said, go with him, listen to him, so now she listened, a war story, and while she empathized, listening to a tale told a thousand times of death and heroes, she could find no glory in it, nor profound meaning.

She would never understand the necessity of war or the camaraderie of soldiers. To her it was another silly man game, fun only until the action starts and friends begin to die and limbs start to go missing and maybe you actually kill someone and, after puking your guts out you decide, maybe, just maybe, this wasn't such a good idea after all.

Men, they are incapable of anticipation, she thought—still listening to Sydney but with half an ear—they are blind to the consequences of their actions, the fallout, the things women spend a lifetime fretting over, evaluating, discarding, hypothecating; a mature behaviour completely alien to most men. Take sex for instance, she thought, working herself up inside. They can't see past their own orgasm, can't know how they will feel the next day, hell, the next second, sheepishly grabbing their scattered clothing, wishing themselves turned to vapor so they might flow beneath the crack of the bedroom door and melt away rather than spend another moment in your presence, confused by their own about-face, embarrassed by their fickleness but not enough to search through it to the underlying truth. Which was what? She had no idea, except as she listened to Sydney's account and saw Brian's wide-eyed response, she thought she glimpsed the truth of it, something about always being hungry, even when you're not.

"They were shooting at this Jap plane; it was coming in real low and we knew about these crazy Kamikaze pilots. Off goes one of its wings but he's still coming on, straight for the hull and they're trying for the other wing, so as he'll flop into the sea but they don't get it and at the last second the plane dips and the one wing explodes against their gun tub and I see men go flying every which way."

He's back there now, a trip he takes every day for the paying public. He is as much a relic of this museum as the planes on the flight deck. She thinks this place is a kind of purgatory for him, a way station, memories left endlessly on hold, the truth of his past, a remembered nightmare populated by the scattered guts of his comrades spread across the flight deck, his homage an expiation of his venial sin, the sin of survival, caught between worlds, left behind to explain and point and remember.

Men don't anticipate. You build a floating highway, stick it full of warplanes and guns and—what did Sydney say—thirty-five hundred men, go trolling for trouble, go out of your way to find it, and guess what—it finds you.

"Alonzo Swann, they finally give him a medal."

"I'm sorry, who?" she asked because she realized hearing the words wasn't much help if you weren't actually listening to them.

"Alonzo Swann. President Reagan, he gave Alonzo a medal for what he did that day. Pulling his buddies out of the mess. All burned up and still pulling people out of harm's way. Took 'em forty years but he got his medal."

She saw the hypocrisy of the equation. Men start wars then give awards for life saving. They pin a medal on you for forgetting to anticipate.

Not now, it was silly to be thinking this now because she hadn't the luxury of philosophy or private thoughts. She had to act.

Lucia looked down the flight deck and it was nearly impossible for her to think of this huge hulking mass of steel out at sea, pretending to be land, floating and bobbing out in the Pacific, nine hundred feet of highway. If the mountain won't come to Mohammed, you take the runway with you.

They had boarded without incident, Sydney nodding to four young men in security uniforms and two maintenance people who stood and watched him walk by, all six dipping their chins almost reverently in return, as if releasing their pain and fright to his care. He had seen action, had told them as much on countless occasions, and they admired him for what he had been through, she saw it in their faces. A man with a broom said to his co-worker, perhaps his wife, he said how now that Sydney was here things would be all right.

A little more organized, perhaps, some leadership, yes, but *all right* was not in the cards today and she did not require her tarot deck for the prediction.

She felt they had an hour or so before the second disaster struck, an hour and a half to figure out how they all might survive, if survival was even remotely possible, if what she had been shown was coming and was as big as it appeared in her semi-conscious state.

Sydney and Brian had wandered into the exhibit area of the aircraft carrier. It was imperative that she yank Sydney out of tour guide mode and into something resembling a CEO, no that wasn't right . . . a CO, that's it. He needed to become the acting CO of the Intrepid and she needed the time to explain to him the facts of life as revealed to her by the voices.

She caught up to them in the hanger where the indoor exhibits were, well, exhibited. It was story time again.

"It was the damnedest thing, son. This Jap plane crashes right through into the hanger deck and explodes. Oh it was an awful mess, men screaming, smoke everywhere, thick and black so as you could hardly see your own hand in front of your face and we were tripping over dead people and there ain't no worse feeling in the world than tripping over your buddies, nothing worse. And we had a song they'd play over the P.A. It was called, *The Bear Went Over The Mountain*. So as the story goes, the CO orders the ship abandoned and one of his aides puts on *The Bear Went Over The Mountain* over the P.A. system because the crew knew that when they heard that song, they were supposed to abandon ship, you know, get the hell off the ship, excuse my profanity. I was on the deck then and we knew something was coming out of the speakers but there was so much damn noise and confusion that we couldn't make out the song. So we're all looking up there, up at the CO's bridge, we can see him in his chair, a mug of coffee in his hand and we're all yelling at him, telling him we can't hear, pointing to our ears and then giving him the safe sign, you know, like when a ball player slides into second and the umpire yells *Safe*. We were doing all this waving and pointing and maybe it's confusing the CO because he doesn't know we can't hear the music and he figures from our hand signals that we don't want to abandon ship, that we want to try to save her. So the bugger, excuse my French, cancels the abandon ship order and we spend the next three hours fighting the flames while several destroyers circle us for protection. And damned if we didn't put out the fire and sail her back to San Francisco."

Sydney pulled Brian over to a far wall to a photo collage of Kamikaze hits on the Intrepid, gaping holes and fire and smoke, dead men wrapped in white and live soldiers turned black by the smoke, their muscles straining, holding hoses, trying to subdue the flames. And Lucia, inspecting the black and white enlargements, had to admire those men for their ability to respond, without thought, without concern for their own welfare. And maybe they were able to do it because the day's dead were already selected and they weren't on the list, but more probably it was another aspect of a man's nature, because it seemed to Lucia, if you lack the capacity to anticipate then you sure as hell better have the capacity to react.

A couple of men in light blue shirts, similar to Sydney's, with the Intrepid insignia on the shoulder, appeared in the doorway to the hanger. The two were remarkably similar in appearance, each in his seventies or thereabouts, gray haired, wiry with only a suggestion of a gut—fit old guys, Lucia said to herself.

After introductions were made, Lucia was told they were Intrepid vets like Sydney who lent their time to the museum, giving some life to an otherwise staid and reverent exhibit. One, whose name was Hernando Torrez, was limping badly while his buddy, Brooklyn resident, Andy Giancarlo, helped him walk.

"I pulled him out from under his kitchen table," Andy was telling Sydney. Andy was in the middle of his morning ritual, he was saying, a ride into Manhattan, a short detour into the 2nd Avenue Deli for bagels, lox and cream cheese, then a brisk walk to his friend's apartment where the coffee would be strong and the conversation, a repetition of the day before with the date changed by one number.

"I hugged the street like I hugged the deck the day that fighter plane came in through the hull," he said, pointing to the spot of the breach.

"Never thought I'd be that scared again. Never. Jesus Christ, what has He done to us?"

Andy had found Hernando in the kitchen of his street level apartment, half buried under a pile of debris, his coffee mug still in his hand. The only place they could agree on was the ship.

"I've been dragging this son of a bitch across Manhattan for the last three hours and the only thing he's had to say is, he's hungry. I ask you, how many more times do I have to save this sorry ass's life?"

"He drags me out of my apartment and forgets the bagels. John Wayne would never forget the bagels."

"John Wayne never ate a bagel," said Andy.

"You know that as being a fact, I suppose?" said Hernando.

"I just know."

It was like watching Bing Crosby and Danny Kaye in White Christmas.

Lucia said, "Sydney, we need to talk," and pulled him away from the group.

Ten minutes later they were all assembled on the flight deck; four security guards, Andy and Hernando, Brian, the married—as it turned out—maintenance couple, and four tourists from Japan, a man and his wife and pre-teen twins, fraternal, boy and girl. The father explained how he and his family had gotten an early start and first stop on their sightseeing tour had been the ship his uncle had been flying high above during the Battle for Leyte Gulf when the Intrepid's gunners had plucked him from the sky.

"We get a lot of Japanese tourists," Sydney had told her moments earlier when they had first spotted the family, huddled together, frightened and confused, with nowhere to go and no way to get there.

"It's a cathartic thing, I suppose," he had said. "Like Germans going to Auschwitz."

Lucia took Brian's hand and wondered if there was ever a right time to let your kids know what a horrible place the world could be. Was there any civilization on earth that did not have reason to apologize to its young, to beg forgiveness for leaving behind a legacy of greed and brutality and lubricity?

"First of all," Sydney said, "I am taking over command of this ship. Does anybody have a problem with that?"

Silence.

"Good. We need to make the ship as watertight as possible. Andy, I want you to form a detail with our security friends here, since you all know the ship so well, and seal the bulkheads, hatches and door-ways. I'm not sure there is much we can do about the glass doors on the hanger deck but maybe we can reinforce the second set of doors and seal them up a bit. Do what you can. I want the superstructure as secure as possible. Understood?"

"Aye aye, sir," said Andy with a limp-wristed salute.

"Enio, you and Floria take care of our guests and Hernando. Take everybody up to the flag bridge. I want everyone in the Admiral's sea cabin."

The keys left Sydney's hand, tracing a slow arc over to Enio.

"Lucia and I are going to free the mooring ropes."

"The two of you," said Andy and it was more of a question.

"There's a chain saw in one of the maintenance rooms, I think. We don't have time to do it any other way."

"That's fine for the rope lines. What about the chains?" asked Andy. "How the hell you gonna undo those two suckers?"

"I guess I'll have to knock the eyes out of the last link fore and aft," said Sydney.

"I guess you will," said Andy.

Hernando said, "You do know what you're doing, right, Sydney? You aren't so far gone as you think you can get her underway with-out engines?"

"We've done it before, don't forget," said Sidney.

"We still had one screw going then," said Andy.

"Ancient history. Let's get to it. There isn't much time."

"'Scuse me for asking," said Hernando, "only, I don't see with much clarity what we're in a hurry for."

Sydney said, "Remember that typhoon we rode out, two hundred mile an hour winds, waves so big you thought they would swallow us up like a snack, us lying down in those stinkin' little shelves they liked to call berths, wishing we were anywhere but where we were? Do you remember all that?"

"Since you bring it up a couple times a day, yes."

"And she rode it through, didn't she? Took a beating but she came out okay, right?"

"Yeah, right."

"So we're going to get ready to do it again."

"So you're saying we're in for a wet one," said Hernando.

"Something like that, yeah."

Andy said, "On any other day I'd say you're nuts, but today I'm not

154

lookin' for explanations. Come on, guys," motioning to his new crew, flat eyed boys with gaping mouths and bad skin, "we've got leaks to plug."

Thirty minutes later they were all cramped into the Admiral's sea cabin, aft of the flag bridge, occupied during active service when the Group Commander was utilizing the Intrepid as his flagship. One deck above was the navigating bridge, the best seat in the house, affording the CO a nearly three hundred and sixty degree panoramic view of the flight deck and the ocean surrounding the ship.

The room seemed too small to Lucia, especially for an Admiral. Normally it was locked, a glass window allowing visitors a staged viewing of the private life of one of its warrior chiefs. On display was a facsimile of the way it would have been kept a half century before, shoes shined and neatly placed on the floor by the side of the bed, which was nothing more than a raised wooden box with a mattress on top. An irregularly shaped shelf bordered the head and one side of the bed, which was built into the wall at a slight angle. A calendar hung by the side of the bed. It was the month of November, 1974 and Lucia had no idea if there was any significance to the month and year. She was not sure why Sydney had picked this particular room. She guessed that if it was safe enough for a fleet Admiral then it must be as good a place as any for them to hide and wait. Wait for what exactly, she was only vaguely certain.

She closed her eyes, sitting on the floor, knees up with her head against the side of the bed. Quiet Japanese emanated from the frightened voices of the Katsuyama family, huddled closely together, the cadence and timbre of the sound, hypnotic, soothing Lucia and relaxing her mind, vanquishing temporarily the floating images projected on the insides of her eyelids, a horrible collection, a grim scrapbook of the worst she had seen this day.

She fell into a fluttering state of semi-consciousness, losing herself, retreating from her immediate surroundings, recalling the words and images she had heard and seen while in the trance state—could it only be two hours since she had fainted?

They had never spoken to her before this, except she now realized the experience with Adam in her apartment the night before was a similar circumstance. She knew it without remembering it or what she may have said. Poor Adam. No wonder he bolted. She must have scared him beyond salvaging. If he thought she was a freak before, what must he be thinking now? How to get him past this? How to make him see that her abilities were not an impediment to a relationship? He's afraid, and she knew of what. Afraid she could see through him, see his truth.

It was his love for Donna he was afraid she would see. He was afraid to share his heart, as if to do so would be counted as a betrayal, to Donna and to Lucia's love for him. What a fool. Lucia knew she could never replace Donna. She loved Adam and was willing to accept all the love he could give her. But she knew Adam; he was an on and off guy, black and white, and a relationship composed of shades of gray frightened and repelled him. She did not know if he would ever be able to accept their relationship except within the context of his life with Donna. What a waste.

She recalled the words of the Masters. Funny, but it did not seem to matter to her who or what they were. Beings from a different universe or another plane of existence, she neither knew nor cared. There was only this intuitive sense of who they were, master spirits, with a tireless benevolence for mankind.

She knew now they had always been there in her life, in different guises: imaginary friend, hallucination, dream—a silent guiding hand. There had been events and incidents during her childhood, most undetected or misdiagnosed by her teachers, therapists and certainly by her parents who watched their child grow up in her own shaped solitude, a happy child but a distant one, who listened with one ear towards the earth and one cocked towards who knew where.

Even Lucia had been fooled for a long time, unable and a little unwilling to consider her abilities at all extraordinary. Part of the problem was reference. Sydney had said it best. Seeing a person's aura was normal for her. She remembered sitting in the bleachers at high school and seeing in her mind the winner of a hundred yard dashing crossing the finish line before the starter's gun had gone off. It was disconcerting—why bother running the race if everybody already knows who's going to win—but it did not seem any different to Lucia than dreaming about a cute boy after seeing him in the school yard. For Lucia, information travelled in both directions, from her mind to reality and vice versa.

It was during early adolescence, that cruel stage when life informs you of your limitations, highlights your differences and shortcomings, then trots them out for all to see, when Lucia finally figured it all out and although she would never claim as dramatic a coming-out party as Carrie at the prom, to her it had much of the same dramatic impact.

156

There was a brown card lying loose in a small brown leather-bound book. The Catholic Girl's Guide. She had found the worn book in an attic box one day when rooting through a trunk full of her mother's antique dolls.

Counsels and Devotions

FOR

GIRLS IN THE ORDINARY WALKS OF LIFE

AND IN PARTICULAR FOR

THE CHILDREN OF MARY

Lucia could rarely get past the title page. She would carefully study the words, consider hidden meanings in the typeface, the font size, the use of capitals and gothic style. And what was an ordinary walk of life? And who were the children of Mary, for whom the book had been particularly written? Her mother said they were virgins, good Catholic girls, and Lucia imagined hidden codes within the pages, visible only to those with their maidenhead intact, unavailable to the fallen, a book whose mysteries were revealed to the chaste, to the pure of heart and body. But she did not know any girls who weren't virgins, and at age thirteen, she couldn't imagine her friends engaging in anything so horrible any time soon so she had no way of testing out her theory, of studying the text with a fallen angel and comparing notes.

No one in her family really knew for sure where the book had come from. There was a dedication on the first blank page, handwritten with fountain ink, a steady, slow hand had written it; *To Elizabeth From Rev. Starky*, it said, and there was a great Aunt named Liz, on Lucia's mother's side, so it was always believed to be hers only how it came to be in their attic, her parents could not recall.

Their church gave Lucia the creeps. Jesus with his bloody hands, hanging helplessly on a stick, the priest, smelling from the obnoxious mixture of Ivory Snow and cigarettes, the fingers of his right hand stained brown, Lucia believed, as a type of empathetic gesture towards the Savior. Sitting in Confession was excruciating for her; the shadow of him lurking behind the screen, his low voice exhuming stale smoke from the depths of his lungs and filling the confessional with poisonous invisible clouds, microscopic priestly detritus escaping into the air.

She would grab the ledge beneath the screen with both hands and run her thumbs along the underside that someone had desecrated with dried chunks of bumpy gum, stuck forever in memorial to the chewer's past sins, and for Lucia it was a kind of penance, breathing in the stale air, touching the foul remainders of someone's wad, *Forgive me Father for I have sinned*, and she had to remember back to her last visit, and recount her sins, pressing her thumbs deeper into the hardened lumps, softening them with the heat from her skin, guilty, never coming completely clean, never revealing the whole truth, walking away, rubbing her palms against her skirt, saying her Hail Marys and Our Fathers, then escaping, head down, out of the church.

Suscipe Sancte Pater Hanc Immaculatam Hostiam.

There was a card in the book. It was a kind of souvenir. A remembrance of the ordination and first mass of a young priest. His calling and calling card. On the front, in all His glory, a plate depicting the crucified Christ, nailed to the cross, the Heavenly Father above Him, two priestly hands holding the plate high, Holy Communion, and the words, the Latin words she did not know, although she could make out 'father' and 'immaculate host' and there was an English blessing on the back, but too many words to be a translation.

A remembrance of my Ordination and First Mass, it said and it was dated, not by hand, rather, printed, a clerical business card, May 12th and 13th, 1951, a Saturday and Sunday, she had checked.

Seipsum Obtulit Immaculatu Deo.

The card was brown and a little faded, gold-embossed highlights around the perimeter of the plate, two gold circles behind the heads of the Christ and the Heavenly Father, rich in detail, sepia tone, the priest holding the plate high over his head, his cuffs detailed in gold, an art museum disguised as a religion, form over substance, arcane language meant to keep the congregation at bay, away from the private domain of the priesthood, the voice of God speaking through His priests, a card heralding the arrival of one more mouthpiece for the Lord.

She was not religious, not like her mother, who every Sunday would drag Lucia with her, the two of them marching smartly along the sidewalk, Lucia's arm chain-linked with her mother's, the men left behind, always refusing each week to attend, and there was this singular image Lucia had of her mother in church, clutching her rosary beads with a white-knuckled intensity, eyes searching the high ceiling for a glimpse of God, kneeling, always kneeling, whispered Latin spoken into her hands, the sun's rays filtering through the stained glass and spreading over her mother, making her glow in a golden wash of ecclesiastical light.

And still it did not move Lucia, did not bring her closer to her mother's God, to Jesus. There were other voices she heard, other gods who spoke to her, who gave her guidance and listened to her complaints. She genuflected, kneeled down, took Communion, went dutifully to Confession, but the counsel she took came from within.

He who has not the Church for his mother, cannot have God for his Father, the little brown book said.

Later she would have a word for it, Gnostic, but for now they were her guardian angels, benevolent helpers who whispered in her ear, appearing before her in the sky and watching over her, always protecting, always comforting.

Until she touched the card.

The book was in her possession for several years. She liked the way it felt, small but weighty, delicate and worn, the patent leather peeling at the corner seams. And the words inside could amuse her, though designed to frighten and cajole. And carrying it around made her mother happy. It became part of Lucia's disguise.

The card slipped out one day. She was in her room after Sunday church, changing into her jeans when the book fell from her bed. There were other strange and beautiful depictions stuck between the pages, one a bookmark, embossed with gold flowers, *Best Wishes For A Happy Feast*, it said, another a petite Get Well card. Lucia tried not to disturb these personal relics, rarely removing them from their resting place. The brown card lay a few inches from the book. As she picked it up she turned it over out of habit.

A remembrance of my Ordination and First Mass

It was dated and there was a name. The new priest had a name and she mouthed it out loud, she said his name clearly and that was when she saw him.

She said his name for no particular reason, heard the words, Jeffrey John Forsythe come out of her mouth and her room suddenly disappeared—no, not completely—it was as if someone had come in and turned off the lights, only it was 1:30 in the afternoon and a beautiful spring day and Lucia's room had a southwestern exposure which made it frightfully hot in summer and wonderfully warm in winter.

There is a scene, a holographic kind of image, slightly out of focus, of a man on the ground, and four men in green uniforms are screaming at him in a language Lucia does not understand. He is lying on the ground and Lucia can see his white collar soiled by the muddy road where he lays, and he is pleading with the men, but not for himself, not in a desperate, terrified way.

He keeps trying to get up but every time he does one of the men shoves the muzzle of his rifle into the small of the priest's back and forces him onto the ground. The soldiers are yelling at him and at each other. They are speaking Spanish, Lucia thinks, and there is a frenetic cadence to their speech that is more frightening than the images she sees.

He is asking them to spare the children, they have done nothing wrong, they are orphans, he says, and he is telling them this in English then switches to Spanish and Lucia somehow understands what he is saying.

He keeps turning his head, trying to make eye contact, trying to break through the dulled humanity of the soldiers. He is explaining the children's plight, the late night visit by rebels to their village, the massacre of their parents before their eyes when one of the soldiers screams *"Sandinista!"* and shoots the priest in the head.

Her parents found Lucia semi-conscious on the floor of her room. A wild tale about a murdered priest did little to ease their concern as Lucia recounted the vision, hysterically crying and holding a faded brown card and sobbing, "It's him, I saw him and watched him die!"

A visit to Emergency revealed no physical ailment and so began a long series of doctor visits: neurologists, psychiatrists, psychologists, homeopaths, none of whom could find the source of Lucia's problem. Lucia made sure of that. Because a day after the vision, she was eating breakfast with her father when she saw him again, the priest, staring out at her from the backside of the newspaper her dad was reading, a kind of publicity photo, from the shoulders up, white collared, younger and very serious, the headline describing the murder of an American priest in San Salvador.

She knew then to say nothing more of the incident, or of her secret

160

talent or ethereal companions. She also realized there had been a change—an escalation or promotion or graduation—and she was no longer a virgin, no longer a child of Mary because her benefactors had bloodied her, had taken away her innocence, and in its stead they had placed prescience.

And only now, while sitting in a cramped room once occupied by men who wielded enormous martial power, with a dozen assorted strangers, waiting for a shared fate so horrible Lucia could not formulate an image in her head to marry to the thought, did she finally understand her role after years of denial, of wasting her talents on parlour games and half hearted advice.

Sydney came over and sat down next to Lucia. They had not said much while Lucia followed the big man around his ship, first to the equipment room for a chainsaw and sledgehammer, then down to the pier where the giant ropes were secured to their moorings. It seemed a pity to cut the ropes but Sydney said there wasn't enough time or manpower to do a proper job of it. When cut through, the ropes sagged towards the hull of the ship. The chainsaw made talk impossible which was fine with Lucia who had run out of anything to say for perhaps the first time in her life.

During a lull, while they were walking from the bow to the stern on the hanger deck, where two huge chain mooring lines were attached at either end, Lucia inquired as to the seaworthiness of the vessel.

"If you mean will she float, sure. We can make her pretty secure. Depends what you have in mind though."

"I saw something terrible, a huge wave engulfing the entire city."

"I'm not sure she's up to something like that," said Sydney and there was no panic in his voice, merely opinion.

"Have you ever had . . . have voices spoken . . . through you?" she asked.

"No, nothing like that. I see colours, is all. Every since I was a boy. When I was eight I had meningitis. They thought I was going to die. My mama said my temperature went to a hundred and six. But I'm still here as you can plainly see. When I woke up after the fever broke, my mama was sitting on the bed, wiping my forehead with a damp cloth, and I thought I was in heaven because she was surrounded by a golden light. I remember I said, Mama, did you die, too? and she laughed and told me it was the fever making me see things, but it never went away."

161

"What did you think it was?"

They were near the stern and Sydney was about to pull the starter cord to the chainsaw, but he stopped and turned to face Lucia.

"I always thought it was a gift from God. For surviving the fever. A special award. He gave me the ability to see people for who they really are, good or bad. The colour tells me about people. It's more than light. It's a message. I think of it as a person's billboard, blinking, *This is me.*"

"So who am I?" she asked timidly a little later, as Sydney swung hard at a spike, held by Lucia against a small round bar embedded inside the last link of the mammoth mooring chain, the ringing sound of metal on metal nullifying the question.

Sitting next to her on the floor of the Admiral's cabin, Sydney put his arm around her and pulled her close. She nestled her head against his chest and sniffed the laundered freshness of his starched blue shirt. It felt good to be hugged by this bear of a man. It made her wonder how different her life might have been had her father taken some time to hold her in his arms. She grabbed for Brian and pulled him close, and he wrapped his little arms almost around her waist.

"I know who you are," he whispered into her hair, and it felt like the nicest thing anyone had ever said to her.

They were all staring at the two of them, the security guards whose names she did not know, the two veterans, the tourists, all of them with their frightened eyes on Lucia and Sydney and the intensity of their collective auras was increasing with each breath taken, filling the room with a holy glow, a rainbow of dazzling light, the room sunlit by an inner star radiating out from each of them.

From outside came a thunderous roar, the sound of furious water, Niagara Falls times ten, increasing until even the Japanese woman's screams could barely be detected. Lucia felt the grip on her shoulder grow tighter, Sydney yelling and pointing for everyone to hold onto something and Andy was shouting too, pointing to his belt and then taking it off and demonstrating, like a stewardess with a seatbelt, how to loop it through the pipes in the ceiling so they'll have something to hang on to. Lucia thought of the movie, Twister, the climactic scene with the two lovers tied by straps to a well pipe, hanging perpendicular to the ground, feet in the air and it is going to look something like that in here soon.

The wave hits the ship and the first sensation is leaving the floor and almost crashing into the ceiling, Lucia's feet slamming into it

162

but the rest of her is pulled down by Sydney's arm. She's upside down, attached to Sydney who has one hand gripped around a small railing at the foot of the bed, the other still holding her, his hand digging into her armpit. She feels Brian holding onto one leg, then one of the Japanese children, the boy, comes crashing into Lucia's chest and Sydney loses his grip.

She hits her head against something and can no longer tell how the ship is faring, she is twirling around, being thrown around like clothes in a dryer, from floor to ceiling to wall, no resistance now, people crashing into her, screaming, the deafening roar of the water, then blackness.

How many times today? Lucia thought. How many times have I seen the darkness? Her world divided between black unconscious and waking light. On the floor again, she thought, though this floor had a decidedly tilted aspect and only then did she realize she had been placed on the Admiral's berth. She moved her head and surveyed the room. Everyone was alive if not robust. The boy who had crashed into her was crying in his mother's arms, bleeding from the corner of his eyebrow, she with a weak, thin gray light emanating from her skin. Sydney was over by Hernando who was sporting a nasty gash to augment his already damaged leg. Everyone else was conscious and appeared unbroken, save for cuts and bruises.

The aircraft carrier was listing to the starboard side, the superstructure leaning towards the water. Lucia pushed her nose against the window. The list was so severe she had to duck her head down low to see anything beyond the horizon. A horizon of mad, brown water.

"I can't see a damn thing," she said to the porthole.

Lucia made her way over to Sydney. Hernando's eyes were closed wincing tight, as Sydney wound a makeshift bandage around the cut.

"Is he okay?" she asked Sydney.

Hernando opened one eye and said, "Gonna take more than a bump on the head to get rid of me. You're the one we were worrying about."

"You got to stop passing out on me, girl," said Sydney.

"How long has it been?" she asked.

"I figure it's been a good half hour since the wave hit," said Sydney. "After I'm finished with Hernando here, I'm going out to do a little reconnaissance."

With some effort, Sydney opened the door and carefully stepped outside.

"I'm coming too," said Lucia, scrambling past the others to the door.

Over the edge of the flight deck they could make out the Jersey shoreline, a changing feature as the headwaters of the wave made their way back towards them, the ship shuddering as it absorbed the conflicting and strange currents.

"They're all gone," Sydney said and it took a moment for Lucia to realize he was referring to the planes and helicopters she had first seen when climbing up the stairs to the flight deck. She saw the sadness in his eyes and could not understand it. With their world disappearing before them, it did not seem appropriate to be wasting any remorse on a few rusting relics of this ship's past. Sydney seemed to sense her detachment, muttering something about an old warrior seeing his life disappear before his eyes. He pointed to the flight deck, the raised port side partially obstructing their view to the west.

"About a twenty degree list, I figure," said Sydney.

"Is that good or bad?" Lucia asked.

"It's never good. I have to go below and see if the flooding is contained. If we're taking in water, we'll have to get off the ship somehow."

He grabbed the side rails and slid down the steep steps to the lower deck where he unsealed a door and climbed back into the superstructure.

Andy came out of the Admiral's quarters and stood next to Lucia. He sucked in a large chest full of air, a seaman's gulp, and he smiled, grasping the railing with both hands to steady himself.

"Hell of a day," he said.

He had a light blue aura and Lucia was struck by the calmness she felt from him. There were so many emotions swirling around her. She felt the intense panic from the people on the ship and beyond, distant places, being bombarded with a myriad of negative emotions; fear, anger, panic, shock swirling in the air, little pinpricks landing on her and distorting her own feelings. But Andy somehow was taking this all in and maintaining a mental ease that Lucia found hard to fathom.

"I worked on the planes," said Andy. "I was part of a crew in charge of making them ready for combat. We were a team. We had our own pilots we were responsible for. Everything we did was to make sure they came back alive. We never had pets in my house. My mother said the apartment was too small. These young pilots, they were like taking care of a pet. Or maybe a racehorse. Most of them were kids, fresh out of college. We took care of them. One day we were running a training exercise and one of our boys lands funny and his plane pitches forward and the propeller breaks off and goes right through the cockpit. I was the first one to the plane and there's blood everywhere and I pull the kid out and only half of him comes with me. I'm holding onto him and half of him's still in the plane. I think about it every day. You never forget something like that. You never stop thanking the good Lord for every day He grants you. And you never forgive Him for what He did to your friends."

As he spoke, the calmness Lucia felt from him was displaced by a sorrow she had never experienced; she saw him on the flight deck with the dead half carcass of the pilot in his arms and felt his tears on her own cheeks and she understood his calm in the face of this new disaster for nothing further could deepen this man's lament, even the end of his world.

The waters continued to recede and the force of their withdrawal was pushing the ship back towards the city. Rudderless and powerless, the giant craft turned slowly in the surging waters. The tops of buildings broke the surface, small islands dotting the seascape.

Lucia wondered if there was a proper response to the annihilation of a way of life, of a culture and country built on the premise of everlasting stability. Was there a dormant gene lying in reserve, waiting for a judgment day to activate and lead the organism through the debris of a civilization destroyed? Do you laugh at the insanity until the laughter turns to tears, then madness? Do you turn and look back, like Lot's wife, or do you force yourself to move forward and never look over your shoulder? Or do you travel, as had Andy, to a more horrible place, a place of memory so painful it made the hopelessness of today seem small and manageable?

For as long as she could remember, Lucia had felt herself to be an emotional barometer, absorbing assorted feelings from invisible sources, living in a world that bore little resemblance to her inner world of feelings. Now, for the first time, these absorbed feelings underscored her outer perceptions like an emotional soundtrack, beating within her in rhythm to the ruination of the outside world, the cries of the dead and dying filling her head with intolerable suffering.

She turned away from the railing, as if her exposed position on the flag bridge was making her more susceptible to the junk floating around in the spiritual plane. Andy placed a sinewy arm around her and hugged her. There was so much vitality in the small man, his

165

bony frame belying the magnificence of his being.

Andy said, "I don't suppose I want to know how you knew this was going to happen."

"It doesn't much matter now. I only wish I knew what's going to happen from this point forward."

"My crystal ball says we get off this ship or we die."

"I don't think we were allowed to survive an earthquake and then this so we could all die out here."

"Then you haven't seen God when He's really pissed," said Andy and he spat over the railing, nailing the flight deck, Lucia was certain, precisely where he had aimed his gob.

"People tend to get the gods they deserve," said Lucia.

"Really. Have you had a chance to think about the number of babies, of small children and decent people who have died this day. Did they get the God they deserved?"

Another flying spittle hit the same spot on the flight deck.

"Perhaps the sins of the father do reign down upon the sons."

"Fact is, I'm not a religious person. And I'm no philosopher. But if the world is being punished for misbehaving then I don't see how the punishment fits the crime. A lot of innocent people died today, God bless their souls. And a God who would do that, who would be so indiscriminate is not a God I wish to follow or obey another day more."

"She's the same God who let you live."

"Then she's fickle and stupid and reminds me a lot of my ex-wife."

Lucia let out a very unfeminine chortle and the somber mood was broken for the moment. Sydney reappeared from below deck, taking the stairs in two leaps.

"We have two major problems," he said, the breaths coming short and fast as he bent over the railing, inspecting something below.

"She's sinking," said Andy.

"It's coming in down somewhere in the berth area near where you and I bunked. If it gets up to the hanger deck we won't have much time."

"Dare I ask about problem number two?" said Lucia.

The carrier's bow now pointed in a southeasterly direction. Sydney leaned on the rail and pointed in the direction of the bow.

"The current is taking us out. Unless we run aground or figure out a way to steer this hulk we're going to drift out to sea."

The wind was picking up, tossing Lucia's bangs across her forehead.

166

As she casually brushed them aside she noticed Andy staring at her.

"What?"

"Nothing," said Andy.

"No really. Do I have food on my face or something?"

"It's nothing. I was just noticing the breeze." Andy licked his index finger and held it up the way you would to get a waiter's attention.

"What do you think we should do?" he asked Sydney.

"I was hoping you had an idea. We have no lifeboats, no engines. I'm not too sure if the rudders are still attached."

"It's getting windy," said Andy.

"Uh huh."

"It's coming off the ocean."

"Sure, but not nearly strong enough to defeat the current."

Andy leaned way over the railing.

"I'm thinking about another pickle we were in."

A big, banana-sized smile appeared on Sydney's face.

"Truk Island," said Sydney.

"Bingo."

"Do you think it will work?"

"Would you have put any money on it working the first time?"

"No, but now we don't even have engines."

"Will somebody please tell me what you're talking about," said Lucia, tugging on Sydney's shirtsleeve.

Sydney said, "In February of 1944 a Jap torpedo plane nailed us with a torpedo. Eleven men were killed. It damaged one of our rudders. We couldn't steer the ship because all of the engine power was coming from one side. We were steaming in a wide circle and we were sitting ducks. Someone came up with the idea of hoisting a sail off the port bow to compensate for the engine imbalance. And it worked. We straightened out and sailed for Pearl Harbor. That sail saved our lives."

"Maybe with a little luck," said Andy, "we can push this baby back towards New Jersey."

"So what do we use for a sail?" asked Lucia.

The two men smiled at each other.

"There's plenty of tarp on board," Sydney said.

"And you think this will work?" said Lucia.

Andy said, "Listen lady, you are on board the Fighting I. This ship has taken many a knockout blow and has somehow come back up swinging. She always makes her way back home."

They went back inside and convened a brief meeting with the others. All of the men followed Andy and Sydney down to the flight deck to search for an adequate makeshift sail. Lucia stayed with the two women and children. She was suddenly overwhelmed by fatigue and coldness. She stuck her hands into the large pockets of Adam's coat and drew it close around her. Her hand found itself grasping something hard and familiar. She withdrew it, knowing it to be Adam's cell phone before her hand presented it to her eyes for inspection.

It was extremely small, accounting for her not detecting it sooner. She began scrolling through Adam's programmed numbers. She stopped when she got to Derek's name. The battery meter was extremely low. She would be allowed maybe one call before the phone went dead. She flipped through a few more names, saw *HOME* and *COACH* listed but she could not imagine landline phones still working.

She so desperately wanted to see Adam again. But she was afraid to try the phone and have it ring and ring, unanswered. She couldn't not try. Not when there was a possibility of saving everyone on the boat. Adam would think of a way.

One shot, she thought. She flipped back to Derek's name and pressed the button marked *SND*.

XIII

A FISH FLOPPED BY THE SIDE of the road, black eyes gaping, dumbfounded and near dead. It lay in a small pool of water, a cruel reminder of the sea that had left it behind.

"Finally, sushi in Montclair," said Derek.

Adam and Derek had made their way down to North Mountain Avenue, picking their way through debris, much of it originating in New York. They passed by a Ray's Pizza sign and Derek was certain it came from the store on Seventh Avenue that he often frequented.

Every home they saw was extensively damaged, windows smashed, walls collapsed, many with missing roofs—one house they passed had been completely shorn from its foundation.

There were bodies, but not too many. Most, Adam figured, would have been swept away or trapped within their homes. The only person Adam had seen alive since the flood was a neighbour a few houses down, a man whose name he did not know. Adam had spotted him standing at the edge of his driveway. Derek had called out, causing the man to turn abruptly and head hurriedly up his driveway.

"It won't still be there," Derek said as they walked carefully up the littered street.

"I don't need any of those negative vibes, man," said Adam.

"Are you kidding? You were born with them."

They came to a high hedge, still standing firm except where a fallen tree had sliced it in two. The only glimpse of the otherwise concealed house came as you crossed the driveway. It was an oddly spectacular home, an architectural misfit in a neighbourhood of stately Tudors and refined Queen Anne Victorians, a bold display of pink stucco and rounded roof tiles. A cement fishpond with a decorative footbridge dominated the landscaping in front.

Adam stood on the trunk and grasped the hedge to steady himself. He slowly surveyed the front lawn area, his eyes stopping at the spot on the driveway where he had seen it numerous times before. His disappointment was immediate. He climbed back off the tree and joined Derek on the sidewalk.

"Well?" said Derek.

"It's not there," said Adam.

"I'm not sure how you thought it would be."

"I don't know. Wishful thinking I guess. Let's go back."

They crossed the street and came to an empty lot between two houses.

"You're sure she said *Intrepid*."

"Yes," said Adam. "How could I be mistaken about that? She didn't say Enterprise or Missouri or Yorktown. She said Intrepid. She said aircraft carrier. I think I'm on safe ground here."

"Fine, I believe you. It's hard to imagine, that's all. It's so fucking incredible to imagine. And only your Lucia could pull something like this off. You have got to marry that girl."

"If we don't find a boat soon she may never have the opportunity to refuse me."

"Right. She has one dime with her life on the line and she calls you. And you still don't get how much she digs you."

"Technically she called you, not me."

"All these years and I'm still running interference for you. By the way, is the thing we're looking for yellow?"

"Where?" asked Adam.

"Right over there," said Derek, pointing across the lot to a back-yard stand of low holly trees.

"That's it," said Adam, and he felt like running, he wanted to know immediately if the boat was damaged but instead he walked slowly, taking in the hull, noting the two propellers facing upwards and the abscence of holes and cracks, trying not to get too optimistic.

The boat had been sitting on its trailer the entire summer. It was a ski boat with twin 100 horsepower engines, two forward seats and two seats facing the rear. It was made of fiberglass, stamped out on the assembly line in one molten moment.

The overturned motors were leaking oil and there were pieces of fiberglass missing but mostly on the gunnels.

"It just might be okay," said Derek.

"Help me turn it over."

The trailer was still attached to the boat which made flipping it a bit difficult.

"Think we should go ask your neighbour if we can borrow it?" asked Derek who was doubled over, catching his breath.

"You go ask him. I'm pulling this back to the house."

Adam pushed from the rear while Derek pulled from the trailer hitch. Their progress was slow and painful. There were frequent stops for breath and to allow screaming joints and muscles to quiet. They were moving along a relatively flat stretch of road and had now come to an intersection where the only choice was uphill.

"We can't do this without a car," said Derek.

"There's too much junk on the road for me to bring the Jeep down here."

"Then how the hell are we going to get it to the water."

"I don't know. I'll think of something."

Derek lay spread-eagled on a lawn, the grass surprisingly dry, not that Derek would have cared. He rubbed the spot near his wound and complained constantly of the throbbing pain.

"I didn't think the end of the world would feel like this," said Derek. "It's kind of like sex with a stranger, don't you think? Anticipation, huge buildup, an explosion and then nothing. You wonder what all the fuss was about. You're satiated but somehow unfulfilled. Anticlimactic. Like, so what do we do now?"

"I don't really know how to respond to something so . . . so puerile."

"Don't think I don't know what that means."

"Good. Then you understand how your boredom with what will be referred to by historians as the worst natural disaster in recorded history—provided humanity survives to write about it—is somehow lost on me."

"You deal with it in your way and I'll deal with it in mine. To me, we just got fucked by the universe. Maybe we deserved it, maybe we had it coming, I don't know. I was having a pretty good time until now and then this happens."

"This isn't about you," said Adam.

"You are wrong about that, my friend. This has happened to my world, my life. From where I sit, this is totally, completely and absolutely about me."

Derek put his arm around Adam and pulled his head into his chest.

"And since you're my best buddy, this is about you too. Don't you feel lucky to be part of my universe?"

"Delighted."

They stood up to continue their task. Derek grabbed Adam's forearm.

"I know that look. You still miss her, don't you?" said Derek.

"Every day. I constantly find myself thinking, what would Donna think of this, or would she like that. Stupid stuff."

"Maybe it's time to stop doing that."

"Maybe."

"I wonder what the gardener is up to."

"What made you think of him?" asked Adam.

"We are all tied together somehow; you, me, our wives, John Walker, even Lucia. I can't think of one of us without thinking of all of us."

"He's probably sitting on his porch with his boots up, sucking back a cool one and taking this all in."

"You ever going to tell me the whole story? You and John Walker that night in the desert?"

"You were there, for Christ's sake. And I've already told you what happened."

"No, I don't think so. I don't think you told me all of it. Not the important stuff."

"We don't have the time for this. I'm going to go get the Jeep and see if I can find a way down to here."

The explosion from the Mercurys shattered the stillness, eradicating the death lull hovering over the neighbourhood. Blue smoke spewed out of the exhaust holes of both engines, one of them deciding whether to stall or continue before finally responding, catching up to the whining sound of its twin.

Adam turned off the engines and the sound of them lingered, like distant thunder.

"No sense in wasting gas. They seem to be working fine."

Adam jumped out and joined Derek and Jenny beside the boat.

Adam had gone back to the shed where he discovered half a case of lawnmower oil, which was used to top up the outboard engines.

"How's your head? You up for this?" asked Adam.

"I'm fine."

"He is like hell," said Jenny. "He should be in bed. He has a concussion. Tell him. Tell him about the blurred vision."

"I have blurred vision. Happy now?"

"How can you tell," said Adam. "You're stoned most of the time."

"I'm serious," Jenny said. "You don't know what's out there. It could be terribly dangerous. I love Lucia. We all do. But this is insanity. He's hurt, Adam. Please make him stay."

Adam had never seen her more beautiful. He was so captivated that he failed to notice it at first, the thin green line of light encasing her entire body.

"What?" she asked, startled by the expression on Adam's face.

"Nothing. You're right. Derek should stay."

"In a pig's ear I'm staying. There's no way you can pull this off by yourself. And I've had hangovers worse than this."

Derek took Jenny in his arms and kissed her.

"Where were you twenty-five years ago?"

"In my crib."

"It was worth the wait. I'll be all right. I have to do this. Adam needs me and honestly, I feel fine."

"Then I'm coming, too," she said.

"That's not a good idea," said Adam.

"Because it's dangerous?"

"Yes."

"But staying alone in this mausoleum, unprotected, is safe?"

Adam was confounded by her logic and stunned by his newfound ability to see what could only be her aura. He tried not to stare but could not take his eyes away from her. It was not only green he saw, there was also a reddish hue with hints of blue and orange. He almost wanted to keep her in her agitated state so he could continue to observe her. He looked past her to the front yard, watched as the greens of the lawns and trees began to emit a translucence before unobserved, shimmering in hues of vibrant colour, alive, and then he remembered seeing something like this once before, on peyote, and the thought of it allowed his anxiety from that experience to unleash itself, breaking the spell and returning Adam to the primary colours of everyday life.

Derek said, "So what do you say? I don't feel too good about leaving her alone here."

"She can come."

They hitched the boat to the back of Adam's Jeep Cherokee. It was slow and arduous as they made their way through Montclair. Adam worked the vehicle from open space to open space, stopping every few yards to remove obstructions or scout around those impossible to move. Jenny displayed an uncanny knack for navigation and soon both men were turning to her for the next instruction when the way clear seemed impossible.

Jenny directed them across lawns and into backyards; she found laneways and easements, the Jeep blazing a trail through the cultured remains of a hundred years of attended gardens, pruned bushes and manicured hedges. Adam, his hands death gripping the steering wheel, offered up a silent prayer of forgiveness for every vandalized bush, each crushed flower garden, as the vehicle slowly made its way through the soggy, littered landscape.

They saw no one alive. Bodies, gray-skinned, some torn and bloody, others in pristine sleep, became a familiar sight. Adam was terrified of running over one. He thought of the little girl, the futility of it, of the burial, having now seen scores of the dead, many of them just as twisted, young and old, in identical need of dignity and a final place of rest, but he could not help them, he had had time for only one symbolic gesture.

One person can only do so much, he thought, as he tried to concentrate on driving the car. There was only so much one could endure. Adam longed for sleep. To close his eyes and wish this day away, if only for a few hours. He wondered if the dreams would stop now. They had been terrifying, but in a perverse way, he would miss them. He was already nostalgic for his private terror, confined as it had been to his inner world, his path of escape always an eye opening away. Now the terror lay before him, eyes wide open.

How much could one endure?

A lot apparently.

There had to be a reason for his survival. It couldn't be an arbitrary accident. He was alive. The people he loved most were alive. There was a reason. Please let there be a reason.

Although the main body of water had withdrawn back towards New York, there were many low-lying areas where shallow lakes and turbulent rivers now formed. They would only know where the new shoreline was when they came upon it. Along the way Adam knew there would be impassable expanses of trapped water; valleys to the east would be choked full, and although the boat could be used to traverse across these areas, there was no guarantee they would be able to find their way out of them to the open water.

"I have an idea," said Adam as they sat, contemplating a dip in the road on Bloomfield Avenue where three to four feet of water had accumulated.

"Does it involve a helicopter?" asked Derek.

"No. A train."

"I doubt they're running today."

"I'm counting on that. The Boonton line runs straight from here to Hoboken. I take it every day. We should be able to follow it to the edge of the flood. With any luck, the trestles will still be in place and above water. I can't think of any other way to the shoreline."

They made their way to the train tracks by cutting back through the commercial area north of Bloomfield Avenue. The tracks crossed at Walnut Street and Adam turned the car onto them.

Almost immediately they ran into trouble where the tracks led under a bridge. Water filled the man-made gorge. Derek got out and made his way onto the bridge, backtracking then leading the car on foot through a wooded area then over the bridge and back to the tracks further down the line.

In Glen Ridge they passed a commuter train flung by the wave from the track, lying dismembered, cars scattered football fields apart like discarded children's toys. Most of the windows were smashed and they could see bodies piled in heaps inside, pressed against the window frames, arms and legs protruding from the openings. Jenny wept silently as they passed. Adam kept his eyes on the track but Derek's were riveted to the carnage.

"That could have been you or Jenny," Derek said.

"Thank God for Lucia," said Adam.

"And you, good buddy. Despite your flirtation with the straight and narrow, in your heart you believed her—you knew something was up."

"Maybe," Adam said and the car went quiet as they continued their tightrope dance down the tracks.

Adam stopped before the trestle crossing the Garden State Parkway. They all got out and walked onto the overpass. The parkway was a raging torrent of water, about ten feet deep, sweeping cars and trees to the south. The vibrations caused by floating debris striking the foundations of the bridge initiated a quick retreat to the car and Adam crossed the watery maelstrom as quickly as he dared.

After close to an hour of agonizingly slow travel—fortunately the only tree in the way was a small one the three of them managed to lift off the tracks—the car approached the ridge overlooking the Passaic River. They were in the northeast corner of Newark though there wasn't much left of the residential section they were passing through. From the tracks they could see foundations and flooded basements and the remains of various building materials tossed everywhere the eye settled; furniture, appliances and personal effects seeded amongst the rubble.

After a while, Adam got used to seeing human carcasses. The further they went, the more numerous were the visible victims of the killer wave. They had yet to see a living person, only birds that seemed crazed; screeching and flying madly in quick loops and high angled turns.

As the car moved onto the crest of the ridge, the swollen Passaic came into view. The river had risen to a prehistoric level, filling half the river valley, obliterating any trace of the train trestle over the river and drowning riverside properties for hundreds of feet on either side. It was an impressive sight but it was eclipsed by something far more surreal.

Adam's attention was first caught by the jet ski's rooster tail, a tall plume of backwash cascading in a rainbow arc. The driver was slaloming around the floating debris. After the momentary shock had passed, Adam saw that the rider had friends, for now three more jet skis came into view.

"I can't fucking believe this," said Derek.

They moved to the edge of the water and walked up the bank a bit. Adam found the whine of the jet ski almost obscene, given the circumstances. Within the mechanical noise he was sure he could hear some human activity up ahead.

About a hundred yards or so up river they came to a wide thoroughfare named Mill Street. The road now poured directly into the river. A mini fleet of outboard motor boats was beached and moored to lampposts and parking meters. A group of young men, Adam counted eleven, decked out in wet suits, stood by the shoreline, hooting and hollering, shouting encouraging invectives to their comrades on the river.

"Hey, we've got company," said one of them, a tall blond youth of about twenty, his skintight body suit accenting his finely tuned frame of hardened muscle. His wet bangs hung down over his forehead in clumps, droplets of waters falling off them and onto his cheeks. He introduced himself as Jim, his eyes never leaving Jenny while he spoke. Derek stepped up to a few inches from the young man's face.

"What exactly are you guys doing out there?" asked Derek.

"What . . . that? It's wild out there, man. There is so much junk in the water. First one to fall loses."

"Loses what?"

"You know. His turn."

The others came over to meet the strangers. They were all bulked up with close shaven hair, surprisingly well tanned considering the time of year and if they told you they were all members of a college football or wrestling team you would have had no problem believing it so. There were tattoos and body piercings in abundance, the former on arms and shoulder blades and ankles, the latter through noses, ears and nipples. Adam thought of his earlier encounter with an entirely dissimilar gang of young men and for some reason this group caused him more uneasiness, as if the danger was hidden and more ambiguous.

The young men had come down the Passaic River from West Paterson, a community on the other side of the same ridge Adam's house was located on. They were old high school buddies, Jim explained, spending most of their summer free time on the Jersey Shore "drinking, fucking and jet skiing—and in that order".

"Man, we thought the season was over and then this. We can't ever use the river you know. It's against the law. But there's no one to fuckin' stop us now."

The accelerated pitch of a jet ski propeller out of water and a scream ended the socializing. The boys ran to their assorted watercraft and headed into the river. One of the contestants had hit a submerged object and was thrown from his ski.

"Were we this stupid and callous when we were their age?" asked Derek, walking with Adam to the edge of the water for a closer look.

"It's a cumulative thing. Like interest."

Derek said, "If this is some kind of cosmic cleansing, then I think the powers that be missed a few spots."

"Don't worry," said Adam. "I think we've only seen phases one and two so far. Let's get out of here. I've got a creepy feeling about these guys and I didn't like the way blondie was sizing up Jenny."

"I wasn't too keen on the way she was zoning on him, either," said Derek.

"I heard that, asshole," said Jenny, following a few footsteps behind. "If I wanted beefcake what in the hell would I be doing with an old hippie with sagging breasts?"

"That's pure muscle, sweetie."

The injured man was brought to shore unconscious. He was bleeding badly from a wound to his forehead and one arm was broken.

"Shit man, what are we going to do now?" one of the other boys asked, appealing to Jim for guidance.

"This sucks. I guess we'll have to take him home. His mother's gonna have a fit when she sees this."

Another boy said, "I thought we were going to go over to New York. Ski through the skyscrapers."

"Have you seen the extent of the flooding on the Hudson?" asked Adam.

"Nah," said Jim. "We've been making our way down the river. Foolin' around. We ran over a couple of bodies and you wouldn't believe the damage they can do to a propeller. That's why we laid up here. We've been doing repairs."

He turned to his group. "Okay everybody. Saddle up, we're going home."

He walked close to Jenny.

"Where you all from?"

Jenny started to say Montclair but was cut off by Adam who said they were tourists.

"Maybe you'd like to come with us. Leave the old folks behind," said Jim, scanning Jenny from pole to pole.

"I'd love to, really. Daddy, can I go with these boys?" she asked Derek.

Adam cut through the idiocy, saying, "Your friend's going to go into shock if he hasn't already. He needs to be kept warm and laid out with his feet above his head. And try not to run over any more bodies on the way home."

He beckoned Derek and Jenny to follow him back towards the car.

"Animals," he whispered under his breath when they were a few yards away.

"We shouldn't have left that boy in their hands," said Jenny as they walked along a side street.

"If we had stayed, two things are for sure. Derek and I get the shit kicked out of us and you have the pleasure of your first gangbang. And then Lucia's toast as well."

"They didn't seem so bad to me. A little insensitive perhaps."

"Forgetting your birthday is insensitive. Running over dead bodies and complaining about propeller damage is disaffection in the extreme," said Adam.

When they got back to the car, Adam pulled off the railway tracks to a street just south called Verona. He backed the trailer to the water's edge then helped Derek slip the boat into the water. Adam put some gear into the boat then they pushed off.

The engines started on the first try. Derek took charge of the driving and they carefully proceeded out into the swollen river.

They were in the middle when the now familiar high-pitched engine noise came to them from the north. Four jet skis and three outboards were bee-lining it in their direction.

Jim was in the lead, on a jet ski. He cut his motor a few yards from their boat and the other craft in his flotilla did the same.

"Out doing some sightseeing?" said Jim.

Adam said, "We've got business to take care of and you're wasting our time."

"Then let me be brief. We want the girl. She said she wanted to come. So give her to us. Now."

"I'm afraid that's not possible," said Adam.

"Hand her over or we'll swamp your boat."

"Over my dead body, fuck head," said Derek.

Adam had been sitting during the exchange. Now he stood, spreading his legs far apart, his shotgun in both hands, held across his body.

"Get the hell out of here . . . now!" he said.

Jim turned to face his friends, a big smile on his face.

"Man's got a gun. Thinks he can scare us all . . . "

The blast of the shotgun tore off the end of Jim's sentence and most of his right foot. The blast also punctured the gas tank, knocking the jet ski onto its side as a slick of gasoline spread along the surface. Jim flailed in the water, screaming for help. No one moved to help him, stunned into inaction by the audacity of Adam's deed and the barrel facing generally in their direction.

Adam said, "We're leaving now. Don't anyone follow us. I suggest you pull your friend out of the water before he drowns. And I've heard of sharks coming this far up river."

Derek put the boat in gear and slowly pulled away. Adam and Jenny watched as the boys scrambled to pull their fallen leader into one of the boats, his screams filling the river valley.

"I'm sorry," said Jenny. "I shouldn't have joked with them."

"Wouldn't have made a bit of difference," said Adam.

Derek half-turned, one hand on the wheel. Adam was still watching the action in the middle of the river.

"Who are you, man? You think you know somebody then boom, laid back Adam disappears. You've turned into Charles Bronson. You are too fucking much. And that bit about the sharks. Brilliant."

"Not really," said Adam, pointing to the shoreline downstream.

There was a commotion in the water about a hundred yards away. Two fins were clearly visible above the water's surface.

Adam said, "All along the coastline it must be banquet time. I saw them before but didn't want to alarm anybody. Just keep all limbs inside the boat."

They met up with the tracks on a high slope on the other side of the river. The three of them yanked the boat onto the cross ties and dragged it to a low concrete wall, painted bright yellow, planted on the outer curve of a winding road coming down off the high cliff.

"Where are we?" asked Jenny.

"We must be close to Arlington Station. I'm going to walk ahead and see how far we'll have to portage." He pronounced it 'por-*taj*' and Jenny eyed him quizzically.

"You know, as in carrying a boat overland between two bodies of water."

"Oh…portage. You're in America now. Talk like an American."

Adam gave her the finger then left the couple and headed down the tracks. He had not travelled more than a couple hundred yards when he was forced to stop. The tracks bit into cliffs looming forty feet above and the narrow gorge was flooded. His view was obstructed as the tracks curved so he could not tell for sure whether or not the water led out to the main body. But he could smell the sea and the gulls in the sky overhead made his heart pound.

He hurried back to the others and the three of them commenced the backbreaking task of lifting and dragging the boat along the tracks.

"Now I know how Sisyphus felt," said Adam.

"I doubt it. You never have sex," said Derek.

"It's a Greek myth, you idiot," said Jenny.

"I knew that."

After many rest stops the boat was placed into the water. Adam did not want to risk breaking a propeller so they used the emergency paddles the previous owner had thoughtfully fitted into the boat.

About a half mile down the man-made cut, the landscape opened up as the town of Kearny emerged out of the water, buildings higher up on the hill only half drowned, the rest of the hillside town submerged. Three-foot waves pounded the small boat and further on, unobstructed save for the odd building breaking the surface, was the shattered skyline of New York City, mostly under water, a uniform archipelago of teeny islands breaking the flat line horizon.

As much as he had tried to imagine it, as clearly as he had seen the destruction on the far horizon from his mountain view in Montclair, nothing could prepare Adam for this sight. He could not help thinking of Charlton Heston in Planet Of The Apes. He half expected to see a broken piece of the Statue of Liberty poking up above the water but she had disappeared.

"Where do you think we should head?" said Derek, who had to shout because the wind was picking up and the waves were pounding into the streets of Kearney behind them.

Adam said nothing, frantic for even a dollop of inspiration.

"I've got to get some speed up or the waves will swamp us," said Derek, gunning the engines, the sudden lurch sending Adam onto his ass below the engines. "This boat isn't meant for the ocean."

"Head for New York," said Adam, recovering, gripping the side of the craft as he maneuvered into one of the rear seats.

They were still several miles away from the city. Derek pointed the bow on an eastern heading using the World Trade Center as his landmark, opening the throttle fully, the boat launching itself off the swells so that at times Adam could hear the propellers churning above the water.

It took twenty minutes to cross the distance from Kearny to Manhattan. Derek maintained as high a speed as possible to stabilize the boat in the rolling swells. Adam had moved to the bow, standing and holding the windscreen for support, directing the craft around a minefield of flotsam and jetsam, although he was not sure he knew the difference between the two. As they approached the sunken skyline, the ruined body of New York acted as a giant breakwater, calming the waters on the west side. Derek eased up on the throttle, bringing the boat back to a cruising speed. The derelict twin towers loomed ominously in front of them.

Adam counted close to thirty floors of one tower above water, most of the floors near the water's surface windowless with exposed twisted steel girders and dangling wires. The second tower was even more severely damaged, shorn at the top, the uppermost portion leaning precipitously towards the water. Further to the north, Adam could make out the fractured structure of the Empire State Building poking up from the surface. He could sense the presence of other office towers just below the surface of wide eddies, round pools of flat water, turning defiantly against the current.

As they trolled by the still undefeated towers, Adam was horrified to see people alive, trapped inside the building, some pressed up against the glass, pounding the windows to attract their attention, silent pleas for help bouncing off the glass while others, situated high up on the exposed girders, yelled down to them for help.

"What should I do?" said Derek as he rotated his head from the water in front of him to the two buildings on either side of the boat.

"You know what to do," said Adam. "We keep going. There is nothing we can do for these people."

"I can't stand this," said Jenny who hid her face in her lap.

There was a crash and a desk flew out from a window, halfway up the bent tower, splashing off the boat's port stern about thirty yards away. Adam and Derek turned at the sound. The desk was quickly followed by a man, his suit jacket trailing behind him like a cape as he fell to the water. He was flailing as he fell, grabbing at nothing before absorbing the fall with his chest. He quickly sank and disappeared.

Another crash and a desk chair was airborne from about ten floors up, this time followed by a woman. Adam turned back to Derek, not prepared to watch her entry. He told Derek to get them out of there. Derek hesitated, his eyes on the woman who had survived the fall and was crying out for help.

"Now!"

Adam glared at his friend. Derek's eyes were tear-filled and Adam could not tell for whom he was crying, the woman in the water, the people trapped inside or for himself. Derek turned back to the controls and slid the throttle forward and within seconds, the towers were far astern.

The wind was blowing in a southwesterly direction so Adam directed Derek to head down the Jersey shore, invisible now beneath several hundred feet of Atlantic Ocean.

"How's the fuel situation?" asked Adam.

"Haven't a clue," said Derek. "We'd better find them soon."

Jenny had recovered and was sitting in one of the rear seats, facing the stern. The towers were still in view and she appeared transfixed upon them.

"Guys, I think you should take a gander at this," she yelled above the engine noise.

Adam saw it. He tapped on Derek's shoulder and pointed. Derek eased up on the throttle.

To the far north the sky had blackened and it was moving south at a visible speed.

"Thunderstorm?" asked Derek.

"I don't know. Maybe worse than that. We have got to find that damn ship," said Adam.

When they turned back around they saw a large box-like structure floating in the water, directly in front of them, perhaps two miles away. Even at that distance there was only one possibility. It was the Intrepid.

By the time the sail had been rigged, and calling it a sail and its placement, rigging, was a slight exaggeration of both words, the wind had changed direction, blowing to the southwest, which, according to Sydney was good news and bad news. The wind-sail combination kept them within sight of the shore, but, acting in harmony with the current, was pushing them much farther south than the location Lucia had given Adam at the time of her phone call. That was hours ago and Sydney didn't give the *Fighting I* much more than an hour before it would slip beneath the waves to its new home which Sydney guessed was somewhere over Staten Island, now submerged in the fathoms of water beneath the Intrepid's keel.

They had gone up to the navigation bridge, Sydney, Andy and Lucia, each positioned along the semi-circular control room, binoculars raised, scanning the horizon—for what? A boat, surely. Lucia had told him to get a boat. But didn't he sometimes use a helicopter service. Maybe he had ordered one this morning. Her mind raced through possibilities but whatever powers of precognition she possessed had deserted her.

"You couldn't have called someone a little closer?" said Andy. "I mean, Montclair. Not a lot of boating in Montclair. And how does he get it to the water? I think we're SOL."

"He'll come," she said.

Andy turned his glasses to the shore.

"I figure a quarter to a third of a mile to shore. Maybe we could swim it."

"If we have to we will," said Sydney. "But don't count on any of us making it to shore. If the current doesn't drag us away, hypothermia will finish us all off."

The ship's list was becoming so severe that the two men had to brace themselves in order to keep their hands free. Lucia was secure in the Captain's chair. The makeshift sail buffeted below them, attached off the port bow, approximately where it had been placed over fifty years before. Sydney and Andy had argued about the exact positioning, Andy prevailing, having been part of the crew that had erected it the first time. It kept the bow in a southerly direction.

"About another hour of daylight," said Sydney, so calmly you could almost believe he was contemplating dinner. He was right though. The sun was in the western sky, business as usual, shining down, oblivious and uncaring of the fate of its worshippers.

Nothing to do now but wait, thought Lucia, calmer now, the monotony of silent floating making her sleepy. The only excitement during the last couple hours had been when the carrier struck something in the water, something submerged and unseen. It made an awful screeching noise but Sydney checked and said the hull had not sustained any further damage. Andy was convinced they had hit one of the upper supports of the Verrazano Bridge.

She was almost asleep when a sound like that of a dentist's drill roused her. She turned in her chair, her chest tightening. Her movement caused Sydney and Andy to come over to her side of the bridge. The three of them raised their binoculars in unison.

"Small outboard," said Andy.

"Really small," said Sydney.

"Let's send it back, then," said Lucia.

Andy and Sydney lowered their binoculars. Lucia's smile produced two more followed by wild cheering and hugging and careful jumping on the tilted deck.

Andy went down to the flag bridge to inform the others. Lucia and Sydney stood on the walkway of the navigation bridge, waving madly at the approaching boat.

Derek brought the boat around to the starboard side while Sydney led Lucia down to the gun tubs. It was very difficult to manage the staircases and decks for fear of falling overboard. When Lucia finally reached the bottom of the last staircase, Adam's craft was not twenty feet off. He stood, arms folded, lips smiling but his eyes searching, examining, as if he wanted to be sure it really was her before he let himself believe it.

Lucia waved, feeling childish, not knowing what to say, tears filling her eyes, her hands leaping up to cover her face as heaving sobs emancipated her, allowing her emotions freedom of movement for the first time all day. But it was only a momentary lapse. Her man was here to save her so she wiped her eyes and locked onto his and this time his were steady and for her and so different; softer with an exposed painful acceptance and she knew at last he truly loved her, without condition or doubt or reluctance; a stripped down, essential love.

"Is somebody going to say something?" asked Derek.

"I'm Sydney."

"I'm Adam Fischer. This is Derek and Jenny. How many on board?"

"Fifteen."

"Fifteen. Okay, let's do three or four on the first trip. Then fit everybody else in two trips. Fuel's a concern so let's get going. I guess it's women and children first."

"What category does that put me in?" asked Lucia.

"There is no category for you. How are you?"

"Better."

"I'm sorry about last night."

"I'm not."

Derek said, "Excuse me but in case you hadn't noticed, the world is coming to an end. Could you two lovebirds save it for when we're on shore."

Adam and Jenny stayed in the boat. The first four offloaded were Brian, the Japanese woman and her two children. Derek headed straight for the closest shoreline and it took about five minutes to find an adequate place to deposit his passengers. He returned to the Intrepid alone and twenty minutes later returned with Lucia, the children's father, the maintenance couple and Hernando. The final trip brought Sydney, Andy and the four security guards. In just over an hour after reaching the Intrepid, everyone was safely on relatively dry land.

The sun was below the horizon when the Intrepid slipped beneath the surface. The sailors saluted and everyone stood, silent, Sydney with eyes swimming in tears, Andy with his chest protruded, Hernando leaning on Andy's shoulder, momentarily oblivious to his pain. The little girl waved goodbye while Brian found stones to heave into the water.

Lucia had her arms around Adam's mid-section, her head snug against his chest. She feared to let him go. She feared this joy she felt would be taken from her if she loosened her grip. She could hear his heart, good and strong, his arm draped around her shoulder pulling her close. It was horrible in a way to feel so good but she had never felt more crystal clear joy in her life than at this moment.

They had said almost nothing to each other since coming ashore, if beaching on a street in a suburban neighbourhood could be labeled a shoreline. Sydney thought they were in or near Edison, New Jersey. It wasn't the time for talk. Their being together said unspoken things, the currency of their feelings for each other traded in gestures and eye contact.

The blackness from the north was more felt than seen. An unnatural warmth began to blow southward and the air had an acrid smell. Andy said it reminded him of burning flesh. Sydney told him to shut up and no one spoke about it after that.

There were no houses left standing intact. Sydney found a relatively dry basement with part of one wall still standing. They pulled together what they could find for bedding. A fire was started thanks to Derek's lighter and some food brought from the Intrepid, shared. Later in the evening the temperature began to fall.

Lucia burrowed close to Adam, wrapping the coat she still wore over his body to form a little cocoon. In the darkness she felt his breath on her face, then his lips were on hers and she thought she would swallow him, her hunger and passion radiating from her mouth to every point of her body. She wanted more but he stopped, hugging her, putting his mouth by her ear.

"I don't know why I couldn't say this before," he whispered.

"You still haven't said it," she answered.

And while she waited for the words, Adam's breath grew heavier and more laboured, and she knew the words would not come. Not tonight. Adam had fallen into a deep, exhausted sleep.

XIV

ADAM WAS TOO TIRED TO SLEEP. There was a tremor pulsating through his body and his mind was full of uncontrollable sounds and images; guitar chords thrashing, loudspeaker announcements, coloured lights and people chanting. And his ears were ringing. Almost twelve continuous hours of sound engineering had taken its toll on his inner ear, minute nerve hairs in his cochlea continuing to dance to phantom sounds.

He rolled over onto his side and explored Donna's bare back. He loved the way the tiny golden hairs at the base of her spine fanned like a feather—it was the first in a long list of attributes he had fallen in love with. He put his hand on her bum and ran it down her thigh. She moaned a little and pushed herself closer. He reached between her thighs and felt her wetness and there was an instant reaction in his groin. This was his private domain now, she had given this to him, ever ready and eager to receive him.

He sidled up close behind her and slid softly into her. It was a quiet kind of ecstasy, a morning wakeup call, and she responded slowly, pushing down on him as he casually moved inside her while cupping one breast in his hand and kissing her neck and shoulders. She turned her head to face him and her lips, partly open, beckoned him for a kiss. The two lovers twisted, human pretzels, finding each other's mouths, their tongues intertwined in a salacious dance. The slow choreography of their union was soon replaced by a desperate frenzy, she pulling him on top and into her, the lovemaking now pure copulation, the fulfillment of a biological imperative, no time for love or tenderness, only the needy, desperate race to conclusion.

It was almost noon. They had gotten back to Grossingers only two hours ago. Incredibly, Jefferson Airplane, the last act to perform, had started their set at 8:30 that morning. The concert had continued through the night. And what a night. Janis Joplin, Sly, The Who.

Donna lay there, gazing up at the ceiling, smoking a cigarette. He watched her and knew he loved her. This was the test. Those first minutes after orgasm told a man everything he needed to know about how he felt towards the woman into whom he had deposited his seed. It had been one of the great unsolved mysteries in Adam's life; how you could be so intimate with a person, take the most private, concealed part of your body and stick it into hers, to trade saliva and sweat and secretions and then seconds after it was all over, to be next to this same person, the object of so much recent desire and instantly feel at best a mild revulsion, seeing the woman with an entirely different set of eyes and a completely rewritten emotional checklist. It was so disconcerting to Adam that he tended to avoid the situation entirely, for the sexual payoff did not cover the angst of feigned affection or the awkwardness of strategic withdrawal with its white lies and 'I'll call you' insincerities.

He was propped up on his elbows, watching as Donna played with her cigarette, making little smoke circles in the air. Even after his body was satiated, his mind was all over her, loving her for her charm and kindness, her sensitivity and innocent flower child nature, all the while watching her tummy rise up and down, admiring her breasts and reaching over and kissing her fingers. He loved to bury his nose in her hair and smell her fragrance and it didn't matter if it contained the residue of a smoky bar or hours of sweat. The pure essence of her turned those other smells into an intoxicating elixir he consumed willingly with his flaring nostrils.

And then there was the fear. His love for Donna was so strong and she was so slight and fragile that he worried over each beat of her heart, every breath of air she inhaled, torturing himself with the thought of losing her.

"What time do we have to go back?" she asked, butting her Marlborough into an amber coloured ashtray on the night table.

"We should get ready now. Joe Cocker is scheduled for a two o'clock start." He rolled out of bed and threw open the heavy curtain, filling the room with sunlight.

"Looks like a nice day. Some idiot said it was going to rain."

He moved back to the bed, grabbing a pair of jeans lying on the floor before heading for the bathroom.

"I'm going to grab a shower, then go see when the next shuttle is heading back to the site."

"Haven't you forgotten something?"

He shrugged.

"You haven't kissed me good morning, yet."

"What do you call what we just did?"

"I call that fucking. Now come over here and kiss me."

He dropped the jeans and knelt over the bed, taking her head in one hand and pulling her lips up to his. Twenty minutes later he took his shower.

The going was slow for the shuttle bus, even with all of the roads leading to the festival closed to public traffic. The scene had all of the confusion of war without the gunfire, Adam thought. There were people everywhere, travelling in both directions, some trying to reach the site, others attempting to extricate themselves from the massed confusion.

Adam momentarily locked eyes with a tall, longhaired man, full bearded, a floppy leather hat keeping an eruption of blond locks out of his face. He wore overalls with a T-shirt underneath and a back-pack, custom made to carry his child, a young girl, about two, who owned beautiful golden curls down past her shoulders that bounced up and down to the rhythm of her father's stride. A fringed bag hung over his shoulder, flopping against the man's side, decorated with an elaborate beaded circular design. A small, delicate woman walked beside him, sharp features highlighting her natural beauty, her long dark hair falling to the small of her back. She wore a native buckskin dress with a high slit up her thigh. She wore no shoes, her feet caked with mud yet they did not seem dirty to Adam. She only came up to the man's armpit and Adam wondered about it, how all the parts manage to fit together. They walked as if in slow-motion and as the van passed by them, the man raised his right hand and gave Adam the peace sign.

The real deal, thought Adam. No mere family outing, this was a pilgrimage. Adam wondered what had motivated them to walk through life in a counter direction, against society's flow, embracing the Age of Aquarius with a fervor Adam was unable to feel.

Everywhere there were people; tents dotting the landscape, small groups of kids around fires, some sitting by the roadside, dumb-founded, maybe a little homesick.

"I saw the weirdest thing last night," Adam said.

They were grabbing some breakfast in the food tent backstage. Donna was talking to a member of Joe Cocker's band, laughing about something and it pleased Adam to see the admiration in the man's

189

eyes. He wasn't bothered by the way men looked at Donna. Hadn't he looked at her the same way when he first saw her, six months before, her body pressed up against the counter at the head shop? What right did he have to deny others the same pleasure or resent its occurrence?

"Sorry sweetie, what did you say?" she said.

"I saw the weirdest thing last night backstage. Just before Janis was going on stage, I saw her chasing this guy around the equipment area, trying to kill him."

"Maybe that explains her performance. I've seen her better."

"Maybe. But this guy she was after. There was something about him. He was enjoying it so much, being chased around. He was goading her, laughing and letting her get close, then he ran away and she gave up. Her band was already warming up so she went straight to the stage from there. Very weird. I'd love to know what that was all about."

Joe Cocker sat nearby. Adam had never met him, had never seen him perform. He knew one of his songs, *Delta Lady*, but knew very little about the Englishman. With his mutton chops and thinning hair, he personified more an English pub bartender than the leader of the opening act on the third day of a music festival making headlines around the world, a gathering no longer about the music—now being labeled a cultural migration of America's youth.

A call had gone out and the faithful had answered. Much of the talk backstage was about revolution, of taking over, a day of reckoning, fuck the establishment, the youth of America shunning the conservative world of their parents. As Adam later sat behind the sound board, unavoidably distracted by the blue-jeaned masses surging behind him, he felt a pressure in his abdomen and a profound sadness. He heard the words in his head, *High water mark*, and knew without thinking what it was he was telling himself. He thought of the hippie family he'd seen earlier that morning, saw them in his mind's eye, walking straight into a psychedelic past, love-beaded anachronisms, history passing them by before the pages were even written. He sighed deeply, thought of Donna and promised to enjoy himself every minute of every hour while the party lasted. He knew it couldn't last forever.

It was a surreal feeling being backstage. There was relative calm and everyone had a job to do, but you could not ignore the seething mass of humanity only a few feet away, nothing more substantial then a fence and some beefy security guards between you and them. Not that you feared for your life, it was more the unsettling feeling you might have sitting atop a huge damn like the Hoover and wondering whether it was possible for the dam to burst.

Adam tried to ignore the big picture and went about his business, conducting his preformative sound check, preparing his equipment for Joe Cocker's arrival on stage. He ran through the day's lineup and smiled. Even without the crowds, without the helicopters and national coverage, without the social implications of a generation coming of age, this was still a day he could tell his children about. The Band, Blood Sweat and Tears, Paul Butterfield, Johnny Winter. And Hendrix. All in one day. Most of the crowd would barely hear it. The rest of the world would see it only in movie theatres. But today, when the music floated off the stage and into the audience and history, Adam Fischer would be at the controls, shaping the sound, molding it into a homogeneous whole and releasing it into the universe.

Adam was back in the food tent, grabbing some grub before beginning what was shaping up to be another marathon session behind the board when he spotted him. The Janis Joplin dude. He was sitting at a table alone, wolfing down his food as if he figured someone might throw him out of the place at any moment. Adam surveyed the tent, saw tables with people he knew, artists milling about, Country Joe holding court at a table nearby, then headed straight for the mystery man, his feet knowing his mind better than his thoughts.

Introductions were made and the conversation settled into cryptic one-liners and mild put-downs for the next half hour. There was a fire in this man's eyes. His name was Derek, and when he spoke his eyes danced, life and light seeming to burst out of them. If you are truly attracted to the things you are not then that might explain Adam's reluctant fondness for this frenetic, irrepressible huckster. And there was no guessing required to know the sort of person Derek was and the kind of havoc he could bring into the life of anyone foolish enough to fly close enough to his flame. He was the boy mothers warned their daughters about. He was the one who showed you how to remove hubcaps and sneak into movie theatres and knew the pharmacist who would sell cigarettes and rubbers to minors. And he was the only kid your age who had actually used a rubber for its manufactured purpose.

"Check that out," said Derek, gesturing towards the entrance of the tent where a lithe, brown-skinned girl with long straight hair tucked behind her ears had entered.

"I do . . . every night," said Adam, grinning and notching another one.

"You are kidding me. She's yours? Shit. Girl's got no taste."

Adam stood and waved Donna over to the table.

"Donna, I'd like you to meet Janis Joplin's best friend, Derek Eaton," said Adam, taking her hand and kissing her quickly.

And maybe this time he did mind; the way Derek was making eye contact with Donna, effortlessly eliciting her laughter and taking the kinds of liberties with his conversation normally reserved for close friends.

"Wherever did you find this rude man?" she asked, laughing as Derek placed two oatmeal cookies with Hershey kisses in the center on each of his breasts, mimicking the swagger of a well-known groupie who had walked by the table.

When Adam left to go back to the sound booth, Derek and Donna were throwing popcorn into each other's mouths but it wasn't jealousy or insecurity he was feeling. Adam knew he was at the center of a day that would be long remembered and revered, a secular Sermon on the Mount, and countless people who had never gotten off their asses would claim they had been there, would in later years describe in minute detail, experiences they had lived vicariously, and here was Adam Fischer, helping to make it happen. Yet all he could think about was Donna and Derek and the fun he was going to miss because he had to get back to work.

For years afterwards, when asked to pick his favourite performance over the three days, Adam always said, without hesitation, Joe Cocker's performance on Sunday afternoon. Part of the reason was his low expectation level. Mostly though, it was the performance. Hendrix was amazing and ran a close second, but by ten in the morning on Monday, after three days and more than sixteen hours behind the control board, it had been all Adam could do to keep his eyes open during Hendrix's thunderous rendition of the *Star Spangled Banner*.

Joe Cocker took the stage under a threatening sky. There were always tales circulating the concert trail of some poor roadie who got himself toasted by falling into electrical wires or touching something metallic with one hand while the other was holding onto a guitar so Adam was always careful; more than once he had been punched to the ground by the force of an electric shock. The stage was a maze of microphone wires, extension cords, lighting fixtures and power amplifiers. It revolved in a circle allowing setup for the next band while performers were on stage. Although a downpour was always a possibility, Adam knew the crew was ill-prepared for anything more than a light shower.

"We're gonna leave ya with the usual thing," Cocker announced near the end of his set, salty droplets falling off his stringy long hair, his sunflower-splashed tie-dyed shirt clinging to his sweaty chest.

Adam had the best seat in the house, about thirty yards from the stage on a raised platform. Normally he fiddled with the dials, riding the levels, searching for a perfect blend of vocals, drums and guitars. Not during Cocker's set, though. After a song or two, he took his hands away from the dials and watched.

The singer moved like he had a disease, a nervous disorder, twitching and pigeon-stepping to the music, playing bass line air guitar with his fingertips, his bear growl of a voice exploding from a deep place inside and into the microphone. Adam had never seen anything like it. It was hard to tell if Cocker would need a stiff drink when he got off stage or a medic.

" . . . The only thing I can say, as I've said to many people . . . is this title . . . ah . . . just about . . . ah . . . puts it all into focus. With A Little Help From My Friends. Remember it."

It only took five minutes for Joe Cocker to pass into rock 'n' roll history.

The frenzied delivery by Cocker and his seizure-like reaction to the music was transmitted into the human sea, dissipating the exhaustion and magnifying the euphoria, much of it drug induced.

A man standing near the sound platform caught Adam's eye. He was dark and solidly built, high cheekbones and long dark hair tied in a ponytail. His yellow deerskin vest seemed to glow in contrast with his deep brown skin. He wore an ornate silver bracelet on one wrist, inlaid with turquoise and coral and an elaborate bone, coral and turquoise necklace, which hung halfway down his chest. It was the man's body movement that caught Adam's attention, though. The man was aping Cocker's every move, twitching and pivoting as if somehow remotely connected to Cocker's body. It was an uncanny instant impersonation and Adam had to pull his eyes away to concentrate on the real thing.

Higher and higher the song soared, the choirboy backing vocals providing a stunning contrast to Cocker's gravel truck vocal delivery. Near the end of the song, a doubled time change, Cocker's body writhing in concurrent meter, his silver-starred, blue leather boots pounding the stage as the song climbed closer and closer to its crescendo, the organ whirling out carnival sounds gone mad, the drummer accelerating the beat while the rest of the band struggled to keep up, all of the clatter combining into one last sustained chord and too quickly it was over, Joe Cocker, exhausted, acknowledging the Grease Band, saying thank you and walking off the stage.

Adam noticed that the dark-skinned man was no longer there.

A member of the stage crew waded through the crowd to the sound platform carrying a giant roll of plastic wrap. Thunderclaps pierced the air with increasing intensity. The canvas tarps suspended above the stage flapped menacingly in the wind. The stagehand started covering the soundboard, unraveling the plastic sheeting over it like it was a large piece of meatloaf. Bill Graham, microphone in hand, repeatedly admonished people to move away from the light towers. Adam glanced up at the tall towers holding the spotlights and wondered how much wind it would take to knock one of them down.

The sky grew darker as large, dull gray clouds moved quickly to obscure the sun. Rain started to fall, lightly at first, the wind delivering it in stinging velocity.

Adam made his way through the mass of bodies to the backstage gate. Some kids were picking up their belongings and heading back to the camping area. Most, with nowhere to go, remained where they were, resigned to the drenching they were about to receive.

The rain was not letting up. Adam had nothing to do but wait it out. He eventually sought temporary shelter in a truck full of sound equipment. He had gone over to the tent to find Donna. She wasn't there and neither was Derek. Most of the artists had sought shelter elsewhere as high winds drove the rain through the eating area.

He was sitting just inside the back doors of the open truck, half-asleep, when he noticed Derek running up to people, stopping to speak to them for a moment then moving on to the next person. He seemed frantic and the feeling in Adam's stomach told him something was horribly wrong.

Adam jumped into the rainstorm and made a straight line for Derek.

"Fuck, there you are," said Derek, out of breath and saturated.

"What's wrong?" asked Adam.

"Your girlfriend. She's freaking out. I took her over to the medical unit."

Adam had never experienced such fury. He grabbed Derek by the lapels of his leather vest and lifted him up onto his tiptoes.

"You fuckin' asshole. What did you give her?"

Derek went limp in Adam's arms, which made it very difficult for Adam to hold him up. It confused Adam to see the calmness in Derek's eyes and he supposed the guy was drugged out on something, too.

"I didn't give her anything. We were sitting there after you left and she just took off. She must have dropped the acid before she came over to sit with us."

Acid. They had talked of doing it together, of lighting some candles and incense, opening a bottle of Mateus and playing their favourite records while they waited for their trip to begin. It hadn't happened because Adam was afraid to do it. Something inside told him tripping was not his bag. The people he knew who took it were party animals. He could not imagine himself laughing hysterically at an ant carrying a dead bee or watching a lava lamp for hours. He knew instinctively an experience like that would tear his head open and he'd never find his way back. Truth be told, he liked being straight, having his world maintained by a status quo of his own design and control. Knobs and buttons.

Derek led Adam through the site to the Freak-Out Tent. The going was slow with muddy rivers flowing down towards the stage, wet blankets, sleeping bags and plastic tarps littering the landscape. The rain was extremely heavy now and people were continuing to move towards the stage, filling the vacuum created by those who had sought shelter from the downpour. Adam stepped on a concealed leg, heard someone wincing in pain as a tarp was lifted by a bearded man lying naked between the exposed thighs of a dark-haired girl with enormous breasts. Quick apologies were made and the couple disappeared beneath the covering.

Another crack of thunder and Adam wondered how they would ever be able to continue the concert. Not that he cared at the moment. The crowd was thinning as they headed further from the stage and with Derek still leading, they made quick progress to the medical area.

Donna wasn't there. She wasn't on the stretcher Derek had left her on.

"Are you sure this is where you left her?" asked Adam, his anxiety increasing with every unknowing moment.

"Of course I'm sure. There are her shoes. Maybe she was feeling better and left. Maybe she left with Hendrix."

"Hendrix?"

"Jimi Hendrix, sure. He was in here before. Lying on a cot near Donna. I swear it."

Adam gave Derek an exasperated grimace then asked him if he could kindly point out the doctor who had treated her.

Derek brought Adam over to a man with a bright orange beard, a stethoscope around his neck, wearing a Woodstock T-shirt. He was frazzled and rheumy-eyed and barely managed to politely tell them to wait while he attended to a dressing on a young girl's arm.

Five minutes later, Adam was describing Donna to the doctor and yes, he had treated her with a few calming words and a compress. He said that she was feeling a bit better and he was pretty sure this Indian guy had taken her out of the clinic.

"What do you mean, an Indian guy?" asked Adam.

"The Hog Farm brought a group of Indians onsite to set up an exhibit and do crafts and native stuff. They're camped right over there," the doctor said, pointing generally towards the entrance. "The guy was helping out, talking people down off their bad trips. He seemed to have a very soothing effect on the patients. I let him do his thing. We need all the help we can get."

The rain had let up only slightly. The wind was less fierce and the steady downpour assumed a more vertical descent. This was Adam's first venture out into the crowd beyond his sound booth. The sight of hundreds of thousands of people fanned out behind him as he sat at the control board had been breathtaking, a human panorama unlike anything he had ever seen. Now as he walked into areas where people were camped, past the Hog Farm tables where food was being doled out, past tents and people huddling in sleeping bags, past nude rain dancers and passed out college kids, people everywhere, every inch of space consumed by a human presence, only then did the magnitude of the festival really begin to make sense. It wasn't about the music. Music was the soundtrack. Music was the calling out. An invitation to connect. To strip down, like the naked dancers, to the very essence of who you were, shedding your job, your family, society's rules and regulations and connecting with your fellow human beings. It really was about peace. Not for everybody. Not for Adam. But he could see it in most of their faces, not minding the rain, the cold and dirt, unashamed, uninhibited, happy. And stoned.

They had erected teepees, smoke billowing from the hole atop each one. Adam pulled open two flaps before he found her in the third. He had imagined any number of scenarios, most of them involving either sex or violence so the scene before him was all the more shocking for its passivity.

Donna sat near the fire in a facsimile of the lotus position, legs crossed. There were other men and women sitting around the fireplace. All were holding hands and chanting the same phrase over and over.

Om mani padme hum. Om mani padme hum.

She was radiant, eyes closed, the fire painting her face with a golden brush. Sitting with her back arched, soaked T-shirt clinging to her breasts, her hardened nipples prominently raised, Adam was paralyzed by her magnificence and his panic was replaced by desire.

Derek coughed insincerely. The group stopped their chanting and rotated towards the entranceway. Donna's eyes were wild, animalistic orbs of delight. She spied Adam and jumped to her feet, running into his arms.

"I'm sorry," she said. "I got so scared," then she pulled him further into the tent and towards the circle.

"You have to meet this wonderful man who helped me."

The wonderful man's back was to the entrance. He had not bothered to turn around to inspect the two interlopers. A long dark braid followed the line of his spine to midway down his back. He looked familiar and when he did finally turn around, smiling, extending his hand, Adam saw the bracelet. The man grasped his forearm, Indian-style Adam supposed, and Adam had no choice but to do the same, his fingers barely covering half the distance around the man's massive forearm, the man's bracelet pressing into Adam's wrist. It felt cool against his skin.

"My name is John Walker," said the man, rising to his feet, "and most people call me John Walker."

Adam started to smile, caught Derek's raised eyebrow, then pulled back the impulse to laugh as the expression on John Walker's face remained impassive.

"I'm Adam Fischer. This is Derek . . . "

"Eaton," said Derek, extending his hand.

"Eaton? Are you Canadian?"

"Yes I am."

"I like your stores," said John Walker. "I've been to Canada many times."

"They're not mine."

"Not yet."

"Not ever."

"Too bad."

Donna said, "Come on Adam. You too, Derek. Sit down with us and meet everybody."

Donna's gaze had physical weight. Adam felt a pressure in his head as he looked into her bloodshot eyes—tiny red blood vessels radiating out from two black suns that were searing his mind.

"Are you okay?" he asked.

"I'm totally fried but I'm fine. Really. I should have told you I dropped acid. I thought it would upset you and you have enough to worry about today. I'm sorry."

She hugged him and he held her close, inhaling the familiar intoxicating essence, her fragile smallness pressed hard against his body. He vowed to himself once more to always protect her and keep her safe.

The soggy intruders sat down as the circle widened to accommodate two more bodies. The heat from the fire reminded Adam how cold he had become and he edged closer, raising his hands to accept the fire's warmth.

Adam and Derek made ten people in the circle. There were brief introductions to the three women and three men scattered around the fireplace.

"We were all at the clinic today," said a big-boned man named Jake. He owned long blond hair, parted in the middle, and a full beard with a drooping moustache that must have gotten in the way when he ate. He had dull, gray, faraway eyes. He reminded Adam of the singer, Shawn Phillips.

Derek was seated next to a blonde girl with the fresh-faced exuberance of a cheerleader. Her curly locks partially obscured her light blue eyes which were dramatically surrounded by eyelashes clumped together into star points by caked mascara, her cheeks freckled, her mouth encased by red, puffy lips.

"So, what are you on?" asked Derek.

"Top of the world," said the girl, who was introduced as Gloria.

"Gotta get me some of that," said Derek.

John Walker interrupted. "We were chanting when you arrived, a

Hindu mantra—it was Jake's suggestion—as a means to quiet our minds. There is great power in silence. If we listen to all of the voices inside of us, if we take heed of every plea, every fear or want or warning, then we will spend our time running in circles, putting out a fire here, throwing water on another spark over there, always running, always chasing the fire.

"Only after quieting the voices can we hear the true guiding voice within each of us. Only by reaching a place of serenity within are we able to connect with the message being sent to each of us by our Creator. Imagine a crowded party and you are on one side of the room and someone is trying to talk to you about something important from the far side of the room. You will not hear the message. Or you will hear bits and pieces, fragments, puzzle pieces for you to play with and waste your time. You have to leave the party behind in order to hear the message."

Derek said, "Why doesn't the messenger just tell everyone else to shut up?"

"Because that's your job," said John Walker. "We must all take responsibility for ourselves, become caretakers of our souls. We must all journey within and find our pure spirit, discover our one path and be open to our true destiny. Drugs can help you see the possibilities of your mind. But know that drugs are like taking cheat notes into an exam. They cannot show you real knowledge. They may lift a veil, show you other dimensional realities, but there is no discrimination, no pacing. You are taken on a transient ride through your psychic landscape at tremendous speeds with uncontrollable input and much of the ride can be terribly frightening for the uninitiated or spiritually unprepared. Many of you learned that lesson today.

"Music on the other hand, music can slowly lead you down into yourself, allowing you to tune into the universal frequencies, to the heart throb of the Earth Mother. Music is a shared, tribal experience. This gathering, this spontaneous coming together of thousands of spiritual warriors to this place is an answer to a call, the jungle drums ringing through the forest, the natives responding. It's only rock 'n' roll, they say. So if it's only rock 'n' roll then why are we all here?"

"For the sex," said Derek. "You know, sex and drugs and rock 'n' roll."

"Sex. Yes. God's gift to his little creations. A way to God and a means by which two people can attain spiritual union. And it feels great. The followers of Tantra Buddhism practice sex as a spiritual meditation. As a way of reaching God. The freedom you are all experiencing to explore the pleasures of your bodies, this time of free love is like what I was saying about drugs. The freedom is illusory. The thrill is temporary. The orgasm is pleasurable to be sure. But there is so much more to be obtained by the act. You must not be indiscriminate. You have no idea how much information about yourselves passes to the other person during sex. Would you tell a total stranger all of your most intimate secrets, your fears and dreams? Why then would you hand over so casually all of the information about yourself on a cellular and genetic level? Such information, if given to the wrong person, may put you in grave spiritual jeopardy. Find someone to love and who loves you. Then you will understand why they call it making love."

Adam slipped his hand into Donna's and squeezed it. She turned and smiled and brought her lips to his ear and whispered, "I love you," and the words and warm breath and the brushing of her lips on his ear sent a chill down his body, causing him to visibly shudder.

John Walker continued to talk and Adam lost himself in the conversation, his arm around Donna, half-listening but mostly absorbed by Donna's presence. Derek leaned over at one point and said, "This guy is good," and Adam was not sure if that was a compliment or not.

Then Adam sat up straight. It had stopped raining.

"Shit, I've got to go. Sorry. I've got to get back to the stage."

He kissed Donna, told her to come to the sound booth later and stood up to leave. John Walker rose and shook Adam's hand.

"I enjoyed this. You speak well," said Adam.

"Thank you."

"And you do one hell of a Joe Cocker impersonation."

"Not bad for a gardener, I guess."

Derek walked with Adam. People were moving back towards the stage. The natural amphitheater had become a soggy brown stew. They passed an area where kids were sliding naked down a river of mud; they reminded Adam of a stone age lost tribe, mud people, every inch of skin covered by brown sludge.

"A gardener. Probably grows pot for a living," said Derek, valiantly trying to keep pace with the quick moving Adam.

"Well, he sure seems to have his shit together. I don't know. I've heard it all before but this was honestly the first time my mind ever shut down and I just sat and listened without judging and analyzing."

"I'll bet you ten to one he fucks one of those girls in there. Donna excluded of course."

"Get your mind out of the gutter."

"Come on. If the Maharishi can hit on Mia Farrow's sister, who can you really trust?"

"I have no defense to that sort of logic."

At ten-thirty on Monday morning, Jimi Hendrix, after jamming his way through a frenetic, free-form display of dexterity followed by a laid back haunting, instrumental number, struck a final chord, thanked the crowd and the Woodstock Music and Art Fair was over. The audience, shrunken to one-tenth of its number from the previous day, began cheering and the noise brought Adam to his senses. The music had carried itself into his waking dream, a dream full of Jimi's distorted guitar and populated by images of people, dirty, half naked, dancing, girls on the shoulders of their boyfriends, breasts exposed and bouncing in time to the music, bearded men, long, dirty hair, garbage and mud, all of it mental trash being put out for the next day's pickup. Adam's hands were still on the controls. An assistant engineer was smiling at him.

"You are fucking incredible, man. I swear you were sound asleep and you were still working the sound, riding the faders perfectly. You are a god."

Donna was asleep at Adam's feet, curled up in a blanket. Derek had come out to the booth after The Band's set and stayed until the last song by Crosby, Stills, Nash and Young, leaving the booth at around four A.M.

Adam's job was done. He woke Donna gently and helped her through the carnage of discarded sleeping bags, ground sheets, canvas tarps, clothing, shoes, beer bottles, broken umbrellas, human excrement, all mixed together in the mud.

They found Derek backstage and it did not come as a surprise to see him with Gloria, the blonde girl from the teepee.

"Look who I found," said Derek.

Gloria smiled sheepishly, her freckles accented in the sunlight.

"The gardener wanted to say goodbye to you two," said Derek. "They're packing up right now so we should go over there if you want to catch him."

It was a lot easier reaching the campsite without the rain and the crowds. John Walker was striking the teepee as they approached, bare chested, the sweat glistening off his lean, sinewy torso.

"Our time together was much too short," said John Walker.

"I agree," said Adam. "Maybe some other time."

"Here. Take this number. Anyone answering the phone will know where I am. I can usually be found in Arizona or New Mexico so if you ever get down there, give me a call."

John Walker took off the bracelet on his right wrist and handed it to Adam. "I want you to have this."

"Oh, I couldn't. It must be very valuable."

"A friend of mine made it. He can make another. You are supposed to have it. Call it a gift between Joe Cocker fans."

Adam was profoundly embarrassed but he slipped the bracelet onto his wrist. It fit perfectly and gave his wrist the same cool tingling feeling as when he had first touched it the day before. He rubbed his thumb over the smooth inlayed stones. It had a turquoise background with three red coral circles positioned in an inverted triangle arrangement, like two eyes and a mouth.

"One day you will learn the meaning of the design. For now it is enough to know that right living is always a matter of choice."

Everybody hugged everybody, Donna holding John Walker tightly, tears in her eyes, thanking him for what he had done for her. She took an earring from her left ear, a gold peace sign, a gift from Adam. She pressed it into John Walker's hand.

"Adam gave these to me. Wear this and think of us," she said.

John Walker smiled, unhooking the beaded earring in his left ear before replacing it with the peace sign. Adam nodded approvingly, delighted by his girlfriend's gesture and by her understanding of his need to reciprocate.

"Gee, what are you going to do with only one earring?" asked Derek, absently pulling on the silver ankh hanging from a loop in his left ear. Donna smiled at Adam who smiled back and cocked his head in Derek's direction.

"Here," she said, "Now you three men are connected forever."

There was much laughter and kibitzing as Gloria helped Derek swap the hoop for the golden stud.

They were standing there, unwilling to break away as Hugh Romney, better known as Wavy Gravy, passed by with a couple of his Hog Farm associates.

"Hey, John Walker, Adam, everyone, hold that pose," he said and nudged one of his mates with a camera to take a picture. After the five had interlinked arms and smiled for the camera, Hugh walked over to John Walker and put his arm around the big man's shoulder.

"Take a shot of just the two of us," said Romney, assuming Adam's place next to John Walker, his toothless smile a gaping, round, black hole. The two couples said goodbye one more time to their new friend, then headed back towards the stage.

PART TWO

I

ADAM WAS BEGINNING TO WORRY about his ears. They were ringing, had been ever since the show last night. There came a point in your career, he decided, when you had to walk out or use plugs. His ears were his bread and butter. Too bad if the band was his biggest production gig ever. His hearing was far more important than sucking up to the label people at a gig.

Donna's plane was delayed.

Adam sat at Phoenix International Airport and listened to his ears ringing.

He disliked earplugs. They wiped out the high end completely and hollowed out the sound. It would be like a surgeon wearing snow mittens to operate.

Phoenix landings were the worst. All the hot air rising made for a bumpy, heart-sucking landing. And Donna hated flying. In her mental state Adam wasn't convinced she should be flying. But she insisted she was okay. And Adam really wanted her to be part of this, to have some time away from New York and be with good friends.

Adam had not seen Joey since she was about six years old. She must be twelve or thirteen now, he thought, and hopefully, the spitting image of Gloria. He envied Derek and Gloria that child.

But not the parents of the two brats seated next to him, treating Frito chips like Frisbees, their mother ignoring them, more interested in carrying on a conversation, in Spanish, with the little monsters' grandmother. And it was an important discussion, something about pink or green towels for the bathroom.

Adam moved to a less occupied area. A soldier sat across from him sucking on the leaking bottom of a snow cone.

Donna was coming and they would talk about their relationship, it would be her idea, about the lack of time together, the desire for a child and Adam would be ready to talk and be cooperative because

207

the only subject he feared could never be an issue between them; that she no longer loved him or thought he didn't love her. Which made any of the other problems merely problems, easily solved when love bound two people together.

Adam hated airport loudspeaker systems. The voices sounded as if they emanated from inside a garbage can. He thought of volunteering his services around the country to put decent speakers into airports.

The arrival screen showed her plane arriving in a half hour.

They will talk about their relationship, about how he's always away and he's the one with a life, and she wants to go back to school, only he's suspicious that she only likes to say she wants to go back to school and hasn't spent any time thinking about sitting in boring classes and taking notes day after day.

It does not matter what they will talk about. He cannot wait to see her, to feel her in his arms. Whoever it was who said lust, infatuation and sex in a relationship dwindle over time had thankfully left Adam and Donna out of the equation. They were a poster couple for Cosmopolitan. Not like they did it every night. But Adam thought about doing it every night. And when they made love, even mediocre 'I'm tired, just go ahead and use me' kind of lovemaking was fabulous. And when they were both into it, which was most of the time, Adam could not imagine a life containing more pure ecstasy than those moments leading up to their mutual climax.

He got self conscious about the growing bulge in his jeans and got up to walk it off.

They went the slow way, eschewing Interstate 17 for the glorious undulating landscape along highways 60 and 89. They took their time, stopping in Wickenburg, first for lunch then a casual stroll through the local museum—an homage to the Old West.

Adam had come to Phoenix as the guest of a record company having its annual convention in a big Scottsdale hotel. It was a perk hard to resist; all expenses paid, first class travel, huge suite, food, parties, live shows.

They went the slow way, for the dramatic change of scenery waiting for them over each desert horizon, and so they could talk.

Adam loved the desert, the space and pristine beauty of it. The city was all about subtle differences, elusive hints and secret codes, a daily slalom course of learned procedures and arcane knowledge. The desert did not care if you knew the latest best restaurant or the quickest way to La Guardia. The desert did not know if you were shit hot or stone cold. There were no hidden layers, no blind alleys, no false ceilings. The desert did not acknowledge you and you loved it for its taciturn indifference.

"I miscarried again."
"How do you know?"
"Is that really what you want to ask me?"
"I'm sorry . . . I'm sorry. Are you okay, baby?"
"No."
"I know."
"Do you?"
"Yes . . . I mean . . . I wanted it as much as you did."
"It?"
"A baby."
"It?"
"I don't know what you want me to say."
"That's the problem."
"Help me."
"Say something that doesn't make me feel like shit."
"I love you."
"I need more than that right now."

They stopped in Jerome late in the afternoon. The sun was low in the sky behind them and the town, built on the eastern exposure of a mountain ridge, was cast in autumn shadows. It was cool and they were inadequately dressed for it, having left a ninety-four-degree Scottsdale a few hours before. There was a windbreaker in the back that Adam had found in his suite along with a goodie bag full of vinyl albums, some CDs, cassettes, magazines, and other assorted promotional items, all of which he'd left behind save for the jacket, a baseball-designed concern with black leather sleeves and collar attached to a black woolen body. Emblazoned on the back was the record label's logo. He placed it around Donna's shoulders and she pulled it tight, one hand grabbing the front of it while the other skewered the space between Adam's arm and body as she pulled him close to her.

They visited a few stores—a head shop where Donna purchased some lavender incense, her favourite, a pottery store run by the pottery maker, and an Indian craft store featuring Hopi and Zuni silver jewelry and native masks.

"That's a nice piece on your wrist," the storeowner had commented.

"A friend gave it to me," said Adam.

"Nice friend."

'I'll be seeing him later. I'll tell him you said so."

Adam wanted to travel while there was still light so they headed back to the rented car.

"I miss the old days," said Donna. "This town, it's so rooted in the sixties. It makes me want to set up shop and watch the rest of the world grow up and go away."

"I like it better now."

"You do not."

"I do."

"What's so great about the eighties?"

"Rock stars live longer. Means more work for me."

"So it's not better to burn out after all."

"Not for me."

Adam opened the passenger door for Donna and she made to get in then stopped, turned and faced him.

"The best thing about my life back then is still the best thing about my life right now. I have you. I can't imagine my life without you. I love you so much, Adam," she said and flung her arms around his neck, tears rolling down her autumn-chilled cheeks. "I'm sorry about before. We'll try again. I'll do better."

"There's nothing you have to try to do to please me. Nothing, understand. That was all taken care of the first time I laid eyes on you."

There was little talk the rest of the way to Sedona. A couple of times Adam slipped his hand into Donna's, partly to reassure her and partly to reassure himself. There were times in the past when he questioned how two so completely opposite people with few common interests and disparate cultural backgrounds could find each other and build a shared life together. A Jewish, existentialist neurotic from Toronto hooking up with a Protestant, All-American, cheerleading beauty from Coral Gables. It made no sense on paper. Other than their combined love of music, Adam would try in vain to find some common ground. He never did and it never mattered because in his heart he knew she was his soul mate, whatever that meant, and he had never felt more comfortable, more in tune with another human being since leaving his mother's womb.

There was an economy between them. A few words could convey

an hour's worth of conversation, a brief caress, a universe of caring love. Their love ignored the differences in their backgrounds, casting off the restrictions of learned behaviour and familial expectations.

The assurance Adam sought as he pressed his palm into hers was not for the continuance of her devotion to him or his to her. That was a given in his world. What he needed and could never have was the guarantee of her, the never-to-be-written warranty on her fragile mortality. His entire life was in the hands of her tiny beating heart. He had given himself over to her completely and knew he could never find his way back if ever he were to lose her.

These were bad thoughts to think, he knew, and he tried to be of the moment, like Derek, and will away the fear of dark tomorrows and gloomy outcomes.

They had decided to take the scenic view. There was an unspoken need to spend some time together—people were calling it quality time these days—to talk and reconnect. As Adam proceeded along highway 89A, his hand firmly holding Donna's, his fingers running up and down the softness of hers, he realized that all of the words they needed to say had been pronounced in but a few seconds of time. All of the feelings they needed to share were being transmitted between the neurons in their fingertips at sub-atomic speeds. Still, it was a breathtaking drive.

The class of '69. Adam had not seen Derek and Gloria together in the same room for at least five years. The last time was at an outdoor festival near Toronto in 1982. Derek had finally, after a decade of trying, put on one hell of a party for his friends. Funded by a consortium of investors with more money than gray stuff, Derek and his cadre of sycophantic, semi-criminal production personnel had staged what would probably be his first and last venture into large-scale concert promotion.

Adam and Derek always got together when Adam was in L.A., which was often. Derek would be full of news of a new deal, a get-rich-quick scheme, trying to draw Adam in, his smile and energy intoxicating. Adam always felt sorry for Derek's new investors. They never had a chance, not against Derek's charm.

John Walker had said over the phone, "The planets are aligning." With Derek, family in tow, headed for a camping trip into the Grand Canyon and Adam in Scottsdale meeting up with Donna, it was absolutely necessary for everyone to come see him in Sedona, he had said. Adam still had the scrap of paper containing John Walker's mysterious phone number, having never bothered to convert the information into an address book. He only felt comfortable keeping it in his snakeskin wallet for some reason.

Adam could count his time spent with John Walker in minutes. They had seen each other briefly and infrequently since Woodstock, once when Adam had flown into Phoenix to see a band play, and twice in New York, the first time a surprise, John Walker showing up unannounced at Adam and Donna's apartment in New York.

He claimed to be in the city attending a conference at the U.N., and Adam's name was in the book. He came in, took an offered beer and, for a couple of hours, he and Adam conversed on a level and with an intensity not previously experienced by Adam, not even with Donna. John Walker had the ability to sit before you and hold up a mirror, a metaphysical reflection that allowed you to perceive yourself from a skewed angle, a little off center, a little bit out of phase. It was disconcerting and fascinating simultaneously and the two hours passed without a single mundane thought, no pee break, the beers barely sipped. Then he said he had to leave and was on his feet before the words had the chance to reach Adam's eardrums. At the door he embraced Adam and Adam remembered him saying, "We must travel together you and I," and Adam had said sure, anytime, and John Walker had said, "No, we must do it at the right time."

A relationship measurable in minutes. A bond feeling like it might last a lifetime. It was one of the great puzzles in Adam's life. Fate or synchronicity or serendipity, naming it made it about as understandable as a botanical classification in Latin.

Their rented car climbed up and down the mountain ranges, the desert cactus giving way to hilly shrub trees, the temperature oscillating with the altitude changes. They had come this way once before, years ago, when money was tight and time was free. They had chosen this route for the same reasons you decide on a second honeymoon—part nostalgia, part reward, part rekindling of the passion fires. Contained within this scenery were the stored memories they both wanted to experience once more.

She dozed off.

He let her sleep, stealing quick glances every few minutes, had always delighted in watching her as she slept, the worry and stress of her life drained away, her face overtaken by an angelic calm. He wondered where she went, what faraway dimension lent her this peace, and could he join her there? In his heart he knew he could not, for though his sleep took him to other places too, they were dark and troublesome, a world of shadows and events too horrible to bring into wakefulness. Not every night. There were peaceful nights, dreams of sweet vision or silly nonsense. The dark nights though, those were the ones he remembered upon waking, the ones that only a hot shower and warm cup of coffee could dispel from his troubled mind.

All roads led to Sedona. Derek and the family were probably already there. John Walker was working at a new place called The Tennis Enchantment, situated in Boynton Canyon, a spectacular setting of red rock cliffs towering close, the resort nestled on the canyon floor. John Walker had gotten them a break on their casitas, meticulously appointed terra cotta cottages scattered throughout the property, connected by winding paths. John Walker said he helped take care of the grounds, did a bit of landscaping, groomed the chipping golf course, did some handiwork, some gardening. It seemed like simple work for so complex a man, a mere gardener, a keeper of shrubs and trees. But Adam knew such thoughts were bankrupt, because he was only viewing John Walker through the lens of Western society, a culture not known for honouring simplicity.

There was hiking planned and something John Walker called a time for healing. He said on the phone it was time for them to travel together. He said he would show Adam the desert beyond the boundaries of the resort. He said the planets were aligning and those words frightened Adam a bit. Adam thought he liked the planets where they were.

Derek was taking his family to the Grand Canyon and the thought of him with Gloria and Joey packed into a vintage VW van made Adam glad he had packed his camera and loaded it with film. Derek had the domestic instincts of a shark. He must have gotten himself in major trouble with Gloria to accede to this type of wholesome family adventure.

Adam often pondered over what exactly had been set in motion that rainy day at Woodstock. Were the planets aligned then, too? How else to explain the genesis of so many interweaving, serious relationships, now tested by time and tempered by the idiosyncrasies of its participants. And if the planets were aligning, if all of them were destined to reconvene, was John Walker the sun around which they all orbited?

Adam did not enjoy the possibility of pre-destination. He felt more comfortable believing he was the master of his own destiny. The idea of a higher power rolling out a web of possibilities for him to choose, ran counter to his belief in a cause and effect universe, where every action has its own specific consequence. Perhaps this weekend would play out as nothing more cosmic than a get together between friends. A few laughs, a few beers and then back to daily routines.

They reached Sedona as the sun was falling out of the western sky. The last rays were striking the tips of the low mountains rising to the north, drawing out the reddish hue of the stone. Donna opened her eyes and raised her head, disoriented at first. Her eyes were drawn to the shining hilltops. The fading light made their rounded peaks glow pink.

"I'm glad we came this way," she said.

II

JOHN WALKER WAS WAITING for them at the resort gate that led to the canyon hiking trails. The sun had risen only an hour before so there was still a sharp, frosty bite to the air. Donna wore khaki shorts and her skin from mid-thigh to her ankle was covered with goose bumps. She wore a bulky knitted sweater over her blouse and had pulled her hands inside the sleeves, crossing her arms across her chest, sleeves flying freely by her side.

Adam was a few paces back, walking with Derek and Gloria, Joey trailing a few steps behind them. Derek wore a Hawaiian shirt, cut-off jeans and rubber thongs. Adam was more suitably dressed in regulation denim, top and bottom, and sneakers. Joey was in overalls and Adam thought he had never seen the child in a dress. Gloria wore a floppy straw sun hat, her fair skin an easy target for the stinging rays of the sun. Her long-sleeved sweatsuit concealed her wonderfully sculpted figure.

John Walker had left them at breakfast, saying he needed to pick up a few supplies before they ventured out into the canyon. Derek had been reluctant to leave the dining room table, preferring the warm sunlight filtering in through the huge windows to the real thing outside. It took a little coaxing and a direct hit to the head from a bun thrown by Adam to move him out of his chair.

"I'm so looking forward to this," Derek said as they approached the gate. "A vortex. What the hell is a vortex?"

"It's an energy spot," said Gloria. "Sedona is known worldwide for its vortices. And you call yourself a hippie."

"No, you call me a hippie. I call myself a free spirit."

"What's a free spirit, Daddy?" asked Joey.

"It's someone who acts like a child and never grows up," said Gloria.

"Like Peter Pan?" asked Joey.

"Just like Peter Pan," said Derek.

"But you can't make me fly like Peter Pan."

"Sure I can. Come here."

Joey ran into Derek's open arms and he whirled the child around by her armpits, Joey screaming to be let down, Derek sticking his tongue out at Gloria on every revolution.

"The man can do no wrong in his daughter's eyes," said Gloria to Adam.

"She's Daddy's little girl."

"Right. If only he'd remember that a little more often."

John Walker bore his mountain man role to perfection. Like Adam, he was dressed in denim. His work shirt had been embellished with coloured beading on both breast pockets, circular designs similar to the ones on Adam's bracelet. His feet were ensconced in heavy duty hiking boots. His face was shaded by a large straw Stetson, his eyes hidden behind mirrored aviator sunglasses. A large inlaid silver belt buckle reflected brightly in the morning sun.

"Derek, the pool's over there," John Walker said, pointing back towards the resort. "Where do you think you're going with those idiotic things on your feet?"

Ten minutes later they were heading up the canyon trail, Derek having traded in his thongs for a pair of sneakers. There were several stops along the way, allowing Joey and Gloria to catch up to the main group and then some more time spent allowing them to rest.

It was a gradual climb and, after a short while, Donna removed her sweater and Gloria climbed out of her sweatpants, daring the sun to find her pink skin.

The canyon walls narrowed on both sides. The ground was thick with both coniferous and deciduous trees. A bed of decaying leaves littered the canyon floor although the path, well travelled, was mostly clear of the autumn carnage. Many trees still held on to their leaves, creating a wall of green, brown and red foliage that partially obscured the red rock cliffs that were gradually hemming them in as they approached the end of the canyon. Having just come from Phoenix, the combination of cool temperature and wooded forest made it hard to believe the desert city lay only a couple of hours to the south.

Adam felt strangely at home in these woods, the smells and sounds spawning memories of summer camping in Northern Ontario along with a pang of youthful longing that penetrated his relaxed state as he laboured up the path.

There had been a brief reunion when Adam and Donna first arrived. Adam found Derek and Gloria in the lounge, Joey being kept amused by a babysitter in their casita. Donna, still dozy from the drive, was resting. John Walker soon joined the table and it was not very long before the conversation turned to their common denominator, Woodstock.

Gloria said, "It was the crowning achievement of our generation. A giant coming-out party that changed people's perceptions about who we were as a social force. After Woodstock, we gained acceptance for our music and our voices were finally heard concerning the environment and our preference for natural living. Listen to the Muzak being piped into this room right now. Ten years ago it would have been Mantovani, now it's The Lovin' Spoonful."

"Actually," chimed in Derek, "it's Mantovani playing The Lovin' Spoonful."

"Very funny. My point is Woodstock allowed our culture, our generation to infiltrate into the mainstream."

"And you think this is a good thing?" said Adam.

"Absolutely. I got tired of calling myself a freak, of being considered a degenerate, getting kicked out of restaurants and having straights turn their noses up at me."

"A bath would have probably solved your problems," said Derek, who immediately ducked, deftly missing a backhander to the shoulder from Gloria.

"You have that look on your face, Adam. Spit it out," she said.

"I think what you call infiltration I call co-opting. What made that time special was that it was ours. The music was ours. The bohemian, vagabond lifestyle was ours. The drugs were definitely ours. And since they, whoever *they* are, couldn't destroy us, they assimilated our culture, absorbed it, skimmed its surface and neutered it. They took the devil's music and put it into shopping malls and elevators. In plain truth, Gloria, we sold out. We gave it away."

"Come on, Adam. You were there. You were at the very center of the greatest coming together of youth in the history of the world. You can't dismiss it that easily."

"I'll tell you how I see it. Remember when you were in high school and you'd catch word of an open house party, how everyone was going to be there, somebody's parents had gone on holiday, and there was going to be booze and drugs and lots of girls, well, and guys too obviously, and you showed up and there were kids everywhere, people spilling out onto the front lawn, guys puking into hedges, broken beer bottles on the driveway and you'd squeeze yourself into the house and if you were lucky you'd find a beer or maybe start drinking one of the ones you brought with you, and you'd look around for people you knew and if you found them, you couldn't really talk to them because the music was so damn loud and finally the police would show up, some neighbour having complained about the noise and everyone would eventually make their way to their cars and split."

Almost out of breath, Adam took a swig of beer then began reading its label, as if it might contain an important message.

"Your point?" she asked.

"My point is," he said, finally putting the beer down, "that's what Woodstock was for me. A party put on by some rich kids, and everyone heard about it and decided to show up. Sure it had social significance; it was a manifestation of the financial emancipation of the country's pampered, white, middle class youth. It was the singular piece of evidence demonstrating the success of the '50's generation. Our parents had succeeded in making their children's lives easier than their own. Think about it. How many black people did you see at Woodstock? Or Hispanics? Or poor people or working stiffs who couldn't dream of taking the time off, let alone finding the money to travel across the country to some rock concert. Ninety percent of the crowd was there to party. And of those who attended, I guarantee if you had polled those kids who showed up, clearly half would have said that, all things considered, they would have rather stayed home. It was only later, when they read about it in Time or Newsweek that it suddenly became a badge of honour to have been in attendance."

"And what does the gardener think?" asked Derek.

John Walker had been sitting quietly, nursing a Becks beer. He put it down, put both hands down on the table and smiled at his friends.

"I thought it made a great movie. I must have gone to see it at least four times."

Then he stood up and did a few bars of *With A Little Help From My Friends*, Joe Cocker style, this reserved, quiet man transformed into a raving rock star wannabe, the patrons agog while Adam, Derek and Gloria split themselves open with laughter, the bartender and waitresses whistling and howling, John Walker finally collapsing into his chair, the seriousness of the conversation, lost and forgotten.

After dinner everyone retired early. Adam and Donna quickly sought the warmth of their covers then of their bodies, making slow and easy love to each other, mouths locked together like amorous leeches, falling asleep quickly when it was over, tangled together, neither willing to let go of the near feeling of oneness.

The final climb to the vortex was mildly treacherous. Joey clung to her father's neck as he negotiated the steep pitch of the rock face, searching for secure footing, everybody using their hands to seek out small crevices. Gloria slipped down a small rock face and sliced her knee on the rough surface, a three-inch gash seeping thick drops of blood. John Walker was quick to open his pack and dress the wound and in minutes Gloria was on her feet, only slightly favouring the injured knee.

There was nothing particularly spectacular about the vortex. The rocky hill flattened out so standing was possible and there was a ledge of rock to sit on. The canyon walls formed a semi-circle of stone around them. Derek turned to Adam and asked, "Can you feel it?" Adam shrugged his shoulders and said nothing.

Donna helped Gloria find a comfortable place to rest her painful leg.

"How do you feel?" asked Donna.

"I'm fine. It doesn't really hurt, just stings a little. I feel wonderful. Really."

"Does it hurt, Mommy?" asked Joey, real concern on her face.

"Not at all. Come on, I'll show you," and Gloria got up and grabbed Joey's hands and the two of them started twirling around, faster and faster they spun, laughing, then Derek cut in and the three of them danced around an imaginary maypole. Adam took heart while watching his friend's troubled family enjoying a pure moment together, but then Derek grabbed Gloria to himself and Joey faded back, left standing alone on the improvised dance floor. Adam could feel her pain, tensed to rise only to feel the pressure of Donna's hand on his forearm so he relaxed and slumped back, disheartened, Joey finding a small boulder and sitting down.

"Can you feel it?" asked Derek.

"Feel what?" asked Gloria.

"The energy in this place. Can you feel it?"

"I thought you meant my leg."

Derek broke from the dance and circled the small rock platform. He swayed as if stoned, caught up in a private moment and Adam could not tell if he was having everyone on or was actually drawing something from the vortex. Adam was betting on the former.

John Walker sat impassively on a natural step in the rock face. He wore a half smile and it was impossible to tell if he was amused or appalled.

"Do you feel anything?" Donna whispered in Adam's ear.

"A little gas from breakfast."

"Seriously."

"There's nothing to feel."

"I think I feel something."

"You're kidding."

"No, I definitely feel something."

"Tell me."

"A slight tingling sensation in my legs."

"Try loosening your belt."

John Walker pulled out a piece of thick green twine from some-where inside his denim jacket and lit the end of it, then blew it out. A line of smoke snaked its way upward a couple of feet until the breezes dispersed it. He walked over to Joey and said a few muffled words then cupped the smoke with his hand and made as if to wash her with it, moving his hand a few inches from her face then down to hcr shoulders and around the back of her head, repeating the process then moving to Gloria and starting the procedure again. When he got to Derek he matched Derek's hypnotic dance, step for step, applying the invisible balm over Derek's head and shoulders. Donna was next and then he stood before Adam.

The smell was part incense, part pot.

"No thanks," said Adam.

"Why are you thanking me?" asked John Walker.

"I'm thanking you for not covering me in smoke."

"It's symbolic. A symbolic cleansing. To clear your spirit."

"I took a shower this morning."

John Walker smiled and sat next to Adam. He gingerly snuffed out the rope with his thumb and index finger.

"You're not buying any of this, are you?" said John Walker.

"Like, as if Derek is. Am I supposed to believe he's communing with nature? He's a freak. I love him but he's a freak. I once saw him smoke a bowl full of compressed alfalfa—he thought it was blond Lebanese hash—and the guy loved it, got high as a kite."

John Walker picked up a small rock and began bouncing it in the palm of his hand. "Derek is open to the possibility. That's what's important. Whether it's an energy vortex or some shitty hashish, he's open to the potentiality of the moment. For better or for worse. And I'm not saying that makes him right and you wrong.

I see two women over there paying the price for his . . . his spontaneity."

"That's a nice word for it."

"And it's not your word, is it? I'll bet you like to inspect your shit before you flush it. I'll bet you've never taken a shit in your life without sliding your butt over and taking a peek."

Donna, who had been hanging on every word, keeled over in laughter. She kept trying to say something, sputtering out words until Adam's glare sobered her but only momentarily, for a new spasm of giggles besieged her.

"I'll take that as a yes," said John Walker, slapping Adam on the back.

Not amused, Adam said, "Not that it's anybody's fucking business, but who doesn't?"

"I don't," said Donna.

"Me either," said John Walker. "Should I ask Gloria?"

"Never mind. What's your point?"

"My point is, you're one constipated son of a bitch. You can't let go, not even of your turds. You have to look back, admire your creation and say goodbye before you flush. Tell me I'm wrong?"

"You're wrong."

"Here, take this." John Walker flipped the rock to Adam, who caught it in both hands. "What do you see?"

"A rock."

"I see a universe."

"I'm happy for you."

"You need to see a universe."

"This will make me a better person?"

"A better human, yes."

Adam could feel it, the walls rising, blocking his view to his heart, a cold, hurtful frankness gathering critical mass as powerful, unretractable words were forming inside his brain to be quick messengered with instructions to his tongue. There was another voice though, a pleading, helpless voice, small, confined, begging to be heard, another message, counteracting the first, weak, barely audible, ignorable, not ignored.

"I suppose it's never too late to improve oneself. What did you have in mind?" Adam felt Donna softly bump her shoulder into his, a signal of what . . . her approval, her empathy, her pride . . . he was not sure.

221

"You need to heal yourself. You need to let the spirits help you. You cannot do this alone. Do you trust what I am saying?"

"I know you mean well. I know you are honest and sincere."

"There is a path I know you will not take willingly. Will you let me show you the way?"

There was such intensity in John Walker's face. Adam felt he had no choice but to say yes.

"Good. Then it's settled. Meet me in the parking lot at seven P.M. Wear loose fitting clothing and bring a bag with a change of clothing and a coat. It gets cold in the evening. Bring a toothbrush, too. Ask Derek if he'd like to come." To Donna he said, "I would ask you and Gloria to come too, but I can't. Not tonight."

"Where are we going?" asked Adam.

"To the desert," he said.

III

A PAIR OF HEADLIGHTS made their way down Boynton Canyon Road. Adam greeted their detection by adding another knot to his already twisting stomach. John Walker had called him a spirit warrior. He felt more like a conscientious objector. Donna had packed his bag and pushed him out the door, telling him it wouldn't harm him to do a little male bonding. He had reminded her how he spent most of his time in small rooms confined for long hours with musicians who themselves were bound together in the modern version of the primitive hunting/gathering group. This to no avail as he found himself on the wrong side of the door to their casita.

The headlights grew larger. Adam turned and faced the door. He thought of his warm bed and Donna in it beside him, the TV on, maybe reading a book or making love, and it seemed so preferable to a night of unknown destinations and uncertain activities. He put his hand in his coat pocket and momentarily held the room key, then let it go and turned away from the door.

It was dusk and the sky was filling with stars. There was little, if any, moonlight so the nearby cliffs were becoming vague outlines on the horizon. It was chilly, the temperature dropping rapidly, Adam's wet breath forming little clouds as he walked to the parking lot.

Derek, uncharacteristically on time, was waiting for Adam in the lot. He sat on the back bumper of his VW van, smoking a joint. He inhaled deeply as Adam approached, slowly letting out a thick white cloud before a hacking cough forced the remaining smoke out of his lungs.

"Want any?" he said, almost gagging on the words, reaching forward with the lit ember.

"Not tonight. I'd rather have a clear head."

"For what?"

"I don't know. I'm not crazy about the idea of going out into the desert at night."

"John Walker said I was really going to enjoy this . . . this thing we're doing."

"Why doesn't that make me feel any better?"

"Relax. You're such an old woman. If the gardener has something special planned for us tonight, you know it's going to be memorable. The guy doesn't trifle around. For sure he's not taking us to some wild reservation party or to a bar to get drunk. Not that I'd mind. No, he's got something heavy planned for us. I think he's been planning it since the day we met him."

"That's just what my stomach's telling me. Shit. What do we really know about this guy?"

"We know we can trust him."

"I suppose."

The headlights were attached to a pickup truck, a late model Dodge. It had a hydraulic winch planted in the middle of the box. There was another man with John Walker.

"This is my brother, Tom," said John Walker.

Tom appeared to be at least a decade younger than John Walker and it was immediately apparent that he had none of the native stoicism John Walker carried with him always. Smiling and unaffected, Tom grasped the two offered hands and shook them heartily.

"At last I get to meet the two hippies," said Tom.

Derek said, "I never imagined John Walker having a mother and father so you're a big surprise. Now is it Tom or Tom Walker?"

"Most people can get my attention with Tom."

"He also answers to — Who wants to go for beer?" said John Walker.

"My brother doesn't approve of my lifestyle. He says I'm not on a warrior's path. I say who wants to be a warrior. Make love not war. Isn't that what you guys say?"

"I traded in my bell bottoms a few years back," said Adam.

"Talk in the car . . . we're late," said John Walker.

They travelled in silence, Tom squeezed into the jump seat, Adam and Derek sharing the front bucket seat. Adam imagined they were heading east but the blackness was disorienting so after a while he settled into the rhythm of the eight-cylinder engine. After forty minutes of rolling along a two-lane highway, John Walker turned onto a dirt road and for another twenty minutes he drove with an abandon rarely exhibited in his personal demeanor. Adam sat, one arm wrapped behind the headrest, the other braced against the glove box, anxiously enduring the ride and the oppressive fear he felt from the black night enveloping them, broken only by the high beams of the truck. The road was nothing more than a glorified rutted trail. It disappeared entirely at times, small shrubs briefly appearing in the lights before being guillotined by the bumper. John Walker would then jerk the wheel back and forth until the path reappeared, the back end fishtailing until the truck eased back into the grooves.

"Not a terribly environmentally friendly drive," said Adam.

"We're late," was all John Walker would offer.

The vehicle slowed as a break in the road came into view. John Walker took the fork and after a few hundred yards, he pulled the truck next to a couple of wrecks near a small dwelling. A small gathering of people sat around a slow-burning fire about thirty feet from what appeared to be the entrance to a hut. John Walker made no move to disembark from the truck. Instead he addressed the occupants.

"I have brought you to a traditional sweat ceremony. You have been invited as my guests. Before we get out and join the others I want to prepare you for what to expect and how you should behave. The conductor of the sweat is a Hopi Elder. There will be three other Elders partaking in the sweat as well. Two are Navajo and one is Hopi but it is not important to you to which tribes any of them belong. What is important is to listen and learn. The conductor will provide you with teachings before we enter the lodge. You are free to ask questions. Do not ask too many. Be respectful. If you seem too self-absorbed or too cynical or analytical you will be shunned and not allowed into the lodge. Listen to the lodge conductor. Do as he says. Listen carefully. Open your hearts to the messages you will receive this night."

John Walker grabbed his bag and got out of the truck. He walked over to the fire and sat down. Adam and Derek gave each other a look then followed John Walker.

There were four men sitting around the fireplace. A fifth was attending to the fire. There were a dozen or more rocks the size of a baby's head or larger, resting on the hot coals. The man tending the fire was sprinkling a fine dust on the rocks, which immediately ignited into a thousand sparks and a puff of smoke. Adam smelled a pungent odour and recognized it as cedar.

Two of the four seated men were quite old, at least seventy. Despite the chilly temperatures, they were already half undressed, their torsos covered only by blankets, the skin on their chests hanging loosely over protruding ribs, their gray hair worn in identical long braids. The other two appeared to be in their mid-forties, one overweight with smooth skin and a stomach that folded over his belt, the other with a ruddy, pot marked face and a strong, acutely defined upper body.

Two women and another man sat away from the fire, by a picnic table, preparing food in large bowls.

John Walker approached one of the older men. The Elder's face was a roadmap of creases, his sun-baked face frozen in a perpetual squint, the crow's feet emanating from the corners of his eyes trailing almost to his cheeks. He had a gentle smile on his face and clear eyes. John Walker went down on his knees before the old man. Reaching into his bag, John Walker retrieved a small leather pouch drawn together by leather thongs. He opened the bag and brought out something Adam could not see.

"What's that?" Adam whispered to Tom.

"Tobacco."

John Walker spoke. "On behalf of myself and my friends I give you this gift of tobacco. I ask that you accept our group into your lodge this night. My friends and I come here to seek guidance from the Creator and to open our hearts, bodies and minds to the four spirits so that we may accept their healing. My friends and I humbly ask you to accept our gift and allow us entrance to the lodge."

John Walker remained motionless, the tobacco still in his hand. The Elder stared at John Walker, then past him to where Adam, Derek and Tom sat. Adam felt naked under the man's intense scrutiny. He fought to maintain eye contact, knowing it would not go well if he looked away. Finally, after a several seconds had passed, the Elder reached for the tobacco and took it from John Walker.

"You and your friends may join us tonight."

John Walker returned to the other side of the fire, smiling as if a great test had been won. The Elder he had addressed now stood up, wrapping the blanket tightly around his shoulders, holding the corners with one hand while the other was raised in what appeared to be a salute.

"I am the lodge conductor. Think of me as the master of ceremonies, if you will. Tonight you will experience the ancient teaching of the sweat." He walked closer to the fire, the red glow lighting his sharp features. He was a deceptively small man. While seated, Adam had imagined him much taller. He wore a beautiful turquoise and silver necklace around his neck, the fire's light reflecting off its many surfaces.

"You see many rocks in the fire. There are seventeen. The People call each of these rocks, grandfather. There is a spirit in each of the grandfathers. Tonight we will free the spirits into the lodge and pay homage to them and acknowledge their passing."

The Elder moved over to the man tending the fire. The man had a pitchfork and was moving the rocks to different spots on the hot coals. Adam tried to count the rocks. He got to twelve but some lay hidden from his view.

"This brother is the fire keeper," said the Elder. "He has great knowledge in the construction of fire and the application of medicines on the flame. He knows how many grandfathers to place in the flames according to our tradition and he vigilantly will mark the progress of the grandfathers until they are ready to release their spirit.

"It is not important that you understand entirely what is happening tonight. It is more important for you to observe and learn. Let your body accept the information surrounding it. Open your heart to the healing spirits entering the lodge tonight. Know that the sweat was given to the People by the Creator to help them come closer to him, to give the People a way by which they are able to commune with the Creator and seek his healing influence. Tonight will be the closest you ever come to your Creator while still in this physical plane. And tonight the Creator will hear your prayers more clearly than he has ever heard them before. The lodge is the womb of the Earth Mother. You will find no safer place since you last crawled from the protection of your own mother's womb, kicking and crying. Tonight we will crawl back into our mother's womb and find the safety and security we have been without since we were forced into this world."

The Elder moved between the fire and the lodge. Adam had been soothed by the sound of the old man's voice, the tone of it calming his stomach although his mind was brimming with trepidation. He was not sure he wanted to confront his Creator. He did not necessarily believe there was a Creator to confront. And he knew with absolute certainty that he did not wish to be proved wrong.

A chill jolted Adam so he pulled his coat closer to his body. Everyone was silent, expectant. The other three Elders sat stone still and they were staring at Adam. It was as if they could read his thoughts and were disapproving of his presence at their ceremony.

"The lodge has four doors," said the lodge conductor, although Adam could only see one, an entrance covered by a tarp. The lodge was igloo shaped, not more than three or four feet high, recessed into the ground. Adam imagined the interior floor must have been dug

227

out because the entrance sloped downwards.

"We will crawl back into the womb," he said. "Through this door we return to the womb of the Earth Mother. As you enter you will give your spirit name. If you do not know your spirit name then give the name the Creator is most likely to recognize you by. You should identify your clan as well. The Creator sometimes needs all the help he can get.

"The lodge has been constructed by bending saplings and tying them together according to our tradition. This door we will enter is facing east. We recognize the directions from which the spirit helpers come. From the east comes the spirit who heals the physical. There are also three spirit doors; the one facing west allows entrance of the spirit who mends the mind, the one facing north, the healer of spirit, and the one facing south welcomes the healing spirit of the heart."

The Elder then walked around the fire. He stopped by Derek and put his hand on his shoulder. "You will sit by the south door," he told him. Tom he told to sit next to Derek near the west door. One of the younger Elders, the fat one, was told to sit on Derek's right near the entrance, John Walker next to the conductor on the other side of the entrance. The other two Elders were to place themselves by the west door. He approached Adam last. "You will sit by the north door." Adam tried to remember which spirit helper came through the north door.

"Which spirit have I got?" Adam whispered to John Walker.

"You will require help from all of them before the night is out," said John Walker.

The men were told to undress and remove all jewelry then line up behind the conductor in the order he had designated.

"Time to remove our clothes gentlemen," said John Walker.

"Are you nuts," said Derek. "It's freezing out here."

"It won't be for long. Take off your clothes. You modest types can leave your underwear on."

"So is this when you drive away with our clothes and leave us naked in the desert?" asked Derek.

"We only do that during the summer. Take off your clothes and form a line as the Elder has instructed. It will get very hot inside. I want you to breathe deeply and slowly. If you feel yourself getting faint, put your head near the ground for a moment. Do not talk unless spoken to."

Derek said, "All this preparation for a steam bath? Shit, we could have stayed at The Enchantment and had one in the health spa."

"I assure you this will be quite different from anything you have ever experienced."

Tom started slowly unbuttoning his shirt. Adam and Derek stood motionless.

"What's going to go on here, Tom?" asked Adam.

"It's like the Elder said. This is a ritual cleansing and healing process. You sit in there and sweat your brains out. Sometimes they pass around a pipe or burn sweet grass. Sometimes they sing songs. There are worse ways to spend an evening. I don't know why JW brought you two here. I know why I'm here. It's another attempt to bring me closer to his world, to the native way. He does not approve of me, of my life, so he tries to improve me, to show me the way of the warrior. I say I don't know why he brought you here. But I do know he has a reason. John Walker always has a reason."

"What the fuck," said Derek, unbuckling his belt.

Adam watched the two men undress. He could not command his hands to do the same. His heart was pounding, an unnamed terror paralyzing him. He watched as the door flap oscillated in the night breezes, distorting his shadow being cast by the fire behind him. Loud cracks from exploding air pockets in the wood broke the stillness and made his heart leap. There was an irrational certainty taking hold telling him his life would forever change once the threshold of this nondescript hut was breached. He tried to locate the source of his discomfort, hoping for a rational impediment to prevent his partaking in this ritual. He could find none. He began to shake uncontrollably, the cold stiffening his joints. And the reason was obvious. He was naked. His hands had obeyed some other signal from his brain while his mind vacillated. He swooped down and picked up his clothes, removing his watch and bracelet and handing them to the fire keeper as the others were doing. Then he got into line according to the Elder's placement, which put him behind John Walker.

There was a mound of earth near the entrance upon which Adam saw a small drum, a pipe, rattles, long feathers with beads attached to their quills and a set of antlers. Each man in turn got on all fours and crawled into the lodge, the lodge conductor entering first with John Walker following.

There was not enough room to stand. The Elder continued on all fours around the perimeter of the lodge, moving clockwise. The flap of the east door allowed some firelight into the dwelling. Adam could barely make out a pit in the center of the room. The Elder came to a halt just before the entrance. Adam stopped and after a few minor calculations, determined he must be near the north side of the dwelling. The others filed in, taking their places in accordance with the Elder's instructions.

Adam knew Derek must be sitting across from him but he could not see any faces and only the hint of legs. Even the young Elder to his right was barely discernable. Adam fought back a wave of claustrophobia as the fire keeper appeared at the entrance, passing items to the last man who had entered, seated near the flap, a man Adam presumed had been sitting over with the women when he first arrived. The Elder to Adam's right, the one with the ruddy complexion whispered to Adam that the man near the entrance was the doorkeeper and he was accepting the articles to be used during the sweat from the fire keeper. The fire keeper disappeared then re-entered, holding a grandfather rock on his pitchfork. The doorkeeper took the antlers and accepted the rock from the fire keeper. There were words spoken in a native tongue, a greeting of some kind. Adam heard Tom say, "Welcome grandfather," in English. The doorkeeper then moved to the pit and placed the rock in the two-foot depression. This procedure was repeated four more times and Adam now joined in and greeted each grandfather as it made its way into the lodge.

The doorkeeper approached the conductor who placed something into the doorkeeper's hand. The doorkeeper moved past Adam, crouching over the pit. He must have sprinkled the rocks with whatever was in his hand because now there was a silent explosion of sparkling light, little starbursts as the material touched the rocks and was instantly vaporized. The lodge filled with the smell of cedar.

The fire keeper returned one last time with a bucket of water, which he placed between the conductor and the doorkeeper, and then he left, moving the flap and fixing it in place, throwing the room into almost total blackness. The only light came from the red-hot grandfathers lining the bottom of the pit. They were streaked with black veins and their redness appeared to throb. They threw enough light for Adam to see the outline of Derek's knees across the pit.

Adam leaned back a little and his head brushed against the slope of the lodge ceiling. The darkness was oppressive. He strained to see as the rocks lost some of their luster.

The conductor began to chant in his native tongue and it had a familiar quality to it. In the pitch-blackness Adam saw the sanctuary of his grandfather's synagogue, the rabbi davening, swaying forward and back, kissing his talus then applying the kiss to the holy script. The old man's chant had a similar cadence, a like intent, as if the way to God was as much a matter of tone as it was of observance.

It was becoming quite warm in the lodge. Adam was tickled by droplets running down his sides from his armpits. His upper lip was moist and his scalp began to itch. He moved one of his feet beneath him to prevent the tip of his penis from touching the ground.

The darkness robbed Adam of the ability to mark the passage of time. He did not know how long the conductor had been praying when he abruptly stopped. There was some rustling then the striking of a match. The flare was blinding and a dancing afterimage burnt itself onto Adam's retina. The conductor applied the match to a long pipe, tobacco fumes filtering their way into Adam's nose.

"Take the pipe and offer a silent prayer of thanks," said the old man. He must have passed it to the left because every few seconds, Adam saw the red embers of the pipe tobacco glowing as another participant sucked back the smoke through the pipe stem. After a few minutes he felt a tap on his arm as the Elder next to him passed him the pipe.

He was unsure what to do. He wanted to ask for directions. But he had been admonished by John Walker to remain quiet. Offer a prayer of thanks, the old man had said. Adam had much to be thankful for. He thought of Donna, of their life, of his career, then sucked back on the stem of the pipe.

He knew as soon as the smoke passed down his throat that he had taken in too much. He quickly exhaled, the smoke stinging his passageway on the trip back up, causing him to hack convulsively. Desperately he tried to hold back the coughing, only to be betrayed by another staccato string of involuntary choking sounds. He was hoping the darkness would conceal his identity.

"My friend has a lot to be thankful for," said John Walker.

Adam added dizziness to his discomfort as the burning sensation receded. He was still holding the pipe when John Walker removed it from his grasp. Then he felt John Walker's hand on his wrist, squeezing it gently, which somehow made his dizziness lessen.

More silence.

Adam heard the ladle being dipped into a bucket then there was a splash and the shock of the steam hitting his face made him flinch. Five times the ladle dipped into the bucket and five times it was emptied over the rocks, the temperature rising with each application, making breathing difficult and hurting Adam's eyes.

"We recognize the healing of mother earth, of the sky world and of the universe. We await you, healer spirit of the body physical."

The pipe made the rounds once again. Adam was careful to gently draw on the pipe, exhaling slowly and giving thanks once again for the good things in his life.

Next an eagle feather was passed from man to man, the Elders and John Walker reciting prayers in the Navajo and Hopi language, Tom mumbling something unintelligible in English, Adam holding the feather for a few seconds, feeling the beads hanging from it, absently counting them before passing it along.

The conductor then sang a song, beating rhythmically on a small drum, a soprano aria, words strung together in a single thread, weaving their way to the heavens. Adam felt a heaviness in his chest, a strange sorrow, as if the pain of a people was visiting his heart. As the conductor wound through his song, the ache in Adam's back from sitting still so long disappeared and he thought he felt a coolness pass over his body. Strange lights, twirling like pinwheels, danced before his eyes. The song soared and Adam's body felt a particular lightness and he imagined himself not sitting but lying on his back, then on his front, then upside down and was amazed with the ease by which he could fool his mind in the darkness.

Then the song stopped. The conductor called out and the flap opened, a gush of cold air filling the lodge. Some of the men were crawling out of the lodge.

"Is that it?" asked Adam.

"No," said John Walker. "It's the end of the first round."

"How many rounds are there?"

"Four, one for each spirit door."

They crawled out of the lodge and sat by the fire.

"Which spirit is next?" asked Adam.

"Yours."

"Mine?"

"You are sitting by the north door. The conductor will next call in the healer of the spirit. If you concentrate you may see him. If you open yourself to him he will heal your wounded soul."

"What makes you think it needs healing?"

"Everyone's soul needs healing. Don't take it so personal."

They sat around, most smoking cigarettes, some engaging in small

232

talk. John Walker warned Derek not to throw anything into the fire except the cigarette he was smoking. They were hand rolled, crafted by one of the women and passed out by the fire keeper, Adam abstaining.

Adam was surprisingly eager to get back into the lodge. After the initial wave of claustrophobia had passed and his body had acclimatized to the searing heat, he had found himself absorbed in the moment, the passage of time untracked and unnoticed. He had no idea if the first round had taken ten minutes or two hours and was going to ask John Walker then thought better of it. It didn't really matter. As he stared at the slow burning fire, he recalled the instant when he had lost himself completely to the conductor's song, feeling the heartbeat of the drum reverberate within him, and the sense of wellbeing, if only for a few seconds, had been worth the initial discomfort of the sweat.

His thoughts were interrupted by the conductor, who was summoning everyone back into the lodge. Adam took his place in the line, confident he had mastered the procedure and could now better appreciate the rituals being performed.

Six more rocks were brought into the lodge and welcomed. Sweet grass was offered to the grandfathers this time and the tiny bits cackled and sparked as they hit the surface of the rocks. The pipe was passed once more around the circle. The tobacco smoke mixed with the sweet grass, producing an intoxicating smell.

Adam was inhaling deeply when the first ladle of water hit the grandfathers. He had not noticed the conductor's movement and the gush of steam in his face made him choke. It seemed much hotter than during the first round. He tensed and listened for the ladle to be placed in the bucket. He braced himself for the second explosion. It came and was more forceful than the first. Adam peered into the pit and saw four brightly glowing grandfathers and two dull ones and he realized the conductor was aiming each ladle at a different rock.

Adam placed his head in his lap, as close to the ground as possible. The change in altitude made the heat only slightly more bearable. His skin was glistening from a combination of his own sweat and the intense humidity. He felt burning hot drops falling on his back and realized it was actually raining in the lodge.

Adam prayed the conductor would not throw more water on the hot rocks but his prayers went unanswered as the ladle made a scraping sound against the bucket and a few seconds later, the whooshing sound of instant evaporation followed another heat rush from which

Adam could find no position of escape. He placed his palms against his eyes, convinced his eyeballs would melt if he did not protect them. His mouth searched near the ground for cooler air. He felt the ground moving beneath him and thought he would faint, then a familiar hand was on his shoulder, gently but firmly pulling him back and forcing him to sit straight; he allowed the hand to guide his body into position, resigned to the pain, to the suffocating torrid heat burrowing into every pore of his skin.

The feather was being passed once again. Adam passed it mindlessly to John Walker. Then John Walker was speaking, half heard words making their way through the dense humidity to Adam's ears. Adam tried to concentrate, thought he was hearing and interpreting, was no longer sure if the words were really getting through to his brain. With all his will, he forced himself to listen.

" . . . ask the spirit to help heal the wounded souls not only of the men in this lodge but beyond this place. I know it is the responsibility of each man to seek his own destiny, to bring the spirit helpers into his life so he may heal himself with their help and so contribute to the repairing of the Earth Mother. I wish to take it upon myself to help my brothers find their way if the spirits so wish it. I ask for the power to be their aide, to seek their guidance and wisdom."

There was silence as Adam imagined the feather passing from John Walker's hand to the lodge conductor's. The conductor's voice was next heard.

"I have spoken of the deterioration of the Earth Mother tonight. I have sung to her, thanking her for her abundance and asking her for guidance. I do not do these things from free choice. It is not I who delivers tonight's message. What is said in this lodge is determined by the Creator and by each of your relationships with the Creator. Even the steam is the Creator's decision. I am merely his vessel. You are merely his vessel. John Walker is correct. We must heal ourselves in order to help the Earth Mother. Like a swaddling infant sucking on its mother's nourishing tit, the Earth Mother needs our nourishment. And like the nursing mother, the degree by which we can provide nourishment for others depends on how well we feed our own spiritual selves. Drink deeply of the spirit helper."

Another swish of the bucket and more water was thrown on the grandfathers.

More drops fell from above, molten beads striking Adam's scalp and shoulders.

Derek saying something about ritual, that he preferred to take his own chances, how you needn't have to rely on invisible spirits to make things happen, the conductor admonishing him, interrupting to say chances are only taken by the ignorant, that a warrior always measures the odds and calls on his allies and spirit helpers to turn the outcome in his favour, if such an outcome is meant to be.

"I don't mean to offend you, brother," said Derek. "I respect your culture and your gods and whatever spirits may visit us this night. I only remind you that there are many cultures in this world, many ways to God and if there are people ignorant of your ways, this does not preclude them from finding themselves on the same path we embark upon this night."

"True, brother. We meet many travellers on the spiritual path, some of this earth, some from other systems. *This* is the People's way. And the People have been travelling this path for millennia, while your ancestors were still living in mud huts, sacrificing to pagan idols and being consumed by their own filth."

More silence, the darkness so immediate, so close it covered Adam like a wet suit.

There was a pecking on his right arm. It grew stronger and his arm began to hurt from it.

"Take the feather," the young Elder whispered.

Adam fought for coherency as he reached once more for the feather. He felt the beads in his fingers, dancing from the bottom of the quill.

"I don't know what to say," said Adam. "I have a good life. I have a super wife and I make lots of money. I can't think of anything lacking in my life."

"We don't need a sob story," said the conductor. "Help us heal the Earth Mother."

For once Adam welcomed the darkness. It hid his humiliation. He fumbled for something redeeming to say. He searched the catalogues of his repertoire and nothing surfaced. He gave up trying. Then he heard these words come from his mouth. "*Life is just a game. You fly your paper plane. There is no end.*"

There was quiet then a deep chortle emanating from where the conductor sat. Soon the entire congregation was laughing. Adam too joined in although he felt left out of the joke.

"That's a good one," said the conductor, and it must have been, for another ladle full of water hit the rocks.

Another song followed, the conductor banging his hand drum while his eerie incantations filled the small room. Adam bowed his head and shut his eyes from the heat. Immediately the room began to spin and Adam watched dispassionately as he fell further and further into a swirling vortex of light and sound. As before, he felt a sudden coolness pass over him and simultaneously a blinding bright light filled the room. He opened his eyes from the shock of it and although the light was still visible, he could not see anyone in the room. He closed his eyes and the light remained. He put his hands over his eyes and the light failed to diminish.

Relaxing, he fell into the brightness, found himself inexplicably able to perceive the brilliant whiteness from a three-hundred-and-sixty-degree perspective. There was a dark shadow coming out of the light. It was huge and as it moved closer it appeared to be loping. Loping? What lopes? thought Adam. Do horses lope? This wasn't a horse. The hind legs drifted to the side, raising the hind quarters higher into the air than the shoulders and head, which appeared to skim the ground. It was the lope of a wolf. The lazy gait of a wolf.

The great beast came towards Adam, out of the light, eclipsing the brilliance, silhouetted against the sun. It stopped before him, stretching its front legs before it, its belly touching the ground, a playful gesture; shy, curious, its tongue hanging from the side of its mouth. Adam was unafraid. The wolf crawled slowly on all fours towards where he sat. Adam froze, concerned that any sudden movement would scare the beast or desiccate the image.

Adam was overcome by a sense of his own well-being, trace memories of his mother, pre-dating his birth, infusing his consciousness with a primordial joy. There was a presence inside him, the listener, the one to whom all questions were asked, the one who listened and passed judgment in silence, the one true voice amongst all the pretenders, and this presence was speaking to the wolf, Adam a bystander to their conversation, a foreigner unable to translate the communication yet knowing that he was the subject matter of the discussion. Then the wolf was gone and the light faded to a quick blindness and Adam lost track of his thoughts.

The splash of cedar-scented water striking Adam's face startled him to full consciousness. He bolted upright, wiping the liquid from his face. The flap had been opened and the participants were crawling out of the lodge.

"Are we boring you, brother?" asked the conductor.

"No Elder. The steam. I must have passed out from the steam."

"I don't think so," said the conductor. "I don't think so at all."

Adam crawled out of the lodge and found a place next to John Walker by the fire. The fire keeper had built it up to a high flame, six grandfathers still awaiting the release of their spirits. Adam noticed the fire keeper entering the lodge to remove the expended rocks. John Walker told him that the rocks were only used once then placed in a strategic location near the lodge.

All eyes were on Adam as they sat by the fire, the cigarettes having been handed out and lit, small clouds of smoke exiting the mouths and nostrils of the smokers, John Walker the only one of the eight, other than Adam, not partaking.

"That was quite a performance you put on," said John Walker.

"I don't know what you mean."

"No? You were howling. In the darkness, if I didn't know better I'd swear a wolf had crawled into the lodge. You made the hairs stand up on my neck and arms. That was very strong medicine."

Adam was going to protest only he felt a deep sense of pride and accomplishment and decided to say nothing.

Derek came over and the two of them had a laugh over Adam quoting the Thunderclap Newman lyric when pressed by the conductor.

"I just about shit myself when you said that. It was perfect. What made you think of it?"

"I don't know. I always thought it would make a great epitaph."

The next two rounds were more enjoyable for Adam, less painful, Adam listening carefully to the prayers of the others as the feather made its rounds. His last two prayers were silent, nonverbal thoughts from the source of his being, his essential self conversing directly with the spirit helpers. He would never be able to describe to Donna these moments of pure communication. He could only feel them.

Before the door opened for the final time, the conductor gave thanks to the Earth Mother by pouring water on the ground.

"We thank you Earth Mother and give you this offering. We thank the helper spirits who visited us this night. We are grateful for the visitation by the helper spirit from the north and thank the Creator for sending the spirit and permitting our new friend to graciously receive his gift."

The conductor encouraged everyone to make an offering of the remaining water, then to drink the holy water. Adam took the first ladle and after making a libation to the Earth Mother, drank the ladle dry. The cedar brew had a strong, bitter taste. A woman entered the tent

237

with bowls of fruit. Adam munched on apple and orange slices, sucking the juices and delighting in their passage down his throat. Adam watched the conductor rub a dripping handful of the cedar tea over his body. The conductor then handed the ladle over to Adam who took some of the scented water in his hand and washed it over his body and under his armpits.

They gathered once more outside by the fire, the fire keeper having built the flames high now that all of the grandfathers had been removed. The conductor prayed before the fire, standing with his arms outstretched, reciting ancient text in a language that while foreign, resonated with an unexplainable familiarity to Adam.

After the final prayer, the women brought more food, big metal pots placed on hooks over the fireplace. Soon steaming helpings of vegetable stew were being poured into bowls and passed around the bonfire. Adam could not remember being hungrier or more satisfied with the simplicity of the ingredients. The talk around the fire became more routine, but it was hard for Adam to imagine any of them having normal lives outside of the sweat.

The conductor brought his plate over to Adam and sat next to him. He dipped some bread into the stew and slurped the gooey mess, letting gravy roll down his cheek before catching it with the back of his hand.

"So you saw the wolf," he said between bites.

"I guess I did."

"You saw the wolf. I saw him come right up to you. I was quite envious."

"Envious? Of me? Why?"

"It is a great honour to be visited by the wolf. He is a great spirit. Frankly, I don't know why he took such a liking to you. He must have wanted to teach you something."

"I don't remember it saying anything to me. It was a hallucination. The steam and the heat, it made me dizzy and I thought I saw a wolf."

A sudden chill made Adam pull his coat close to his throat.

"It wasn't a hallucination. Ask John Walker. Ask the other Elders. We all saw the spirit wolf. He has chosen you. There was a lesson you need to remember. Perhaps tomorrow you two will meet up again."

Adam looked at his watch. It was after midnight. It had been four hours since they arrived but if his watch had shown only a few minutes having passed he would have been no more surprised than by the passage of a few days. Something had changed. Inside he felt a new sensation, a slightly altered perspective, as if he had been fitted with contact lenses without his knowledge.

People started to get up. All of the Elders got in their cars and left. The fire keeper, whose name was George and one of the cooks, a young woman named Rose, who happened to be George's daughter, remained by the fire.

"Feel like taking a dump?" asked John Walker. He was sitting next to Adam.

"No, but thanks for asking," said Adam.

"Still constipated then. The sweat didn't loosen you up?"

Adam ignored the question. "Hadn't we better be going?"

"We'll go in a few minutes."

"Anybody feel like smoking a joint?" asked Derek. Without waiting for an answer, he pulled one from behind his ear and, pinching one end between his thumb and index finger, inserted the entire doobie in his mouth, pulling it out slowly to apply a veneer of saliva over the paper. Reinserted and locked between his lips, he found a small branch and stuck it into the coals before carefully bringing the burning twig close to his face. The joint flared to life, Derek stoking it with two deep inhales before passing it to Tom.

John Walker said, "George here is a Navajo Road Man."

This did not seem to require a response in Adam's opinion. Yet John Walker glared at Adam as if waiting for him to say something.

George had the joint. He held it the way you hold a cigarette in a strong wind; cupped inside his hand, pinched between his thumb and index finger, mouth sucking on the exposed tip, his hand glowing like a lantern with each drag.

"There's a ceremony tomorrow," said George, the cannabis fumes flowing lazily out of his mouth. "We never used to let non-Indians attend. But I don't give a shit about that. John Walker wants the three of you to come. He says you are his brothers. And with a brother like Tom, I guess a man needs to look farther afield."

"You're such a lizard turd," said Tom, picking up a pebble and tossing it at George's head.

"Then I must be making you pretty hungry," said George, easily evading the soft toss.

"What sort of ceremony?" asked Derek.

"It's a peyote ceremony," said John Walker.

"I'm in," said Derek, smiling, slapping John Walker on the back.

"It's not an acid test, you jerk. It's like the sweat, a place for healing, a place where powerful spirits mediate with your soul to negotiate new insights and alter your consciousness."

"Sounds like an acid test."

"You don't fool me, Derek. Behind this façade of the clown is a serious person."

"True, but dig a little deeper and you'll hit the fool again," said Adam. He passed the joint without taking a toke. "Listen, I'd love to get together like this again but I want to spend some time with Donna so count me out."

"She can come if she wants . . . and I can't count you out," said John Walker.

"Dare I ask why?"

"You've already been invited."

"So uninvite me."

"I can't. I didn't invite you. The wolf did."

IV

ADAM SLEPT UNTIL NOON. It was a dreamless sleep, deep and heavy, the slow climb to consciousness forced upon him by a shaft of sunlight drawn across his face, his body stiff, frozen in the same position he had first assumed after crawling into bed next to Donna some time after two A.M.

The light in his eyes as he awoke mimicked the brilliance of the vision in the sweat and remembering the wolf snapped Adam awake. He raised himself onto his elbows, saw the time and Donna's impression in the sheets gone cold and relaxed back into his pillows.

He had actually enjoyed the sweat. It was the type of experience that always plays better after the fact; an arduous task achieved, like canoe tripping or mountain climbing, memories cleansed of physical pain and discomfort, leaving behind only achievement and remembered highlights. He already felt an almost nostalgic regret, an impossible wish for frozen time, where all the players and all the actions are fed into an eternal loop, to be replayed at one's leisure. He missed the lodge conductor, had been warmed by his avuncular radiance and hypnotized by the mantra-like quality of his voice.

Stepping outside the casita after showering and dressing, Adam saw a man hunched over a small plant, a spade in one hand and shears in the other. It was incongruous to see John Walker tending to the grounds of the resort. Adam could not lose hold of the conceit that his friend, whose comportment and personality were of the highest order, would literally stoop to so low an occupation. And despite knowing this said far more about Adam than it did of John Walker, there it was, the secret wish of a more exalted position in life for his friend. Because John Walker's life exposed a significant flaw in his own; the wasted pursuit of success as defined by the accumulation of wealth, fame and power. Everything Adam had worked to achieve, all of his single-minded, myopic goals had been laid low by this man pruning a shrub, who went about this simple task with the same dedication and purpose that Adam and most people he knew reserved for more prestigious tasks and lucrative activities.

"Sleep well?" asked John Walker, continuing his work on the plant, his back to Adam.

"Like a baby. Eyes in the back of your head?"

"No, just ears on the sides."

John Walker stood up and stretched. Except for the bandana around his shoulder length hair, he was wearing the same clothing as the night before.

"Didn't go home last night?"

"Naw. I crashed in the tool shop."

"Want to use my shower?" said Adam, nodding towards the door.

"Not unless I want to get fired. There's one in the employees' locker area. Do I smell?"

"You have a campfire quality to you."

"How are you feeling about last night?"

"I enjoyed it. It'll take me a while to digest what went on. I'm a little confused by the vision I had."

"The wolf."

"Yes the wolf. If it was a hallucination, how did you and the Elders see it too?"

"It wasn't a hallucination. And we didn't exactly see what you saw. We knew he was in the lodge. We knew he was visiting you. It's very odd, actually. The Elders were frankly shocked that he revealed himself to you."

"Who revealed himself? All I saw was a wolf."

"I can't really explain it to you. He came in the form of a wolf. Not a spirit really, or a guardian angel. A teacher, a powerful teacher."

"It didn't say anything to me."

"He did, only not in words. Tonight we'll know more. I have a feeling he'll come back tonight."

Adam's heart started to race at the prospect of another ordeal, no matter how pleasant the last one felt after the fact.

"This isn't feeling like a holiday. I want to spend some time with Donna. Why is it so damn important for you to have me do this?"

John Walker tilted his head back. His eyes were almost closed and he absorbed the morning sun's rays with a wry, forced smile on his face.

"I have a certain gift, Adam. Call it the gift of intuition. The first day we met, during the rainstorm, I instantly knew our fates were

242

intertwined. I accepted it without question. I saw something in you then, and I see it now. It is something hiding inside you. It is something I am attempting, in the short time we have together, to allow you to discover for yourself. There is much power within you. As great as your life is now, you have barely scratched the surface. I know this to be true. Either what I'm saying resonates inside you or it doesn't. If it does, then come with us tonight. At the very least you will partake in a ceremony few white men get to experience. You will undergo, first hand, a holy ritual nearly lost to the overbearing influence of the white man and his luring of our children away from the old ways. There is not enough time for you to catch but a glimpse of the possibilities inside you. But maybe a glimpse is enough."

Adam found Donna by the pool. It was about sixty-eight degrees but Donna did not seem to mind, stretched out as she was on a cot in her bikini, suntan oil glistening off her smooth brown skin.

"So, who did your back?" asked Adam as he sat down next to her.

"I had the pool boys get in line. Two guys on my legs, two on my arms and the lucky winner who got to undo my top and rub my back."

"Slut." He moved to kiss her cheek, but she quickly flipped her head to the other side, swatting him with her ponytail.

"A girl's gotta do what a girl's gotta do. Especially when her husband's out with the boys to all hours of the night. And I hear you guys are going out again tonight. Some holiday."

"I won't go."

"Yes you will." She turned back towards him and sat up, their knees touching as she put her hands in his.

"John Walker told me everything this morning. He says you need this. That's good enough for me."

"Need what, exactly?"

"A swift kick in your spiritual butt. Listen honey, I love you to pieces and I believe in you and will always be there for you. But you need to lighten up a little. You're a moody, brooding little boy who needs to grow up. If John Walker can help you along, I'll find a good book to read and wait for my man to come home."

"He said you could come."

"Uh uh. You go play with the boys without me. But I want a full report. Did you really see a wolf?"

"Maybe. I think I fell asleep and dreamt one."

"Far out. Why don't we go back to the room and do a little howling at the moon before you go."

It was a much further drive to George's teepee than it had been to the sweat lodge. That's where John Walker said they were going, to George's teepee. Adam asked if he actually lived in a teepee and John Walker told him not to ask stupid questions. John Walker had swung the pickup truck onto Highway 17 a few minutes after six, heading north, and two hours later they were still driving, travelling east along Interstate 40. The desert was present but not visible, the only detectable signs of life coming from house lights well off the road and the headlights from the occasional westbound vehicle. Twenty-four hours had passed in a flash and it felt to Adam as if they were on the same journey as the night before, a continuation interrupted by a few insignificant hours of sunlight.

John Walker pulled into a gas station in Winslow. Adam smiled as a verse from an Eagles song started playing in his head. It was *Take It Easy*, the second verse, a guy fantasy about a girl and her pickup truck. Always the same imagery materializing whenever he heard the song.

In the middle of nowhere. Alone, insecure, not knowing anybody. Maybe you're a drifter or on a personal journey of discovery or maybe you're running away from something or someone. And your esteem has hit rock bottom. And you're broke and wondering whom to call with the change jangling in your pocket. It's hot and the sun is beating on you so bad you're starting to take it personally and you'd like to go sit in a restaurant except they've already kicked you out of the only decent diner in town because of the way you're dressed. Maybe because of the way you smell. And then you see her. A country girl, driving a pickup, a shimmering mirage rolling slowly towards you, blonde hair tied in pig tails, wearing a denim shirt with sleeves carefully rolled up over her elbows, two hands on the wheel. She's slowing down, maybe to take a better look, maybe to negotiate the intersection. The passenger window is open and she follows you with her eyes, her head turning away from the road, both of you locked, eyeball to eyeball in a momentary spell, then caution makes her return her concentration to the road and you watch the back of the truck until you can't see it anymore. And your day is made, the change in your pocket feels like a million bucks.

That, for Adam, was the power of rock 'n' roll. It let you feel for a moment like the change in your pockets was a million bucks. Whenever Adam heard that Eagles song he thought of the day he and Donna had met. How she had slowed down to take a look at him. And had seen something worth stopping for. Maybe the girl in the song had made a U-turn and gone back. He always wanted to think so.

"Hey man, we're in Winslow, Arizona," said Derek, who on this trip had picked the cramped jump seat next to Tom over Adam's lap.

"I know," said Adam.

"We should get out and take a picture."

"We don't have a camera."

"I have to pee."

Derek crawled between the two front seats and out through the driver's door. John Walker was outside, filling the tank. By the time Derek got back to the car, John Walker had pulled away from the gas tanks and the motor was running. Adam got out to let Derek in the back.

"I got you something," said Derek, reaching into a brown paper bag. He pulled out a postcard and handed it to Adam. Adam looked at the picture and smiled. His eyes misted a little. He hugged his friend.

"Nobody knows you better than me," said Derek into Adam's ear.

"Frightening, but true," said Adam, releasing his friend.

They got back in the car and John Walker pulled out onto the road. Adam played with the card in his hand; a building with the name *Winslow* in three-foot-high letters displayed high on its wall, facing the street. Downtown Winslow on a busy day. Lots of traffic. People and cars and trucks.

V

THE TEEPEE WAS LARGER than Adam had imagined. Much larger than the plastic one his parents had bought for him on the occasion of his tenth birthday, which included a bow and arrow set and a pair of moccasins. At four foot eight, he had been unable to stand totally straight in it. This one, George's teepee, rose a good twenty feet from the ground.

George came out to greet them when he heard the truck pull up. Rose was there and three other men were introduced to the new arrivals. They were young men, late twenties or early thirties and Adam thought if he passed any of them on the street he would not have necessarily pegged them as native. Two of the three wore their hair short, military style. George introduced them; Jeremy and Simon were brothers, fraternal twins, tall and bulky, linebacker material, both clad in jeans and flannel shirts. The third one was introduced as Benito, smaller, with jet-black hair, curly, but greased back. He was oddly attired in black pants and a frilly white shirt, over which he wore a black-with-gold-trimmed bolero, the ensemble finished off by shiny black cowboy boots.

"I'm a waiter in a Mexican restaurant," said Benito, in answer to Adam's unspoken curiosity. "I came straight from work."

"We call him Zorro," said Jeremy, or was it Simon.

"I'm a big fan of yours, Mr. Fischer," said Benito. "I always read the credits on my record albums and your name is on some of my favourites. I can't believe I'm standing in front of the guy who produced Frozen Hell."

"So you're the one," said Adam.

Benito scratched his head, puzzled, not knowing what to say.

"You're the one who bought that record. I had to travel all this way to find you."

"You do yourself a grave injustice. All of my friends love it."

Derek said, "Do all of your friends partake in the peyote ceremony?"

"Yes."

"I think we have our answer."

Benito laughed and slapped his side in an exaggerated manner, congratulating Derek on his funny joke. George finally brought some order to the gathering by telling Benito to shut up and stop making an ass of himself in front of the guests.

"We are about to enter the teepee. For those of you entering the teepee for the first time, there is nothing I can tell you about Peyote Religion. It will reveal itself to you as it sees fit. You must use peyote the right way. I cannot tell you the right way from the wrong way. This you yourself must discover. All I can say is you must give yourself totally, reverently to Father Peyote or it will go badly for you."

Once again into the breach, thought Adam. That last admonishment shoveled a mother lode of acid into his stomach. He had very little experience with psychedelics, acid and mescaline a couple of times, and while the experiences were not wholly unpleasant, some of the side effects had made the trips seem not worth taking again.

They entered the teepee and circled the central fire in a clockwise fashion, much as they had done the night before in the sweat lodge. At the back of the teepee was a small crescent-shaped mound in front of which a fire blazed. There was just enough room behind the mound for one man to sit. George took his position there and everyone else sat in a semi-circle facing him.

A plant lay on top of the crescent mound. It had a long central root like a carrot, the portion which grew above ground not more than an inch or so tall, a small smooth-skinned cactus, dull green with a flat top on which short tufts of white hair sprung from small furrows.

Jeremy and Simon sat on either side of George. Jeremy picked up a drum near the edge of the teepee and began banging on it slowly to a heartbeat rhythm. Simon reached towards the fire and sprinkled a fine dust on it, and like the night before, the teepee soon filled with the burnt offering of cedar.

The fire cast huge shadows on the sides of the teepee. Adam watched the smoke funnel its way up to the opening at the top. It was surprisingly smoke-free in the teepee, fragrant with the smell of burning wood but not hard on the eyes or throat.

The drumming stopped.

"I will speak in English in honour of our guests," said the Road Man, for George had transformed himself into his leadership role.

"The Peyote Religion is a religion and a medicine and a source of power. We seek the supernatural to heal us from within, to make us better and stronger people. As we sing our songs this night, as we make our prayers, concentrate on the peyote plant. Pray to Father Peyote to give you the insight you require. If you need to vomit, ask permission to leave the tent. If you get too sick, this is not a good sign from Father Peyote. Give your body time to adjust. Do not languish in wild hallucinations. They are not true visions. Seek only the revealed inner visions."

George the Road Man then nodded to Jeremy and the drumbeat was taken up once again. George began to sing, a high pitched chant emanating from deep within his chest, B to C#, two notes wavering back and forth, a song of yearning, a song from a man to his gods. He held a cane in one hand and a gourd in the other. Adam's mind floated with the melody, and unlike most music he heard, he could not think of a thing to make it better or bigger or more commercially palatable. It made Adam think that his own work had the spiritual value of a Saturday morning cartoon.

After the song, Simon picked up a gourd and passed it around, first to Benito on his left, who dipped his hand into it before passing it to Rose. Tom took the gourd from Rose, grabbing a handful of peyote buttons. He passed the gourd to John Walker who put his hand into the gourd and retrieved the peyote. He passed the gourd to Adam and as he did so, he opened his hand wide, showing Adam four buttons. Adam took four buttons out of the gourd then passed it along to Derek. Once Jeremy and George had taken their share, Adam watched as the first buttons were eaten.

"Chew slowly," John Walker said.

Adam put a button to his lips. It had a horrible, alien presence in his mouth, the topside fuzz touching the roof of his mouth, eliciting a gag reflex he managed to control. Gingerly he bit into the side of it, and the aroma wafting up to his olfactory receptors was powerfully foreign. He tried to locate a place where he might discreetly spit the button out. Carefully he chewed, slowly biting into the soft flesh of the cactus, his saliva mixing in with the severed bits, now cleaved in two, working both sides of his mouth, slowly chewing, counting, and after twenty-three bites it was gone.

Derek leaned over and put his lips to Adam's ear.

"Kinda tastes like chicken," he said.

It took several minutes to consume the four buttons, Adam guessing that at least twenty minutes had transpired. The consumption was slow and deliberate on everybody's part. Adam watched the Road

Man as he chewed, eyes closed in meditation, the chewing a kind of physical mantra, repeated and repeated, slow and sure. John Walker also had his eyes closed, lines of concentration accented across his forehead. Benito was watching Adam watch everyone else and every time their eyes locked, Benito would wink a conspirator's wink, or raise one eyebrow as a signal—of what, Adam had no idea.

The Road Man took a burning ember from the fire and lit a hand rolled cigarette, the tobacco hanging out like the tassels on the end of a cob of corn. It ignited instantly, George taking the cigarette out of his mouth momentarily and blowing out the flame. Jeremy, Simon and Benito also lit up. Tom passed several cigarettes over to John Walker who handed one each to Adam and Derek.

"I don't smoke," said Adam.

"Don't inhale if you like but please light it up."

Derek lit his and took a deep drag, exhaling slowly and raising his eyebrows in approval.

Simon stood and sprinkled more vegetation on the fire. This time a different fragrance, earthier, more herbal than woodsy, almost like pot.

"Sage," whispered John Walker.

The Road Man took up the cane in his left hand and the gourd in his right. The drumbeats rang out once more as Jeremy and the Road Man sang a duet. Rose swayed seductively to the beat, her neck making small circles around her shoulders while her chest heaved in and out. It started to get very warm in the teepee. The light from the fire seemed brighter, the shadows more pronounced as the drum beat fell further into the distance, as if it had been taken outside and played out in the desert.

The cane and gourd were passed to Benito who did a serviceable job on a song, but he was no match for the Road Man. Then it was Rose's turn and the sound of her voice stunned Adam, a pressure point building on the back of his neck as her sweet voice filled the tent and his heart. He tried to think about how he would record her, what microphone to use, which studio would suit her voice, which setting on the Lexicon he would use; he tried to think of these things but he could not focus on them. He could only hear her voice and feel it osmotically reach into his muscles and bones, vibrating through his body as if his ears were hearing it from the inside.

That was the feeling—his heart and lungs and liver and all the other gooey tubes and tissue were on the outside and he was trapped inside his epidermal shell.

He looked around the teepee, at the people sitting Indian style on the bare ass of the desert, a glass-eyed group, images hitting his retinas like chopped meat through a grinder while fumes and songs left trails in the air.

The gourd took a turn round the circle and he grabbed another one, there was another button in his mouth and it felt like he was frothing, actually frothing at the mouth, so he wiped his lips and sure enough there was green bubbly spit on his hand.

Someone handed him the cane and the gourd. The cane was more of a rattle. He shook it and it made a little noise. He could not remember John Walker having sung, but maybe he had.

The Road Man said, "Sing," so Adam put out a verse of a Beatles song, a song off of Rubber Soul—how appropriate—a song of love, soul love. He sung *In My Life* and Rose smiled at him, weaving her body, and he was into it, he wasn't a bad singer. The words formed in his mind on a large banner which he read off, and he saw the notes floating by, heard the guitars, key of A, John Lennon's lament of faded memories and everlasting love, and Adam felt hot tears rolling out of his eyes as he sang.

Simon was chewing another button.

Rose stared at the plant lying on the crescent mound.

Derek wore a stupid grin, his eyes red and puffy, his skin dotted with giant pores; greasy, dirt-filled holes peppered across the landscape of his face. Adam had to look away.

A sudden wave of nausea made his heart race, the teepee suddenly too small to fit his body, panic exacerbating the upset in his stomach. He raised his hand, a frightened schoolboy needing the teacher to take him to the bathroom. He heard himself say he was going to be sick then he felt the strong hand of John Walker lift him up and lead him towards the entrance.

Adam could barely walk. The ground seemed slanted, an uphill climb, the earth rising to confront his every step. He wanted to go home, he wanted this to be over, he wanted it to be tomorrow. If only he could get to tomorrow. How easily it normally was to make it be tomorrow, only now, with this poison in his system he may never see the dawn, for how will he live through this night?

His heart was beating so hard it hurt his chest. His entire body rumbled with each beat.

John Walker led him a ways from the teepee and let Adam get down on all fours. The nausea was overwhelming. Death seemed the only solution. Then the contents of his stomach flung themselves out of his body, his vocal chords evoking an otherworldly howl as the vomit splattered onto the ground. Heave after convulsive heave was heralded by a shattering unholy retch, until the muscles surrounding his stomach were pulled so tight, it was impossible to continue.

Adam slumped down, falling onto his side. He lay there quietly, mindful of the soggy chunks of peyote and bits of dinner lying on the ground. His heart decelerated to a jogging rhythm and a sense of wellbeing shooed the panic away.

Rose came over near to where Adam lay, leaned forward holding her hair back and daintily puked a little, silently, with dignity and lack of drama. She wiped her mouth with her sleeve and smiled at Adam and it would have warmed his heart only it was so dark he could not really see her.

"Do you think you can get up now?" asked John Walker. He reached down and, grasping Adam's hand, pulled him to his feet. It was disorienting in the dark. It took a moment for Adam to steady himself. Rose came up beside him and slipped her arm around his waist. With John Walker on the other side, they walked back to the teepee.

"Father Peyote was a little upset with you, I think," said John Walker. "When we go back in, I want you to stop fooling around and monitoring what everybody else is doing. Stop indulging yourself. This isn't some acid trip you're on. Shut out the hallucinations. Get inside of yourself. Concentrate on the plant. I want your eyes only on the plant. Stop thinking, okay?"

"Fine."

"I liked your song," said Rose.

"I liked yours."

The drumbeat had picked up again while they were outside. Adam took his place next to Derek who was slumped forward, eyes closed. The Road Man was in the middle of an incantation, a loud exhortation, arms raised towards the hole at the top of the teepee.

Adam snuck a peek at Rose, then at Benito, and in doing so, a fractured image of Rose repeated, like a shuffled deck of cards, across his field of vision. Hippies had a name for it—trails. It was fun. You moved your head and your brain forgot to shut off the picture it had just seen, creating a time-lapsed image. Adam remembered John Walker's warning and stopped the practice.

The cactus lay atop the mound, on its side, a dead soldier, sacrificed on the field of battle.

He stared at it.

He stared at it until his eyes screamed to his brain to blink, damn it, before we shrivel up like prunes!

Peyote and the drum beat.

Each beat of the drum and the plant glowed a little.

Each beat of the drum and a little life was breathed into the plant.

It grew dark with each beat of the drum.

A black night with a single star; a sun piercing the ebony sky.

The plant began to shimmer.

It got up and danced, diminutive tendrils having grown out from the main root and inside the root, a glowing heartbeat matching the beat of the drum.

It comes to him. It dances across the threshold to a spot before his eyes. It leaves a trail of golden dust. He is no longer sure if his eyes are open or shut. It does not matter. He is unaware of the transformation. He only knows it is the wolf before him now. Playful, nipping at his pants. He goes to pat it and it shies away. It runs a bit then stops, its eyes beckoning him. Impatiently it stamps its paw, dragging it slowly along the ground. Back it bounds towards him then pivots and gallops away then stops. Slowly it turns its head, tongue hung over to one side. It compels him with its deep, blue eyes.

He makes to stand only he is frozen in place. He cannot find the will to move his arms, to uncork his legs. It is black and he cannot see anything but the wolf. He cannot even feel his body. They float together in a black universe.

There is another presence. Someone else in the darkness. He cannot see him. But he feels his presence. It is the gardener.

"Go with him," he says.

"I can't move."

"Yes you can. All you need is the intent. You need to want to go with him."

"I can't find my body."

"You don't need your body. You are spirit. Use your spirit body to move."

"Come with me."

"I will follow."

"I am afraid."

"Fear is the darkness. Shed it and the light will follow."

He tries to move. He pulls against the anchor, but it holds him fast in place. The wolf eventually wanders away until it is nothing more than a shiny pinhole in the distance and finally it is black once more.

A bird was singing. Three times its voice rang out. Adam heard the fluttering of wings. He felt dampness on his forehead. He opened his eyes and saw the Road Man with a thin tube in his mouth, his cheeks puffing as a fourth call went out. Someone had put more wood on the fire—Simon was rubbing soot off his hands. Adam noticed he was leaning on John Walker's shoulder and that a cold compress was being applied to his forehead.

"We will break for a while. Time to relax and have some water," said the Road Man who broke into song and continued for several minutes. Other rituals were performed that Adam watched with detached indifference, as if viewed from beneath several layers of gauze. Simon brought some water into the teepee. More tobacco was consumed, some of it laid next to the altar mound, some of it sprinkled into the fire along with cedar. Benito poured some water on the ground and then it was passed around in a cup for everyone to drink.

The Road Man rose and stretched. He handed the cane and gourd to Jeremy and moved out of the teepee. Adam heard the whistle again, four times, then again from a different position, then one final time as he imagined George walking around the teepee. George re-entered the teepee and sat down for a smoke. Rose and Benito then moved to the entrance of the teepee and went out into the darkness.

At some point during the evening another woman had arrived. There was a fire blazing the same distance from the teepee as the fire had been from the sweat lodge the night before. John Walker led Adam to a place near the fire. Derek sat down, babbling about bunny rabbits. Adam gawked at the flames, thoughtless, all functions on automatic. He was so stoned he was past caring, so detached it felt as if he observed himself from the other side of the fire. And what a pathetic figure he made with his red crazed eyes and twelve-hour stubble and vomit stains on his corduroy shirt.

It was midnight. The ceremony would proceed until first light. This was the one and only break. There would be more singing, more contemplation, more peyote buttons.

"You almost went with him."
"Yes, but I was stuck."

"You weren't stuck. You wouldn't let go."

"No, I tried. Something wouldn't let go of me."

"*You* wouldn't let go of you. He might not come back now. But if he does, you must follow. Or all of this will have been in vain for you."

"Where will he take me?"

"To where you need to go."

"It was your voice I heard. You were there."

"Yes."

"Will you come if I go?"

"If he lets me."

Adam was oblivious as to how long they had been sitting outside by the fire. He guessed not much more than a half hour. He was starting to get cold. He began shaking uncontrollably so John Walker moved him closer to the fire and the new woman, the one tending the fire and helping out, materialized with a blanket to throw over his shoulders.

He could not recall walking back to the teepee. Suddenly, it was as before. The Road Man was singing, cane and gourd in hand, the drum compelling his attention, the plant beckoning his intention. More peyote was passed around and Adam chewed on another button, unaware of the movement of his jaws. Time became a confusing element and was abandoned.

Another button and Adam found himself constantly chewing a wad in his mouth, a cow's cud of peyote fibers lodged in his cheek. Farther and farther he drifted, aimlessly floating, geometric patterns and iridescent colours, a kaleidoscopic cerebral display, firing in his brain.

He was singing again. The cane was in his hand and he was singing an ancient dirge, and he listened to himself and could not understand the words. He was speaking in tongues, he imagined, the foreign sounds flung into the teepee, and he could see these words, ancient symbols floating in the air, caught by the updraft of the fire and spiraling out through the hole to the night sky and they were familiar, these letters, and somewhere inside a tiny voice suggested they might be Hebrew and it slowly dawned on him where and when he had learned this song, a long time ago, when he was twelve years old, studying for his Bar Mitzvah, the Torah portion he sang to the congregation, long forgotten, some pocket of his brain awakened by Father Peyote—only a deity would ask for an encore.

254

He did not remember stopping or passing the cane. He lost track of where he was as he fell deeper within. He floated upwards, lying prone on his stomach, and he could seem a clock from his perch, a clock with only nine hour marks, nine circles, unevenly spaced. It glowed at the center and it wasn't a clock, the hour marks were moving, they were heads bobbing to the sound of a drum, his head and the others, the fire casting dancing shadows against the walls of the teepee, everything moving to the beat of the drum.

The Road Man looked up. He looked up at Adam.

"He is leaving," said the Road Man.

"I will follow him so he doesn't become lost," said John Walker.

Adam was caught in the updraft, sucked out of the hole at the apex. Higher he rose as a golden thread trailed behind him, leading back down into the teepee, now receding far below him. The earth melted away and all was blackness. He floated there awhile, tethered to his golden string, peaceful blackness—this must have been what it was like inside his mother's womb—surrounding him, swaddling him, such joy, his heart would burst if he had brought it with him.

Out of the darkness it came and even before he could make out any more of it than a pinprick of light, he knew what it was. It was coming back for him. The wolf came within a few feet and paced back and forth, tongue hanging, it had been a long run, and this time Adam heard his thoughts, this time he knew he was being asked to take a journey, to let go and follow. There was an admonishment as well. He was told he would do well to hang onto the thread, to not let go and even though these thoughts were not communicated with words, Adam understood that his only way back was by this thin golden connection.

They travelled together through a universe of suns, of spinning planets and exploding stars. The speed was tremendous yet effortless. The loping gait of the wolf was easy to follow. Adam was thrilled by the sights. There were others present, spirit travellers making their way along the same portal as he. There was so much love present it almost ached to feel it. He wanted to stop and touch everything but the wolf kept moving, its eyes piercing, making it perfectly clear there were to be no stopovers on this trip.

They were heading for a light in the distance, a star or a moon or planet. It grew and grew in size until it monopolized Adam's entire field of vision. He wanted to shield his eyes but he had no mechanism for blocking out the light. They were flying into a sun. He felt no heat. There was only the whiteness. He felt himself slipping into the white, losing track of the wolf, falling, falling into the middle of the white, then, as if descending through the clouds in a jet plane, the way became clear and he saw familiar signs of life, green fields, a stand of trees, a road and farms dotting a checkered landscape. There were horses and men and it all appeared very familiar, like the opening an oft-read book. He fell lower and lower to the ground and there were people, many people, then his feet were on the ground.

— ◆ —

The rain should be making a difference, it should be cooling me off but the heat is so oppressive and my backpack so damn heavy and I can't remember the last time I got a full night's sleep.

I know this place, I say to myself, been here before, seen this road, felt the soreness in my boots, the strain of keeping up, don't want to let the folks back home down, don't want to look bad in front of the other men. There's a fight up ahead and I'm scared and I know every thought, every detail, every heartbeat has come before, a déja vu and only part of me knows what that means.

"I know this place," I say.

"What do you know?" asks a familiar voice and there by the side of the road stands the gardener, misplaced in his denim shirt and pants, his cowboy boots covered with flecks of mud.

"I know this place. I have been here before. No, more than that, I have stepped each step, thought each thought, breathed each breath. I am me yet I am him. We are both joined here together. It's hard to explain."

"Who are you?"

The gardener falls into step next to me and no one seems to notice or care. He's wearing his mirror sunglasses and I've never seen anything quite like them before, but that's not the truth of it; I have a pair only I can't quite remember where they are or how I got hold of them.

"My family name is Templeton. Christian name, Joshua. Just like our commanding officer."

"Do you know where you are?" asks the gardener.

"Damn right I do. We crossed over into Pennsylvania about two and a half hours back."

"What year is it?"

"That's a good one. It's 1863. July 1st, 1863."

"Do you know who Adam is?"

"Yes."

"Do you see what's trailing behind you?"

"Yes. It's the golden thread the wolf warned me about."

"So tell me about how you got here."

I think back to the day I enlisted. I had walked about fifteen miles to Dexter. My parents didn't want me to go. My mom, she's French Canadian and my daddy, well, he's all for freeing the slaves, being as he's a farmer and having to do most of the work himself, but I'm the only help he's got and besides, my mom thinks I'm too young to go fight a war. Maybe I was too young when it started but I just turned seventeen and there are lots of boys I know younger than me signing up.

I guess I was late to the recruiting office because I never did end up being placed in the regiment from our area. There were so many of us Maine boys enlisting that they created a kind of orphan unit, the 20th Maine, made up of men from all over, Down Easters, others from Bangor, Augusta and Milo and places all the way up to the Canadian border.

We carry no town's flag. We represent no county. We are Maine boys and that brings us all together in a way local geography never could.

We are entering a town called Hanover.

"Stuart's boys been this way," says private William Merrill. He's from somewhere out Freeport ways, six feet tall and a lot older than me. He was a machinist before the war, and that sounds pretty important to me. We're in the same company, Company K, and we're on this hot dusty road, only the rain has kept it down some, and we've been marching through mud and rain for days now and there's surely a fight ahead 'cause Stuart's cavalry is the smoke to Lee's fire.

I am so tired I don't know how I will be able to lift my musket let alone kill somebody with it. We've covered at least fifty miles in the last two days and we've been marching since before dawn and now the smell of war is reaching my nostrils.

Horses lie dead in the streets. Wagons are burning and some stores have been looted. A store owner comes out when we arrive, waving Confederate notes in his hand, yelling at us to go make this money as worthless as the sons of bitches who gave it to him when they confiscated his dry goods. It's nice to be welcomed for a change. Walking through Virginia towns is no picnic. If scowls were bullets then I'd be up in heaven, or wherever you go, a thousand times over.

"Do you see anybody you know?" asks the gardener.

I had forgotten he was there and think that, for a while, maybe he wasn't.

"Sure. I know everybody in my company. And a lot of the others."

"But do you *know* anybody?"

And I think about it and figure I understand what he means and say, no, I know only him.

There is a company on each side of the column, a skirmish line to protect either flank. We had caught sight of cavalry now and then throughout the day but no real contact. Now I see the companies returning to the column and they are leading us to a field. We are praying we will be allowed to bivouac for the night. We have no idea where the Rebel army is. There are plenty of rumours. There are always plenty of rumours.

We stack our rifles and forage for water and wood. The farmers must hate us for taking their fence rails but we're the ones who are going to be doing the bleeding so that's how I justify it to myself.

We start fires and try to get some sleep. Our tents and provisions were left behind during the march and we are hoping they will arrive tonight and we won't have to march any further.

Me and William Merrill—I call him Billy and he doesn't seem to mind—have an arrangement. There are lots of brothers and cousins fighting together and they watch over each other, going into battle with their backs to one another. Literally covering each other's back, as the saying goes. So Billy and I have teamed up. Ever since Fredericksburg, a night I would sooner forget, when he and I hid behind the dead bodies of our fallen comrades while Johnny Reb shot down at us from behind their damnable wall, ever since then, while we laid on the freezing ground all through the night, hugging each other for warmth and not caring about the impropriety of it all, we made a pact saying that if the good Lord would see us through this night, then we would honour His favour by seeing each other through the rest of this war. Billy is a good head taller than me and about half again as wide so I figure I got the better of the bargain.

He's pretty well hung, too. Something happened a few days back that I'm hesitant to write to my folks about though I feel no shame about it. I've seen a lot of crazy things this past year but this one takes the cake. We were fording a small stream and nobody wanted to wait for the pontoons because it wasn't much of a stream, only a few feet deep and not too wide. So a couple of soldiers start taking off their boots, then a few start removing their pants and before long, the entire 1st Division is butt naked, three thousand of us wading across the river with our gear and weapons held high over our heads.

Billy took one look at my manhood and asked the Lord why He'd bothered giving me one at all. Billy, being twenty-one, knows all about women. He told me if you didn't use it for God's intended purpose it will eventually shrivel up and fall off. I didn't believe him of course. Seeing his though, I have to wonder if there might be a grain of truth to it.

I lay with my head on my backpack as the sun goes down, too tired to sleep. Billy is fast asleep nearby and the gardener sits cross-legged a few feet off, picking at long stalks of grass.

Not too far away I see our commanding officer, pacing back and forth, talking to his adjutant who also happens to be his brother. Nobody minds though because Lieutenant Chamberlain is a fine man and no one holds it against him that his brother commands the regiment.

More rumours abound about an attack on two of our corps west of here. The Rebs have beaten back our boys through a town called Gettysburg and killed General Reynolds to boot, but I decide not to believe any of it, then, just after the sun goes down there are officers riding back and forth, a lot of commotion and I get this feeling in my stomach and I know what we heard was true.

"To Gettysburg!" becomes the rallying cry and our regiment forms up quickly as we are travelling light, and before I have time to think about it, we are marching into the darkness.

It is a pleasant evening, warm and moonlit and I am only a bit itchy. I boiled my uniform a few days back and have thankfully been free of lice. Why God made those disgusting little creatures is something I cannot imagine unless it's His way of not making war too enjoyable, as if being shot at or wounded or worse isn't enough.

We pass through Pennsylvania towns and are given a hero's welcome. Many young girls, some single, some left behind by soldiers fighting in this very army, are out to greet us. They offer us water and milk and some have baked bread and sweet rolls. Flags are waving and we are serenaded with patriotic songs.

As we march through a town called McSherrystown, a girl about my age, with long golden hair, sees me and comes over and walks with me for a bit. She puts her arm through mine and I must admit, I feel a swollen pride even in the face of Billy's unkind taunts. She tells me to take care of myself and teach those Rebels a lesson, then, on the outskirts of her town, she puts her arms around me and gives me a kiss, right on my mouth, the best kiss I've ever had, and the boys are whooping it up and patting me on the back and though embarrassed, I turn one last time and wave before the blackness envelopes her, the golden thread briefly casting light on her tear-stained face.

We march and march and march. You learn to fall into yourself, to stop the voice inside howling in pain or the one begging you to stop and lie down. You concentrate on the back of the man in front of you, or on his shoes and you shut out the rest. Least ways, that's how I do it and I don't figure I'm particularly unique, though my mom would respectfully disagree.

The gardener leaves me alone, walking easily on the shoulder of the road and I know he is there if I need him, though for the life of me I cannot quite remember why I might require his help.

I think of my family and the farm and I wish I was back there now, helping daddy with the chores or learning my letters with mom's help. We practice French together and it gives her such delight to hear me speak in her native tongue. I wonder if I will ever see them again. I do not fear for my life too much. I just know it will break my mom's heart if I fail to return and that weighs heavily upon me. It is not good to think such thoughts on the eve of battle so I push them from my mind.

Rumours spread down the column like a line of lit gunpowder. "McLellan is back in command!" they yell from in front and yesterday it was Meade and later on there is tale of George Washington himself being seen roaming the hills of this Pennsylvania town we're headed for and I don't for a second believe a spot of it, but I pick up the chorus on any account and shout the information, such as it is, over my shoulder to my comrades in the rear of me.

Men are falling out, dog-tired from all of the marching. Most will stagger in an hour or so after we halt. Some will show up riding on provision wagons or ambulances. A few we will never see again. I wonder where those men go. Surely not home to their loved ones. I cannot imagine the disgrace awaiting the man who walks into his hometown a deserter. Whenever I think I can go on no longer, I see the eyes of my daddy and somehow I struggle forward.

We have been marching west and now the column is slowing as we maneuver off the road and begin a southerly course. I see the lights of many campfires far off in the distance to our right and know we are near our other corps. After a short march we are told to fall out and the men drop in their tracks. It is no exaggeration to say most are asleep before their bodies hit the ground.

"Is it all right if I lie on my back? I don't want to damage the strand."

"Don't worry about it. Only your spirit can damage it."

Sometimes, an hour of rest can feel worse than a night with no sleep. We are awakened before dawn and my head is swimming so, I feel as if I have spent the night in a tavern drinking cheap whiskey. Of course, I have never spent a night in a tavern, never mind drinking cheap whiskey, but I imagine this is how it must feel the next morning.

Billy has kept some bread in his pocket, given to him by one of last night's benefactors and it is hard and good and better than the indigestible hardtack we normally eat when neither time nor availability allow for more wholesome meals. Oh how I miss breakfast at our table, mom frying up fresh eggs and pancakes, hot coffee brewing on the stove. The thought of it can make a man crazy so it's best to dwell on other things.

"Are you hungry?" I ask the gardener, and he smiles, shaking his head, no.

We march again and it is a particularly warm morning. In the distance we hear some sporadic musket fire and cannon. I am wondering if we will engage today and believe we will probably be held in reserve.

Billy says, "There's only one thing a man has to do right in his life. Don't matter if you be high born or low. Free man or slave."

"And what might that be?" I ask.

"Find yourself a good woman. One which won't make you wish'd you'd never been born."

"How 'bout earning a living or learning a skill like you done or going to college like the Colonel?"

"Don't mean shit if'n you have to come home each night to a shrewish female."

"And this matter is occupying your mind just now?"

"Yup."

"You're one strange man, William Merrill."

We meet up with Twelfth Corps and halt for a while. The town of Gettysburg lies only a mile or so to the northwest. Our division moves farther south and we finally fall out in a peach orchard. We stack arms and small fires are lit. There is a battle going on somewhere but I can't tell from where because a ridge lies between us and where the action is taking place. I am quite certain we will be engaged by tomorrow.

It is Meade who leads us now. The entire Army of the Potomac is lined up along this ridge before me, waiting for the Rebel army to show itself. We take comfort in that. No one wants to face another Fredericksburg.

I am not aware of falling asleep until the sound of artillery awakens me. I rise quickly and stuff my pockets with the twenty extra rounds of ammunition Billy has secured on my behalf during my slumber. Most of yesterday's battle occurred on two hills to our right, less than a mile away. One is deeply wooded and the prospect of heading in that direction fills me with dread. This new cannon fire however, is occurring off to our left.

Our brigade responds and is first into line as we push off at the double quick. My heart is pounding and I must slow it down or I will have no energy for the fight. We march as the crow flies, across a road then into bush and wet areas, the going difficult as we drag ourselves over rocks and fences and small rock walls, until we reach the crest of the ridge and a breathtaking panorama reveals itself to me.

For at least a mile across, the most magnificent flat fields of wheat and orchard lands extend from right to left for as far as I can see, interrupted by farmhouses and, in one area, close by and to our left, a low depression of gigantic rocks, from which the crackle of musket fire and the smoke of artillery are now emanating. On the horizon lies another ridge, cloaked by trees, and a misty cloud of smoke filing up from those trees tells me where the Rebel army lies in wait. I feel part of a Roman spectacle, a player in one of the stories of antiquity told to me by my mother.

Our brigade commander, Colonel Vincent, another college man, rides by and I hear him say something about 'That damn fool Sickles', whose Third Corps has pushed forward about a mile to our front. Billy says Third Corps was supposed to be where we are standing now and that's why our Corps was brought up to this position. I see Sickle's troops engaged in front of me, stretched out for at least a mile. We pass by a peach orchard then a wheat field as we proceed south along the ridge. There is terrible fighting to our right at the far end of the wheat field. Men are staggering back through the tall grass, some dragging comrades who are unable to walk. There are explosions everywhere and the sound is horrible. My view is somewhat obscured but, from the sounds of battle down and to our left, I imagine Sickle's flank is being threatened near the huge rocks and since we are ordered to halt at this position, I presume we have been called up to reinforce his flank and rear.

"I had no idea." It is the gardener talking, staring out at the smoke-filled horizon, mute horror consuming his eyes.

"I had no idea," he says again and turns to me. "Thank you, Adam. Thank you for bringing me here and showing me this."

I don't know what to say. I merely nod. I haven't the time to wonder what he is talking about or why he is thanking me. Or even whether it is me he is trying to thank.

I close my eyes and imagine myself loading my Enfield. It is a good rifle and I have fired it several times though I think I have hit no enemy with a shot from it. I wish to kill no man. I am a patriot and I understand the importance of this war, a war not fought for land or wealth or power, rather, for an idea, that all men are created equal. But murder is murder and I do not know how to explain the great reluctance I feel to take another man's life over a point of philosophy. My mom says the great philosophers fought each other with words. My daddy says the politicians made the war and now expect the nation's young to go out and prove their side right. I load my rifle in my mind. I take aim. I fire.

The sound of bugles snaps me to attention. The drummer boys set the marching beat and we are on the move again, double quick, following a farmer's livestock path running parallel with the ridge. To the south, not a few minutes away, a rocky hill juts out from the ridge like the period at the end of an exclamation mark. The 44th New York is in our front and we follow. They have found a road that winds around the east side of the hill. We are suddenly in the thick of it. Rebel artillery shells are overshooting the hill on our right and hitting the trees above us. Deadly splinters and exploding shot rain down upon us. I nearly trip over a fallen soldier, who bleeds profusely from a concussion to his temple. Tree limbs snap with a sound more frightening than musket fire. A thick branch falls in my path and I stumble and fall, smashing my knee into a rough-edged rock.

There is no time to attend to my injury. I can still walk and that is good enough. We move lower down the east side of the slope to avoid the bursting shells and lethal falling tree limbs.

We come around to the south side of the hill which I see is a narrow spur running down towards the east from the crest of the hill and before us lies a shaded hollow, widening to our right as it bends around our hill, and, rising up just beyond our position, a larger hill looms, a mass of trees obscuring the slope. I strain to see into the dark tangle of green and know if Johnny Reb decides to attack us from down that further hill, we won't know he's upon us until the first man falls.

I appraise our hill. It is bare for the most of it, logged for its trees, exposing a jagged surface of rocks and boulders, placed by nature in no detectable pattern. It is some comfort to see that if the time comes to fall back, there will be plenty of cover for the lot of us.

We are ordered to form 'Right in front', a shuffling maneuver executed while we face in the direction we expect to engage the enemy. We know from training that this maneuver is designed to put us quickly into position when a fight is imminent, when more carefully planned formations are abandoned for lack of time. Company B is sent out as a skirmish line and I thank the good Lord I am in Company K. I watch them descend into the hollow, moving to our left, then, as if enveloped by a fog, they disappear into the foliage.

Our regiment is the second last in line. To my left, the 16th Michigan has formed a line across the hollow between the two hills. Our regiment is wedged between the 16th on our left and the 83rd Pennsylvania on our right a ways up the hill. I am feeling secure knowing two regiments bookend us but this is short lived for I watch as the 16th is moved to our rear and back over the top of the hill, disappearing somewhere on our right.

Something is bothering me. We are told to load and make ready. I go through the mechanical action, stuffing the minié ball cartridge down the muzzle, then ramming it into position down the barrel, all the while scouting to my left. We infantry soldiers are an ignorant lot. We never know where we are marching to or who we are fighting until we have already arrived and are fiercely engaged. But, having passed by the whole Union army this morning and afternoon, I am aware of something I confess would have stood me better not to have known. There is no Union army past our left or to our front. As I look down the left side of our line, beyond it I see nothing. I can only imagine the presence of Company B, probably a hundred or so yards off. We are positioned at the end of a line of soldiers, over ninety thousand strong so I am told, strung out over two miles along a ridge. And our little regiment is the last in line. I know I pray in vain for reinforcements, for other troops to complement our position.

It becomes quiet. The shelling has stopped. Maybe they are through for the day. It is getting late. The sun is beginning its descent. Perhaps they are heading back towards their own lines. But the musket fire is getting louder. By small degrees its volume increases and the sound of men's voices begins to carry to our position. Our brigade is engaged. There is shouting and gunfire coming from the top of the hill. I look up to the crest on my right. Our troops are positioned on the far side. I can only see a few officers with binoculars facing west. I wish I knew what was going on. I stand at the ready and wait to meet my fate.

"Why have you brought me here?" I ask the gardener.

"It is you who have brought me here," he replies.

I hadn't noticed before how the golden thread flows back from me for several rods before turning upwards and vanishing into the air.

"Where does it go?" I ask.

"Back to you."

"Where am I?"

"You are here . . . and there."

For a moment I see in my mind a campfire and people seated around it. Then a bullet whizzes by me, shredding a leaf above my head and I freeze. The air is filled with bullets passing over our heads and leaves begin to fall like rain, creating a green rug where we stand. They are shooting high but their aim is lowering upon us.

I see them. The gray men. They come from around the southwest side of the hill, engaging the 83rd beside us and now coming upon our line. My company is third in line from the right. Billy yells at me to take cover and I realize I am standing stock still, frozen to the ground, watching the gray men inch closer as they find rocks from which to take aim and fire their deadly volleys.

There is a huge explosion and smoke as our regiment opens fire. The sound of it makes me jump and I drop my rifle then quickly retrieve it. Our line scatters, men scrambling behind rocks and trees. We are no longer a straight line, rather a jagged collection of dots along the bottom of the hill. Some men clamber up the spur to more defensible positions, throwing up rocks and logs for protection.

Billy and I find a huge rock to hide behind. There are at least six of us taking refuge behind it. We are sitting against the rock with our backs to the enemy and on the count of three, Billy and I jump up and fire our weapons. There is no aiming, no target. I see gray uniforms and point in the general direction of their positions. I know in my heart I have aimed high. I swear I do not do this on purpose. It is a first shot and I have fifty-nine more chances to improve my aim.

Fifty-nine more chances to kill someone. And God knows how many thousands of chances to be killed.

The Rebels are not charging. They are satisfied with a steady, aimed fire, and already I see some of our boys down, their cries of agony a most unbearable sound. Lieutenant Nichols walks behind us, urging us to close our lines, reassuring us, telling us to take careful aim, to load properly, to keep up the fire. Billy and I throw a few more shots into the battle. He is grinning at me and I can't tell if it is madness or fear.

He is waiting for me the next time I pop up for a shot. He has sat there patiently, waiting for my head to appear, like a groundhog peering out of its hole. I only know this when a bullet bites a small piece out of my uniform collar. Then I see him, I see the smoke from his rifle and the grin on his face. It is a grin telling me he has found his range. It is a grin telling me next time he will not miss. And still I manage to fire high.

I sit back down and something I have seen in that brief moment begins to register. I call Lieutenant Nichols and tell him he might want to observe the vale beyond the Rebs shooting at us. I am sure I saw many more gray uniforms moving to our left behind those in the fight. He takes my advice, then climbs up the spur. A moment later, he returns with Colonel Chamberlain, who amazes me when he leaps onto our boulder in full view of the enemy. He climbs down untouched and shouts an order into Lieutenant Nichols' ear. Lieutenant Nichols then goes down the company line, ordering us to keep up a covering fire while we sidestep to our left, creating more distance between ourselves, lengthening our line while those positioned behind fill the gaps, all the while moving further up the hill to lessen the length of our front.

Billy and I abandon our giant rock and move a few paces left and back, firing a shot each as we go, finding new cover about twenty or thirty feet up the hill. There is a lull and we hastily throw up rocks to create a small wall behind which we lie prone with our guns resting over top our meager breastwork.

The maneuver has lengthened our line and brought more order to it. On either side of me men lay protected by rocks or logs or trees. Some stand behind large trees, others kneel behind large boulders. Most have their bellies to the ground. There are men lying near me I recognize as cooks and drivers and ambulance attendants. Never before have I seen them bear arms yet they are filling the holes created by the thinning of our line. My heart swells at the thought of their valor and I have renewed vigor to match their courage.

I cannot see how far we are now extended to the left and fear the Rebels will flank us and attack us from the rear. Not too far down the line to my left, I see our colours raised by a fallen log and large rock ledge. I see where our line bends at that point, forming a right angle to our own south-facing line. As I am thusly observing them, our men let loose a unified rifle exchange and never before have I heard such a noise. Far down the hill, out of my line of sight, I hear screams and know the left side of the line has engaged the enemy and sent many of them to their Maker.

A bullet ricocheting off a rock near my head flings grit into my eyes and brings my senses back to the issue before me. Billy says they are from Alabama and, in concert with their brethren attacking our left, the gray men to our front commence an attack on our position. Bullets fly and I do my best to draw a bead on any moving thing. There is a man, a boy really, blond hair dangling from under his Rebel cap, loading his rifle from behind a tree, and although it is a respectable tree, it is not half the width of the boy. I aim my rifle and line up a shot into his stomach, then decide a bullet to the head would be more humane, but perhaps a shot in the leg would do the trick, but he could die from such a wound so I decide on his foot. Is it any wonder that with so much indecision I miss him entirely and slam a bullet into the base of the tree? He does not even flinch, sees me, knows it is I who owns the poor marksmanship and smiles. Then he raises his rifle and shoots at me.

I duck and have to resist the urge to immediately pop up again as I am confused by my sense of familiarity with this boy's face. It was his smile. Billy says they're coming and the thought leaves me momentarily as a few brave Rebs rush our position and many rifles are raised against them and they all fall not three feet from where I lay, their bodies riddled with holes, one of them turned on his side, eyes open, wild with the surprise the impact has brought.

I see the blond boy dart from behind the tree to the safety of the other side of the huge rock Billy and I had shared and Colonel Chamberlain had earlier mounted. Many of our boys try to shoot him down during his mad dash but he arrives unharmed and disappears behind the rock. I watch as others attempt his exploit and many men fall to our rifles before they reach the rock. Those that do survive the trip, which I do not believe number even ten, are pinned down by our fire and that of the 83rd Pennsylvania on our right.

Time passes unnoticed. The rebels charge and are repulsed. The left seems to be having the worst of it. At one point I turn at the sound of much struggling and am horrified to see our men and more than a dozen Rebs locked in a mortal barroom brawl, rifles swung like clubs, fist to fist, men choking each other and smashing each other senseless. Then the frenzy subsides and our men are once again secure behind rocks and trees.

The Rebels in our front are making little headway. The contours of the spur, with our units on one side of a slight V in the ridge and the 83rd on the other, have created a crossfire situation and the Rebels are confronted with bullets coming at them from two different directions. Word comes down the line that the left and center are taking a terrible beating. Officers attempt to pull the two companies on our right out of the line to reinforce the left but there is much confusion, other men believing we are in retreat and abandoning their positions, so the two companies are quickly put back into their original position next to us.

During a lull in the action, Billy hops over our thrown-up breastwork and relieves a dead Reb of his Springfield rifle and cartridges. I watch as he displays it to me, his back to the bottom of the hill. I tell him to get down and he laughs. A blond head captures my interest. The boy has popped up from behind the rock. He takes careful aim as I scream for Billy to get down. Instead, Billy turns back down the hill as a bullet strikes him on the bridge of his nose.

Billy is thrown back towards me, his head smashing against our little wall, the back of his skull cracking open with an awful thud, blood covering the rocks and my face. My anger is piqued as I raise my rifle to fell the slayer of my friend.

He is still standing, admiring his handiwork. He sees me yet still he does not move. I take careful aim and am about to pull the trigger when he removes his hat, as if to invite his execution.

I cannot believe my eyes. I lower my gun. I slump to the ground. I turn to the gardener who has sat silently with his back to a tree during the entire engagement.

"I know that boy behind the rock," I say.

He nods his head without turning.

It is Derek. Derek has killed my friend. I do not understand. Derek is my friend. How could he do this to me? How is it we face each other as mortal enemies?

The battle does not care of my dilemma. Confederates break through over on the left and I watch as one of our men takes a bayonet through the forehead, his killer felled by the pistol shot from an officer's revolver. It is a gun in the hand of Lieutenant Chamberlain who fights valiantly amongst our foes.

I am on my back loading my weapon. I feel a hand on my shoulder. "One at a time," says the gardener.

I return my eyes to my rifle and see that in my daze I have stuffed several cartridges into the barrel. With some effort I remove them and re-load. Not counting the ruined ones, I have less than a handful of cartridges left. The fighting has turned from a long line of raised rifles to small pockets of men partnered with similar small pockets of the enemy. Each group has picked their counterparts on the other side to harass and kill. There is no more line. Men lie dead or wounded all over the hillside. I drag Billy over the rocks and wipe the blood from his forehead. His is a peaceful countenance, betrayed only by the grotesque hole between his eyes. Now I have no one to watch my back. Tears flow freely down my cheeks as I hold the head of my friend. I wish for yesterday. I wish for an hour ago. I try to think of a way to make this right but to no avail. Billy is dead and his soul has departed.

Lieutenant Nichols is inspecting us for ammunition and it is determined that I have five rounds left. He pries open my hand closed shut as if by rigor mortis and suggests I put the cartridges to better use. There are men around me who have run out and are searching the dead for ammunition. The Lieutenant urges me again to keep up the fire. I load and fire, load and fire, five times and each bullet hits the rock where Derek hides. He pops up and taunts me, watches me ram the minié ball into place, sees me take aim, and each time he ducks before I am able to send him to his grave.

"That's mighty fancy shootin'," he yells to me from behind the rock.

His mocking infuriates me and it is a familiar feeling. Everything is familiar and nothing is clear. I want to kill the boy, this person I know as Derek, yet I want to love him as well. He has killed my friend and I decide I do not care if he too is my friend. I will make him pay for his deed.

There is another lull. The Rebels who had broken through our line on the crest of the spur have been repelled, leaving behind the bodies of their comrades, most dead, some screaming in pain, others dragging themselves back down the hill. Many of our own men lie scattered between the two forces, deadly fire passing inches above their bodies and sometimes lower, finding their mark with a telltale vulgar thud. The wounded cry out for help, some weeping quietly for their loved ones, for wives and mothers, others clutching their wounds in unbearable agony, one soldier, one of theirs, rocking back and forth, holding his guts in his bloody hands, pushing them back into a gaping dark hole made by a bayonet.

I think I must go mad. There is madness all around me. We have been fighting for hours, the sun is low in the sky, there is no more ammunition, and still the fight is carried, our bloodlust unrelenting, slowed only by fatigue and our shrinking numbers. I watch in horror as one of our men smashes a soldier's head with a rock, up and down goes the rock in his hand, until there is nothing left of the man's head but a shredded mess of tissue and bone and still it is not enough. An officer orders him to stop, puts his pistol to the man's ear, the rock held high above the crazed man's head, his eyes darting, threatening to roll right out of their sockets, then he lets go of the rock and covers his face with his hands, sobbing, the stab of sanity more painful than the point of a bayonet.

Derek is out there. I know him from before. I know him from after.

Our center is gone, withered away by the attacks on either side of the right angle created by our line. Men are pulled back from there, leaving a trail of our dead and wounded in clumps around the rock ledge where first our colours were placed. The regiment colours still fly, clutched by a soldier who stands painfully against a tree, but further back. I know another thrust by the enemy and they will be among us.

"Bayonet!" our company commander orders, screaming to be heard over the din of battle.

"Bayonet!" cry the men down the line.

The gardener points to my scabbard then flicks his finger towards the muzzle of my gun.

I unsheathe my bayonet and fix it into place. My reluctance to shoot a man is multiplied by the prospect of sticking someone with the point of my blade.

The middle of the line has regained its original position, easing towards the rock ledge, bayonets fixed, preparing for the charge, our men peering over the edge to see what confronts them. I watch the left close rank with the middle and disappear over the far crest. Then we are all up and over our barricades, running carelessly down the hill, a misstep as deadly as an enemy bullet, a high-pitched scream, our own Rebel yell, and the gray coats are falling back, running away, those of us with bullets, stopping to take careful aim and finding the exposed backs of our enemies.

I head straight for the large rock. Part of me sees the confusion our charge has rendered. Confederate soldiers are throwing down their weapons as others from positions to our left are being chased down the vale towards the way they have come, running directly in front of the fire from the rest of the brigade up on the hill. Some of the Rebs are stopping to take aim and fire, only to be cut down by our troops. It is a glorious scene and I want to be part of it but I only have eyes for the rock. Just a few seconds have passed since we left the top of the hill, but everything is different.

As I run towards the looming boulder, I am no longer a soldier fighting for my country. Everything grows dim around me except the rock, which takes on a dull, unfocused light. I see him bolt from the rock's custody and make for the trees to my front. I take chase, dropping my rifle as I go, arms pumping, and I feel as if I am back at school, chasing the village bully who has grabbed my cap from my head.

He heads for the trees, for the large hill we have faced all afternoon. He begins to ascend the hill, clutching for rocks and trees as he scrambles, at times on all fours. He is fit and wiry, bounding over obstacles like a cat, yet somehow I find the strength to keep pace. I am not two rods in his rear, and he hears me, glances back now and then to see where I am and always there is the grin, as if someone has tacked the corners of his mouth to his cheeks.

He veers to the left to avoid an outcropping of unassailable stone, working his way around to the eastern side of the slope. The pain in my knee from the earlier fall a lifetime ago reminds me of its presence but I am unheedful.

The sight of Union soldiers surprises both of us and the soldiers as well. I recognize them as the skirmish line sent out at the beginning of the fight. Company B is moving up the hill as we pass them at right angles. They open a path for us to pass, seeming to recognize the personal nature of my pursuit.

The east side of the hill is grown dark, the sun almost done with this day, the thick foliage blocking what little light remains of the faltering dusk. I am near blown and I wonder what I will do if I catch him. Will I bash his brains out? Will he attempt the same to mine? It is a fleeting thought for I have no will for debate. I am almost upon him now, having gained, little by little, until the branches he pushes aside are springing back at me like the swat from a riding crop.

He stumbles and I lunge for him, my arms reaching around his waist as we both fall, rolling down the slippery slope locked together until my head meets the trunk of a tree and it is the end for me.

When my eyes open, I think I have passed out for no more than a few seconds. Night has arrived, a full moon enabling me to see only the vague outline of trees surrounding me. My head pounds ferociously, each heartbeat a hammer blow, so painful I think I must faint from it. I struggle to rise and find I cannot lift my head more than a few inches without the blackness overwhelming me. I put a hand to my forehead and feel a lump the size of a mountain and a stickiness I cannot wipe from my fingers. I am sure I am done for and relax back into the soft mattress of decaying leaves.

I hear someone coming. He curses as I imagine his foot striking an unseen stone or exposed root. He slows, his approach careful, then he stops.

"Where are you, Yank?" says a voice.

I do not know what to do. It is him, the golden-haired boy. Derek. My friend. I know him from before. From before I came to this place. He is my friend. I seek out the gardener and think I see him but it is so dark in this dense forest that I am not sure; it could be a boulder shaped to a man's proportions.

"Over here," I say and hold my breath.

There is more movement, twigs snapping under the weight of his feet as he approaches.

"Say again."

"Over here, to your right."

His steps are louder, only a few feet separate us. I am calm for I know he will not harm me. My brains would be seeping into the underbrush by now if he intended me any violence.

He bends down beside me, bouncing on his haunches, and he puts a hand on my forehead, avoiding the damaged area.

"You're getting hot. You'll die for sure out here. But it ain't so bad as it may seem. Not for you least ways. We're surrounded by Yanks. They're all over this mountain top."

He cradles my head and puts a canteen to my lips. I welcome the lukewarm fluid. In my pain I have not noticed how dreadfully parched is my throat.

A shaft of moonlight throws a bluish light on his face. It is sweat-stained and filthy, his blond locks clumped together in saber points. His easy charm shields the fear but his eyes cannot hide it from me. He moves to adjust the canteen, the moonlight falling across his shoulders, and the shock of seeing a Union lieutenant's coat on his body makes me choke on the water in my mouth.

"They will shoot you for sure when they catch you with that on," I say. "Have you no respect for the dead?"

He takes the canteen back and allows himself a long swallow.

"Well, I've got to tell you," he says. "He wasn't exactly dead."

"Not exactly dead?"

"Not exactly."

"I could start hollerin' and they'd be upon you like flies on shit."

"And I could cut your throat out but neither is likely to happen, right?"

He is right. I release my strength, sinking back into his arm. I am unable to do him harm as he is incapable of hurting me and we both know this.

"I'm sorry I killed your friend. I mean, I'm not sorry I killed him. I'm only sorry he was your friend."

"We promised to watch each other's back."

"Well, that's what friends are for, now ain't they? And you're madder 'n' hell at me cause he's dead and you're alive and you think maybe he's watching you so you have to put on a good show for him and ease your mind at the same time. I don't blame you. I seen enough ghosts rise off the battlefield to believe in the hereafter."

I want to protest, belittle his opinion, make mockery of his deductions only there is the ring of truth in what he says. I feel exposed, as if he can see inside me and hear my thoughts.

"I suppose," he goes on, "that being your friend's grim reaper, his obligation to you has fallen upon my shoulders. My name is Levi Coppersmith."

He extends his hand. I tell him my name. We shake and I want to tell him how pleased I am to make his acquaintance but the words seem unnecessary.

"Come on, get up."

He rises and puts his hands under my armpits and tries to lift me. I cry out and he stops, putting his hand over my mouth as he puts me back onto the ground. He pours some water on a handkerchief produced from the lieutenant's coat and applies it to my wound. He explains to me that his reconnaissance has revealed a farmhouse a couple hundred yards to the east where many of the wounded are being taken. He intends to drag me there and would appreciate it if I could assist him in his undertaking.

"But surely they will find you out and kill you."

"Ah hell, I've been through worse scrapes than this. You just do as I say and before an hour is passed I promise you a soft bed and someone to doctor your head."

After several false starts and muffled cries, he manages to drape my left arm over his shoulders, holding my wrist with one hand while the other grabs onto my waist. I am slightly bigger than he but he is strong, his body hardened, much like my own, from the daily ordeal of being in an army constantly on the march. We make our way slowly through the trees, following the contour of the hill until I imagine us on the eastern slope. He leads me from moonlit patch to moonlit patch as the way is treacherous. I know he fears that another fall will finish the job on my head.

We gain flat land and through the trees I hear the sound of men, some full voiced, barking orders, others, wounded, dying, crying into the still night.

"Who goes there?" says a voice in the darkness.

I feel Levi poke me in my side and realize he wants me to respond to the hail.

"20th Maine," I answer.

"All right. Come forward. Slowly."

We approach a farmer's stonewall. A platoon of Union soldiers stands on either side.

"Got wounded here," says Levi, keeping his head down, his cheek resting on my chest. We are allowed passage through the picket line and directed to the farmhouse where an aid station has been set up.

"You boys from Maine sure know how to fight," says one of the soldiers as we pass.

I say, "Those Alabama boys sure seemed to have the hang of it, too."

"Ain't that the truth," says the soldier as Levi gives my wrist a squeeze.

We cross a field to the farm buildings. There is a barn and a house nearby. There are numerous campfires and our way is well lit, and oh that it were not. We must be careful to not step on the dead and the dying, for wounded soldiers, mostly Union but some Rebs as well, lie scattered across the yard. The barn has been converted into a makeshift field hospital and the surgeons are busy with their ghoulish carpentry, sawing through flesh and bone, men nearby begging to be taken next, begging to rid themselves of a limb no longer wanted, desperate to relieve themselves from the unbearable pain contained in their wounds.

I think back to the early days of the war, the excitement of it, the sense of adventure, of gallantry, men marching off to teach those Southerners a lesson and have a good time while they were at it. Who among us saw this? And how difficult was it to imagine? As Levi leads me through the maze of these suffering souls, some cursing, some begging God for mercy and some, as always, repeating the names of their far off loved ones, I wonder why we were blind to the only possible conclusion of our hasty decision to fight. In war, men die. And in this war, they die horribly and painfully and too often, slowly.

"Why don't you leave me here in the yard and hightail it back to your own lines?"

"I promised you a bed, didn't I? You see any out here?"

We near the house. There is light coming from every window and I see many people moving past. Two girls and an older woman are in the kitchen and many Union soldiers are moving in and out of the front door.

My head slumps and I notice that in his haste and in the darkness, Levi has put the boots he liberated from the wounded lieutenant on the wrong feet.

"Those boots must be awfully comfortable," I say.

"Damn near feel custom-made for my feet," he replies.

"And how many custom-made boots have you had occasion to wear?" I ask.

"These would be the first," he says.

There are guards posted outside of the house and one reacts to our approach.

"You can't take him in there. It's full up and only officers are allowed in now."

Levi moves us into the light shining through a window and straightens himself, bringing me onto my toes.

"I don't believe I saw the salute you must have given me, Corporal."

"Sorry sir," says the guard, hastily saluting then standing at attention.

"Now this here boy not only saved my life, he also happens to be the son of Senator Springfield from Maine. Now stand aside while I have someone tend to his wounds."

The guard complies and we enter the house through the cellar kitchen door. There are lanterns burning in the basement and the floor is covered with the wounded.

"Senator Springfield?"

"All I could think of was my rifle," says Levi.

"And what if that soldier had been from Maine?"

"He had a Third Corps badge on. I figured since you're from Fifth Corps, he must be from someplace else."

"The 4th Maine is in Third Corps."

"Oops."

"Just let me do the talking from now on."

"Whatever you say, Private."

We find a space and Levi gently lowers me to the ground. The dirt floor is hard but it is a warm place and I only want to close my eyes and sleep. I begin to drift away when a hand shakes my shoulder.

"None of that, Private." It is Levi, back with a cup of beef tea. It tastes delicious though I know it is nothing more substantial than water boiled with a few cow bones. I ignore the scalding heat and sip it quickly.

"You fall asleep with a knock on the head like the one you got and you're likely as not to wake up from it."

Levi settles in beside me and brings his mouth close to my ear.

"Mighty fine nurses you got in this Yankee army of yours. I asked one of them to stop by and pay you a little visit. Here, I grabbed this off a dead man they were carrying out."

He places a rolled blanket under my head. It hurts tremendously to have my head tilted up but I am able to see the room and, after a few moments the pain subsides to an acceptable level.

There are men lying in every available space in the basement. Most, I notice, are officers. There are several women in long, plain dresses, some by the stoves and ovens preparing soups and bread, others tending to the men spread out on the floor. We are lying near a doorway to another room in the basement. There is a wounded officer lying next to me, Levi between us and obscuring the man's uniform so I cannot tell his rank. He is attended to by another soldier who holds a candle near his fallen comrade's face. The injured soldier locks eyes with mine and offers me a weak smile. Levi adjusts himself and I see from the officer's collar that he is a general.

Two young girls, younger than me, are helping the nurses, and the man with the candle calls out to one of them. He asks for some bread and the girl is off in search of some.

"Where did your friend fall?" says the man with the candle to Levi.

"Over yonder by that hill out back," says Levi.

"I can't quite place the accent. What regiment you boys from?"

I say, "The 20ᵗʰ Maine."

The man with the candle is a lieutenant and he moves it forward to better see us.

"Well I'll be. You boys put on a fine show today. We saw your charge from the top of the rocky hill. This fine gentleman lying next to you is General Weed."

I knew the General as one of the brigade commanders in our Division.

"You Maine men do have some of the oddest accents I have ever heard. You ever spend any time in the South, Lieutenant?"

"Some. I was stationed at Fort Sumter when the war broke out."

"Is that a fact? I had a friend stationed there."

The girl returns with some bread for the General. Her name is Tillie, she tells the General, and she is staying at the farm because her parents thought it was safer out here than in town, where she lives. The General seems to come more to life as she prattles on and I sit back and listen to the aimless chatter, glad of it, the ordinariness of it, taking me far from the battlefield, farther than the quarter mile separating its blood-drenched ground from where I lie.

The General is bandaged in the arm and his chest is wrapped in a bloodied dressing. I fear it does not go well for him. The girl takes her leave, beckoned by her friend, but not before the General extracts a promise from her to return in the morning.

"Now don't forget your promise," he says and I think it is he who will forget as his eyes shut before the reply is made and he drifts off to unconsciousness.

A nurse comes by to dress the wounds to my leg and head. Levi takes the opportunity to move away from me and the prying questions of the General's adjutant, as that is who I believe the man with the candle must be. The nurse is gentle and kind, washing the dried blood and dirt from my head wound, a deep cut she says, and she produces a needle and tells me to be brave, and I think that after today, her request will not be a difficult challenge. Still, I wince and whimper and shy away and she has to hold my head still as she sews me up.

Levi returns with freshly baked bread and a report of the goings on outside. He says the entire yard has filled with the wounded from both sides. The surgeons are doing bumper business, he says, and limbs are piling up. He had managed to converse with a couple of his compatriots and they were mostly Alabama and Texas boys. He says they are under guard but not being treated too badly. Out there, he says, nobody is getting treated too well. At least, he says, the Union doctors have chloroform, which he makes a point of telling me is a luxury item in the Confederate army, as if it were a matter of courage to face the saw with full faculties.

I think of the gardener and although I do not see him, I sense he remains nearby. The glow of the golden thread is wavering, and I fear my time here is running out. I know now I will never see my parents again but I cannot tell who inside me is making such a conclusion.

"I guess you were in a pretty big hurry getting dressed this morning," says the Lieutenant next to us.

Neither Levi nor I care to respond.

"Your boots. You've got them on backwards."

Levi says, "A trick I learned from my pappy. Helps break them in quicker."

Just then, the General begins coughing, dark blood easing out of the corners of his mouth. He grabs the Lieutenant by the arm and raises himself slightly, his eyes crazed and alone, trying to speak only he is choking on his own blood, spraying the Lieutenant's uniform with a coarse, red mist, mouthing words that the Lieutenant must lean over to hear. The coughing abates and the General whispers something then collapses and I think at that moment he dies for I see a light around his body, a shimmering silvery glow. It gathers itself up into a tight mass near his stomach then ascends through the ceiling of the basement.

The Lieutenant gets to his feet and I presume he is going to report the passing of his superior to command. Before he leaves, he turns to us and says he will see us later, his eyes never wavering from Levi's.

"You should go now, under cover of darkness," I say.

"There's no way I can make it back to my lines tonight. I'll leave at first light," says Levi.

"Do you reckon he knows?" I ask.

"I reckon he does," says Levi.

There is a minor commotion at the entrance to the cellar as a stretcher is brought into the kitchen, attended to by three civilians;

a man and his wife and a girl, who I figure, like Miss Tillie of Gettysburg, is a bit younger than me. They are fretting over the body lying prone in the stretcher, and as there is a little bit of space on my left, they head towards us and place the stretcher down beside Levi and me.

My curiosity is aroused, even through the dull cloud enveloping my senses, except Levi is between the stretcher and me and the family is blocking my view of the invalid. I imagine he must be a local Pennsylvania boy as there were many on the battlefield today, some fighting next to us on the hill. How fortunate is the man to have his family around him at a time of such pain and fear and loneliness. Oh, to have my mother attending to me, making rich stews for me to eat and preparing her secret Indian poultices to draw the poisons from my wounds and quickly heal them.

A nurse brings one of the surgeon officers to our corner of the basement. She shoos the relatives and Levi away to make room for the doctor. I wish to see the soldier's face, half expecting to see General Meade himself lying next to me but what greets my eyes stops my heart and the gasp from my lips distracts the doctor and nurse who glance my way until my rank registers and they return to attending the wounded stranger.

She is a beautiful young girl, older than her sister, for the resemblance to the younger girl is obvious, with long, wavy brown hair and skin so pale I think perhaps in a stronger light I could see through it. Her eyes are closed and her mouth is parted slightly, her breath laboured. She is injured above her left breast, near the shoulder and the surgeon is unwrapping the temporary bandage that has been placed upon it. She is the most beautiful girl I have ever seen. And I have seen her before. She is Donna.

I turn and the gardener is there beside me.

"It is Donna," I say.

"I know."

"How is she here?"

"This is her time, her place. Same as it is for you."

"I don't know who I am."

"Yes you do. You are Joshua Templeton. You are Adam Fischer."

"What am I doing here?"

"I don't know. I didn't bring you. The wolf did."

I turn back to her. The doctor's attention to her wound has disturbed her delirium and she opens her eyes. She turns her head towards me and gazes into my eyes and I am stunned beyond words by her beauty, her eyes penetrating through me more easily than the sharp end of a Rebel bayonet, and I suddenly know the inspiration behind the poems my mom insisted on reading to me, recall her telling me that one day I would understand their meaning and that day has come for I am certain I look upon the only woman I will ever love. And I see her with two sets of eyes and know we both love her, have always loved her.

Her right breast is momentarily exposed as the doctor conducts his examination and it is the most perfect thing I have ever seen, a firm, rounded mound topped off by an intoxicating chocolate brown nipple, and I begin to ache in my loins as the warm feeling of longing moves up into my belly. I flinch, embarrassed with guilty delight and mortified that her eyes are still watching mine, aware of the liberty I have taken, but she does not seem to mind. She will not abandon my eyes and I see a large tear fall to the blanket underneath her head as the surgeon probes the wound, her bravery betrayed by a steady stream of uncontrollable tears rolling one after the other down her cheek.

There are only a couple of feet between us and her hand traverses the distance and finds mine and the strength of her grip surprises me. Her hand is cold and smooth, so soft and puffy, the softest thing I have ever touched. My soldier's hand must feel as if I am wearing woolen gloves. I see a glowing where our hands are joined and notice my golden thread has regained its former luster. Without a word spoken I feel I know this girl as I have known no other.

The surgeon finishes his ministrations and raises himself as far as the ceiling will permit. The girl withdraws her hand but it is too late; he has already seen our joining.

He commands her to rest and to me he says not to bother her too much for she is gravely injured and needs to be kept quiet. The nurse goes to fetch her family members who have escaped this den of suffering to catch a few breaths of air free of the stench of the dead and dying.

"Are you badly hurt?" she asks and her voice, while thinned by the shock of her injury, has the texture of fine velvet, at least that is what comes to mind, as I am not sure if I have ever been in the presence of velvet, fine or otherwise. It is a small voice, sing-song lyrical, a voice I would never tire of listening to, even if it were to recite to me nothing more stimulating than the inventory of a dry goods store or a voter list.

I say, "Not too bad, I think."

I am afraid to ask her the same question and instead, ask her if she is in much pain.

"It hurt dreadfully bad at first but I was given some syrup and it has dulled my senses."

She tells me of her accident, how she and her family lived on a farm a little ways to the east of here, and on account of the Rebel shells overshooting the hill where our brigade had been fighting all day, they were raining down instead on their homestead. She and her family were seeking safer accommodations, loaded up on a wagon, not far gone from their house, when a solid shot burst in the air above them, sending its deadly fragments to the ground, one of which found lodging in her chest below the shoulder.

"I thank God that no one else in my family was hurt," she says, and her selfless gratitude makes me think of something my mother used to say to me, about never judging a book by its cover, and I know now that sometimes you can.

Her family has returned and Levi with them. He has made acquaintanceship with her sister, a near carbon copy of the beauty lying beside me. I think perhaps I know her too, but I am too smitten with her sister to concentrate and besides, the hammering in my head has grown worse from the exertion of my pleasantries with the young lady whose name remains unknown to me.

Her mother is weeping, attending to her injured daughter's covers while her father, hat in his hand, fidgeting with it by rotating its rim through his fingers, hovers at the foot of her bed, whispering "Courage" over and over.

"Mother, this young man has been keeping me company while you were away and I am afraid we have not been properly introduced."

"Why Clara my love," says the mother, "The Lieutenant informs me that you are lying next to a senator's son. From Maine. Imagine that. Right here in this awful little room lay so many fine gentlemen. Still, this is not a proper place for a young lady. I have asked the nurse to find you a more suitable location for the night."

I cannot but notice Levi's silly grin, his one eye winking at me as if inflicted with a bit of dust.

"I am comfortable here mother. If only I knew this young man's name."

"Joshua Templeton at your service, ma'am."

She tries to tell me her full name, instead a coughing fit replaces those delicate syllables. I am reluctantly certain that she is in a bad way. The metal is still inside her and already her bandage darkens, her life force draining away. I call upon God to spare her, to make any bargain He chooses with me so long as she will live.

The nurse returns with two attendants who prepare to move my dear Clara. I say her name over and over in my mind. Clara. Donna.

They are taking her to a room upstairs, occupied by one man, I hear the nurse relate, who is wrapped in gauze, horribly burned, having had the misfortune of being the driver of a caisson that blew up of its own accord early yesterday in front of the farm house.

"Miss Tillie, who witnessed the tragedy, says the poor soul was flung thirty feet into the air," says the nurse. She says there is a nurse in his room and Clara will be well attended.

As they lift her, she reaches for my hand.

"Please come visit me before you leave," she says.

"You can rest assured I will," I say.

Her eyes haunt me long after they have taken her away, branded into my memory by their tender longing and despite the fetid vapors of men dirty and dying, her scent of lavender lingers for minutes after she is gone. My mind drifts back to the morning of this day and the person I see rising to begin the march to this place is no longer me, or rather, I see now another me, an expanded, wiser me, as if in one day I have lived a lifetime of experience. Today I have known death and pain, fear and exhilaration, loneliness, despair, hatred and friendship and now love. I am overwhelmed with emotion and cannot stop the tears from coming.

Levi sits beside me and rests his back against the wall by my head. I turn away so he will not see me crying.

"I never seen a Northern girl I liked 'til now. And damn if there weren't two of them. And you, ya young buck, practically on your deathbeds, the two of you, and carrying on like that. Did my heart good to see it. Good to know it's still possible to be like regular folks. With all the marching and killing, I wasn't sure I could act normal again. You ever feel that way?"

I nod my head and remain quiet, lying so he cannot see my face. A favourite poem of my mother's is playing in my head. It is by a man named Blake. I never liked or understood it until now.

"Love seeketh not Itself to please,
Nor for itself hath any care;

282

But for another gives it ease,
And builds a Heaven in Hell's despair."

So sang a little Clod of Clay,
Trodden with a cattle's feet;
But a Pebble of the brook,
Warbled out these metres meet:

"Love seeketh only Self to please,
To bind another to its delight;
Joys in another's loss of ease,
And builds a Hell in Heaven's despite."

I would gladly give of my soul to make her well. Yet, I earnestly hope she is troubled by our separation. I want to free her of all her earthly troubles and still bind herself to me forever. The clay and the pebble, I finally realize, are but two sides of a single coin.

Levi tells me about going outside and seeing the Lieutenant standing nearby, talking to a group of soldiers and taking an inordinate interest in Levi, as were the other men in the group. He says he has reconsidered my advice and might as well take his chances out in the woods rather than get trapped in this cellar. He reckons it's eleven o'clock and will leave around midnight.

He spends most of the hour telling me about his life in Alabama, and it is a harsh life, subsistence living my daddy calls it, his father a dirt-poor farmer, working a few acres of land, lending himself out as a handyman for those who cannot afford slaves of their own, Levi's mother having died when his younger brother was born. He was three then and remembers nothing of her. They live outside a town I've never heard of, in a State I cannot fathom, as the description of it and the life Levi has led is as foreign to my experience as would be, I imagine, the life lived by someone from France or Spain.

Like many poor boys from both sides of the line, to Levi the war seemed a glorious opportunity to break free from the dreariness of his daily life, a grand adventure leading beyond the confines of the farm and the few miles between it and the closest town.

"I've marched across most of this damn country by now and there have been some grand sights—cities and mountains and long valleys. But when I close my eyes, all I see are the dead and the wounded. I see arms blowed off and men ripped open. I'll tell you, I wish now I'd never left my daddy's farm."

At midnight, or thereabouts, he prepares to leave. He quietly loads his Springfield and sticks some bread into his shirt.

"If'n anything happens to me," he says, "you don't know nothing about me being a Confederate. Do you understand? There ain't no use in the two of us getting into trouble."

"I can't lie. I can help you. I will tell them how you helped me. Perhaps I should go to them now and they will let you go."

I am crazed with fear for him. There seems to be a bottomless well in my heart providing me with the rich emotions of love on this bleak day of death and destruction.

"You will do me a great dishonour if you do not save yourself. I saved your life. You are beholding to me. And I say to you, save yourself. Do we have an understanding?"

I nod my head.

"Besides, I've been in worse fixes than this. Maybe after the war we will meet as friends."

He cups my bicep in his hand and I his, and we hold each other for a moment. I stare into his eyes and they are the eyes of a dead man.

He rises and walks out the door. A few minutes later I hear scuffling and men shouting, someone yelling "Halt!" then a few shots ring out and the commotion dies down.

Presently, the Lieutenant is by my side. He tells me my friend was a rebel spy who has shot a guard while trying to sneak away to his own lines, was wounded in the leg, captured and will be executed at dawn.

"So how is it that an officer from your own regiment is a complete stranger to you?" he asks.

"I keep to my own company. He looked familiar. Besides, he saved my life. I seriously doubt he is a spy. Why would he bring me here when he could have left me out in the woods to die?"

The Lieutenant guffaws and if I were well enough, I would have risked a court martial for one good punch to his face.

"What better way to sneak behind our lines than to escort a wounded soldier to a field hospital. Do you realize, boy, General Meade is not one mile down this road right now. Wouldn't he be a prize for your Reb friend to bag."

"I know an honourable man when I see one. Like your dead General here lying beside me. If he is a Rebel, then I'll wager he was only trying to save his skin after saving mine."

284

"Maybe so," says the Lieutenant, slumping down on the wall next to the dead man. "Maybe so. Don't really matter though cause he'll be shot at sunup."

It is hard for me not to think that God has taken a sudden and pre-occupied interest in me, devising a wonderfully devilish world for me to inhabit, as if I were the sun around which every thing in creation has suddenly decided to revolve around. My daddy likes to say, life is a test and you pass or you fail according to how well you follow the laws of God. If this day be a test, then I do not know which laws I am supposed to adhere to.

I turn to the spot where she laid before they took her upstairs. The gardener sits there now.

I say to him, "What am I supposed to do? Do I let them kill him without trying to save him?"

"Ask yourself what you can do."

"I don't see as how I can do anything."

"Stop thinking with your brain and start thinking with your heart."

I mull this over and the hours pass slowly. I sleep in fits and starts, a continual theme of shooting and fighting never leaving me. Asleep or awake, I am back on the hill, poor Billy, me and Levi, the sights and sounds of the battle renewed and repeated, uncontrollable and unstoppable as I pass in and out of consciousness. Each time I open my eyes I see the Lieutenant slumped asleep against the wall, still at his post, keeping vigil over the fallen General. Only when thoughts of Clara occupy my mind to the exclusion of all others do I finally find peace and sleep.

I startle at the sound of the first rooster. Never have I wished to hear a sound less. The rooster's signaling of the dawn has woken many of the crazed wounded and a new round of moaning begins in the vicinity of where I lay. The Lieutenant gets up and asks if I want to see this thing done. My head says no but my heart says yes and I nod my assent.

He helps me to my feet and takes me outside. I almost pass out from the attempt as it has been some twelve hours since I last stood. My age occurs to me and I feel so much older than I did at the start of yesterday. Not only my body. My mind feels older, as if countless dawns have passed since the last one I saw.

What an awful spectacle greets my eyes. In the darkness of the night before, one could only imagine the numbers of men brought to this place to be treated or to die. Now in the growing light, I see the ground littered with countless bodies, some moving, some still as rocks, some making awful sounds, some silenced by the pain or the stopping of their hearts. This is wrong, I think. To ask a man to die for his country may be honourable, but to leave him lying in unbearable pain while his life ebbs away, unattended, without the means by which he can be released from his misery, is an unholy disgrace and it sickens me to see the countenance of so many contorted and fearful faces.

I am led past a fence where a pile of sawed-off arms and legs reaches higher than the fence posts, hundreds of hands reaching absently into the air, countless feet that will never touch the ground again. It is a sight one's eyes are not designed to see, a scene so terrible I have not the will to digest it.

We pass by a surgeon's table outside of the barn that is full of men screaming to be taken next and three men are holding down a soldier while his leg is being removed. I can smell a trace of chloroform in the air. I watch the saw rip through the man's flesh as he squirms and yells and there does not seem to be much art to it.

At first there is only a solitary tree, off to one side of the yard, a gnarly crab apple tree, a shade tree with a small table underneath. Then arrives a cadre of soldiers, dopey from being roused this early in the morning, marching to a quick kill before some warm coffee and a bit of breakfast. Behind them comes Levi, flanked by two guards, one of them supporting him as he hops on his good leg, the other crudely bandaged with a piece of cloth, tied tight to prevent the prisoner the satisfaction of bleeding to death.

He passes close by and gives me a casual glance, devoid of recognition; so convincing is his expressionless face that for a moment I think he has not realized who I am. He is led past us to the tree and his hands are bound behind his back. There is no priest, no offer of last words, only a canvas bag placed over his head, a clearing away by the guards and detail officer, then the command to aim and fire.

He twists and falls onto his back, landing heavily in a dusty cloud. They have blasted his heart to bits and I think he was dead before the ground stopped his fall. I stagger over to him and kneel down to remove the bag from his head. He is smiling at me, eyes closed, his face so unlike the many I have seen lying on the battlefield or dying in the yard. It is peace I see. It is a peace I envy and think I will never know.

I watch large tears fall to the ground by his side, making little puffs of dust. I think of Billy and how bad it felt to watch him fall and this is even more hurtful to me, and I mean no disrespect to Billy. Billy and I were friends but this boy who lies broken before me has stolen my heart. I think of his father and brother and their little farm, of the son and brother who will never return, of the friend I will never get to know. I think of the place he described to me and I see in my mind a map of the United States and it occurs to me that he and I have met about halfway between where we were both raised and it seems appropriate somehow, our two worlds coming together at this god-forsaken place. I wipe my eyes and look up in time to see the same light as I saw leave the General, gathering itself about Levi's stomach before shooting into the sky, disappearing in an instant.

"Did you see that?" I ask the gardener.

"Yes I did."

"What was it?"

"Why do you ask me questions you already know the answer to?"

"It was his spirit."

"Yes."

"I will meet up with it again."

"Yes."

"I am glad for that."

They take his body away and I wonder aloud if he will be properly buried. The Lieutenant scoffs at my concern. He tells me to look around the yard, at the dead piled in wagons and gathered together in long rows by the fence. He will fare no better or worse than the others, he says, and takes leave of me, saying he must attend to the disposition of the General, and I assume by that he means a burial of more import than the one my friend will receive, for I am certain it is not the General's personality he refers to, he being stone cold dead and long past human exchange.

My thoughts return to the living, to Clara, and thinking of her, I realize she has not been out of my mind for a second since last I saw her. Even when my thoughts have been elsewhere, or I have been dreaming, I have felt her inside me, as if her eyes and mine have joined and I see the world with a combined vision.

There is much traffic on the road next to the farm. Troops, cavalry, ambulances, artillery and provision wagons all wager for a piece of the road. There is much shouting and confusion and I tire of it, desiring only an end to this war, for the fight has gone out of me. My head throbs less though it is still tender to the touch. I find myself standing in front of a window on the porch of the farmhouse. I see my reflection and wonder for a moment whether some wretched stranger is standing on the other side of the window staring out at me. The image I see has little bearing to the face I have grown accustomed to viewing from a reflecting surface. Even in the dim light I see a face unshaven, my bandaged head obscuring my fine head of hair, so described by my mom, and my eyes, puffy and forlorn, calling to mind the vacancy of the dead. Hardly the bearing of a man about to go courting the woman of his dreams.

I step inside and the place is bedlam, nurses and attendants scurrying to feed and treat the injured men lying in every conceivable space of floor throughout the house. I see the girl, Tillie, who had brought the bread for the General and his aide to eat and she is crying a little. I approach and ask if she remembers me from the night before and she does, relating to me how she kept her promise to the General and paid him a visit as soon as she arose, only she found him dead and isn't war the most horrible thing! I assure her that it is, then inquire as to the whereabouts of the young lady, Clara, who was brought upstairs late in the evening. Miss Tillie informs me she is certain Miss Clara was removed to a room upstairs, but having not had the opportunity to further inquire as to the injured girl's condition this morning, she is ignorant of her current state. Clara's sister and Miss Tillie are classmates, she tells me, both attending the Young Ladies' Seminary.

I take my leave and head up the stairs. I ask a nurse coming down where I might find the young woman, Clara, who is known to be convalescing on the second floor and she stares at me in a way that sets my heart pounding. She says nothing while pointing to a door past the landing. I proceed with haste, bounding up the remaining steps then slowing my gait as I reach the door. I tap lightly and wait. Never, even in battle, has my heart raced so. I begin to get a little dizzy, waiting for a response to my knocking. Finally, the door opens and it is the sister who has answered my tapping.

She is tear-stained and although she has opened the door only enough to reveal herself to me, I can nonetheless see over her head into the room where her parents are holding vigil, the mother sitting next to the bed, her head buried in the folds of the blanket covering her child while the father stands silently by her side. Clara's face is hidden from me but the meaning of the scene is so vividly clear that I visibly slump, growing smaller into myself, my heart doing an about face and nearly stopping.

"Who is at the door, Sarah?" asks the father, not caring to turn and see for himself.

"Just the boy from the cellar," she says.

"Tell him to go away," he says.

She looks up at me, her petite face contorted with an unaccustomed pain and puts her hand gently on my chest and pushes me away from the door, moving herself into the hallway and closing the door behind her.

"She is dead," I say.

"Yes, she died early this morning. I do not know what I will ever do without her."

She begins to sob and her tears threaten to bring on my own. I fight to control myself, but as I do so, I feel a heaviness, a dead thing growing inside me, a dark cloud of despair obscuring my heart and robbing me of the sense to feel.

She puts her head on my chest and I feel her hot tears as they penetrate my shirt. I pat her on the back and say "There, there" and feel awkward and confused. In the same hour I have lost my friend and my love; my mind is incapable of containing the experience and my heart has lost its ability to do anything more than be the pump it was designed to be.

She recovers and pushes away from me, patting down the front of her dress to give her hands something to do. She then reaches into a pleat in her dress and retrieves a folded piece of pale pink writing paper. She hands it to me.

"A few hours ago, before the sun came up, Clara asked me to obtain a piece of paper and a pencil. She was too weak to write so she asked me to put down the words."

She turns and puts her hand on the doorknob, then turns back and throws her arms around my neck, reaching up and putting her lips near my ear.

"I only hope I find a boy someday to smite me the way you did my Clara," she whispers, then kisses me on the cheek. My eyes linger on the piece of paper in my hand and when I finally raise them, I am alone in the hallway.

I find myself on the porch, not really remembering the steps I took to get here. If anything there is more activity in the yard and on the road than before and all I can think of is the need for a quiet space so I can read the note. I hold it to my nose briefly, thinking perhaps she must have touched it when proofing her sister's hand and yes, there is a trace of her and I breathe her deeply inside me.

I need to be away from this place. I walk towards the road. The noise from the men and the traffic seems far distant. I hear a voice, someone yelling, "Hey, 20ᵗʰ Maine!" and it seems directed my way so I turn slowly around and sure enough, a soldier from my regiment approaches me.

He is a private from Company I named Wescott and I do not know him nor he me. He has been sent by the Colonel to check on our wounded and I cannot give him any information other than the state of my own well being. He informs me of the regiment's new position about a mile from here, just off the Taneytown Road and, since he is pointing up the road we stand beside, I assume that name and this road are one and the same. He recommends I rejoin my company, as we were badly bled yesterday and are down to less than half of our strength.

It is impossible to walk along the road so I wait and wait until I can cross it without risk of being trampled. I continue for fifty yards or so then begin walking north, parallel with the road. There are great artillery craters where I walk and occasionally I come upon an unexploded shell. A row of trees between two fields beckons me and I find some shade, resting my back against the rough bark of a tree. My heart is again racing as I open the letter. These are the words I read:

My Dear Joshua;

I hope this letter finds you recovering from your grievous wound. When I saw you lying there beside me with your bandaged head, I thought you favored a picture book creation of a fallen hero. My comparison is not meant to reduce you to a caricature, rather to illustrate the impact of your pose on me when I first laid eyes on you.

You must be a very brave soldier, as only your eyes betrayed you. In them I saw the deep pain you were suffering. Your stoicism was a shining inspiration to me because at that moment I so desperately wanted to cry out and beg God to make the pain go away.

I do not know what made me reach for your hand. I only

know that when I did, God answered my unspoken prayer, for the moment we touched, the pain in my chest abated. I was overcome by a joyful spirit and as impudent as it may be for me to say such things, I did wonder what effect your arms might have had if wrapped around me.

I fear this day must be my last, as I grow weaker with each passing hour. I wish we had had the time to become better acquainted. I cannot explain the kinship I am feeling towards a total stranger. I can only believe that God sent you to me so that I might hear for a moment the beginning notes of true love. I hope this letter does not offend. It is too late for me to say other than what I feel. I wish you a long and prosperous journey through life.

Yours forever,

Clara MacDonald

I do not know how many times I read the letter or how long I have sat beneath the tree. I only stop when a tear threatens to smudge her sister's hand. By the time I tuck it into my breast pocket, I have committed the note to memory and can repeat it without thinking.

My gaze shifts to the road where I am unable at first to make out more than ghostly images travelling both ways along the rutted track, having too long focused my eyes but a few inches from my face. I am hesitant to rise for there is a general and widespread reluctance on my part to do anything, paralyzed not only in body but in every part of me. I feel as would a starving man, having been led to a feast beyond imagination, who is then forced to watch as it is thrown to the dogs, ripped apart in his presence while he salivates and wonders what might have been.

"What might have been?" I ask the gardener, who has joined me in the shade of the tree or perhaps I am only now noticing his presence.

"Better to concentrate on what will be."

"Why is it better?"

"Because a pilot can only change the course in front of him, not the wake behind him."

"Why am I here?"

"You are always here."

"I want to go home now."

"It's not up to me."

"Who then?"

He does not answer. I rise and leave him sitting under the tree. I possess only one clear thought and it is to return to the regiment. I do not want to examine the reason. I hear it though without thinking, without forming the words in my head. I wish to join my love and my friend and perhaps the regiment will fight again today and send me to them.

I tramp through the fields, my course and my life running parallel to the activity on the road. There is fighting to the north where a lone hill looms up from the forest. I move closer to the road as there are many trees ahead, my footsteps becoming more laboured, each step requiring thought and encouragement. My will has abandoned me, unable to cope with the fickle path God has guided me down, the joys and sorrows of the last day incomprehensible, making me unable to rest on any one thought to the exclusion of all others. I try to see only Clara's face and it is soon replaced by Levi's or by the contorted faces of the dead. I try to hear only her voice and then musket fire, men screaming and exploding artillery rounds drown out her soft tones. I reach into my pocket and put the letter to my nose and breathe in a hint of lavender and, for a moment, she is there beside me, but it does not last, for the stink of gunpowder and the stench of men's exposed entrails seep into my nostrils.

I cross the road during a rare lull in traffic. I pass by a small white dwelling near the road where many senior officers are bent over a table reviewing maps being held in place by various heavy objects such as field glasses and stones. The man at the center of this concentrated activity I soon realize is none other than General Meade. I assume the other men are corps and division commanders but they are not known to me. I pass by close and for a moment they all pause, four well-appointed Generals distracted by my passing. I feel compelled to salute and stop and do so. Only General Meade returns my salute. I listen to myself ask for directions to my regiment and am astounded, not only by my audacity but by the reaction to my question, for it is General Meade who calls for an aide and orders him to assist "this brave soldier who helped save the day yesterday." Then they return to their maps and I am forgotten. The aide leads me away from the conferring Generals.

The aide is not sure, but he thinks I may have passed my regiment a ways back down the road. I am too tired to retrace my steps so I wander away from the road and find a shady spot next to an empty caisson and lower myself to the ground.

I drift into a waking dream, one in which Clara and I are married, living on a farm near my parents. We are on the front porch of our house on a warm summer evening, the light of the sun casting long shadows towards where we sit. There are three small children in the front yard, two boys and the youngest, a girl, chasing chickens with sticks and Clara is ever watchful, warning the children not to hurt the birds, a glowing pride in her eyes as she watches over her young and healthy brood. I am close enough to reach for her hand and the feel of it is the same as the day she first placed it in mine. She is in full bloom as a woman yet even after bearing three children, she remains as lithe and beautiful as the day we first met. I feel to be the luckiest man on earth for what she has brought into my life—her love, her wisdom, her charity. We sit in silence, no need for words, the children's laughter like music to us. I am content. I am happy. I am deeply in love with my wife.

The artillery shell explodes so close to me that the concussion reopens the wound to my head. A wall of dirt rains down on me. I feel the warm trickle of blood in my eyebrow and touch my forehead to determine the extent of the damage. I push my fingers under the bandage and feel the loosened scab, withdrawing them to inspect the red drops running in little rivulets down my fingers. Another shell explodes then another and another. Someone taps me on the shoulder. An officer is beckoning me towards a low wall. I scramble towards it and push my body as close to it as the laws of nature will allow. A direct hit and the caisson I was sleeping under disappears in an instant, evaporating in an exploding cloud of shell fragments and dirt. A violent wind hurls bits of wood and stone against me, stinging the back of my head and legs.

Men are yelling and running about, mainly artillerymen, organizing the placement of guns and the transfer of shells from the caissons to the waiting chambers of the Napoleons. I am glad I am not an artilleryman. They fight from a distance and know not who they kill or injure. Even a rifle seems too impersonal a weapon to me. If I am to take a man's life, or he mine, I want it to happen in front of me so he knows me and I, him.

I peer over the wall and see that I am about a hundred yards from the crest of the ridge. Our boys are hidden behind walls and small breastworks and our artillery fires from positions closer to me. The Rebel guns are mostly overshooting the crest and the shells are falling near my position and back towards the road and beyond. I watch as General Meade and his staff abandon their headquarters for safer ground.

I sink back and close my eyes, trying to relax and ease the strain in my body but the ground shakes so with each explosion that I fear my teeth will crack each time my head bounces off the ground. I think of the evil men do in the name of God and country. I have seen the ways of battle and the cruelty in it, and I wonder if there is any real difference in the natural constitution of each man. My mom says there is good in everyone. But so too does evil there reside. And it is surely only our conduct that separates us, and at best, only by small degrees.

The pounding continues and I begin to adjust to the shaking ground, the ear splitting explosions and the proximity to my own demise. I imagine that after a while, even Hell must become bearable. I remove Clara's note and open it onto the ground, protecting it in a small space between my chest and the wall. After a while, I can no longer hear the shells bursting and instead hear her voice, as if she were lying beside me, nestled between my body and the wall, and she is reading the letter to me, repeating each word slowly. We lie together and the world disappears and I think I am aware of a delirium overtaking me, like a laudanum-induced stupor, but I am past caring, for the real world has become a nightmarish hell for me and my withdrawal seems more substantial than the ground I lie sprawled upon.

I do not know how long the bombardment lasts. The sun has moved so I guess a couple of hours have passed. There is still a bit of the soldier left in me and he is telling me to get ready for a Rebel assault now that the artillery has silenced. I tell Clara not to worry—I will protect her. I lie with her for some time, listening as the sounds of battle draw closer to the ridge. Finally, our boys begin to fire at will and the noise is like popcorn bursting in a pot. Clara is frightened and I make little shooing sounds to soothe her.

Reinforcements run past me to the crest. Batteries are rolled up the ridge, filled, I imagine with canister and case, the better to wreak havoc on advancing infantry lines. Clara has gone and only the note lies next to me. I must go find Clara. I must go to her.

I stand up and start towards the ridge. There is a beautiful copse of trees on the crest and I head for it. I see, with a detached indifference, several hundred Rebs making it to the crest, breaching the low walls and engaging our boys in close combat. One group of Rebs are blown to bits when a cannon lets loose a canister shell a few feet from their advance, tearing an entire company to shreds. The fighting is fierce but it does not interest or bother me. I walk towards the trees. My Clara is hidden there.

Men are falling around me. There is no room to load so rifles become clubs, some men using the butt to strike, others the barrel. Blue and Gray surround me but I am unseen.

He comes out from amongst the trees. He is large with red facial hair covering every bit of his face except his small black eyes. His gray uniform is a rag-tag concoction and he wears no shoes. He has fixed his bayonet in anticipation of breaching the wall. I am closest to him and I offer an inviting target as I carry no weapon. He lunges towards me, covering the twenty yards or so separating us in a few giant strides. I see the point of his blade set to strike me in the chest. His cadence appears to slow, so much so that I am able to take in everything about me. Soldiers are moving at unnatural speeds, men lunging and falling with ballet-like grace. I sense something and turn around. The gardener stands there and, pacing nearby, the wolf. The golden thread is shimmering as it leads away from me and up into the sky, blinking off and on like a firefly and at times, briefly disappearing. The gardener is yelling to me only my ears hear nothing, not his voice nor the sounds of battle.

I turn back to the hairy Rebel who has come for my life. His is a face of pure hatred, having accumulated enough rage since leaving the safety of his lines and marching through the hellfire thrown at him by our guns, to split me open and rip my heart out as a trophy. Behind him, leaning against a tree, I see Clara and she is waving at me, her face awash in alarm, her head shaking violently and I am confused by her signal.

A few more inches and the bayonet will find me and I will be with her. One well-placed thrust and my sad journey will end.

The wolf is beside me and its furious eyes brand me; I am blinded for an instant by a vision of a long life, well lived, a life of hard work and trials and heartache and the joys that make the dark moments worth the struggle. I see a dark-haired woman, not Clara, and two sons and old age and releasing death. I see these images and instantly know them to be unexplored paths, for the path I have chosen each time at this moment has at the end of it a small gravestone marker with my name and company and regiment engraved in black upon it.

And that is when I turn back and within a fragment of time, decide finally to parry the blow with my left forearm, knocking the gun barrel aside and smashing my right fist into the throat of the Reb who would have had me skewered on the end of his Springfield. I turn towards the copse of trees. Clara is gone.

And then I feel the pull of the golden thread and the wolf is at my side and we are flying above the battleground and hurtling back through the void.

VI

ADAM BECAME AWARE of two things simultaneously. He could hear a woman praying close by and he was breathing in dirt through his nose. He altered the latter by shifting his head so his face was not resting against the ground and he witnessed the former by opening his eyes. He could not see anything more coherent than distorted shapes fused with the background, one of the figures swaying to the rhythm of the prayer.

He listened for a while, content where he was, his body feeling phantom and strange, his mind no longer certain where all of the parts were located. He knew there must be arms and legs still attached to his body, but their prolonged stillness had caused him to lose all sense of them.

Adam's nose smelled tobacco and, as his vision sharpened, he recognized the praying shape as the woman who had arrived late after the ceremony had started. In her mouth was a hand rolled cigarette from which she took deep drags between prayers, the red ember glowing and crackling as she inhaled. In front of her sat a bucket with a ladle hooked over the rim.

Adam was not clear where he was although it felt familiar and comfortable. The sense of a recent absence was strong in him. Beyond the praying he heard other voices but was unable to take much meaning from any of it. He heard a voice saying something about someone having returned but he did not know who had returned nor from where. He tried to move and was shocked by the heaviness of his body. There had been such lightness before, effortless flight at incredible speeds.

His eyes opened wide as the skin on his face blanched. He rose quickly to his knees, only to have a wave of dizziness send his head back towards the ground. He felt for a wound—it should have been above his left eye—and found only smooth skin coated with slippery sweat. He was on his knees and his head was resting on the cleavage between his thighs, coherency fueled by the adrenaline flooding into his bloodstream.

It was the peyote, he remembered. His head was swimming in a drugged stupor, though less intense than earlier in the evening. He must have passed out and been swept away by an incredible hallucination. He felt a pair of hands on his shoulders and knew it was John Walker's touch. He was slowly lifted, his head adjusting by degrees to the effects of gravity on his inner ear.

"Take some deep breaths and sit quietly," said John Walker.

Adam did as he was told and slowly the room stopped moving and he could make out everyone sitting around the fire, still in their same places, with the addition of the woman with the pail.

"Where have you been, man?" said Derek, and even if there had been a reply on Adam's lips, which there wasn't, the Road Man's call for quiet while cigarettes were passed around, ended all conversation.

Everybody was smoking and Adam realized that he was too and inhaling and enjoying it. He began to remember the hallucination and it seemed so real, his memory invested with an actual inventory of experience. His watch said it was 5:10 in the morning. He started to panic a little when he realized his last waking memory was some time after twelve. The dream had gone on for hours or at least he had been passed out for all of that time.

Following the Road Man's lead, everyone put down their tobacco. The woman with the bucket poured out some water and drank it. She passed the water around and everyone took a drink. When it came to Adam, he drank it slowly, his throat so parched it hurt for the water to pass over his inflamed passageway. When each person had taken water, the woman picked up the bucket and left.

The Road Man sang another song and Adam tried not to think about his strange dream. He wanted to wait until he was alone before he thought about it. It had a queer quality. He did not so much remember it as feel it.

Derek reached over and brushed some dirt from Adam's face. Derek was a good friend, a nut bar to be sure, but someone who had stuck by Adam, not judging him, faithful, trustworthy, freely giving his love. And Adam always assumed he had given as well as he had received. Yet now, with Derek's questioning eyes on him, Adam saw so clearly how he was always the one holding back, releasing his love and affection in small doses. How foolish of me, thought Adam. He felt an uninhibited outpouring of affection for his friend. He leaned over and hugged Derek about the neck and whispered to him that he loved him.

"I love you too, man," Derek whispered back.

Another man might have been put off or embarrassed by Adam's action. Then again, another man might wear socks occasionally. Not Derek. Adam saw only joy in Derek's eyes and even a small tear.

"I was worried about you for a while there. George said you were okay and to leave you be. You should have seen yourself. I thought you were having seizures or something. And every time you moved or jerked, John Walker made the same movement. It was pretty freaky, I gotta tell you."

Adam turned to John Walker. He was sitting with his head bowed and his eyes closed. He must have sensed something because he raised his head slightly and opened his eyes. Then he winked and closed them again.

The water woman reappeared with corn bread and fruit. She withdrew then returned with cooked meat, its origin unknown to Adam; goat or beef, he presumed. The food was placed around the fire and Adam was tempted to grab something but when he saw no one else move, he held back.

The Road Man spoke. "Our time is finished. The sun is rising to signal the end of the ceremony. It is time to reflect on our insights, eat, then sleep."

The Road Man picked up the gourd and cane and began to sing as Simon applied more cedar to the fire. Jeremy banged on the drum. The Road Man began to pray again, his hands over a plate of meat. Then Jeremy commenced spooning food onto plates and passing them to his left.

Adam watched as Rose ripped strips of meat off a rib, chewing it slowly and methodically. Benito seemed to require a simultaneous sampling of the menu as meat, bread and fruit entered his mouth in quick succession. The Road Man munched carefully on a piece of melon. No one spoke while the food was consumed.

The first few bites of food made Adam's stomach contract, sending sharp pains to his sides. He chewed very slowly and after a few swallows, began to feel better. He was still extremely stoned, but happily so, light and colour magnified and sharp, his thoughts as random as the snow swirling around a winter scene in a shaken glass ball.

He had so much to tell Donna. The thought of her made his heart leap. A sudden terror gripped him while pictures from the dream played before him and he wondered at their meaning. Why had Donna died? Why would he dream of such a thing? It was the peyote. It had to be the peyote. It had found his darkest fear and played on the thought of losing her. It manufactured an elaborate melodrama and played it out while he was under a drug-induced psychosis. Adam took a few deep breaths and bit into the meat, satisfied he had solved the conundrum.

When the food was all consumed, the water woman gathered the plates and took them outside. Cedar was passed around the circle and everyone tossed it into the fire. This signaled the end of the ceremony and everyone got up and left the teepee. Only the Road Man remained behind and Adam could hear him in earnest prayer. When he was finished, George brought the gourd, cane and drum outside.

The fire was freshly built up, the flames reaching four or five feet into the air. A pink strip defined the eastern horizon as the sun raced towards the dawn. It was chilly and Adam moved close to the fire. John Walker took the spot next to Adam.

"The Road Man is very impressed with you," said John Walker.

Adam looked across the fire to where George sat, the water woman huddled next to him. She was talking to George and he was nodding in agreement or compliance, it was difficult to tell, his eyes fixed on Adam's.

"Is that his wife?"

"Yes."

"Why is he staring at me?"

"He is not sure what to make of you. He's not sure he likes the implications of what happened to you last night."

"What did I do?"

"It's not so much what you did, it's what the wolf did."

"I dreamt about a wolf. So what?"

"Don't be a fool. You really think you were dreaming? You weren't dreaming. The wolf is a powerful guiding spirit. He wanted to give you something so he came to you several times until he got your attention. Traditionally, the wolf spirit should have had nothing to do with you. It is a spirit of the People. I told you whites are normally forbidden from partaking in the peyote ceremony. It's not prejudice. Would a rabbi marry two Catholics? No. But he shouldn't care if there are Gentiles in the congregation. George is an open-minded guy. He didn't mind if I brought you and Derek. But he got a little more than he bargained for."

"How so?"

"You stole the show. You were the bit player who the audience unexpectedly goes wild for. None of us have ever seen a spirit power adopt a white man before. George doesn't resent you for it. He just does not understand how such a thing could happen. Father Peyote granted you a priceless gift last night. You should feel honoured."

John Walker smelled of all of the things they had burned in the fire last night; sage, cedar and tobacco. Adam searched for a dent in this serious delivery and detected none.

"It was a dream. A vivid dream. A fabulous, trippy dream. But that's all it was."

"Then what was I doing there? How do I know the wolf came to you?"

Adam sat there trying to remember if he had told John Walker about the wolf. His head began to swim a little as he recalled the sweat and the howling and the conductor telling him he had seen the wolf come up to Adam.

"I dreamt you were there. I must have told you about it."

"This is the first time we have spoken since leaving the teepee."

"I don't believe this. How could you know about my dream?"

"Because I was there."

"Where?"

"In Gettysburg. With you. And Levi. And Clara."

Adam bolted up to his feet. He had a blanket wrapped around him and as he stepped backwards his foot pinned a corner of it to the ground, catapulting him backwards. That cracked everybody up, with the exception of John Walker and George.

John Walker stood and walked over to the fallen Adam, who lay where he had landed, sulking and embarrassed. He sat down near Adam's head and patted him on the shoulder.

John Walker said, "Remember two nights ago. You quoted lines from a song. Did you mean what you said?"

"I don't remember what I said."

"You said life was just a game. You said there is no end. You said something about a paper plane. What did you mean by it?"

"I don't know. It's a line from a song. It popped into my head. I didn't know what to say."

"So you didn't mean it."

"And the point is . . . "

"The point is, you're right. There is no end. Last night you and I took a spirit journey to another world and visited one of your past lives."

"And you believe that."

301

"It doesn't require belief. Certain things are true whether you believe in them or not. I am not required to believe in air. I only have to breathe it."

Adam took the blanket and pulled it over his head, curling up into a fetal position.

"Leave me alone, please. I'm very tired."

"Rest my friend. We can talk later. Your body is weak. We'll leave soon and you can sleep in the car."

Adam was thinking how he never fell asleep in cars. The blanket was warm and smelled of leather and smoke. It was thick and allowed in very little light. Adam relaxed and let his body melt into the contours of the ground. The next thing he remembered, he was being helped to his casita by Derek and John Walker, groggy, disoriented and strangely elated.

VII

IT LAY UNOPENED on his desk. It was not a working desk. Adam had found it in an antique store upstate on one of their frequent weekend outings. It had been an impulse buy, the roll top irresistible to Adam, who addictively opened and closed it while under the subtle scrutiny and increasing consternation of the shop owner. All the way to the cash register Donna had pleaded with him; we don't have room, it isn't practical, it doesn't go with our furniture. And she was right on all counts. It got tucked into a corner of the spare bedroom and Adam used it as a repository for his keys and spare change, the desk too small to do any real work on, and besides, he had no real work to do at home, a one-foot pile of Billboard magazines taking up most of the work space, his mail tucked into little slots built into the back. One side of the desk remained uncluttered however, and occupying the space was the unopened letter, conspicuous in its isolation.

The desk did not even have a chair. Adam sat at the edge of the bed, another weekend purchase, for of course a spare bedroom had to have a spare bed to go with it. It was wrought iron, distressed, not faux, the real thing, peeling paint chips on the floor to prove its rusty, chipped surface was earned by years of neglect and oxidization. People paid good money to have their furniture damaged and Adam was not sophisticated enough to sort out the sense in that. What kind of society was he living in where even the furniture lied about its age?

He sat on the edge, the low iron railing running across the foot of the bed making comfort a lost desire as he balanced one cheek on the rail, the other on the mattress.

He read the return address. Very official-looking. Then he reached into one of the mail slots in the back of the desk and pulled out the other two letters.

Three letters, triplets, the first having arrived weeks ago, the second earlier last week and the last one, today. He placed them one on

303

top of the other, today's on the bottom; he wanted to read it last.

The first one was from the Alabama Department of Archives and History in Montgomery. Adam's wrists were resting on the edge of the desk, fingers spread wide, the little appendages awaiting the command to begin tearing open the letter. His heart beat faster, the way it used to when he was a teenager, hand on the phone, dialing the girl's number then hanging up before the first ring. Finally, he said, "Fuck it" and tore open the envelope and this is what he read:

February 23, 1988

Dear Mr. Fischer;

Thank you for your inquiry. Your request was not as unusual as you made it out to be. We get many requests like yours every year. The information you seek is as follows:

A private named Levi Coppersmith was recruited into the 15th Alabama Regiment some time in July of 1861. According to the Regimental Muster Rolls, he was from a small town called Jack. He is listed as being in Company K, single and seventeen years of age when he enlisted. Our records show that he was killed or captured on July 2, 1863, presumably during his Regiment's assault on Little Round Top during the Battle of Gettysburg.

Thank you very much for the cassettes you sent. My daughter was quite thrilled to receive them. I hope this has been of some help to you.

Yours truly,

Eleanor Stanton
Research Clerk

Adam took a deep breath, having not breathed at all for the last thirty seconds or so. Without stopping to think, he opened the second letter, sent to him from the Maine State Archives office.

March 17, 1988

Dear Mr. A. Fischer;

Re: Pvt. Joshua Templeton

We are pleased to provide you with the following information:

1. Pvt. Joshua Templeton enlisted some time during the summer of 1862. He was from the town of Dexter.
2. He was seconded to the 20th Maine Regiment, Company K.
3. He was seventeen years of age and unmarried at his time of enlistment.
4. He was killed in battle on July 3, 1863 and is buried at the Gettysburg National Cemetery.

I should bring to your attention one curiosity. Pvt. Templeton is listed as killed on July 3rd. This means killed on the battlefield. Please note that since the 20th Maine was not engaged on July 3rd, having been sent into reserve earlier that morning, it seems more likely that Pvt. Templeton died on July 3rd from wounds received on July 2nd, during heavy fighting in and around Little Round Top.

Thank you for the cassettes you sent me. Unfortunately, we are not allowed to receive gifts from the public so they will be returned under separate cover.

Yours sincerely,

Theodore Richmond
Archival Research

Adam put down the letter and lay back on the bed. There was a pain in his chest and he wondered if that was the point where the bayonet had entered the body of Joshua Templeton and killed him. It was much too surreal, beyond his ability to comprehend, the idea of reincarnation, of past life regression. He had read many books since the trip to Arizona and in every one of them he found a way to dismiss the findings, to belittle the anecdotal accounts and find more rational reasons for the described paranormal experiences. But here it was in his hand. How in the world was he going to rationalize himself out of this one?

He picked up the third letter. This was the one he had waited for, letting the other two sit in a slot at the back of his desk. He listened for Donna who was resting in the bedroom. Assured she was asleep, he opened the last letter.

It was return addressed to one Susan Allen c/o Gettysburg National Military Park. Adam opened a folded three-ringed piece of lined paper and read these words, written in neatly handwritten script on both sides:

Dear Mr. Fischer;

It was so nice to speak to you on the phone. I field many requests here at the Visitor's Center, some of them from serious scholars and many from Civil War buffs and people who are just plain curious. Your requests were rather unique ones. At least you weren't asking me to track down ghosts for you. You wouldn't believe how many visitors have come into the center, visibly shaken, swearing they have seen a dead soldier walking around the battlefield. Almost daily, people complain about jammed camera equipment, and folks around here blame it on the spirits. I can't say I've seen any ghosts, yet on a particularly beautiful evening, I will drive out into the park, and climb Little Round Top to watch the sun go down, and there have definitely been times when I truly felt I was not alone there.

I went out into the National Cemetery and your Private Templeton is indeed buried there. He is in Section 15, row E, if you ever get a chance to come down here to see for yourself. As I told you, the original Evergreen Cemetery is next to the Gettysburg National Cemetery. I searched the headstones for the name you gave me. Sure enough, I found a headstone with the name Clara MacDonald, who was born in 1846 and died on July 3, 1863. For some reason I walked off the distance between the two plots. It's about 260 feet. Then I purchased red roses with the money you sent me in case I found the headstone, and placed them on the grave. I know you didn't ask this, but I kept back one rose and put it on the grave of Private Templeton. Actually, I kept back two. I took the petals from one and dropped them between the two graves. Call me a hopeless romantic.

I am so happy you shared your story of these two young lovers with me. Surprising as it may seem, I have never been too interested in the Civil War. Growing up in Gettysburg and working at the Visitors Center gift shop, you tend to O.D. on all the history. And I never took much interest in my genealogy. Hearing the story as you have researched it, I am so grateful to you for shedding light on my family history. Without your call, I would never have known that Clara MacDonald's sister Sarah, was my great-great-great grandmother.

It was my pleasure to help you with your project. And thank you for the cassettes. I am getting a compact disc player for my birthday so maybe when I do, I'll hit you up for some CDs.

Yours affectionately,

Susan Allen
April 29, 1988.

Adam figured if he didn't blink, the tears in his eyes would recede without spilling over onto his cheeks. He put the letter back into its envelope, and, gathering the other two, placed them in one of the slots at the back of his desk, then closed the roll top.

PART THREE

MY CAREER IN THE MUSIC BUSINESS is over. Without electricity, I have no job. Maybe I should have listened to my mother and gone to med school. People always need doctors.

A tourniquet has been applied to the invisible lifeblood feeding our world. I walk around my house and all I see are obsolete relics; useless electrical machines made grotesque and garish by their lack of function. It has only been a couple of weeks since an earthquake and tidal wave destroyed New York City—as well as, I would imagine, much of the eastern seaboard coastline—and already the life I had, the one I shared with everybody else, the fun one filled with cars and lights and exotic locales and fine restaurants, has receded to a faraway place, entombed inside a hidden layer of gray matter. I feel I am connecting into an ancestral mind frame, one far more potent with possibility, genetically amorphous, equipped with an adaptable jungle awareness, spawned perhaps by an unused portion of my brain that has overgrown my modern mind with its dependency on convenience and speed, replacing it with a different rhythm, an ancient, tribal mentality where one's inner life takes paramount control.

You always think of yourself as in the middle of history, writing a page or two in the middle of the book. You never imagine yourself reading the last chapter with you as a main character.

It is past midnight and I cannot sleep. The house is full of strangers, refugees from the Intrepid. I tiptoe down the hall and look in on Lucia. Her covers are half off and her bum is exposed. I allow myself to imagine slipping under the sheets beside her and as my stomach rolls, I close the door. Lucia has nailed onto the door a black iron star she picked up outside the Whitehorse Tavern. I press myself close, my head resting on the cool metal of the star, listening to her breathing. I am so messed up over her. I want her but I can't allow myself to have her. I know Donna wouldn't care. But I care.

Only two weeks since the rescue. After spending a horrible night in an exposed basement, we had some hard decisions to make. I invited everyone back to my house—that sounds so funny—but the four young men who did security on the aircraft carrier decided to head off on their own and the maintenance couple were gone when we woke that first morning. Our new friends included a Japanese family of four, three veterans from the Intrepid and the boy, Brian, whom Lucia and one of the vets, a guy named Sydney, had rescued from a sodomite.

We left our boat behind and headed off on foot. It was almost out of fuel and there was no guarantee we would be able to find any and besides, we couldn't fit that many people into it without fear of capsizing. It took us better than two days to reach my car.

Shall I relate to you, dear reader, whoever you may be, of the death and destruction we witnessed on our little journey, of bodies bloated to double their size, purple- and black-skinned, their clothing ripped open by the building pressure, the stink of death so vile that we were forced to wrap makeshift scarves around our faces with only our eyes exposed, and if we could have walked blindfolded, we would have covered them as well?

Can you imagine the extent of the destruction we saw as we walked, not a single building undamaged, passing through neighbourhoods reduced to nothing more than a series of flooded basement holes, many with floating rats bobbing on the surface, the debris so thick, we were forced to make hundreds of detours to navigate our way through it?

Or maybe I should describe in detail the sadness we all felt, walking with our eyes averted, avoiding the ground and the relentless sight of dead children and toys and clothing and the everyday items of living callously strewn in our path, or how the children in our party cried all of the time, even in their sleep, or how when sadness left you, the void was immediately filled with the kind of fear that you think will make you crazy.

We moved as a military unit, Sydney on point, myself at the head of the main group and Andy and Derek on picket duty fifty yards to either side of our rear. Rudimentary hand signals were learned.

We did not see too many people the first day. A dense fog and a sky as dark as I have ever seen made for limited visibility. Near the town of Linden, Sydney spotted a group of six youths, probably curiosity-seekers as they were not visibly armed, but we took cover anyway and waited for them to clear the area.

"We have to find more weapons," said Sydney. My shotgun was our only line of defense and I had given it over to Sydney while he was on point. We searched every town for a sporting goods store and near the end of the first day, we found the remnants of such a store with guns and ammunition scattered a few hundred yards around. We took as many weapons as we could carry. We now had an arsenal of shotguns, handguns and one M-16 rifle. Lucia, Jenny and the children carried as much ammunition as they could stuff in their pockets or carry in the plastic bags that Brian had developed the habit of collecting off the ground. We tested the ammunition and found most of the shotgun shells useless, ruined by the flood.

Lucia was usually by my side as we walked. Sometimes we held hands. We said little the first day. I was glad for that. I felt horribly guilty for having left her alone in her apartment after her seizure, or whatever it was I had witnessed. She seemed changed somehow, distant, unnaturally quiet and composed. I was used to her voice filling every blank space. This was a different Lucia. Everybody was different, I suppose. Except for Derek. I wanted to spend a minute inside his head to see what it felt like to be emotionally oblivious.

After a while, even the vile landscape became monotonous and my mind began to wander. I was thinking of the future and could not imagine it. How would we feed ourselves? How would we defend ourselves from the predators who were sure to rise from the ashes of this devastation? I thought of Lucia and wondered if I would ever be able to remove the place Donna occupies in my heart.

I know it is not Donna inside me. I know she is happy wherever she has gone and if she is watching me from that place, she would want me to live my life and move on. I know such a place exists. For a long time I have tried to forget or trivialize the out-of-body experience I had several years ago. It was easy to blame it on the drugs and atmosphere of the peyote ceremony. But I know what happened was probably not a dream. Certainly the people I dreamed were real. And maybe Donna is Clara. The truth is, there is no point in my analyzing what happened because the significance of it still eludes me.

I cannot sleep so I write. Normally, on a night like this, I would steal away to my studio in the basement and doodle around, work on a mix or play some keyboards. Now all I have is an acoustic guitar to play and I'm a total hack player so it's not much fun for me.

Sydney is outside somewhere, guarding us. At 4:00 A.M. it will be my turn. Towards the road I can barely make out the body swinging slightly in the breeze.

"We need a scarecrow," Andy had said.

The second night in the house I awoke to the sound of breaking glass. I got up so suddenly that I blacked out and fell back onto the bed where I waited until my heart fed my brain with enough blood to allow me to stand. I grabbed the handgun on my night table and headed downstairs. In the living room I met up with Sydney who was armed and naked. Only when I saw him did I realize I was naked, too.

"Kitchen," he whispered, pointing for me to take the left side of the entrance to the pantry. We could hear cupboards opening and low voices. Sydney took a quick peek then held two fingers up to me. Then he held his fist before me and silently counted with his fingers, one, two, three.

We jumped into the kitchen and there was enough light from the moon in the western sky to allow us to see an elderly man and woman, bedraggled, the man's corporate haircut gone to seed, his sport jacket ripped and soiled, a poor match for the pajama bottoms he wore. The woman wore a tracksuit, her long gray hair a twisted mess, her regal cheekbones accenting her gauntness so that in the dark, her features were ghoulish. Her eyes darted from the guns to our dangling dicks.

I lowered my gun and Sydney yelled at me to keep them covered.

"What are you doing here?" Sydney asked.

"We're hungry," said the man.

"We didn't know anyone was living here," said the woman.

"Now you know," said Sydney. "You have ten seconds to get out of here and then I'm going to blow both of your heads off."

"I never saw old people move so quickly," I said at breakfast the next morning, a hearty meal of porridge and Spam, fried over an open fire outside.

I wish I had had a camera the day I showed everyone my basement pantry. Derek once dragged me to a lecture in New York by a Cherokee medicine man who insisted everybody should have two years of food stockpiled for the end of the world. I guess I half believed him because the next day I took my housekeeper to Costco and we purchased five thousand dollars worth of non-perishable supplies. I had more inventory in my pantry than a convenience store.

"You weren't really going to shoot them, were you?" asked Lucia.

"No," answered Sydney. "I only wanted to scare them. They may be living with other people and I wanted the message sent loud and clear: this is a place to be avoided."

And that is when Andy came up with the idea of a scarecrow. Lucia and Jenny were appalled at the suggestion. We asked our Japanese friend, whose name is Peter, and who is, unfortunately, the only member of his family who speaks fluent English, what he thought, and he was the one who suggested the sign. He said that he and his wife, Nancy, saw something similar once in a Western movie. So we decided to do it.

After breakfast we took the wheelbarrow and went searching for a body. It was a short search. We were fortunate to find a man who had survived the flood and had only been dead for a day or so. He appeared to be a murder victim as his head sat in a large pool of blood. He smelled pretty bad so we flipped on who would wheel him home. Derek lost.

We picked a tree by the end of the driveway and strung him up by looping a rope through his armpits and around his chest. Peter was a graphic artist in Japan and he made the sign. We argued for a while about what it should say. We settled for the following:

Keep out. This man didn't.

I watch him sway in the breeze and wonder at the heartlessness of it. I think of the girl I buried right after the wave and now see the futility of my action, the mopish banality of my burying one girl when I had so many to choose from. A few weeks ago my sophisticated, modern self might have been tormented for days, hell, years over such hypocrisy and the callous disregard for the dignity of my fellow man. But this new survival-driven mindset, this return to a more primal state of consciousness does not allow me such luxury. I watch him swing and only hope it does some good for all of us.

NOVEMBER 9

Lucia spends most of her time in the backyard with the three kids. Brian is teaching Henry and Susie English words while they in turn teach him Japanese. They chase each other around the yard, pointing at trees and doors and rotting squirrels and identifying them in their adopted tongues.

Lucia is mad at me. She is still upset about the scarecrow. She says it's bad karma and inappropriate with children in the house. I said to her I didn't think it was possible to keep reality away from them. Their scarring is already complete. Brian has been having night terrors, reliving the collapse of his family's apartment and Susie alternates between manic, uncontrolled bursts of energy and sullen, can't-get-out-of-bed, lethargy. Henry has recurring nightmares about the family we found in the car.

We reached my Cherokee on the second day. The water level was continually lowering. We had walked north, keeping to the ridge running along the western side of the Passaic river valley. New York City came in and out of view as heavy banks of fog moved slowly along the surface of the calm ocean. The city was still mostly underwater.

315

It was a riveting sight and I found myself constantly glancing over and marveling at the flawed beauty of the broken skyscrapers, reminding me of deadwood trees in a misty forest swamp.

We backtracked the Jeep slowly along the train tracks, Sydney and Derek sitting on the roof, the kids cramped into the back, faces pressed against the windows. The trip back was uneventful. We were almost at the house when we came upon a green Jeep Cherokee, almost identical to mine except for the colour. I saw the hose connected to the tailpipe and immediately knew what we would find in the car.

I jumped out and made for the driver's side door. A dull gray cloud filled the interior, obscuring my view of all but the crown of someone's head in the back, which was pressed against the window. The car was still running. I opened the door and the driver fell out, followed by a choking cloud of car exhaust. We pulled the occupants out and laid them on a nearby lawn. Mother, father, two little girls, an infant and a pre-schooler, all dead save for the infant, who had been found wrapped in her sister's arms, a swaddling blanket covering her face and delaying the inevitable. The baby died in Lucia's arms not twenty minutes after we found it.

I had an overwhelming urge to kick the man in the head. To defile him in some way. To knock out the teeth of this gutless lump of shit. But Lucia, seeing my rage, put her hand on my arm.

"He wasn't raised for this," she said. "You can't blame him for not knowing what to do. They force you to play by the rules, they train you from the cradle how to behave, what to strive for, who to marry, how many children to have. Then the rulebook gets thrown away and a man like this one panics. He can't see his way through this monstrous dilemma. He hasn't the first clue what to do. He is scared to the foundation of his soul. So he takes the only empowering action left to him. He forfeits his life and the lives of his family. He moves on. He moves out of the way. You can't hate him for that."

But I do. Her lecture does prevent my foot from rearranging his face, however.

Henry is crying. He understands enough to know what has happened. His face is buried in his mother's chest and he is asking her why the man did that to his family. He is asking if the same thing is going to happen to him and his sister. He is saying this in Japanese as we drive away from the scene and sometimes language is universal and you do not need to understand the words to know what is being said.

I can't sleep. My body is racing, ready for flight and I cannot convince it to rest. Sometimes, when I close my eyes, the world collapses inside me and a panic rush climbs up from my stomach and my eyes bolt open. It is 3:30 in the morning and I am sitting in bed. Earlier, I took out my prescription vial of Valium and counted the little blue ten-milligram pills. I have twenty-three and a half left. I desperately want to take at least a half, five milligrams, just to take the edge off and let me sleep. But now each pill is more valuable to me than a vial full of three-carat diamonds. If I use them now, what will happen when I run out and really need them?

I flex my left knee. It is swollen from the long walk. I took an Advil and should really take another but they too are in short supply. I wonder about all the people out there and all the medication they require and then I think of Darwin and his theory and surely it is being put to the test.

I am jerking off a lot lately. More than I have done in years. It feels so juvenile but it's the only way I can keep my mind off Lucia, who lies sleeping only a couple of feet away from me in the next room. I want to go to her; I fantasize about making love to her until I get so hard I have to relieve myself or I will never fall asleep. I tell myself that if my mind is willing to have sex with her, what is the difference if I allow my body to do the same? It's sinning without the benefit of the sin.

It is awkward between us now. There was this incredible catharsis when we spent that first night together after the rescue. I felt as if I had broken through my debilitating guilt and anguish over Donna's death. And I had, for a few hours. But the revealing rays of the morning sun brought it all back and I felt myself withdrawing to a safer place, to an emotionally mute plot of gray matter where I can relax and feel nothing.

DECEMBER 10

Have I mentioned the weather? We have not seen the sun since the day of the Change. That's my new euphemism for the earthquake and tidal wave that destroyed my world. Things are, after all, changed. An ugly gray gloom descended upon us from the north not long after we unloaded everybody onto dry land. The sky has grown more and more gray with each passing day, blocking out increasing amounts of sunlight. This is not your normal haze. There is much speculation in our house as to the cause. Everything from enormous fires to a nuclear exchange to a meteor crash.

We had our first snowstorm a few days ago and it hasn't let up for three days. There must be four feet of snow piled up outside. Today it is bitterly cold, 10° F, which at least has prevented any more snow from falling. The house is freezing. We gather for most of the day in the living room, burning the cords of wood I have out back for now. Kindling is at a premium so yesterday I thought it would be fun to start the fire with my stock certificates. We burned about three million dollars worth of Microsoft, Sun Microsystems and Nike stock. Peter thought it unwise to do this as other markets may still be open. He does not say so but I know he is wondering whether Japan is below water or has been spared this devastation.

We have precious little news. A man showed up on our front lawn today. He was tightly compacted into a beige parka with a fur-trimmed hood. He waved a white rag tied onto the end of a broom. Sydney stationed Andy and Derek at the door to cover us as he and I went out to see what the man wanted.

He said he was my neighbour from a couple of houses down the road. I think he was the man Derek and I saw when we went to find the boat. I could only see his nose and mouth as he had ski goggles on, a thin graying moustache framing his upper lip and dark veins in his nose indicating old age or too much alcohol or both.

He told us there were twenty-three people living in his house. He and his wife had been living alone. He was a retired lawyer. They had lived in Montclair for thirty-five years and both husband and wife were active in the community, he told us. Being so high up on the ridge, theirs was the only intact house to seek shelter in for their many friends who had survived the wave, except now, food was low and people were starting to get sick.

"People call this the mean house," he said, nodding his head towards our hanging man, more snowman than scarecrow now.

"We have no quarrel with anyone who respects the boundaries of this property," said Sydney.

"You threatened to kill my wife's gynecologist and his wife."

"They should stay out of other people's kitchens."

"They were hungry. We all are. We didn't know this house was occupied."

"Now you know."

"Could we talk inside?" the man asked and I was about to say sure, when Sydney said, "No."

"Could you spare some food, then?"

Sydney said, "No."

"Wait a second," I said. "We might have some food to spare. But you'll have to earn it."

"How?"

"Tell us something we don't already know," I said.

"Like what?"

"Like what in the hell happened."

The pencil thin moustache stretched into a half smile.

"Well I don't know much," he said. "One of my guests is a local cop. He told me that some time between the quake and the wave, a report came into the police station regarding an immense explosion somewhere above the Arctic Circle." The cop had said the information was sketchy, that something had been tracked by radar but it was unclear whether it was a nuclear strike or something natural like a meteor.

I went back to the house and brought out six boxes of Kraft macaroni and then Sydney sent him on his way.

"I hope those boxes don't cost any of us our lives," said Sydney, who watched the man until he disappeared from sight.

"Come on, Sydney, a few boxes of macaroni aren't going to make any difference one way or the other."

"It's not our supplies I'm worried about. Now there are going to be twenty-three starving people out there who know we have food to spare."

"What's that guy going to do . . . sue us if we don't give him any more food?"

"You don't get it, do you my friend? The people in his camp are starving. Stop thinking of them as your benign, professional neighbours. Mark my words, one day soon we will pay for your generosity."

We walked back to the house. The snow was cold and dry, little tornadoes skirting the surface of the drifts, my legs almost disappearing with each laboured step. My mind anticipated a warm foyer, an assumed memory, for there was only the absence of wind to differentiate our crossing the threshold.

"I am not a cruel man," said Sydney as we removed our jackets. "God has placed these people in my care. He has placed Lucia in my care. The only way to keep all of us alive is to ignore the plight of everybody else. Not that you don't feel badly for what other people are going through, or empathize with their condition. But there is no

319

room for charity now. Charity means the forfeiture of all of our lives. If I manage to keep the people in this house alive at the expense of others, then I am willing to meet my Maker on those terms."

DECEMBER 15

It was a plan conceived in desperation. And if not for Sydney, it may very well have succeeded and someone else would be telling this story. As it is, I can barely stop my hand from shaking long enough to write while the event is still fresh in my head, although I fear that ten years from now I shall be able to recite the occurrence with the identical clarity I possess today.

Lucia lies next to me in bed. Between us is Brian. There is much fear in the house, surpassed only by exhaustion. It started in the pre-dawn when Derek went to spell off Hernando who had drawn last night's midnight shift. Hernando's leg was healing slowly, probably fractured slightly, but he insisted on contributing so a cane was fashioned for him, using a broom pole and nailing a handle to it. With the increasingly cold weather, those on guard have been using the entranceway to the portico as a kind of guardhouse from where they initiate their rounds and hide from the incessant wind. Derek had gone to the entrance and, not finding Hernando there, had called out for him. After several minutes had passed, Derek became concerned and awakened Andy, who has converted my ground-floor study into a bedroom for himself and Hernando. The two made their way through the snow, each taking an opposite track around the house.

Derek found Hernando near the coach house. He was dead with a wound to his chest. His shotgun and handgun were missing. Andy came back into the house and woke up myself, Sydney and Peter. We carried Hernando into the kitchen and laid him on the table.

"Knife wound," said Andy. "Long knife, probably a bayonet. Took him from behind and the thing went right through him."

"Didn't take him very long to die," said Sydney. "Very little blood."

I listened and was appalled by their clinical assessment. Where was the outrage, the sense of loss? Their lifelong buddy laid out before them and everything was professional and analytical.

"You figure it was the guns they were after?" asked Derek.

"Maybe," said Sydney.

We put Hernando back outside in the snow and waited for everyone to wake up before we gave them the news. Lucia insisted upon a proper burial. And while we were at it, she had said, we could take down the scarecrow and bury him too, since he seemed to be having a diminishing effect.

"A funeral's not such a great idea," said Sydney.

"Why not?" demanded Lucia.

"For one, there's a killer out there. For two, the ground's too hard."

In the end, Lucia got her way. We were able to dig a shallow grave in the backyard, about midpoint between the coach house and the main building. Sydney wouldn't let anyone go down to the end of the driveway to retrieve the scarecrow, which Lucia continued to resent.

Before the ceremony was to commence, Sydney pulled me aside.

"You ever killed anyone before?" he asked.

I answered in the emphatic negative. He then told me to get my semi-automatic handgun and stuff it into my pants. Discreetly, he went round to the other men and held short conferences with them. As we headed out the door we all gave each other knowing glances. Sydney did not follow us out, disappearing into the house.

Andy presided over the ceremony. He described Hernando's wartime days as part of a maintenance crew assigned to keeping the flyboys aloft. He spoke of the personal pride Hernando took from his work, how he cared for his pilots, and that's how he thought of them, as *his* pilots, knowing he had done everything possible to make their aircraft safe and airworthy.

"And when one of our boys failed to make it back to the ship, we all took it bad. But Hernando, he seemed to die a little with each loss. Long after the rest of us had left the flight deck, Hernando would remain topside, standing near the stern, searching the sky in the vain hope that a black dot would appear on the horizon, praying for the return of our missing pilot. He was a fine man who loved his work and loved our boys. And they loved him. All of the other pilots envied those who had Hernando working on their planes . . . "

The women were facing the grave, their eyes on Andy. The men were standing a little further away, our bodies half turned away from the grave with our heads twisting back over our shoulders. It was a Mafia-styled funeral, replete with bodyguards feigning nonchalance and making a poor showing of it.

I sensed we were being watched but maybe it was only Sydney's paranoia I was buying into.

The first shot caught Peter in the chest. He lurched backwards and fell into Lucia, knocking her down. Nancy and her children started to scream. I drew my gun as the woods to my right came alive with movement. Derek dropped to one knee and took aim. Andy already had his gun out and was grabbing behind him at Nancy, imploring her to get up and take the children into the house. I called out to Lucia and Jenny to grab Brian and run.

Lucia caught my eye and for a moment the light seemed to change and we were alone and it was a peaceful scene, the snow unblemished, with only the wind between us. Then a scream reached me and I pivoted in the direction of the sound. They were coming for our food.

There were at least fifteen of them. Their leader was a burly man, mid-thirties maybe, holding in his hand what had to be Hernando's shotgun. He was raising it to take aim at one of us when the crack of an M-16 tore his face away. Sydney, I knew, had stationed himself by the second-story window on the staircase landing.

They charged at us now, a rag-tag army of middle-aged men and women, some with handguns and rifles, others with makeshift weapons; a baseball bat, a golf club, one woman wielding a metal rake, another wielding a large kitchen knife in one hand and a revolver in the other. The knife wielder was in the lead, her cheeks red and puffing as she leapt through the snow and the determination in her eyes frightened me as I realized I was her intended target. She was fumbling with the gun as she ran, attempting to cock the hammer with the hand that still held the knife. I took aim at her head, then thought no, I'll wound her in the leg, but no, I might miss and this was all feeling so familiar until something inside took over and I aimed for her chest and shot her dead through the heart. She recoiled backwards, falling ten feet away from me. She coughed and a red spray floated over her mouth momentarily and seemed to hold there as if frozen before the wind whipped it away.

A whizzing sound sped past me. I whipped around in time to see a man running at me and shooting off a handgun. It was almost sad to watch him try to manage the gun while negotiating the drifts in the yard. I took careful aim and this time there was no thought, only a carefully placed bullet in the man's chest.

Andy and Derek were firing carefully and many of their shots were followed by painful screams and bodies falling into the snow. The M-16 was firing almost every other second and the ranks of our enemy thinned with every step forward.

I could see the madness in their faces. They were past caring, having abandoned their upbringing, their civility, their humanity with each passing day of gnawing hunger. It almost felt like shooting down rabid animals.

One man made it to Andy and fired his gun straight into Andy's head but his clip was spent and all it made was a clicking sound. He stood there, clicking and clicking the hammer against the empty chamber. Andy, who had been kneeling, stood up and glared at the man but did nothing. Then the M-16 rang out and the man flew backwards several feet, his neck half severed from the force of the bullet.

Derek was fighting hand-to-hand with the woman who had broken into our kitchen. They were dancing around the grave, she swinging a three or five wood and he with his gun in his hand and no inclination to use it. He was smiling, goading her into mistimed swings, incensing her. I turned to the house and yelled to Sydney not to kill her. It wasn't her fault. Derek had a way with women.

The woman finally fell to the ground sobbing. Sydney came out and assessed the damage with Andy. I watched as Andy put a humane bullet into the head of one of the attackers. Sydney gathered up the weapons. We escorted the woman around the battlefield and she identified the dead. We had killed two doctors (a heart surgeon and the woman's husband, the gynecologist), a dentist, two real estate agents, the cop, three housewives, a clothing designer and a writer for the New York Times. Four men had turned and fled back through my neighbour's property.

My backyard had the blemished disorder of a lunar landscape, potmarked with craters where the dead lay. The brilliant white snow made a stunning backdrop for the blood splattered over it, reminding me of an abstract work I had once viewed at the MOMA.

We let the woman go and then dragged the bodies into an open area, piled them up, doused them with gasoline and set them on fire. Then we extended the grave and added Peter to it, covering our two friends over as best we could before retreating to the safety of the house.

DECEMBER 20

Five days and there have been no further disturbances. The snow continues to fall and the gray of the day is so close and thick, I fear the entire sky has sunk to near head level and that if you were to climb up a tree you might poke your head through it and look up into the blackness of space. It is impossible to tell the time without a watch. I have developed a nervous tick, continually shaking my left arm to make sure my automatic Rolex does not unwind itself from lack of movement. I go outside and try to guess the sun's position but the texture of the light never changes from hour to hour. Sometimes I fall onto my back and make snow angels and dream of hot chocolate and harrowing trips on my sled down the big hill near our house, and I wish it was my mother and not Sydney fixing lunch.

I cannot stand staying in the house. I have no one to talk to. Derek and Jenny keep pretty much to themselves, coming out of their room to take meals, sometimes hanging out in the living room near the fire but mostly they are out of sight, creating their own world within the confines of their bedroom. Lucia is busy with Nancy, taking care of the children. They have structured a schooling schedule for them and Lucia is busy teaching Nancy and her children English and Brian basic reading, writing and math skills. When I feel like company, I usually can find Sydney and Andy together, cleaning weapons or taking inventory or doing something militaristic, I imagine mainly to make themselves feel useful and to ease their minds with the familiarity of structure.

I sit and listen to war stories mainly, and I am envious of the fierce pride revealed by the tone of their voices and the light in their eyes, both of them animated and alive while describing every detail, sometimes correcting each other, like old lovers, as to dates or names.

Sydney seldom talks of his life before the Navy. He loosened up a bit yesterday and told me he was raised in the Bronx—not far from where Colin Powell grew up, he said with real pride. His mother died when he was five and he was raised by his aunt, living in a house with five cousins and a part-time uncle. His dad was a hard worker, he said, and a conscientious father, only he had little time to spend with his son because he worked on the presses for the New York Times and spent most of the day sleeping. His aunt gave him all of the attention she could afford, but with five of her own to raise, Sydney had plenty of time on his own. He was a loner, big for his age, never picked on but never included, content to watch schoolyard games from the wrong side of a chain link fence. When the war started, he lied about his age and enlisted at fifteen.

Sydney had the ageless quality many black men possess. Some quick math and a surprise when I realize he has to be at least seventy-four or five.

"Can you imagine the shock of it? I had never been to Manhattan in my life, never travelled more than five square blocks from my home, and here I was on an aircraft carrier, being carried halfway round the world, to island ports with exotic names and women who were beautiful and willing and three square meals a day to boot. I mean, I would have paid the Navy instead of the other way around. At least until the shooting started."

I asked Sydney how he felt about there being no black pilots, no black officers on the ship. He and Andy gave each other a raised eyebrow and then he answered me.

"My daddy went down to that newspaper every day and worked on the white man's machines so as they would have their newspaper on the stands for other white folks to read. It didn't feel any different for me on the ship. That was just the way of it back then. And I'll tell you, not once during my tour of duty did any white sailor remind me of the colour of my skin. You can't know what it feels like to live together in cramped berths, to eat together and work together on those planes. Hell, we even suntanned on the flight deck with our pink-skinned brothers. There was no room for race on board that ship."

Andy said, "There was this black fellow, and he was assigned to washing the heads everyday and maintaining the showers. And he was one sorry son of a bitch, always complaining about not having signed up so as he could clean toilets. Then one day we got hit by a kamikaze plane and he came top side to see the damage and it was the last time he left the lower decks until we sailed into Pearl Harbor."

Andy and Sydney had a good chuckle over that one but I found it not terribly amusing and I guessed it was a story that had been told and re-told until the mere mention of it elicited a bottled laughter.

I leave them and wander the halls of my mansion, absently running my fingers in wavy motions along the corridor walls, venturing into darkened rooms for no reason, as if by constantly moving, my thoughts will be unable to linger long on any disagreeable topic. But they are persistent, buzzing thoughts, quick and penetrating and no sooner have I rid myself of one than another enters my consciousness and begins to suck at my soul.

A month ago I had never shot at anything more animated than a clay pigeon. Since then I have killed and maimed. A month or so ago I thought confronting those hoodlums on the driveway with my shotgun was the outrageous act of a madman. Today it does not even seem worthy of remembering. I replay shooting the woman with the knife and I watch as another Adam pulls the trigger, not me.

I used to read about a senseless murder or rape or a vicious assault and be appalled by the inhumanity it conjured up and I would soothe myself by wondering how someone could do such a thing and I would attempt to dissociate myself from the act. But unspoken was the fear that maybe we all draw upon the same repertoire, and all it takes is the right set of circumstances to place yourself into the shoes of a killer, and even a split second of letting those thoughts take hold churns your guts and makes you wish you belonged to another more benign species. I know I do.

I begin to doubt whether I will ever have another peaceful night's sleep. I think you can fall so far away from yourself that it becomes impossible to find your way back to the place where good things are still possible, where hope fuels your actions and sees you through the lost times. The Christians will tell you any soul can be saved. It's good advertising. It appeals to a broad demographic. But I think you can get low enough that even Jesus himself won't find you.

DECEMBER 26

It wasn't much of a Christmas tree. Derek and I climbed up into the Eagle Rock Reserve. He wielded the axe while I manned the shotgun. It was mainly a deciduous forest and we had to make do with a sapling that was more overgrown fern than fir tree. I didn't have a tree stand which made sense since I am Jewish and do not, as a rule, celebrate Christmas, so we found some two-by-fours and fashioned a tripod with nails and placed the lame little tree into the opening at the top.

The three women and I searched the house for presents. I never throw anything away so the girls had a field day in my attic. Old newspapers and magazines served as wrapping paper and electrical cords from my studio were used to deck the halls with holly. Jenny fashioned ornaments from tin foil and we hooked them on the wires with plastic straws and string. We even had music. One of my Gramophones still works thanks to a little encouragement and ingenuity applied to it by Andy. I searched through my collection of 78's until I found some Christmas records—Bing Crosby singing *White Christmas* and Gene Autry doing *Rudolph the Red Nosed Reindeer*.

Brian spends most nights in Lucia's room and it was he who woke me up, telling me he was sure Santa had been to our house. We were all roused from sleep and brought down to the living room by the children. I sat with Lucia and she put her hand in mine and it felt so good I thought I would cry.

Brian opened his present—it was a pair of binoculars—then ran to the window facing the front lawn and said he would spy for us so we would know if any bad men were coming. Henry eyed my childhood baseball glove like it was the lost appendage of a dissected giant. He eventually slipped it on and begged Andy to throw him the ball I had buried in the pocket of the mitt.

There were presents for the adults as well. I gave Sydney a hunting knife I kept for no particular reason, and to Andy I gave a box of Havana cigars a friend of mine from Toronto had given me. To Derek and Jenny, I gave a Valium each, which they both immediately popped into their mouths before kissing me each on either cheek. Nancy had fancied an old floppy leather hat of Donna's she found in a box in the attic, so I gave it to her. Lucia had helped me with the gifts and had made me promise not to give her anything.

"This is for you," she said, reaching into the folds of her bathrobe—it was mine, actually—and handing me an envelope.

"I thought you said no presents."

"No. I said you shouldn't give me one. Go ahead. Open it."

"I'll bet it's a gift certificate for the Gap."

I slipped my finger under the flap and tore open the envelope. Inside was a single piece of paper. The four corners had the word *Coupon* written in red and in the center was written, *One massage—redeemable tonight.*

She came to me after everyone had retired for the evening. Our Christmas dinner had been an indulgence—canned tuna and canned peas and canned pineapple slices. I could barely eat or look at Lucia during the meal because each time I did, my heart and adrenal glands mistakenly prepared me for combat.

She did not say a word other than to tell me to take off all of my clothes and lie on my stomach. She had brought a candle with her, an extravagance, since they were in short supply. She climbed onto the bed and pulled the sheet down my back to my buttocks. I was already tense and the chill in the bedroom only exacerbated it.

She began to run her hands up and down my back and I had forgotten what an incredible masseuse she was. Her hands were warm and soon the temperature of the room didn't bother me. She worked on my back in silence and after a while she pulled the sheet off me entirely and used her bathrobe like a tent to cover the both of us.

She was naked underneath the bathrobe as I could feel the heat of her radiating onto my skin. She shifted her position so that she sat atop my left leg with her clit on my thigh, hot and smooth as she moved back and forth to the rhythm of her hands. I got so excited I thought my cock would break in two as it was pointing originally towards my feet and now wished to do a 180° turn. I raised one hip and allowed it to swing around to a more comfortable position. As I did so, Lucia put her hand on my raised hip and turned me over onto my back. She placed her hands on my stomach and slid herself down my leg and took me full into her mouth. Her breasts were full with nipples extended and the sight of them unleashed my desire and I was powerless to stop my seed from seeking the cause of such pleasuring.

The orgasm was painful, part seizure, part emotional rupture, so much so that I imagined each drop as a tear, shed for my lost soul and for all of the suffering around me and finally, for Donna. I wanted to tell Lucia to stop, that I couldn't stand the joy, didn't deserve the ecstasy but instead I let the tears from my loins disappear into her while fresh ones fell from my eyes.

She stopped and gazed at me with a partially fed hunger in her eyes, and I felt badly that it was only I who had been satisfied but then she moved with a feline grace and quickness and slid me inside her and it was as if we had only begun, my renewed vigor surprising me. I pulled her down to me as I shoved myself deeply into her. Her lips were primed with hot liquid and she tasted of her and me as we kissed, our tongues exploring each other as if we had no other sense but taste.

In a single rolling motion we exchanged altitudes and I pushed myself up onto my elbows so I could watch her, her face contorted with eyes squeezed shut, her lower lip sucked back into her mouth. My eyes travelled the length of her body; she had her hands hooked onto each of her thighs, opening herself as wide as she could for me, and beyond the visual ecstasy provoked by her pose, I was moved by the token of this total acceptance of me, the throwing wide open of her, and it brought back to life something I did not know was dead until that moment. Only in this rush to life did I begin to recognize how far I had fallen into a living decay, how each day since Donna's death and more so since the Change, I had drifted further and further from the simple act of living. And I resented it a bit, this being woken from a kind of fitful sleep, where the tossing and turning of a life dulled to a nub was nevertheless preferable to the pain of feeling.

We made love for a long while and then when the sheer excitement of it had dissipated, we just fucked, no kissing, no caressing or sucking, only animal coupling, my head on the pillow next to hers, facing away, watching the sepia reflection of us on the bay window, not distracted or disinterested—wholly content to stay inside her while locked in a perpetual motion. And then, when exhaustion threatened to burst our hearts, we stopped, but still we did not disengage, the swelling of me inside her remaining steadfast, and we lay there, me on top, the sweat between our bodies growing cold from the air and still we did not move. We had become a single entity, forever fused, neither of us willing to let the other slip away to a separate season.

JANUARY 23

Lucia is sleeping the sleep of the dead. There is no movement from her, only a slight heave of her chest. She is pressed heavily into the sheets as if the cells in her body have compressed themselves and given her increased mass. I had to carry her from the living room after her reading, as she was far too weak to even raise herself from the couch. I know it is only rest she requires but I worry about her stamina now that the voice has returned.

Our group is in a far better frame of mind ever since Brian let everyone know at breakfast how he goes to sleep in Lucia's bed and wakes up in mine between Lucia and myself. I was totally unaware of the tension I had been creating by my moods during the days prior to Christmas. I was only vaguely aware at the time of the way my attitude seeped into a room and rearranged the psychic furniture. Though I had sometimes noticed Derek's withdrawal from me, I had not really given the reasons for it much thought, preferring my solitude to the company of even the best of friends. The old Derek has come back to me and today we went up into the reserve to hunt deer and killed two tree stumps and a sign.

The light from the moon spreads over our bed and gives Lucia's skin a deathly bluish tint. I tell myself she is strong but I only see someone vulnerable lying there. I am on the threshold of believing Lucia can save me. Perhaps I needed to fall away from her before she could bring me back. I feel like I'm a motor accident casualty who is learning to walk again.

As I come more to life, my awakened spirit has found its way into my dreams. The peyote ceremony of years ago has been on my mind and several nights this week, when I have been able to sleep for more than a few dozen minutes, I am there, facing the bayonet as it races towards me and sometimes I move to avoid it and sometimes I let it penetrate my chest. Each time it does, I awaken terrified and the first time I let the bayonet strike, my eyes could detect no light and I was certain I had been placed in a casket and buried in the ground.

John Walker once said I was being given a second chance. For the first time since my strange journey to that other place, I am unafraid to accept the possibility of the past life experience having been for my benefit, the bestowing of a gift, transmitted from one dimensional reality to another. And I finally begin to glean the task before me. If there was purpose to my visit to another time and life, then must it not have been so that I could, in this life, recognize the bayonet and parry the thrust. In the moribund conclusion to Joshua Templeton's life I begin to see a parable, a story of opportunity lost, of a task left uncompleted. And I recognize how my alter ego fell victim to the shroud of despair when love seemed forever lost.

Lucia gave her first reading tonight. It seemed a great waste of a valuable resource for her not to use her abilities for the benefit of the group. I understood her reluctance. It was one thing to tell somebody about a job offer about to be made, or to foresee a new lover on the horizon. What would she see when there was no horizon?

I said to her, "Remember the night before this all happened? You explained to me how you were only allowed to see what they would let you see. So do you think the rules have changed? Shouldn't you see if we can get some answers?"

She agreed and Derek went first. They both insisted we all attend the reading. We gathered in the living room and built a great fire. Lucia sat on a couch with her back to the flames and a yellow halo formed around her from the thrown light. Derek shuffled Lucia's deck of tarot cards, including the six of cups, which I had returned to her.

"Are you planning a trip?" she asked and there was mockery in her voice.

"No," said Derek.

"You are going on a long journey but you will not be alone."

She opened more cards onto the table, dealing them out fast and making a crisp sound with each.

"Joey waits for you. I see her sitting on a rock, waiting for your coming."

More cards were dealt.

"You will go to the west of here. There is much danger along the path you will take. You must . . . "

She stopped and her head fell, her chin resting on her sternum. Jenny went to grab her but I pulled her back. Lucia slowly lifted her head back up, her eyes closed though we could all see them moving behind her eyelids, back and forth as if she were reading or watching a tennis match. Then her head nodded slightly as if she were agreeing or acknowledging something being said to her. Finally she spoke and said these words, which I wrote down as best I could:

"There is a spirit who wishes to address you. He says he is a Master spirit and we are wise to heed his words."

A mild jolt lifted Lucia's body and then she spoke in the same voice I had heard in Lucia's Village apartment.

"We are the guide known to this incarnate body. You seek out your enemies in the wrong places. They are not on the outside. You have but one enemy and its name is Fear. Conquer your fears and your enemies will be vanquished. Do not interfere with the lives of others. Your weapons will not protect you. Only love will protect you. Now is the time to distill your knowledge into wisdom. The excesses of humankind have destroyed this world. The Earth is returning to a pristine state of balance and harmony. There is wisdom in nature and the delicate balance it decrees. Respect the Earth Mother. The world is cleaving into two. The time of the lizard is passing. Many will leave their human experience at this time. They require no help from any of you. You have chosen to stay. There will be pain for each of you. That is your choice. It was your decision to accept this time and this place. You too will know the time of your leaving. You must move away from those in transition. You must move into another space. The entity called Adam will take you from this place. There is little time. You must leave when the sparks ignite the fire. The way has been previously revealed. Find your way to the island near Gobean. Go by way of Malton and Klehma. There you will find others to guide you. Leave this place."

Lucia's chin fell back into her chest. This time I did not stop Jenny when she went to Lucia and held her.

"It's the same message as before," said Sydney.

Sydney related the untold story of the appearance of the voice prior to their reaching the Intrepid.

"I remember most of it. She said, or it said, we needed to conquer our fears, and we would be judged on how we accepted our pain. Pretty much the same message as tonight. Except then he named me as Lucia's guardian, least ways, that's how I interpreted it. I got this funny feeling while listening to this voice. I heard myself say, mission accomplished."

We let Lucia rest on the couch and when she woke up, I told her of the message she revealed. Lucia had no memory of anything past her reading with Derek. I asked her if Gobean meant anything to her. She said no.

After I put Lucia to bed I searched the dictionary for the word *Gobean* then *Malton*. I looked them up in an old set of Encyclopedias gathering dust and rotting smells in the attic. The words showed up exactly nowhere. Even if I had the full might of the Internet at my disposal, I sense my search would have been fruitless. This is a new word, revealed to us tonight, of a safe haven, a destination we must somehow find. *I* must find. Why me? Where inside me do I uncover this information?

I can no longer deny the presence of things unseen, be they other worlds or dimensions or spirits. I can no longer ascribe to a world ruled solely by chaos and random selection. There must be an order. There must be purpose to all acts, even those of the so-called inanimate. If life is just a game, a labyrinthine game of chess, then my piece is about to be moved.

After putting Lucia to bed I took an axe and went to the end of the front yard and cut down the scarecrow.

APRIL 16

After our ordeal in Harrisburg, we decided to leave the Interstate Highway system and try our luck on less-travelled alternate routes. No one said anything when I turned south onto Route 15, with its mileage signs indicating Gettysburg, not thirty miles away.

I figure we have enough gas to get us close to Indianapolis. After the tank runs dry we are prepared to proceed on bicycle or even on foot if it comes to that. It took us days to siphon gas tanks from derelict cars and there was only so much we could carry in the Cherokee, given all of our food supplies and camping equipment plus the gas generator. With four bicycles mounted on the roof rack we must make an inviting target.

It was Sydney who finally deciphered the ambiguous message received from the Master. None of us could figure out what leaving *when the sparks ignite the fire* meant. Sydney had been tinkering with my Jeep ever since the day it died, right after we returned to my house from the rescue on the Jersey shore. I had tried to move it into the garage but the battery was dead. I thought at the time maybe I had left the headlights or map light on. But then, every car we came across in town had a dead battery. Even the Duracells lying around the house and in my remote controls and flashlights had all run dry. It made the circumstances surrounding the Change feel all the more purposeful.

We were eating dinner a month ago when Sydney put down his fork and announced his solution to the puzzle.

"When the sparks ignite the fire. It's so obvious. The Master was talking about internal combustion. He's saying, when you figure out how to get your car going, you can leave." Sydney was so excited he jumped out of his chair and started walking around the table.

"Not to put down the Master, but I could have told you that," said Derek.

"No, you don't get it. It's a test. Like cutting off Medusa's head," said Sydney. "They want the four of you to leave but they know you have too far to go without a car. I know I am right. They were telling me to fix your damn car."

The solution to the riddle and the problem was deceptively simple. Sydney scoured the neighbourhood for a gas generator. He found one in a neighbour's garage. He and Andy then modified it in order to charge the battery without blowing it up. When the engine started the sound of it was foreign and delightful. And Sydney was wise to insist we take it with us, as, despite a perfectly operating fan belt and generator, the car continued to die on us every forty minutes or so.

The problem was the Susquehanna River. There was this big mother of a river and we had to get across it. I suggested we head south and cross using Highway 30, which was in a less populated area. Derek and Jenny were all for trying one of the Harrisburg bridges and Lucia just shrugged her shoulders.

She had scarcely uttered a word since leaving Montclair. It was hard for all of us to leave behind Sydney and Brian and the rest of our little family, but for Lucia it was devastating. It took weeks to convince her that Brian was better off with Sydney, that we had no way of knowing what lay ahead and at least here, in my house, Brian would be safe.

After Lucia's first trance channel experience, there had been several more visitations by the Masters. There were at least three different entities speaking through Lucia. Each had its own personality and particular message and area of interest. We all sensed there was a hierarchy and that each of the three Master voices was responsible for the diffusion of distinct types of information and advice.

The first Master I experienced in Lucia's apartment came across as superior to the other two. He was austere and authoritative and spoke in general terms. It was the first Master who made it clear who was to leave and who was to stay. The second Master's voice had a gentler tone and manner, friendlier and less caustic. It was like the difference between the God of Abraham and the God of the New Testament. The third Master, I sensed, was of a lower order than the other two. He was the dispenser of practical instruction. It was the third Master who told us to head for St. Louis when we asked him where Malton was located. He also told us that Gobean and our island destination were in Arizona, which had us all scratching our heads.

But it was Sydney who pushed us out the door. Lucia continued to use the cold and stormy weather as an excuse for us not to leave. She did everything to delay our departure, desperate to remain with Sydney and Brian. She had cramps, there was too much snow on the ground, Brian needed her, but finally Sydney had had enough.

"You ain't doing anybody any good sitting here on the edge of the world. They need you out there," Sydney said, motioning with his shoulder to the west. "And like the man said, you're supposed to go when sparks ignite the fire."

"But what about Brian? He needs me," she said.

"Don't you worry about Brian. There'll be more than enough love and guidance left in this house after you're gone. And don't think we won't meet up again. You go find what's going on out there and then send word back to us."

The kissing and hugging went on for several minutes. Sydney wrapped me up in his huge arms and whispered to me to be careful and to take care of his girl. I told him to treat the house as if it was his own because I knew I would likely never see it again.

I was nervous about using the highways. I imagined a hungry and desperate population, with shortages of everything but ammunition. I drove expecting to hear the pop of breaking glass after passing under each bridge, after rounding each curve in the road. There were no cars moving in either direction. Thousands of them littered the shoulders, with many left in the middle of the highway, making high speeds near suicidal.

Derek commented on how he had expected to see the remnants of a massive exodus away from the urban areas. But we realized that between the earthquake and the wave there would have been no reason to flee since there had been no warning of either event.

We did witness a sporadic migration west. We passed small pockets of people, refugees, carrying their worldly goods on their backs or in makeshift wagons and carts. Like us, they had waited until spring before venturing out to seek what we all hoped was a less hostile environment, both climatically and socially. Only the cold and dark had not gone away with the coming of April.

We were afraid to stop near large groups of people. The sound of our vehicle approaching compelled them to stop and stare. It was painful to see the desperation in their faces as we drove past. Several times, mothers held out their children to us and I pretended I did not understand the meaning of the gesture and stared straight ahead. Our car was silent in tribute to the suffering outside because we knew many of the people we passed would soon be dead. It was while I was thinking of these poor souls struggling through the snow that I spotted a couple and child, having a meal on the trunk of a car. Without taking any consensus on the matter, even with myself, I pulled the car over and stopped a few yards past the family.

They were dressed in hooded parkas. The boy was about eleven and he had the haunted expression of the undernourished. The husband and wife were in their thirties and even through the thick clothing, I could see the bulk of the man, his massive forearms barely able to squeeze through the sleeves of the parka. His wife fairly disappeared beside him. They were from Allentown and were heading for St. Louis. The man, who said he ran a body repair shop, had heard rumours of a safe haven near Champaign, Illinois.

"We met some travellers heading east to retrieve families and friends and they told some pretty weird tales. This one guy said he'd been to a new city where the sun shone every day. He said you could travel for three hundred or so miles in any direction before you hit the fog and the cold. He said the climate was different too, like a cool

335

fall day. And there was plenty of food and people were inventing all kinds of new machinery, utilizing the power of the sun. Sounds too good to be true but hell, we're sure as shootin' gonna die if we stay where we are."

I asked him if the place had a name. He said, "Matter of fact, that guy did call it something . . . Molten, or something close to that." Before we drove away we gave them a little food over the protestations of the man's wife, who said we'd eventually need it and then regret having been so generous.

We skirted most of Harrisburg but finally had to turn west along Route 581 and into the downtown section. The city was deserted. Although there were no signs of natural destruction, many of the buildings we saw were burnt or damaged. Derek said, what nature had failed to do, the looters had managed to accomplish. There were no visible signs of electric power, even in areas undamaged by earthquake or flood. The entire country appeared to be turned off.

The higher a civilization evolves the quicker it falls, I thought. In ancient times, a civilization was destroyed by laying waste to its temples and palaces then dispersing its people into slavery or assimilation. This took time and a great deal of manpower and effort. Now all you had to do was turn out the lights.

The J. Harris Bridge was one of four bridges in Harrisburg and it was the biggest. Next to it on the north side were two smaller, older bridges, made of stone, consisting of a series of arches that reminded me of the way I would draw a bridge as a kid in grade school.

Every car we passed on the approach to the bridge was burned out. Inside many were the charred remains of the occupants. Jenny, her head stuck out of the window for a more panoramic view, said she felt she was in the middle of a war documentary, entering the outskirts of a town under siege. I could see her through the rear view mirror. Never could I have imagined her resilience in the face of the tragedy of losing her family and facing the ordeals we had all been through these last five months.

"Look out!" cried Lucia and I had been so busy admiring Jenny that I failed to notice a chair in the middle of the road with a person sitting in it, right at the foot of the bridge. I hit the brakes.

He was a little man, draped in a blanket with a shotgun poking through the folds, sitting on a patio chair. I could see where two of the nylon seat straps had broken and were trailing on the ground, making the man's rump sink further into the seat. He had on a gray

Stetson, which, being several sizes too big for the head upon which it was perched, came to rest on the bridge of his nose. Long gray hair of a shade almost identical to the hat, flowed freely from under its brim.

It was only after standing and putting a hand up for us to stop did the outline of large breasts pressed against the blanket reveal the true gender of the person flagging us down.

She came to the window with the barrel pointed at knee level.

"What d'ya want?" she asked. She was old and battered, with a mouth naturally drawn into a frown.

"We don't want anything. We just want to cross the bridge."

"Well now, that's something, ain't it?"

We had brought two handguns and two rifles with us that I rationalized to Lucia as necessary for hunting since we could probably not rely on the drive-thru windows at McDonald's or Wendy's during our trip. My hand was slowly reaching for the semi-automatic under my seat when I felt Lucia's hand grab my wrist.

I said, "I suppose it is. So what's it to you?"

"What's it to me, the boy says," and she slapped her side and gave out a cackle and her teeth were gray like her hair where they weren't missing entirely.

She said, "I own this damn bridge, is what it is to me."

"Really," I said. "Last time I crossed, it belonged to the government."

She let out another howl then said, "Last time you was here there was a government. Now I ask you, smart mouth, where you think your government officials are now? I'll tell you where. They's all dead. I hear'd tell that all those Washington folks went off to their secret hideouts and ended up drowned like the rats they all were. So don't give me no crap about government. I am the government of this here bridge."

Lucia told me to ask her what she wanted, which I did as politely as possible.

"This here is a toll bridge now so you best pay up or turn this yuppie-mobile around and find another way across."

"How much?"

"First I got to see what you got. We usually only get walkers these days so it's much easier to assess the toll. Now get out of the car." She raised the barrel to my face and I heard Lucia tell Derek and Jenny to do as the woman said. The old woman ordered us over to the side of the bridge then she put two fingers to her mouth and let out a

337

whistle that rang in my ears for seconds after. I could hear the sound of shod hooves against pavement and then the head and torso of a man appeared above the crest of the bridge and, a second later, the body of the horse on which the man rode. More followed and by the time they pulled up to our car, it did not require a lot of math to determine how badly outnumbered we were.

Seven of the most dismal excuses for human beings dismounted from the horses. It was hard to imagine any of them as babies, being cooed at by loving mothers. They were unshaven and gap-toothed and wore what was obviously the wardrobe of other travellers, for most of them had on expensive winter coats and footwear ranging from Timberland to Kodiak. They all stared at Jenny and Lucia with a stupid, dazed hunger and one of them remarked how these were the best yet.

"Drake, check the damn car," said the woman and one of the men moved to the Cherokee and opened the back hatch.

"Ooo wee, it is party time tonight," said Drake, a frail man of about sixty who was permanently bent to one side and had a look of perpetual absence about him. "Now just how in the world did these folks think to get all these goodies across our river?"

One of the men, a huge pig-faced lout, his gut spilling out from under the hunting jacket he wore, came close to us and stood in front of Jenny. His black stubble accentuated the folds of skin under his chin. He unzipped Jenny's coat and pushed it back onto her shoulders.

"Will you take a look at these? We got us some Playboy honkers to play with, boys." He grabbed Jenny's breasts and squeezed hard enough to bring tears to her eyes. I could see Derek turning senseless and I gave him a slight shake of my head. There was no point in dying just yet.

The other men approached us. Lucia took my hand and whispered to me to take Jenny's and with my eyes, I indicated for her to grab onto Derek.

I began to get lightheaded and there was a tingling sensation in both of my hands. Lucia's eyes were closed. The men were close and they smelled of a lifetime of dereliction. There was a haze developing around them and perhaps they were starting to notice something too, because their expressions changed to wide-eyed gapes.

I thought something was happening to my eyes because the fog grew denser, rising up around the men. They were yelling at each other, confused, the fear in their high-pitched voices making my hatred for them distill into pity.

I could barely move my head. I turned slightly and from the corner of my eye saw Lucia. She was glowing; a purple and white band of light enveloped her like a cocoon. Far off I could hear the old woman screaming at the men, calling them foul names and imploring them to find us in the fog. Then the aura around Lucia flashed white-hot and there was a small popping sound and the light and the fog disappeared.

We were alone on the bridge. Jenny fixed her coat around her and Derek took her into his arms. Our car was still there and so were the horses but the men and the old woman were nowhere in sight. I was squinting. I could feel the sun on the back of my neck. I turned and shielded my eyes. It had suddenly turned into a bright and clear day after months of constant haze and cold.

"What happened?" I asked.

"Listen," said Lucia.

"I don't hear anything," I said.

"Look," she said.

"I don't see anything."

"All of you, look closely at the car."

I stared at the Cherokee. I did not recall it being such a bright red colour. Everything appeared clear and rich. Then I saw it. A slight shimmering disturbance highlighted against the red backdrop of the Jeep. And there was a noise to go with it, an insignificant sound, muted, barely detectable. I recognized the spectral shape. It was the little woman.

Jenny saw it too. "What did you do, Lucia?"

"We all did it."

Derek started to bounce up and down, grabbing Lucia by both hands and screaming, "Holy shit!" over and over again. Jenny and I watched, perplexed. Derek came over and grabbed each of us by an arm.

"It's Brigadoon, man. It's fucking Brigadoon."

We got back into our car. Something the first Master had said was starting to make sense to me. He said the world was cleaving in two. Lucia urged us to get over the bridge as quickly as possible. I could sense the men and the old woman all around the car. It was as if I was dreaming them into existence. Or maybe I had it backwards.

Instinctively, I reached down for the handle of the gun under my seat as we drove away. I wasn't surprised to find it missing.

The haze and cold returned not long after we started heading south on Route 15. No one had asked where I was heading. No one had said much of anything since the incident on the bridge. I was hoping this sunny, springtime world we had slipped into would last longer than the hour it took for the brilliant greens and pinks of the budding trees and the pure whiteness of the snowy landscape to dissipate into the same dull, featureless grayness we had been encased in these past several months. Whatever phenomenon had come to our rescue had withdrawn and left us back in the real world. Or maybe we had entered a tantalizing preview of the real world and had been thrown back into the horrible dream we take for reality.

I have no explanation for our timely escape on the bridge, and quite frankly, I am past caring. The golden rule seems to be—if you took it for granted, it's gone. If you valued it or depended upon it, it was false. The only thing left untouched and thriving is love. I know I should be crazy by now. A process begun years ago during my out-of-body experience at a peyote ceremony and culminating with the destruction of the world I grew up in should have turned my mind to the consistency of Jell-O. But I actually feel pretty good. And the reason is so simple. I love Lucia.

APRIL 17

It took us most of today to drive to Gettysburg. We slept in the car by the side of the road last night, Derek and I taking turns staying awake and alert for any sign of danger. The road was fairly clear but the battery was working for shorter and shorter periods and I am not sure how much longer we will be able to keep the car running.

This is my first visit to Gettysburg—in this life at least. I know it to be two hundred miles from Montclair and under normal circumstances, should have taken no more than three hours to drive. Still, I am pleased with our progress since I half expected us to all be dead by now.

As we drove down the Taneytown Road, my eyes roamed across to the fields on the east side of the road. My teeth began to chatter as I imagined myself—as I saw Joshua Templeton—tramping over the fields, a letter in his breast pocket, eyes misting as he fumbled towards his untimely demise. I was stunned by the familiarity of the place. I suppose the reason I had never come here before was the fear of confirming the inevitable truth of my astral experience. There was

340

no question but that this was the place to which I came during the peyote ceremony.

I remember at the time not wanting to describe my out-of-body experience to my wife or Derek, but they insisted. I described it vaguely and as a wild hallucination. Donna was delighted by the thought of our coupling through different incarnations. Her premature death during the battle of Gettysburg seemed not to bother her at all. Derek too, was enamored with both this apparent confirmation of life after life and his heroic efforts on my behalf. Donna later asked John Walker if he had actually dreamed the same dream or had I only imagined him there. John Walker said dream sharing was an ancient practice and that yes, he had shared the experience with me and was present as a guide and keeper of the connection. He did not expand on the subject. After that, I never talked about it and no one ever queried me about it again—until recently—not even Donna.

But somebody had told Lucia. There was still enough light to see well into the heavily wooded areas and the ridge on our right.

"This is your special place," she said.

"Yes. How did you know?"

Derek said, "I told her years ago. You were going through an extremely moody period, although to the untrained and uninitiated, it would have seemed like the normal you."

"Does it feel familiar?" asked Lucia.

"It's like a mirror out there. Memories reflecting off every surface. There are less trees than I remember, but it's the same place."

"So where did they shoot me?" Derek asked.

"In the heart mostly."

It was the first laugh of the day, which was a pathetic reminder of the gloomy atmosphere in the car.

"I'll show you later. We should pull off and figure out our sleeping arrangements."

The two Round Tops loomed to our right, obscuring what little light still filtered through the haze. The larger of the two, Big Round Top was dark and heavily wooded and the sight of it made me cold. We passed by a farm and it was modern and at first I did not realize where I was, but then I saw a sign near the road stating that Second Corp had set up a field hospital on the Weikart's farm, so I knew this had to be the place. I pulled into the short driveway and turned off the car. Was this really the place that had been besieged by the debris of dying men strewn across its yard? I wanted to say something to Derek, to point out the location where I was pretty sure Levi had been killed but before I could, I heard Derek breathe the word "Shit." He was staring straight at it. Lucia also seemed awestruck by the place.

We sat in silence. There were slight moments when the light shifted and I thought I could see the place as it was then, the hellish sounds of the men on the ground a distant echo, and I have no idea if it was a synaptic recall or dimensional static. The world has become a mysterious place for me and I am no longer able to question any possibility. And there is peace of mind in surrendering myself to the unknowable. I started the car and pulled out of the driveway.

I turned onto Wright Avenue and headed into the park, the two Round Tops bookends on either side of the road. We came upon a makeshift roadblock, a small tree placed across the roadway. Two men approached us and at first it did not register as unusual to me that both of them were dressed in Union uniforms. I was in a place where confusion had first been born in me, and had they been two ghosts, it likely would not have given me much in the way of pause. But they were not ghosts. They were boys, not yet teenagers, and when they said, "Halt, who goes there?" they had squeaky high voices and fresh faces and there was far more nervousness than bluster in their delivery. They examined the car as if they had never seen one before and I was starting to actually believe we had slipped back in time or through another dimension when one of the lads said, "Gee mister, how did you get your Jeep going?"

"I used the key."

"None of our cars work. Even the ones with gas."

Lucia leaned over and asked, "What are you boys doing out here?"

"Reenacting."

"Reenacting what?" she asked.

The way the two boys reacted, you would have thought Lucia had asked for directions to Alpha Centauri or the composition of cement.

"This is Gettysburg, lady," said the older of the two, a freckly redhead with curly locks falling out from his cap.

"What regiment you from, son?" I said to the younger of the two, a boy of nine or ten whose uniform seemed to wear him rather than the other way around. His eyes moved continuously as he thought hard for the answer. Finally he near shouted out, "20th Maine, Company B, Sir!"

The boys led us down the road to a parking lot where we got out and followed them to their camp. We came to a little river and before us rose an anomalous formation of huge smooth rocks, some towering twenty feet or more above our heads.

"Devil's Den," I whispered.

I had seen it briefly before we went into position on the small spur where our particular part of the battle had taken place. We were on the crest of the hill and I had spotted some fierce fighting and remember seeing the rocks and men in both uniforms scrambling between and over them, puffs of smoke indicating where the batteries lay hidden, their shells tearing through the treetops above our heads and causing a deadly rain of shrapnel and severed tree limbs to fall amongst us.

It was almost dark and the silence of the rocks belied their terrible history. I felt as though this was a between-worlds place, a spot where the gate between the spirit and human worlds had been stuck open.

There was a small building on the other side of the river and the boys led us towards it by way of a small bridge. Four tents were pitched on higher ground, protected from the wind by the rocks. A small group of similarly attired boys sat by a fire and they eyed us with more than a hint of suspicion.

It was a small A-frame building, built of stone. A wide stone path led to the base of it and it was an odd-looking building because it had no door or window facing the path. Beyond the hut were trees that eventually sloped up to Big Round Top. We passed to the left side of the building and there were two doors on this side, one marked *Electrical*, the other *Men*. It was a bathroom. Without anyone knocking, the door to the men's room opened and a woman stepped out. The light from a lantern spilled out from behind her, creating a veil of darkness over her face. Lucia let out a little gasp. She had an expression of shocked recognition on her face. The woman appeared to be in her forties but I could only make out the shape of her face where the light caught her angled cheeks and the ridge of her nose. She stood with a patrician air, arms folded across her chest, studying no one but Lucia.

"My name is Cynthia Adler. Welcome to the headquarters of the 20th Maine."

She moved aside to let us into the building. Someone had knocked out the wall between the two bathrooms. The electrical room was accessed through a hole punched through its inner wall. It served as a pantry and storage area. A crude living area had been fashioned from odd pieces of furniture; a single mattress straddled the two bathrooms lying between the urinals on the men's side and the toilets on the women's side. A three-legged folding chair stood next to two crates supporting a piece of plywood upon which lay a notepad, a small pile of books, all exclusively devoted to the Civil War, a coke can with dried Baby's Breath stuck through the hole and a framed picture of our hostess, a man—presumably her husband—and two boys, the younger of the two having led us to his mom. There were roots and herbs tied in bunches hanging from the walls of the building, giving the air in the room a sweet, compost smell. A blanket on the floor near the women's entrance on the far side of the building served as a rug. The woman motioned for us to sit on it while she took up a commanding position on the lone chair.

In the light I could see her fine features. She had straight, perfect teeth that were too large for her mouth as they pressed against her thin, wide lips. Her skin was taut, pale and smooth. She was dressed in jeans and work boots and wore a lumber jacket over a sweater. Her hair was pulled back and tied in a ponytail. She had the air of good breeding and I figured you could give her an hour and a hot bath and a gown from Saks and she could just as easily host a New York fundraiser or attend the opening of La Bohème at the Met, as entertain us in this hut.

"I didn't think there was anybody left in the town," she said and still she did not take her eyes off Lucia.

"We didn't see any," I said.

She said, "Most of the old timers are still around, off in the hills or living on the farms of friends. Most people left town after the electricity and water stopped flowing. So you're not from around here."

"Just passing through," I said.

"Civil War buffs?"

"Not really, no. I was here once before."

"So, apparently, was I," said Derek who was laughing until no one joined in and he stopped.

"And you," said the woman, addressing Lucia, "have you been here before?"

"Yes, once when I was young," said Lucia.

"Do you see what I see?" said the woman.

"Yes."

"Good." A big smile showed off her teeth and removed the tension from the room. She had an equine grace about her so peculiar to the rich.

"You must be hungry. Everybody is nowadays. Let's have some names and then I'll take you out to meet my troops."

We went out to the fire and sat amongst the boys. There were twelve of them and over a dinner of baked sweet potatoes and vegetable stew plus some Kraft dinner, courtesy of us, we heard the story of how they came to be in this place.

They were Civil War reenactors from Maine. When her two boys were toddlers, Cynthia Adler said she had anticipated a future disturbed by early morning drives to the hockey rink and tedious Sunday afternoons attending Little League baseball games. She told us she could never have imagined becoming a reenactor mom, driving her kids and their friends hundreds of miles each summer to various reenactment events. Nothing in her life had suggested she would become a recognized expert on Civil War battledress and uniform making. And she loved it. Winters became a time of planning and organizing and sewing.

"These boys are wearing uniforms of an identical weave to those worn by the actual soldiers," she said. "Every button is an exact reproduction and is sewn into the uniform utilizing the same threads and the same methods as those of a hundred and fifty years ago."

They had been in Petersburg for a staged reenactment and were on their way back to Maine when the shit hit the fan.

"We were about fifteen miles away from here. There was an earthquake, more of a tremor really, then the sky grew dark. We pulled off the road for the night. The next day our two vans went dead. All of the cars around us were dead, too. Luckily we weren't on a major freeway. The only thing I could think to do was bring the children here."

Jenny asked, "Who was driving the other van?"

There was silence for a moment and then Cynthia explained that there was another mom on the trip and how one night, she went out to collect firewood and never returned. One of the boys started to weep, the missing woman's son, and his friends put their arms around him and let him cry.

"I never found her body. I think she strayed too far from the camp." She failed to amplify upon the point and we took that as a request to not ask any more questions on the subject.

Later, after the boys had turned in and we had pitched our own tents, Lucia and I were invited into Cynthia's dwelling. Derek and Jenny had already retired to their tent.

Cynthia offered us some tea then bade us sit down on the floor.

She took Lucia by the hand and held it for several seconds, regarding Lucia's long fingers before saying, "You have the most magnificent aura I have ever seen."

Lucia said, "It's funny how I can see everybody else's but I never think of my own because I can't see it. I'm not even sure what colour it is."

"It's a brilliant purple, fringed in white. When I first saw you it was as if I was basking in a violet sun."

"Yours is a deep orange and it is radiating out from just below your navel."

"The second chakra."

"Sex and creativity."

"That would explain my day job. I write Harlequin novels."

I was profoundly confused.

I said, "Lucia stopped seeing auras right before the earthquake hit New York."

"That's right. But as it turned out, there were no auras to see. The wave made sure of that."

"What wave?" asked Cynthia.

She sat poker-faced while we gave her a quick history of our adventures since the Change.

"I had no idea," she said after we had finished. "We have been fairly isolated since we arrived here. I've seen more ghosts than people. I knew something horrible had happened. I dream of great fires. One night, we camped up on Big Round Top and to the north I saw what I thought were the Northern Lights only it couldn't be them, not with the constant haze blocking out the sky. It was as if somewhere far off the world burned out of control."

I had been half listening, half drifting away into my own thoughts. I was remembering something, one of those memories you come across by accident every now and again, part of your personal Apocrypha, and you can never know if it actually happened because the passage of time and the distortion it leaves in its wake has camouflaged your ability to backtrack it to its beginnings; you think it happened but you can never be sure it did.

"I had a dream once," I said, and only after I said it did I realize I had interrupted Cynthia. They both turned and looked at me strangely, as if they had forgotten I wasn't a chair.

"It was a long time ago when I was a child. I think I dreamed it more than once. There were two parts to the dream. In both I was floating high above the earth. In one I saw a huge explosion on a tropical island followed by a wave submerging the island. Then I travelled north to witness a huge asteroid or comet falling to the earth near the North Pole."

"What an interesting colour he has," said Cynthia.

"He has no idea," said Lucia.

I was growing uncomfortable with their patronizing banter although I must admit there was a bit of envy mixed in as well and I found myself for the first time wishing I shared some of Lucia's—and evidently Cynthia's—talents. And by opening myself up to the desire I spontaneously unleashed bound memories and misplaced experiences; how could I have forgotten my dreams or so easily dismissed the little unexplained events that transpired almost daily—knowing who was on the phone before I picked up the handset or my gut telling me to stay home when I wanted to go into New York and later finding out the Lincoln Tunnel was shut down. Then Jenny's green glow right after the tidal wave came to mind and it was suspicious, my completely forgetting about it, and as these thoughts passed by my mind's eye I looked intently at my two female companions and slowly the light glowing from a source within each of them began to reveal itself to me.

"It makes sense, though," Cynthia said.

"What does?" asked Lucia.

"An asteroid. It makes sense. The haze, the tidal wave, the light to the north. He may have something there."

I heard her but did not reply. I was no longer interested in the conversation. They were my dreams, after all. The telling of them did nothing to impart the range of conflicting emotions they had imposed on me—the fear and confusion that carried itself into my waking hours as I stumbled absentmindedly to school, compulsively scouring the heavens, a fifth-grade Chicken Little, waiting for the sky to fall. Or sometimes I would remember the exhilaration of weightless flight, a sensation so real I actually believed I had left my bedroom during the night and, like Peter Pan, travelled to a magical place. Eventually I was cured. The psychiatrist explained it all to me. Something about my sexual urges; exploding volcanoes and hurtling rocks and stones nothing more than symbolic orgasms, nocturnal wet dreams of the subconscious prepubescent mind.

I did not want to move. I was in love. I loved the way the room was lit by the energy of my companions, two suns intermingling their rays and warming me with their combined light. I loved the quiet of the night and the smell of cold air and I loved this place with its improbable rocks. As soon as we came here I felt the solemn peace that the carnage of a century and half ago had earned and I could sense the warding-off effect of all those deaths, as if the spirits of those men were saying, 'Enough already, no more bad things can happen here'.

Somewhere faraway I heard a banjo and it took a few seconds before the sound of it struck me as unusual given the time of night and our isolation.

"Who's playing the banjo?" I asked.

"Oh that," said Cynthia. "He's one of the members of the 15th Alabama over on Warfield Ridge. Nothing to worry about. They never attack before five P.M."

APRIL 18

A day of dreams. It started last evening when I went to bed. I dreamt mad dreams all night. I normally dread the idea of sleeping in a tent. I don't even like hotel beds. So it came as somewhat of a surprise when I found myself quickly drifting off after our visit with Cynthia. The banjo played on and after I lost consciousness, it continued to play in my dream.

I saw mostly Confederate soldiers, walking without purpose through our campsite. Some wore the semblance of a uniform but most were in the clothes they had worn the day they left for the war, work clothes mostly, denim pants and work shirts, a few Texans clad in skins, footwear ranging from heavy boots to nothing but dirt. They did not talk to each other, did not in any way acknowledge each other's presence other than to navigate so as not to bump into one other.

One of them came up to me, an officer, wearing a gray hat with a wide brim and a feather stuck in the hatband. He wore a cape over his shoulders and owned a fine pair of riding boots that fitted neatly over a pair of britches. He wore his beard in a goatee and when he spoke, the gold in his teeth glinted from a light source within since there was no sun.

"So you have returned," he said.

"Yes," I said.

"They don't usually come back."

"Who?"

"The left behind. If they manage to find their way out then that's it, that's the last we see of them."

"I'm here on a visit."

"Most cordial of you. So why aren't you up there?"

"Where?"

"The hill. Up on the hill."

"I don't know."

"You best get on up there. They'll be needing you come tomorrow."

"I'm confused."

"That's more like it."

"I don't understand."

"I do declare."

When Lucia woke me from the dream she said I was making noises like I was suffocating.

We sat around the fire, eating breakfast. The boys executed the meal in military fashion. Cynthia's eldest son, a tall blond lad of about twelve watched over a pot of bubbling peach sauce while another boy worked a frying pan full of corn fritters. A third commanded a pile of plates, which he held out until they were brimming with food then passed them along to a line of waiting hands. In another pot a concoction of roots and herbs was steeping.

There was still a lot of snow on the ground and I was curious as to how this small group was able to sustain itself through the winter.

"Where do you find this stuff?" I asked Cynthia who had joined us. She wore a long denim skirt, cut mid-calf, with square-toed boots and on top, a bulky loosely woven beige sweater. A red bandana was tied Indian style around her head to hold back her shoulder-length strawberry-blonde hair. Even in the muted light of the overcast morning, she radiated a beauty extending far beyond her physical appearance. It was easy to understand the mutual attraction held by Lucia and this woman.

"Haven't you already witnessed the cracks in the world?" she asked. "Lucia told me about your little disappearing act on the bridge."

"What does that have to do with your food?"

"Perhaps a little demonstration is in order."

After breakfast, Cynthia's little men put down their utensils and joined her as she began to climb to the top of the rocks. She motioned for us to follow. We climbed a well-travelled path to the top of the great stones. One huge rock we passed rested atop two others, creating a small passageway underneath it and you had to wonder what force had placed it in such an odd location.

Once on top we found Cynthia already seated on a flat section of rock and we joined her in a circle. I sat facing Little Round Top and the loneliness of the place stilled my thoughts. Derek too seemed mesmerized—his eyes were steadfast on the hill, as if something long forgotten was suddenly upon his mind.

I was sitting next to a chubby little boy of around eight and he took my hand and his touch brought me back to the circle. Lucia on my right also took a hand. Cynthia said nothing. She closed her eyes and the boys followed her lead. Derek, sitting across from me, rolled his eyes. I winked before shutting mine.

The picture of our group burned as an afterimage. It was a peculiar scene, twelve boys in Union battledress, right down to the buttons on their tunics, two middle-aged men who may have faced each other in another life near this very spot and three spectacular women, each unique, beautiful, vigorous; in charge, yet seductively vulnerable. I should have thought it odd and uncomfortable to be sitting in this place. I normally would have expected a feeling of dissociation to come over me, keeping me separate from the others. Not this time. I relaxed and began to float over the group. I saw the crowns of our heads below me and it reminded me of another time, in a teepee, with a similar circle around a fireplace.

The inner scene grew brighter and warmer. Long shadows grew out from the trees by the river as the snow receded to small dirty strips by the river's edge or lay hidden in clumps under the protection of coniferous trees. Insects buzzed around us as loud as motor saws and flowers poked their heads out from the soft, wet dirt. Then someone let go of my hand and I fell back down into the circle and opened my eyes.

It was the same scene. The sun shone and warm breezes buffeted against my face. Derek caught my eye and mouthed the words, 'Holy shit', he of uncharacteristic sensitivity in deference to the average age of the circle.

"Like the bridge," said Jenny and everyone in our group nodded.

"I hope we saved enough for the Alabama boys," said Cynthia. "Quickly, Johnny, David, go gather up more peaches. Eric, you take Timothy and cross over the road and harvest more corn."

We got up and headed back down to the camp.

"If only we could figure out how to maintain this shift for longer periods of time. You see, after an hour or so we slip back into the old world."

"But the things you gather go with you," I said.

"Yes. Anything we can bring back to the camp transits with us."

"What did you mean about the Alabama boys?"

We were at the river's edge and a more idyllic scene I could not remember. The current was slow and steady, the water so clear that in small eddies near the shore it became a transparent window to the world on the river's bed. Small fish hung suspended, breathing slowly in the rich waters.

"Those Alabama boys are crazy. There are six of them and they travelled up here after the day . . . well . . . you know what day I mean. They are reenactors, only I think circumstances have kind of taken them over the edge to the point where they aren't pretending anymore. They keep launching their attack everyday at the same time Colonel Oates led his 15th Alabama against the 20th Maine during the second day of the battle."

Jenny said, "And they aren't in this world?"

"No, this is our refuge. If only we could stay here. If only we knew how."

Derek asked, "What do you do when they come?"

"We go up to Little Round Top and wait for them."

"Why go where they expect you to be?" I asked.

"You don't want to stay here, not if you know the history of this battle. The Devil's Den was a terrible place to be during the late afternoon of the second day. It's impossible ground to defend or maneuver in. At least on Little Round Top we have the high ground and we know what to expect. They may be a crazy bunch but they follow a precise schedule and they attack with historical accuracy."

"They're actually trying to kill you?" asked Lucia.

"Not at first they weren't. It was cordial, if not friendly, in the beginning. They are a confused ignorant lot; boy-men who have spent too much energy on play acting and pretending. They were ill equipped to deal with whatever devastation occurred down south. So they came here, to a place they've been coming to every summer for years. For a while we were glad for the company and, despite our being from Maine, the Alabama boys felt they had more in common with us, being reenactors, then with most folks. Then something happened. There was a terrible winter storm. Went on for days. We all squeezed into the hut and waited it out. When the weather let up, they were waiting for us. They had guns and they took all of our food. Then the leader came up to me and I barely recognized him because he had lost about twenty pounds and his expression was altered, as if some essential part of him had gone missing. He put his mouth close to my ear and told me that starting tomorrow, the reenactments would re-commence, except this time they'd be using bullets so maybe there'd be only one battle to worry about.

"All night I prayed for deliverance. I prayed to God to give me clarity, to show me how to protect our group. My boys—all of them, not just my sons—are a brave bunch. That night they posted pickets in case of a night attack. The next day we went up to Little Round Top. I sent a lookout up into the New York monument— it's the high tower you can see on top of the hill—and when the lookout yelled down a warning, I formed the circle. I had seen it in my dreams. I had no idea what good it would do but there was no point in putting up a fight. We had no weapons. We closed our eyes and when we opened them, we had slipped out of their world and into this one."

"What time do they usually attack?" asked Jenny.

When Derek and I both answered "5:15" all three women turned in our direction.

"History students, then?" asked Cynthia.

"Reenactors . . . in a manner of speaking," I said.

Derek pulled me aside to speak privately.

He said, "We ought to shoo these rednecks away. We could scare the hell out of them."

I said, "Our guns disappeared during our little shift on the bridge. What are we going to scare them with?"

"With the ones that reappeared after we slipped back into the gloom."

"Gloom or sunlight. I'm not ever pointing another gun at a person."

"You don't have to. These oafs have been preying on children for months. When they hear a few shots go over their heads, all we'll see of them is the crack of their asses sneaking out over their belt tops as they run away."

Derek was energized in a way I remembered young Levi being.

"You're starting to remember things aren't you? This place, it's triggering past life memories."

"Hell no. I'm just pissed. I like Cynthia. I like her kids. I want to kick those hillbilly asses all the way back to Alabama."

"So how did you know the time of the original attack?"

"You told me. Years ago back in Sedona."

I was certain I had never told him any such thing.

I had never spoken to Lucia of my night at the peyote ceremony and my incredible journey back through time. We went for a walk mid-morning, starting east between the two Round Tops and out to the Taneytown Road, then north towards the town of Gettysburg. Along the way I described in detail the events as I experienced them through the eyes of Joshua Templeton. She listened without comment and as I heard myself talk, I began to perspire while the story unraveled freely and unabridged.

We took a road that went west into an area of numerous monuments—statues of soldiers, bas-relief commemoratives and cannons littered the grounds. It was fascinating and only vaguely familiar. Even though I had taken an obsessive interest in corroborating my astral experience to this place and had spent much time determining the existence of Joshua Templeton and Levi and Clara, I had not bothered to learn much more about the actual battle.

The terrain I remembered and the ground I now walked upon had the same distorted reality as a visit to one's childhood neighbourhood after a long absence, with its missing buildings and unfamiliar ones and there's a McDonald's on the lot where you played baseball and tooled around on your bike and maybe kissed your first girl.

We came to an area riddled with statues and memorials and nearby stood a small group of trees, fenced in, with a large monument in front of them.

"There were many more trees," I said.

Lucia approached the monument and read for a moment.

"It's called the High Water Mark. This is where the Confederates penetrated the Union lines on the third day. During Picket's Charge."

"I know." I could not walk any closer to the monument. My feet stood on the ground as if encased in cement.

"What's wrong?" said Lucia, coming back to where I stood.

"This is where I died."

"I thought you said the last thing you remembered was avoiding the soldier's bayonet."

"Right. But only because I knew the wolf wanted me to. It was the reason it brought me back here. To take me to this point and show me the mistake I made in that life. A simple object lesson in wrong living . . . and dying. I think now that maybe Joshua had been born for that precise moment and when that moment came to pass, he failed the test. So I guess

I'm repeating a grade. I guess I have to pass the test this time or be condemned to repeat it again and again until I get it right."

"What do you think the test is?"

"You are the test."

"Me?"

"Yes. When Donna died I wanted to die too. Her death sucked every bit of vitality out of me. I wasn't suicidal, I was just over. My life was over. I had no energy for the smallest challenge. Like getting out of bed. Like having a conversation or reading the newspaper. And when I wasn't feeling dried up and dead inside, the guilt would take over. I would replay it over and over in my head. If only I had been able to get her to the hospital sooner."

"Adam, she died of a brain aneurysm. There was nothing you could have done to save her."

"Maybe. But there was something so fragile about Donna. I always knew it. I always knew."

"You've got to let go of all that, Adam. You have to."

"That's it, don't you see? I have to parry the blow. I have to go on. I have to let myself love you and not feel as though I am betraying my love for Donna. I have to live. I have to live with you. I love you so much Lucia."

"I love you, too. I have always loved you. Always."

We kissed, mixing the wetness of our lips with the salty tears flowing down both of our cheeks. My feet felt lighter and the heavy heart of Joshua Templeton was replaced by the strong beating of my own.

We walked over to the Evergreen Cemetery. It took a few minutes of reading headstones to find the one with Clara MacDonald's name on it. I brushed the snow off the mound and uncovered a dozen roses, preserved under the snow, still red and vital.

"I pay a girl, a relative actually, to put flowers on her grave."

I knelt down and put my hand on the ground. I don't know what I thought I was doing. Maybe I was trying to feel the spirit of Clara and Donna. I so wanted to feel her presence. I wanted to know that everything was all right.

The wind picked up and I cocked my head to see the full sky, which was dark, gray and formless. I thought there might be a sign, a signal from the spirit world but it was only the wind.

"She wrote me the most beautiful letter."

"Yes, you told me."

"I have it memorized. I never told Donna about it. It was so damn confusing. I felt guilty for thinking about another woman, even though it wasn't really another woman. It was Donna. Different time, different place, same Donna. Same eyes. The way she looked at me. I felt like I had wives in two countries except my visa had expired and I could never go back and be with the other one. Is this upsetting you?"

"No. I've waited years for this. For you to share this with me."

"Good. Sometimes, when I had difficulty sleeping, which was often, I would recall all of the words in the letter, repeating them to myself over and over again until I fell asleep. I would then dream of her, of Clara, and sometimes it was Donna, and then later, often it was you."

"We are all connected to you and you to each one of us. And Derek and Jenny and John Walker, we are all connected, like beads on a string."

"So I broke the string back then . . . here . . . "

"Maybe."

Later, we stood at the gates of the Gettysburg National Cemetery. I stared into the grounds.

"Row E," I said.

We walked in and paid our respects to my alter ego.

"What a waste," I said, as we stood before Joshua Templeton's name, engraved along with the names of his fallen comrades along a concrete bar embedded in the ground. "He was so young. I was so young. So confused by the love and hurt I was feeling. Events truly conspired to give me little chance to make the right decision, to think things through and come out the other side with a deeper understanding of my emotions and what to do with them. Instead, I let the bayonet make my choices for me."

"Oh happy dagger, this is thy sheath," said Lucia, thumping her chest with her fist.

"Wrong gender. That's Juliet's line."

"Yes, but the inspiration is identical."

"I suppose it is."

Lucia took my hand into hers and drew me towards her.

"How did you track down Clara MacDonald's living relative?"

"I hired a local genealogist. He found her by following the family lineage from Clara's sister, Sarah MacDonald. She's the one who wrote the letter for her dying sister."

"Sit down, I want to try something," said Lucia.

I did not question her and, after clearing a little snow, we sat facing each other next to Joshua's marker.

"Now hold my hands and do whatever you did earlier this morning in the circle," she said.

I closed my eyes. I tried to concentrate on nothing in particular but I had to wonder what Lucia was trying to accomplish and then there was the cold ground, seeping through my coat and pants and freezing my ass. Lucia's hands were soft and warm and I felt a tingling sensation emanating from her fingertips and penetrating my skin. It crept up my arms and into my chest until I could feel the heat from my body escaping out from the collar of my shirt. I lost all sense of the now and drifted with her energy into a black stillness.

We travelled together through the void. The blackness eventually opened up to bright sunshine and we were flying high above a wooded, hilly landscape. I recognized it instantly as the time and place of Joshua's last moments. Lucia held my hand and we watched from above, like two Greek gods surveying their latest interference with the lives of mortal men. We hovered over the battle, and I noticed other beings around us, spectral observers admiring the demonstration.

"Why are we here?" I asked.

"There is something you need to see now. Something you weren't allowed to see before."

We drew closer to the fighting. The sounds were somehow muted, as if we were watching the battle through thick glass.

"There," said Lucia.

I followed her finger and there, a few feet below us, walked Joshua Templeton, heading towards the advancing Confederate line. The forlorn expression on his face was a pitiful sight and so out of place with the twisted dementia etched on the faces of the combatants locked in their death-crazed dance. I watched as the red-headed Confederate soldier charged, Joshua blocking the lunging bayonet with his arm, or almost so, for the blade found the soft flesh and muscle of his triceps, impaling his arm while Joshua smashed the soldier in the jaw with his right fist, causing the man to fall and hit his head sharply on the ground. The Reb's rifle hung suspended from Adam's arm until he gathered up his courage and tore the bayonet out of the wound.

A drummer boy serving as a stretcher-bearer grabbed the good arm of the prostrate Joshua and helped him regain his feet, leading him away from the front line. We followed Joshua as he wandered off, down the Taneytown Road, holding his left arm against his body, using his right hand as a tourniquet, squeezing his upper arm to stem the flow of blood.

We watched as he staggered down the road. In vain he searched for the letter, his hands frisking his body, every pocket ransacked, and when he finally gave up, the hurt in his face gained ground on the pain.

I knew where he was heading. I knew he remembered Clara telling him how her farm was a bit east of the Weikart farm.

After a time, he wandered up a long laneway. A sign by the road told him he was entering the Macdonald farm. There were wounded soldiers everywhere, the field hospital unable to cope with the number of injured. On Joshua walked to the farmhouse, the sleeve of his tunic blood soaked, glistening in the hot sun and attracting thirsty flies.

A girl came out of the farmhouse. She called back into the house, then came running towards Joshua. I identified the dress she wore as the one Clara's sister, Sarah, had been wearing when she had given Joshua Clara's letter. I was watching Joshua's reaction. I could feel his blurred vision and dizziness. I saw the release in his eyes when he saw her coming to him. Joshua stumbled to his knees, the girl arriving in time to prevent his complete collapse to the ground. She helped him to his feet and as they rose up together, she absently hooked her long hair behind one ear, the western sun lighting up her face and my heart nearly stopped for it was not the same Sarah I remembered. It was Lucia.

"I don't understand. It couldn't have been you. I would have recognized you."

"It was me. It was always me."

Sarah carried Joshua into the farmhouse as Lucia and I were pulled back towards the sky. As the scene receded below me I recalled the vision Joshua had had, as the rebel soldier was lunging with his bayonet, of a farm and a wife and children. This was the future Joshua had forsaken in his grief, the potential of a life with Sarah as fulfilling and meaningful as one with Clara might have been.

When I opened my eyes the sun was shining. It was warm like earlier in the day after our circle meditation. There was no snow and the ground was soft and damp, the musty smell of spring filling my nostrils. Lucia sat across from me, her eyes open and searching mine for some hint of what I was thinking.

"How did you know?" I asked.

"John Walker. Remember the first time I met him. He was staying at your house while he attended a seminar in New York. You asked me to come out and meet him. Don't you remember how shocked he was to see me? Later he told me why. It wasn't Derek who first told me about what happened that night in Arizona. It was John Walker. He recognized me as Clara's sister. He told me I had a very important role to play in your life. He said I was your messenger. He said I was also your message."

"Message received," I said and took her in my arms and held her for several minutes. It was when I released her that I noticed it.

"Look," I said, pointing to the grave markers.

Lucia said, "Somewhere in Maine there are two headstones under a big oak tree with the names of Joshua and Sarah Templeton etched upon them, and they lived into the next century and watched their children grow and held their grandchildren in their arms and died when there were no more challenges in their lives to conquer."

I did not doubt her words because, in this particular world at least, where the sun shone brightly, the marker we sat facing no longer bore the name of Joshua Templeton.

It is a place I now know as Little Round Top. Joshua Templeton never knew the name of the hill he fought on. By the time Lucia and I made our way back down there, Cynthia's twelve little soldiers were already in position along the crest of the spur, having spread themselves out in a 'V' from a square block monument that marked the spot, I realized, where I had seen the regimental colours planted that day so long ago.

It was the same place yet so different. The left side of the spur had been hacked away to make way for a dirt road, long unused, its surface concealed by brown, rotting leaves and fallen branches. On the right, a park road ran between Vincent's Spur and the crest of Little Round Top. It had been elevated, making the original gully between the spur and the hill much more shallow. This had the effect of greatly reducing the sense of isolation I remember Joshua feeling as his regiment positioned itself along the top of the spur, cut off from the rest of the Brigade by the gully now filled in. There were fewer trees and I could swear there were fewer rocks, even though to a first time visitor, the place must seem strewn with them.

It did not feel like I'd been here before. It felt more like I lived here. Every inch of the place bred the familiarity normally reserved for the everyday sameness of home. Any vestige of a lingering doubt concerning the existence of my past life was dispelled as I stood near the place where I watched my friend Billy die.

Derek came up from the car with our guns.

"This place really gives me the creeps," he said.

"It should. See that rock down there. You were behind it and every now and again you would pop up and take a shot at me. Then one time, you popped up as my friend jumped out to grab a fallen soldier's rifle and you shot him in the head."

"Bummer. But, I guess I learned my lesson, 'cause I'm a peace-lovin', make-love-not-war pussy in this life."

"Really? Interesting statement from a guy holding a shotgun in either hand and two handguns tucked into his pants."

"Sometimes you have to be cruel to be kind."

"Do you realize that your entire personal philosophy is nothing more than an amalgam of pop lyrics?"

"Que sera sera."

I was sick of guns. I did not want to intimidate anyone anymore. I had no desire to find my way back to a mindset where shooting someone was an option. The words of the Master were more than a warning. Their impact was immediate and persuasive. It was a simple and ancient command—thou shalt not kill. Unless we say so, they might well have added.

"So what's the plan?" asked Derek.

"We shoot over their heads and hope they run away once they realize some big boys with big toys have come to play."

"And if they don't go away?"

"Then we hope Cynthia and Lucia can summon the shift in a hurry."

Lucia and I had taken advantage of our journey to what was becoming referred to by me as the *sun world* by stripping off some of our clothing near the cemetery and having sex. It was urgent, no frills, giggly lovemaking, the kind where your wits stay with you —no more creative than two rutting animals.

By the time we were done, the sun had disappeared and we had slipped back to the real world. Not that I had the slightest idea anymore what was real. Reality had become for me a multi-layered sediment. There was the world we inhabited, a three dimensional surface layer. But now we had begun to reach down into other layers, utilizing, I imagine, some unused portion of our brain, and it was going to take time and effort before we would be able to shed the atrophy completely and sustain these newfound levels of consciousness. Perhaps our bodies were undergoing subtle genetic changes that allowed us to maintain these vibratory dimensional frequencies, enabling Lucia and Cynthia and, to a lesser degree, the rest of us, to lift the veil concealing the invisible worlds, worlds I was starting to imagine must contain the inhabitants of mankind's myths and legends, from fairy people and leprechauns to extraterrestrial beings.

When I think back to my astral journey to this place and John Walker's presence throughout my time here, how else to explain it except as a form of wizardry? If there was a divine intent to the earth's devastation and destruction, then I believe it was to remind us that the world is a place of magic. And no one had forgotten this better than me.

I took a position near where Joshua had lain in wait for the oncoming 15th Alabama. Derek stood behind the 20th Maine monument at the furthest extension of the crest of the spur. The boys had been told to hold their position until the Alabama boys saw them, then they were to withdraw to the top of Little Round Top where the women were stationed by the 44th New York monument.

They showed up at 5:15 P.M. on the dot, as Derek and I had intuitively known. They crossed the hollow between the two Round Tops and were not too particular about seeking cover, walking carelessly, their voices carrying clearly to our position.

They were a feral lot. Even from a couple hundred feet, they bore scant resemblance to civilized men. I recognized their leader from Cynthia's description. He was tall and bent against the wind that had come up suddenly. He dragged his rifle by the muzzle, as if it was a reluctant dog. His feet were bound in rags and his once proud Rebel uniform was now a patchwork of gaping holes and shorn appendages, his bare arms poking through half sleeves. The others were variations on a theme, each of them, desperate and devolved in appearance. They walked abreast and at times you lost the individuals, seeing instead a moving gray wall, and I guessed that if you held them up against the lifeless, smoke-painted sky, they would probably blend in so thoroughly as to be undetectable. Closer they came and I saw their faces and they wore the vacuous expression of the undead. I told the children to go.

The gray men arrived at the foot of the hill below us and slipped behind the same rock where I had first seen Levi.

The leader stood up so that his head and shoulders were above the rock. "You kiddies ready for a little re-writin' of history?" he yelled.

I nodded to Derek and we both let loose a shot which ricocheted off the big boulder.

The leader stood there, stunned, then ducked back behind the rock. I heard one of them say "Shit, what was that?" then the leader started laughing.

"Well now, that sure as hell beats your disappearing act," he said from behind the rock. "One thing to shoot at a rock, 'nother thing to aim at a man. You boys gonna be able to do that?"

I said, "We boys have done it before, so why don't you fellows put down your guns and never come this way again so we won't have to prove it to you."

There was a pause and then he spoke. "Reinforcements. They went out and got fuckin' reinforcements. I told Rick here this was gonna be fun. No, he said, they was just a bunch of runny-nosed spoiled brats. Like shootin' pigs in a pen. No fun in that, he said. So you some farmer they talked into saving their hides?"

"No, we're pretty much city folk," said Derek.

"Two of you. Shit, there's two of you."

"Come on, guys," I said, "this is pointless. There's absolutely no reason for this. These are kids up here. They're no danger to you. Why don't you boys head back to where you came from and we can all get on with trying to survive this thing."

"Can't do that, Yankee. See, I had a dream. Colonel Oates himself visited me and told me to avenge his defeat. And that's what we aim to do. We're gonna take this damn hill once and for all."

He stopped talking. Derek shrugged his shoulders. I had a really bad feeling suddenly. There would be no easy way out of this. I tried but was unable to see through the trees to know whether Lucia was within earshot of what was being said down here. I could only hope that the circle had commenced its meditation. Six shells in my weapon. I was praying I would have no need of any of them.

It wasn't a bad rendition of the Rebel Yell. Only six of them but the sound they produced made the hairs on the back of my neck stand up as quick and straight as enlisted men called to attention. They rushed towards us, leaping over stones, bent forward against the grade of the hill.

It all slowed down for me, took on the quality of a macabre ballet, like before, when the bayonet was seconds from entering my chest. I could see their eyes and was terrified by their crazed and rabid glare, their faces animated by a demon's desire to fulfill a maniacal bloodlust. One of them fell and at first I thought he had stumbled until I saw the red stain on his chest and heard him chortle, a bubbly half-scream, his lungs shot through, not enough air for a full-scale howl. Derek, I saw, was already targeting another of our attackers.

One man, older than the rest by a decade or two, stopped to assist his fallen friend, putting his ear close to the man's mouth, listening, trying to make sense of the gurgling sounds until Derek's next shot ripped through the older man's forehead, a mass of skull and brains smashing against a rock as the man flew backwards, landing dead in a contorted clump twenty feet further down the hill.

And still the muzzle of my shotgun faced the dirt.

Three of the men ran back for cover but the leader came on, thirty feet between us as I raised my shotgun. He stopped by a small tree and went down onto one knee, raising his rifle as he did so. I took aim. There was plenty of exposed torso, and one leg was in plain sight. His head was half hidden behind the stock of his rifle. A shot to the chest would kill him for sure. His knee was inviting but he would probably bleed to death from a severed artery. There just wasn't a good place.

It did not feel like I'd imagined it would. You think something travelling so fast would slide on through like a finger stuck into a pie. Instead, it felt as though my head had stopped the progress of a wrecking ball because the power of the bullet entering my forehead slammed me so hard that I only saw for a slice of time as I flew backwards through the air, an unexpected cloudless blue sky and treetops lit to a golden brown by the long rays of the setting sun. I was happy to see the sun again.

No pain. I float over my body. It is a sorry sight—a heavy, ugly, dead thing, a smart hole between its eyes, a pillow of blood growing slowly from where the bullet has exited. Pathetic creature. Over there is Derek, avenging, killing my slayer, the others running. No matter.

The light. So attractive. I am a spirit moth, drawn towards the brilliant whiteness. It does not blind. No need to blink. Lightness. I am freed from the weight of life. Love, so much love. The light is love. Maybe I will see Moses or Buddha or Hendrix.

There are forms in the light. Coming to greet me. One brief glance at the drama below. No regrets. Silly. A silly life. A few lessons learned. Not a bad attempt.

They come to greet me, spirits known and unknown. So clear now how the puzzle pieces fit together.

One stands alone. Not standing, actually. Formless energy. But I have not yet shed the vestments of life and I see her as standing. Alone. So beautiful. "You are early," she says. "It is not the right time. They are sending you back. The entity must discover its soul purpose. You must return."

I do not want to hear these words. I want to stay. With her. But there is no debate. It is not my decision. Disappointed. Reluctant. It grows even brighter. I feel heavy and thick as I fall away from them, from her. I am lowered back into the world of atoms. The sun is in my eyes and I blink.

She is fading. God, it is so beautiful there.

EPILOGUE

FIVE YEARS LATER

"Garbage defines a civilization. Primitive man left behind his skeleton, a few crude tools and child-like drawings. Rome littered the known world with roads and aqueducts. The early Native American barely touched the ground, only a sprinkle of arrowheads and pottery abandoned for children and archeologists to unearth. And what has America bequeathed to the world? Plastic. And twisted steel and shattered McDonald's signs and secret mountains full of enough radioactive material to contaminate the entire globe. Worse still, we remain plagued by the living remnants of a soulless culture—depraved people, lunatics, paramilitary fascists, cult followers, murderers and rapists who have embraced the destruction of our world as an affirmation of their own deviance."

Lucia waited for the 'Right on's' and the 'Here here's' to subside before continuing. Adam sat on the podium directly behind Lucia, between Cynthia and John Walker, feeling disoriented and out of place. He envied the man behind the sound board, stage left, and wished he were once again cocooned within the confines of his equipment, oblivious to everything except the sound, his mind nothing more than a mental abacus of sliding faders and turning dials. He detested this side of the performance. The exposed side.

He let his mind and eyes wander. He guessed there were at least two thousand people at the community meeting. Almost the entire population of the Isle of Sedona. The security forces would be missing of course, stationed at outposts ringing the island and on the mainland shoreline. The clinic would have left a skeletal staff behind to care for the infirmed. A few scientists working on timely experiments would not be amongst the gathered. Joey and Tom were absent with leave while they prepared for tomorrow. Derek and Jenny were also missing, probably off the island, scavenging for the festival. Everyone else though, would be in attendance.

The canyon floor made a natural amphitheatre in reverse with the platform on the narrow high ground and the audience fanning out below. Lifting his eyes, Adam strained to focus on the expanse of water lapping gently against the red rock shoreline less than a mile distant, so brilliantly blue that he was barely able to detect where the sky touched the sea. Adam was still in awe of the idea of Sedona as an island.

" . . . And so tomorrow the grand experiment begins. With the combined effort of our friends in the spirit centers of Malton, Klehma, Gobean, Shalahah and Wahanee we intend to once and for all time, remove ourselves from the Fourth World permanently and completely. It has been an exhausting several years for those of us responsible for the temporary maintenance of the nexus between the Fourth and Fifth Worlds. We believe Maasaw will close the seam to the Fourth World forever. Finally, we will be able to turn our focus and energies to the creation of a spirit center, here amongst the red rocks of Sedona, as was always intended."

Adam absently rubbed his temple, mention of the old world bringing back phantom pain and tenderness to the area. And not a little fear. Ever since that day on the hill, when Lucia, Cynthia and the rest of the group had brought about a shift to the sun world, simultaneously withdrawing Adam from the old world and death, he had wondered whether somewhere out there on the other side of the nexus he lay, a rotting corpse, atop a small rocky slope in southern Pennsylvania. Lucia said it was possible. Many dimensions, many realities, she said. If Joshua Templeton could live and die simultaneously, then why should Adam expect any less or more?

For the last five years Lucia had devoted herself to maintaining the sun world—or Fifth World, as it was now being called—around their party, afraid to let Adam slip back into the Fourth World and lose him to the bullet that had ripped through his brain. Sedona, like the other energy centers dotted across the country, was already more or less permanently stabilized, but there remained great evil in the outlying areas and there was always the threat of an attack by roving bands of outlaws. Sedona was an especially inviting target for these frighteningly insane people, who somehow were unpredictably capable of breaching the fragile crack between the two worlds.

Adam watched the faces in the crowd. Their unified, raptured expressions and manner of clothing hearkened back to the communal era of the '60s. It was a diverse group; many white people but generously seeded with Hopi, Navajo, Havasupai, Zuni, Afro-Americans and Hispanics. There were Christians and Jews, the educated and the impoverished, sinners and the sinned upon—all stood before the stage on equal footing. It had been that way ever since the moment each of them had waded across the shallow waters of the Bay of Harmony from the shore two miles to the east and placed their feet and their fates on the pebbled shore of this island of red rock cliffs and sheltered canyons.

Adam thought of the day he and his companions had finally reached this longed for destination after years of travel across America. Nothing in Adam's life could have prepared him—especially after months in the desert—for the breathtaking splendor of the red jeweled island rising out of water so blue and still.

After the rally, John Walker and Adam walked together down the path to the village.

"You live a charmed life, you know," said John Walker. "Two extraordinary women have loved you. Personally, I don't get it. The gods act in mysterious ways."

"You're jealous, you old fart," said Adam.

The two men walked with arms around each other's shoulders. Their affection for each other was a tangible presence that passing villagers could not help but notice, most stopping and stepping aside to let the two Elders continue undisturbed through the narrow village walkways.

"Jealous? Of you? Ha! I am only jealous of the time I have wasted in my life nursemaiding your psyche."

"Who asked you?"

"You did. Before you were born. The second I laid eyes on you I knew our destinies were intertwined."

"Really. Then that leaves only one question left unanswered."

"And that would be . . . "

"When do they return and pick you up?"

"Who?"

"The people from your planet."

"I don't know."

"I was kidding."

"I still don't know."

Adam looked into John Walker's eyes. They were noncommittal, poker eyes. He could be from another planet, thought Adam. Nothing could surprise him anymore.

"But they won't come soon?" said Adam.

"No, not soon."

"Good, then. Let's go grab some lunch."

At the southern end of the island, running between a tall rocky hill which used to draw thousands of tourists to its scenic lookout, and Boynton Canyon a couple of miles to the north, lay a strip of old Highway 89A. It ran fairly straight, the eastern end ducking into the old commercial area of Sedona before sliding into the sea. The west end rose out of the water in a relatively straight line and it was there where Joey intended to touch down. Tom waited about five hundred yards up the road. His eyes were stuck to a pair of binoculars and he held his breath as the F-16 grew larger, its flaps and landing gear down.

Joey sucked back some air. This would have been a hard exercise even during the height of her training and readiness—no ILS guidance system to guide her flight path, an undulating road with barely a single stretch long enough to entertain a 200 knot landing, and most disconcerting, an untested landing gear, repaired by an auto mechanic over a period of years with makeshift parts and a fair bit of improvisation. There was some comfort in knowing that the mechanic was your husband and he would not let you fly if he thought you were in danger, still, there was no sure way of knowing if the gear would hold until she bounced it against the pavement.

She made her final approach, swinging the aircraft in an easy loop before pulling the nose towards the road. The blue water sped past underneath as the highway grew larger on the horizon. Tom had lit two fires on either side of the road at the shoreline. Two thin columns of gray smoke spiraled slowly into the still sky, framing Joey's approach.

She could not believe it was over five years since the throttle and stick were last in her hands when it meant something. Sure, hardly a day had passed without her climbing into the cockpit and pretending there was some system to check, when really all she wanted to do was put her hands on the controls and shut her eyes. Many were the times when Tom would find her passed out at the controls, and it was when he gently woke her that he would whisper into her ear a promise of a day when her bird would fly again.

In the beginning, long before the community was established, Tom's overtures both mechanical and romantic were met by a high wall and kept at a polite distance by Joey. But one day Tom disappeared without telling her or John Walker what he was up to and, when he returned several days later, his pickup held six drums of jet fuel and twenty-four thousand rounds of ammunition for the six-barrel cannon. That gesture brought down the first wall and not long after, the second was breached. It happened when the two were working on the damaged wheel and their hands grazed against each other. Tom looked at Joey in a manner that made her throat go red and he saw it and it was like a roadside neon sign blinking out *Good Food*, so he pulled her to him and kissed her and she liked it in a way she had never liked a kiss before and after that, there was an unspoken understanding that lasted until the day they recited their wedding vows.

Joey kept the nose of the jet up a little higher than normal, nervous that the front landing gear might not withstand the impact of a normal landing. Her AOA indicator was useless without an airport ILS signal beacon so she had to guess and figured the drag of the elevated nose was slowing her down so she pushed the nose down a little and increased the throttle. Her air speed jumped to 210 knots, a little fast, but she wanted to hit the runway and be able to pull up with enough lift to get back off the ground if she felt the need to abort the landing, especially if it meant gaining enough altitude to enable her to eject safely.

The sea was only a hundred feet below. The landing reminded her of coming into LaGuardia. As a passenger it had always been a bit disconcerting for her to watch the water come closer and closer until, a few feet from landing, the runway appeared. At least in the driver's seat you saw the dry land in front of you.

Tom watched the Falcon fall gently from the sky. She could see him now, half a mile down the runway. Got to do this right for him, she thought. All these years together, unified in their goal to get the plane back in the air, and now it all came down to a few feet of air between her and the pavement.

The back wheels hit a bit hard, two puffs of blue smoke accompanied by a shrill shriek and then the nose descended, slowly, an eternity of dissected seconds until she felt the jerk of the front wheel pounding into the center of the highway. She applied the wheel brakes and waited for something bad to happen.

The plane came to a full stop next to the truck. Tom came running to the plane and hopped up onto the wing. Joey opened the canopy and she could not unbuckle herself fast enough. Tom was whooping and groping and when she was finally free he lifted her out of the cockpit. They spilled out onto the ground, jumping and hugging each other then rolling around on the desert floor like a couple of coyote pups.

She had a headache and her heart was racing so she laid down to rest. Lucia was unused to public speaking, of having a large group of people gather to receive her words. The slow movement of so many bodies pressed together, the suspension of individual thought to the collective ear of the group, it was dizzying, it was syrupy and intoxicating and it should have felt good, only all it did was make her head hurt. Put some words to music, give her a lyric sheet and a band behind her and there was no problem. But up there, alone, testing people's faith with her version of the truth—it was foreign and it was painful. She scoffed at the belief by some that she was the White Brother of Hopi legend.

Lucia was worried about the experiment. No, whom was she kidding—she was worried about Adam. She had come so close to losing him on the hilltop—why had he insisted on scaring those Alabama assholes—and ever since then, it had been a daily concern for her, physically and mentally exhausting, like having a child in and out of remission, only there are no doctors to help you, no prescriptions to fill.

Adam was unaware of the many times during their long journey when, after having left behind the safety and spiritual radiance of Malton, her own energies had flagged and the old world had begun to reappear and, simultaneously, Adam had started to disappear, in the way a drop of dye disperses into clear water. Only with Cynthia and Jenny's diligence was the crack between the worlds kept closed and Adam kept safe. But it had taken its measure on Lucia's body. She was always tired, her breath shortened by the slightest exertion. She was sure all she needed was some time alone to re-energize and relax her weary body and spirit for the demanding day ahead.

She drifted and dreamt of Malton. Or maybe she was still awake and only daydreaming. Malton was the dream. A Midwestern oasis. They first noticed it when they passed through Indianapolis. A corporeal oppression dissipating from their world. The Jeep had been long abandoned. It was not much use after their group swelled to seventeen people, with a majority of them under the age of twelve. There had been endless days walking along old Route 40, the National Road, America's first highway, a pilgrim's route, all faces lit by the western sun, drawn to the seductive energy, then finally reaching the edge of the vortex's influence and folding into its arms. Next followed glorious weeks of sharing and communion, the group finally reaching the center, Malton; energy vortex, center of fruition and attainment, agricultural collectives, biotechnology, markets full of tomatoes the size of a man's skull and pumpkins big enough to sleep in.

For three hundred and fifty miles in every direction, including straight up into space, the vortex protected and enriched those within its umbrella. Lucia had quickly fallen in with other adepts, and communal sessions were held where many Masters spoke to the population through their chosen trance channel. Lucia, it was soon discovered, was a conduit for a committee, its number unknown, made up of extraterrestrial spirits from the star system Sirius. Fantastic stories were told by the extraterrestrial spirits through the trance channels of alien bioengineering and DNA manipulation, of race after race utilizing the Earth's strategic cosmic accessibility to create a genetic storehouse of living experiments.

All of mankind's notions about space travel and theories of relativity were made naively redundant by the revelation of other dimensions and portals existing on the planet through which alien beings entered Earth's confining third-dimensional reality. There were some UFO's as it turned out, used more as alien marketing tools than transportation. They were unnecessary when the ability to enter higher dimensions was possible.

Much communication about light and the evolution to a higher consciousness, teachings of the seven chakras, and of a movement into a more fluid bodily state, revelations about the many alien cultures that have moved on and off the planet, seeding it and letting it grow.

The nature of the Prime Creator revealed, Lord of a free-will universe and much discussion about a race of lizard beings, of a huge portal in the Middle East through which they had entered the world and integrated, maintaining down through the ages their own bloodlines while manipulating mankind's DNA to enslave us, creating a natural human inclination throughout history for war and greed and hatred, all of it psychic food for the palate of these reptilian parasites.

And now a change, the earth precipitating the activation of a dozen strands of DNA, each person undergoing a transformation towards the light.

A new freedom emerging, a breaking free from the insidious manipulation by governments and media, the turning away from the controlling addiction of television and ubiquitous radio transmissions, all designed to stunt spiritual growth and keep you dumb and far away from your own internal truth.

Of transition and a phase shift of the third dimension, separating those who were ready for the opening up of their consciousness and those stuck in the old world, of those connecting to the universal flow of information and those of an obstructed bent, enslaved and mind controlled, still trying to make sense of a world no longer able to support their misplaced values, still feeding the lizard race with sickness and insanity.

The new goal, to keep the frequency, to allow the structural biochemical and genetic alternations to effect a permanent change in the collective body of mankind.

It is time, the Masters said, to remember who you are, to become more intuitive, to remove the blocks placed by those invested in negativity and to begin to operate in a multitude of dimensional realities and to help those further down the spiritual evolutionary trail to quicken their pace and catch up with the others. It is an honour, they said, to be alive at this time, to have secured the approval of your ancestral spirit group to incarnate into this world, all of you spirit warriors, human manifestations of the intentions of your spiritual family, given a test, a mission before conception, and now was the time to discover your purpose and complete the assignment.

They said your external world is but a symbolic reflection of your internal thoughts. They said it is vital to shape your human experience with right thinking. They said there is no death.

She and Adam had many discussions about the new information. He held an advantage in that she was incapable of remembering any information that was transmitted through her. But there were so many others with her abilities. The information was repeated by other entities through fellow trance channels and recorded and reproduced and placed into learning centers for further study and accessibility.

There were also psychic readings, public and private, and it became clear from her readings of her friends that Adam, Derek, Jenny, Cynthia, Donna, Sydney, Brian—all of the people close to her, living and dead—were part of a spiritual collective, trading parts and roles through different incarnations. And there were grades of relationships—Adam, herself and Donna strongly connected and, at the top was the spirit leader. And as much as he would balk at the sugges-

372

tion, it was clear to Lucia that John Walker led this group.

Lucia got up, her mind too active to sleep. She walked over to Adam's desk. She could see from his window the sparkling blue water in the distance. So beautiful. Too shallow for even a sailboat. A few canoes and rowboats skimming the surface near the shore. People lounging near the water's edge. It made her almost long for the chaos of New York City.

She wondered often of Sydney and Brian. She had contacted Sydney more than once on the astral plane so at least she knew they were all right. She longed for a reunion with all of them. There had also been unexpected astral contact with Gloria, who was safe and happy in Gobean, a booming spirit city to the south near the abandoned Phoenix. Derek and Joey had been planning a trip to go find her but Jenny's latest pregnancy had delayed the trip.

Lucia ran her finger along the wooden desk, littered with man stuff, an uncontrollable smile springing up when she saw the motley pile of makeshift journals Adam had kept since the early days of the earth changes—four high school composition books, a couple of three ringed binders, a steno pad, several sections of loose leaf paper bound together at their corners by tree sap and toilet paper, rolled up like a torah—at the time, a blasphemous waste of a rare and precious commodity on Adam's part.

Every morning, after breakfast, Adam sat there and wrote. Music no longer interested him. Of all of us, she thought, Adam was the most changed. Happier, free with his love, a kind man and generous, yet at times Lucia felt as if he were a benign sort of Frankenstein, a person disassembled by events and circumstances then put back together without benefit of a blueprint.

She picked up a few freshly written pages, his almost indecipherable scrawl filling every line. Lately, he had been editing his journals into a more cohesive record of their journey from New York. She knew he would not mind so she sat down and drew a page close and this is what she read:

I am getting old. That is how the Elders greeted my fifty-fifth birthday. No cake, no surprise celebration in my honour, only an admonishment. The Elders say it is time for me to compile my journals and edit them into a coherent whole. There are fewer days ahead of me than behind, one wise soul warns me. I tell them they don't call all of us Elder for nothing and

373

point out those who pre-date me. But, I have to admit, none of them by much more than a few years. My good friend, John Walker, leads the cabal against me. Who else? I am convinced his sole mission in this life has been to be a thorn in my side. And I thank the Prime Creator every day for sending him to me. I do not know where I would be right now if John Walker had never entered my life. Dead, I suppose. Certainly not sitting in the warm sunlight on the Isle of Sedona.

I have much material to examine and I hardly know where to begin. My dear wife, whose strength normally equals that of a woman half her age, has been extremely tired and listless lately but she insists on lugging box after box to our study. I finally told her to stop. I will soon run out of room to even move from my chair. I think that is her plan. To seal me in and not let me out until my editor's work is completed.

The sheer volume of my journal making should not surprise me. I have tried to put pen to page every day, if only for a few minutes, and I do not believe more than a handful of suns have set in the last five years without my scribbling something down.

There are many contributions I have made to this community in which I take great pride. But lately, I have tired of community involvement and have created this façade of the isolated writer, daily wrestling with his muse. I am accorded great respect and yet no one has ever read a word I have written. Now I am about to be found out for the fraud I have perpetuated these past couple of years.

I do not relish the idea of returning to the world I left behind five years ago, even if only in memory. The time span is not so long but it was a different world and by no means a better one. During the time of the Change I witnessed many terrible things, human suffering of epic proportions and atrocities so horrible I hesitate to think of them again, let alone relive them through my journals. It was not all doom and gloom, however. There were glorious moments as well and I intend to include as many of them as I can find in my notes.

Of my life before the Change, I have little to say. I think back to my first fifty years and it is a vague dream I recall, the machinations of a little man preoccupied with little things. Now I am an old man preoccupied with little things. The time before the Change has been documented to the nth degree and

I am not predisposed nor qualified to comment on it. Certainly, the Elders have no interest in my opinions of the Fourth World. I understand their motivation. My journals are significant for the events I lived through and, more importantly, for the person with whom I travelled. There is no person more revered in our community than my dear Lucia.

There is a saying, 'Well begun is half done', by an ancient man named Horace. So how do I begin to compile a tale so extreme, so impossibly significant, that if I hadn't lived through it, I would have difficulty believing any of it. I suppose since this is very much Lucia's story, I should probably start with the day Derek, Jenny and I rescued her party from the sinking aircraft carrier, Intrepid. Now that was a day for the history books. A day when history ended. It was the most vivid twenty-four hours of my life, burned into my memory with indelible clarity. As terrifying as the events of that day were, and believe me, there are not words invented to adequately describe the paralyzing fear we were all subjected to, still, I thank the Prime Creator for allowing me to see it, to experience the fury of the provoked Earth Mother. I was born for that moment. This I know more clearly than are the blue waters surrounding our hilly enclave.

As I began the process of reviewing the yellowing sheets containing my scribble, I would read a paragraph here, a page there. I noted dates and sections I wished to read, smiling at some passages, my heart sinking at others. As I poured over my meandering discourse, I recalled a line I once read in a work by Oscar Wilde. He said, 'Every man nowadays has his disciples, and it is always Judas who writes the biography.' Self-deprecating yes, but it is apparent to me now, as it was then, that in the company of Derek and Jenny and Lucia, I was the weakest link in the chain.

Lucia put the page down and wiped the tears from her eyes. Not true, she thought. Not true at all.

Everyone seemed to have something to do except for Adam. The community had taken on the collective manner of a beehive, beginning in the early hours of the morning as scores of villagers, apparently responding to the same inner alarm clock, spilled out into the streets in precisely timed unison before even the sun had managed to crest the horizon. If anticipation were a measurable item, then today it would be off the scale.

Lucia was gone when Adam awoke so he made his way to Derek and Jenny's place and had breakfast with them.

"It should be quite a show," said Derek between mouthfuls of scooped papaya.

"If it works," said Adam.

"I meant the festival."

Adam started to laugh until he choked on the strawberry in his mouth. Jenny came over and gave him a few good whacks in the back. When he had enough air back in his lungs he said, "Derek, it's good to know that in these times of momentous change, some things never do."

"Meaning?"

"Meaning, the greatest single event in the history of mankind—give or take a few here and there—is about to occur and all you can think about is your party."

"But I'm in charge of the festival. It's *my* party. I have to think about it."

"And it's going to be a great party."

"Better than Woodstock."

"Woodstock Schmoodstock."

An incensed Janis Joplin came to mind but Adam knew better than to ask again what had made her so mad. It was one more mystery he would take to his grave without solving.

After breakfast the three of them hired mules and made their way to the airstrip. There were long stretches of silence and Adam spent most of it observing his friends. Derek was so completely in his element that he seemed to have reversed the aging process. There were a few lines around his eyes and across his forehead but they were more from constant exposure to the sun than the passage of time. With his buckskin britches, white flowing work shirt and red bandana holding back his mostly blond hair—there was a hint of gray at the temples—he could have been mistaken for an Apache warrior, as long as you squinted and did not rest your eyes for too long on the mule.

Jenny sat astride her mount in maternal majesty, her firm, round belly proudly exposed beneath the flowered peasant's dress she wore. Derek and Jenny's first child—Adam's godson and namesake—had been born six months after their arrival in Sedona. And if there had been an awkward coolness between Derek and Joey when they were initially reunited, baby Adam caused any rift between father and daughter to evaporate. Joey and Tom now spent as many nights at Derek's dinner table as they did at their own and Jenny usually had to pry baby Adam away from Joey when it was his time for bed.

Tom and his crew were working over every inch of the F-16, like ants on a dead bee, readying the aircraft for its first and last mission. Joey was removing tape from the fuselage where a freshly painted symbol had been placed.

"Jewish star. Your grandparents would be so proud—if they were Jewish, which I recall they weren't," said Derek, admiring the black and white interlaced triangles.

"It's Solomon's seal, Daddy," said Joey, giving him a hug and quick kiss. "John Walker suggested it. He said it symbolizes the union of body and soul."

"Well, you just make sure you don't separate the two today. Okay baby?"

They hugged for long seconds. Adam winked at Jenny and they smiled at each other. Adam saw for a moment in Joey the little girl who had climbed to the vortex with him so many years ago; it was impossible to imagine then how important her role would become in the deliverance of this place from the mad reach of the mob gathering on its borders. There had been reports this morning of brigade strength bands of wandering outsiders not twenty miles from the island. This had to work and it had to work today.

"Don't worry about me, Daddy. I've got the easy part."

"No baby. I always reserve that role for myself."

Derek gently fingered the peace sign earring in Joey's earlobe. "Where did you get this?" he asked.

"John Walker gave it to me. He has that picture from Woodstock. He told me the story of the earring exchange a long time ago. He said Donna is my guardian angel. It's for good luck."

Derek reached for his left earlobe and removed his earring, which had not been disturbed for decades.

"Let's double your luck then," he said, handing her the earring. "They looked better on Donna anyway."

Adam found Lucia at the vortex. Since he had no formal role in the proceedings, he decided to stay near his wife lest she need his support, moral or otherwise. He stayed out of the way, up on a rock ledge, allowing himself an overhead view of Lucia and her fellow adepts as well as a partially obstructed view of the southeastern shoreline.

Lucia's group was composed of twenty-three men and women; a diverse assortment of trance channels, clairvoyants, healers, shamans, diviners and one fellow whose specialty was snake charming. John Walker and Cynthia flanked either side of Lucia. The group started to gather in a circle around the vortex portal. It was marked by a stone cairn on top of which lay a peyote plant.

Adam saw it and was overwhelmed with memories. He saw John Walker smiling up at him and the mischievous dance of his friend's eyes made Adam unsure whether the plant had any significance to the ceremony or had been placed there by John Walker as a joke. Only John Walker would pick the most inappropriate of times to develop a sense of humour.

There was still almost a half hour left until noon. Adam wondered how things were going at the five spiritual centers. It was one thing to coordinate two thousand people on a small island. How must events be transpiring in places like Malton, where easily five million people were spread over a radius of three hundred and fifty miles? He prayed for all of the locations to be ready. The coordinated event was designed to proceed at noon, Mountain Time.

Down at the shoreline, all around the island, hundreds of people began to wade out into the still blue waters of Harmony Bay. Entire families walked out together, hand in hand, while the elderly, those who could manage, strayed only a few feet from shore. Many of the disabled had insisted they be included so nurses and relatives guided wheelchairs into the water, some venturing hundreds of yards from the shore. In every direction, people moved slowly out into the tepid, salty water, their only instruction—to stop when you feel you are in a good place. By ten to twelve the island was surrounded by its population, a still forest of humanity ringing the red rock island.

Derek and Jenny with little Adam in tow, had walked west along the old highway and when it left the shore for the sea they just kept on walking. It was easy going with the asphalt under their feet and the water only up to their thighs, Derek carrying Adam piggyback style. When they had gone out about two hundred yards they stopped and faced back towards the shore.

Soon thereafter, the sound of a jet engine filled the air with its violent howl. A few seconds later and the nose of the F-16 raced towards them, heading west down the highway. A few hundred feet from the end of dry land it rose at a sharp angle, Derek and Jenny observing the landing gear receding back into the belly of the aircraft as it soared over their heads.

Adam watched the F-16 head out towards the sea then bank left one hundred and eighty degrees. When it reached an easterly heading, the plane arched up into the sky and raced towards its cruising altitude. Adam shielded his eyes until the plane was but a black dot on the horizon.

It had become formalized. The circle was tight and the people were still; each assumed a meditative posture. Most sat in a variation of the lotus position. One person, a woman Adam knew named Madeleine, lay forward in the prostrate position adopted by followers of Islam. John Walker sat as Adam had seen him do so many times, back straight, hands resting on each folded knee. Lucia was leaning forward, her head down and Adam was sure her eyes would be closed.

A clap of thunder rolling in from the east diverted Adam's attention. The eastern sky was growing dark in the distance. Adam knew a wandering mob could be found on the ground below the storm clouds, literally travelling under a dark cloud. Similar groups had been repelled in the past but hopefully, after today, there would be no further need to fear for the security of the island.

The sun was directly overhead. The rock cairn threw off almost no shadow. It was time.

At first Joey thought it must be a malfunction. She was cresting the storm clouds when the LNH light started flashing and the howl from the threat-warning panel went off. A quick peek at the threat-warning indicator showed a small green square heading for the center of the round screen. And her plane was the center. A SAM missile? How was it possible?

She banked right and rolled over, releasing flares and chaff as she pulled the nose down towards the ground. The jet sliced through the clouds and she watched as the missile passed close by, heading for the chaff in her wake. At seven thousand feet she broke through the clouds and on the ground she saw a column—its formation scattered and undisciplined—with a number of makeshift armored vehicles. "Damn, I wish I had a few Mavericks," she cursed as she switched to guns. Her watch told her she had little time to play with this band of scum.

She eyeballed a soldier standing on a flatbed, shouldering a mobile missile launcher pointed in her direction. She let loose her cannon about a hundred yards in front of the truck and watched as men ran ninety degrees away from the torn-up desert floor, and then the spray hit the truck—men and metal blowing into the air as the gas tank exploded. Joey had no time for a second run. She pulled back to gain altitude and kicked in the afterburners. It was time to get the show on the road. The island was closing fast. At thirty-eight thousand feet she leveled off the aircraft and increased the afterburners, watching her airspeed climb to 650 knots. The drag on the plane's nose caused a violent shuddering throughout the aircraft, the sticks in both hands vibrating like two electric dildos in overdrive. The Sea of Harmony was speeding below her. She switched to full afterburners and watched her airspeed pass through Mach 1 as the red rocks passed directly below her aircraft.

Adam had heard some more thunder only it was different—staccato sounding and abrupt and then there was the light from an explosion. A small dot finally appeared on the horizon and Adam watched as Joey arced her plane into a higher altitude, a white plume of smoke following her up into the stratosphere. He kept switching from the sky to Lucia and her group. Something was happening. There was a coloured light around each person; for most it was a purplish glow, fringed by white, emanating from the forehead and encasing each of them in an egg shape. Cynthia was encased in an orange radiance, traces of purple and white pulsating on the perimeter while John Walker was almost entirely encased by a white light, the quality of which Adam had seen once before when the light had beckoned him five years ago on the hill.

Adam shielded his eyes to search for the plane but the sun was directly overhead and he could not find it. The sound of the Falcon's engine was reaching him however, a dull roar audible as the plane made its approach. For a moment he saw her as the plane eclipsed the sun, Adam wincing as an intense afterimage burned red in the center of his vision.

It mattered not that he was expecting it. Nothing could prepare his senses for the intensity of the sonic boom. He did not so much hear it as feel it activate every neuron as it echoed throughout his body. With the sound wave still reverberating against the canyon walls, Adam witnessed a rippling sensation in the atmosphere around the circle below, like the shimmering ascension of air as it is heated by a radiator. Adam shook his head, thinking his eardrums had been pierced since the ensuing silence seemed unnatural and impossible.

The disturbance in the air around the cairn grew and began to revolve, a barely visible whirlpool of energy engulfing the circle. Adam felt nothing, no wind but there was a tingling sensation in his mouth, as if his fillings were being magnetized. As the whirlpool gathered speed it grew in height and width. The individual auras of the circle members began to commingle with the twirling energy, thin fibers of coloured light twisting round the swirling tornado, still attached to their owners but stretching out from them and wrapping around, spooling endlessly. Adam guessed there was a finite amount of energy available in each person and he began to fear the phenomenon. Then he was engulfed within the cyclonic force as well and, although he could not see it, he knew his energy too was bound up in the whirlpool.

From the shallow waters far below the vortex, Derek watched as a translucent plume rose from the center of the island, near where he knew the ceremony was taking place. He held tightly onto Jenny's hand and flinched when a spark jumped from his free hand to the person standing thirty feet away from him in the water. There were more sparks flying across the water connecting each person by a static thread. The water too was charged—Jenny started giggling from the sensations running up her legs.

Adam's mind stilled. He watched Lucia in silent amazement. Her body was wavering, becoming fluid, as if the force of the whirlpool was scattering her molecules. The circle began to come undone, liquid bits of each of them following their auras into the whirling mix. At the center was the cairn and atop it, the peyote plant stood, animated, as if conducting. Adam raised his hands to his face and saw that he too was coming apart, his fingers growing into long spaghetti tendrils, stretching into the irresistible force, painless, delightful even—willingly falling into the energy stew.

Once taken up into the spinning force, the sense of movement abruptly ceased. Adam was no longer aware of his body and this was not a surprise to him as he was familiar with this state. He recognized Lucia and John Walker and was not confused by how it was possible to detect and feel what was no longer actually visible. The spirit circle hovered over the vortex and waited.

Adam peers into the vortex and a galaxy of light and images rise up and dazzle him—a celestial kaleidoscope. Many spirits start to ascend out from the opened portal, some human, others alien and still others, animal in nature. As they emerge they are sucked high up to the top of the whirlpool then scatter into the air. Adam understands he is witnessing a re-seeding of the earth with new spirits from other worlds, other dimensions.

A figure rises out of the vortex, horrible to look upon. But Adam does not fear it. He is aware of not thinking solely his own thoughts but the thoughts of the entire group and the entire group is aware of his thoughts and there is a combined sharing; and perchance it is John Walker conducting the group for Adam is certain the voice in his mind is John Walker's. There is only one word being repeated within the circle and it is a word of relief, a word of reverence, a name, and the name is Maasaw.

Maasaw ascends slowly and hovers a few feet above the portal. His face is awful, childlike in its simplicity; two large black pools for eyes and a similar round opening for a mouth only with razor sharp fangs hanging from that hole, the three facial circles positioned identically to the coral circles on Adam's silver bracelet. The apparition has pale skin and is covered with caked blood and blotches of coloured paint. Many feathers of different lengths and origins are haphazardly arranged about the top of his head. He is draped in a cape of animal hides, cinched by a belt with a gourd hanging from it, another one hanging from a cord about his neck. He holds in front of him a torch that burns with the intensity of acetylene and in his other hand is grasped a cane or stick of no discernible function.

"It's a planting stick," says a voice and Adam instantly knows all he needs to know about the stick.

"I am the first and I am the last," says the figure.

He says he was the one who opened the Fourth World and he will be the one to close it. His speech is a lamentation of the loss of the Covenant between his People and himself. He has foretold the closing of the Fourth World but knowing this does not lessen his disappointment. He admonishes the gathered to follow the Pattern of Life or the Earth Mother will rise up again and rid herself of despoilers and contaminators.

Many spirits continue to spiral up to the top of the funnel and these he says are being brought into the Fifth World just as many wounded human spirits of the Fourth World are being returned to the underworld while still others will move on to the spirit world, their work having been completed in this human materialization.

The lessons continue and the concept of time is lost to the collective consciousness of the group. Then Maasaw says he must go do as the Prime Creator has directed him and close the Fourth World forever. As he ascends up through the spiraling funnel he names a time and place for the continuance of his instructions, for he says he will guide the People of the Fifth World.

Once Maasaw has gone each mind unravels from the communal bundle and Adam is returned to a state of individuation, able to differentiate his thoughts from the others and digest with his own brand of cognition, the extraordinary world he has entered.

Adam is thrown into a jet stream of ascending energy and memory. He is surrounded by familial spirit energy. He is touched by the spirit of his mother, of his father, a lattice work of interlocking love, and it is a glorious feeling beyond description. Lost memories of intimate detail are instantly available, of olden lives and relationships, each successive spirit manifestation intended for the furtherance of a mutual transcendence. It all makes so much sense in here.

Donna is present. His capacity expands to embrace her. They form into one.

"We succeeded this time," she says to him.

"You are magnificent," he says.

And then enveloping them is Lucia and John Walker and they form a ball of energy and cling together, silent, thankful, happy.

Adam does not notice the wolf at first. He has stopped all thought and is drunk with the loving energy of his spirit mates. The wolf strikes a familiar pose, legs stretched forward, tongue wagging. The group disengages and Adam faces his guardian spirit guide.

"Are we going on another trip then, you and me?" he says to the wolf.

Lucia is nearest to Adam. Her spirit body radiates as though a thousand mini suns have been placed all over her. Donna is similarly glowing and her hand is clasped in Lucia's.

"He is here for me," says Lucia.

"I want to come too."

"Be patient," says Donna. "You are always in such a hurry."

Lucia says, "In a heartbeat we will be reunited. All of us. We must go now. I love you forever. We all love you forever."

Their spirits pass through Adam's and he knows he will burst from the intensity of their love. They recede quickly, following the gallop of the wolf. John Walker is beside him now. "Look behind you," he says and Adam sees the golden thread falling far below to the earth. "You know the drill. Time to return."

When Adam first opened his eyes his disorientation was complete. He did not recognize where he was nor could he initially understand why he had fallen asleep on a rocky ledge. After a few seconds though, he was inundated with a flurry of thoughts and images that frightened him to his feet. He heard a commotion and when he leaned over the ledge he saw a congregation of people hovering over something, their heads blocking his view.

Adam climbed down the ledge and pushed his way to the center of the circle. A man, the snake charmer, was hunched over the prone body of Lucia. He was applying CPR, alternating between mouth-to-mouth resuscitation and heart massage. John Walker stood next to Adam. He placed his hand in Adam's, pulled him away and led him back down the canyon path to the village and home.

—◆—

Three days later Adam returned to the vortex with John Walker and Derek. Jenny was under doctor's orders to rest and despite her protestations, was forced to stay behind. Adam carried an urn containing Lucia's ashes; she had been cremated the day before at a public funeral.

The men climbed in silence. It was a beautiful day, the blue sky visible in patches and streaks above the forest, the light of the sun finding its way between the trees to create blankets of light on the canyon floor. The smell of composting leaves was dominant, but there was also cedar and juniper and the smoke from a distant fire in the air.

When they reached the vortex, Adam climbed up onto the ledge he had occupied during the ceremony and stood, admiring the vista monopolized by the calm waters of the Sea of Harmony. He waited for a sign and was answered with a sudden gust of wind. He immediately overturned the urn and watched as the ashes danced in the breeze, twirling in a snake figure before dispersing into the air.

Derek and John Walker watched from below. Adam knew Derek must be itching to return to the festival site. Today was his big day.

An incredible phenomenon had occurred ever since Maasaw had closed the Fourth World. Thousands of people had almost simultaneously begun to appear on the mainland shore—pilgrims, refugees, all manner of people—drawn to the energy of the island. Everyone was delighted when Gloria showed up unexpectedly, arriving in time for Lucia's funeral and the pending birth of her grandchild.

Derek had decided to move the festival to the mainland, as the island could not accommodate the influx and all around the staging area, a small village had grown up, literally over night. John Walker had remarked that perhaps a sister community would grow out of this gathering. Already artisans and trades had set up booths while open-air kitchens spontaneously appeared to feed those without provisions. The mood was festive and giving and peaceful. Diverse arrays of performing artists were among the newcomers. Derek had even persuaded John Walker to recreate that legendary performance from Woodstock.

Adam came down off the cliff and the three of them stood in easy silence amongst the stones and spirits of this holy place.

"It's amazing," said Adam, "but I really don't feel sad this time. I can feel her inside me. Both of them inside me."

"I have something for you," said John Walker. "Something I picked up that you left behind a long, long time ago."

John Walker reached into his pocket and pulled out a weathered piece of folded pink paper, its edges softened and worn.

"They both wrote you this letter," said John Walker. "One composed and the other transcribed. It is a gift from the two of them."

Adam took the note from John Walker but did not unfold it. He held it for a moment, gently rubbing his thumb along its surface, gazing skyward as he silently recalled its content. Then he lifted it to his nose. Past the musty smell of another century there was still the hint of lavender.

Acknowledgments

This was a collaborative effort on many levels. I wish to thank those who helped, encouraged and guided me through this wonderful odyssey. To my beautiful wife, Trish, thank you for supporting my efforts and maintaining your belief when mine was faltering. Thanks to the other Trish, Trish Perrine for her research. It was a thrill for me to meet Michael Lang and discuss Woodstock with the man who made it happen. Thanks also to Lee Blumer who made the introduction to Michael and also provided information on Woodstock. The crewmembers of the Intrepid were never without a new story about their venerated ship. I wish to single out Hector Giannasca and Joe Liotta who freely related their personal experiences and inspired the characters of Andy and Hernando. Thanks to Cindy Quist, a real reenactor mom, for her enthusiasm and for inviting me to my first Civil War reenactment. My sister Andrea took on the unenviable task of proofreading an early draft. I am now enlightened on the correct use of the hyphen. Most of what I learned about Native American sweat and peyote ceremonies came via my brother-in-law, Dr. Ed Connors, a clinical psychologist and published expert on native teenage suicide. I greatly appreciated those of my trusted friends and family members who took the time to read various drafts: Steve Reid, Dorothy Connors, Kathie Fasken, Trish Secretan, Jodie McKeown and Daniel Klaus. I will be forever indebted to Laura Nenych for her brilliant (and swift) final proof and edit. Thanks to Teresa Winckler for helping me with permission clearances. I borrowed Peter Danson's high school yearbook caption for the book—with his permission, of course. Without Cynthia Frank, this book would have never seen a bookstore's shelf. Thanks also to Michael, Sheri and everyone at Cypress House. Thank you Patrick and Annette for a stunning cover. Special thanks to Colette, who made me aware of the gift of time I was being granted back in the summer of 1997, and who said that I'd better use it to write. Finally, without having had the benefit of reading Julia Cameron's book, *The Artist's Way*, I doubt this book would have ever materialized.

HISTORICAL NOTES

ALL OF THE CIVIL WAR OFFICERS mentioned in Part Two of the novel are historical. William Merrill of Company K is listed as killed in action on July 2, 1883, although the circumstances of his death in the book are purely my creation. The character of Miss Tillie is historical. In her book, *At Gettysburg, or What A Girl Saw And Heard Of The Battle,* Mrs. Tillie Pierce Alleman claims that, contrary to most published reports, General Weed did not die on Little Round Top, but rather, died during the night in the cellar of the Weikart farmhouse. I defer to Mrs. Alleman. Pvt. William Jordan, a private with the 15th Alabama, wrote in his memoir, *Incidents During the Civil War,* about his scamper to a great boulder where he remained during the battle of Little Round Top. My descriptions of the activities of the 20th Maine are as historically accurate as current research reveals. My camera froze the first time I visited Little Round Top when I tried to take a picture of the setting sun through the arch in the 44th New York Infantry monument. It was only later that night that I read of similar 'ghostly' occurrences happening frequently in and about the area. The Miami Pop Festival was an actual event. It was the first pop festival I ever attended. I can still smell the incense when I think about my many visits to The Great Train Robbery in Miami. Given the fact that there were hundreds of thousands of witnesses, it seemed incredible to me that there is still debate as to whether Janis Joplin went on stage before or after Sly and the Family Stone at Woodstock. Michael Lang is adamant that Janis went on after Sly. The Enchantment is a fabulous resort—I highly recommend it—and the nearby vortex is as I described it. I have never flown an F-16, but I feel like I have, thanks to the Falcon 3.0 PC flight simulator and the many hours I spent going head to head with members of the Flight 649 Falcon Challenge Ladder. I am greatly indebted to the following authors and intuitives whose research and instruction were invaluable to me:

Thomas E. Mails, *The Hopi Survival Kit*

Armin W. Geertz, *The Invention Of Prophecy — Continuity and Meaning in Hopi Indian Religion*

Thomas A. Desjardin, *Stand Firm Ye Boys From Maine*

Joshua Lawrence Chamberlain, *"Bayonet! Forward" — My Civil War Reminiscences*

Lt. Frank A. Haskell & Col. William C. Oates, *Gettysburg*

Shelby Foote, *Fredericksburg to Meridian*

William Hutton, *Coming Earth Changes — The Latest Evidence*

Brian L. Weiss, M.D., *Many Lives, Many Masters*

Barbara Marciniak, *Bringers of the Dawn — Teachings from the Pleiadians*

John Stenger, *The Global Family lecture*, New York, 1990

Lori Wilkins, *I Am America Map*

Robert Anton Wilson, *Cosmic Trigger — Final Secret of the Illuminati*

Carlos Castaneda, *The teachings of Don Juan: a Yaqui way of knowledge*

Peggy Beck, Anna Walters & Nia Francisco, *The Sacred—Ways of Knowledge, Sources of Life*

David S. Blanchard, *Elements of Mohawk Leadership*